CATHERINE PADMORE completed a PhD in writing at Deakin University in 2002. *Sibyl's Cave* is her first novel and was shortlisted for *The Australian/* Vogel Award in 2001.

Sibyl's Cave

CATHERINE PADMORE

ALLEN&UNWIN

First published in 2004

This project has been assisted by the Commonwealth
Government through the Australia Council, its arts
funding and advisory board.

Allen & Unwin
83 Alexander Street
Crows Nest NSW 2065
Australia
Phone: (61 2) 8425 0100
Fax: (61 2) 9906 2218
Email: info@allenandunwin.com
Web: www.allenandunwin.com

National Library of Australia
Cataloguing-in-Publication entry:

Padmore, Catherine.
   Sibyl's cave.

   ISBN 1 86508 952 4.

   I. Title.

A823.4

Set in 11.5/14 pt Adobe Garamond by Bookhouse, Sydney
Printed in Australia by McPherson's Printing Group

10 9 8 7 6 5 4 3 2 1

Dad

14.96

Contents

Island

New South Wales 1990

Billie sits at the end of the wharf with her toes in the river and a sketchbook on her knees. Splintered planks prickle her buttocks through her summer dress. Ample buttocks, she thinks, feeling her centre of gravity between them and the spread of her thighs. She leans forward until her reflection wobbles in the river, framed by chunky grey locks escaped from her bun and with a streak of orange at her temple. Creased as a crumpled photograph, the face in the water is unfamiliar. It's me, she realises. When did I get that old?

The back of Billie's neck roasts in the afternoon sun. She knows it won't burn; in the morning her skin will be one shade darker. Terracotta, like the cliffs opposite. Cool green water makes the heat bearable, and she swirls her feet so tiny waves lap at her calves. Fifteen years, she thinks, since I first came to this rocky peak in the Hawkesbury River. Driving north from Sydney along the old Pacific Highway, on a whim she'd flicked her indicator right and followed a pot-holed road to its end by the wide river. A ferry waited at the marina. For me, she'd thought. She paid a silver coin and let the ferry chug her to the island. Later, in her battered atlas, Billie found the island ten kilometres due west of the Pacific Ocean, near the great salty delta of Broken Bay.

Fifteen years, Billie thinks, shaking her head. She watches the escarpment across the river. Soon the sun will set behind the island and its last rays will illuminate the cliffs. She knows the pattern. In the tackle box beside her, she shuffles through pencils and rolled-up paint tubes until her fingers find pastels in the right colours. She waits, poised with sketchbook and pastel stub. Here it comes. The sandstone glows orange, and the clefts in the rock deepen to rose.

A neat gesture, five fluid strokes, and the bluffs across the river exist twice—once in the flesh and again, in thick pastel, on the cream pages of the sketchbook. Billie moves the pastel instinctively, her eyes on the sandstone, not the page. She has given up chasing the changing shades—they're too fast. She focuses on one hue only, blending ochre and skin pink and orange and burnt sienna with her fingertips.

When she watches the sandstone, the river noises fade: the steady chug of the ferry approaching the wharf, children shouting in the shallows, even the shrill lorikeets that dive from the jacaranda branches. As the light intensifies, the world recedes. I am two eyes, she thinks, and fingers to guide the pastel. She holds her breath. The colours peak. Orange slides into rich pink, then purple. All within a minute.

The shadows deepen, and she feels a strange grief as the light fades. She breathes again, aware of a tingling in her palms, as if they had reached over the water to scuff the rocks. In the liminal moment between day and night, still as the violet river, the tingling draws a memory to the surface. Moving across the paper automatically, her hands inscribe another image of the mainland on the page, while her mind explores the memory.

Compelled, she draws, peripherally aware of the ferry unloading its last passengers for the day and returning to its mooring by the marina. She draws until there is barely enough light to see. Channel markers glow green and red, offering safe passage across the night river, and lamps flicker on along the wharf, bathing the planks in harsh yellow.

Blinking in the light, released from her fugue, Billie lifts her pastel from the sketchbook. She stretches cramped fingers, then flips through the pages she has filled. The jagged lines of the sandstone cliffs dominate the first pages, but other images follow—windows carved into a rocky promontory, a man with black curly hair and a woman with a headscarf. Words encircle these sketches, sentence fragments in her spiky writing.

What she finds does not surprise her. She is used to the drawings that appear unbidden, squeezed between landscapes and portraits, when she thinks she is drawing from life. Books just like this one, smudged volumes of observation and recollection, line the shelves in her studio. She strokes the pages—lightly, so not to smear the faces captured in them with her stained fingertips—before closing the sketchbook.

Slow, stiff, Billie lifts her feet from the water and stands, forcing limbs to move after too long in one position. Her joints creak and groan, reminding her of their sixty years. Almost sixty-one, with her birthday early in the new year. Sit still much longer, she thinks, and you'll petrify, transformed into another sandstone outcrop to be worn down by the river.

Tackle box in hand, she tucks her sketchbook under her arm and begins the walk home. Behind her, as she turns her head to stare back at the river, wet footprints mark the winding path to her house on top of the island.

Cibelle

Campania 1936

The child lay down on a rock at the edge of the glittering sea. It was hard, digging into her scalp and spine, but she wriggled until she found a warm dent to rest her bottom. Stretching, the child scraped her hands over the rock until her fingertips stung. There were smooth pebbles, too, glassy black beads trapped in the pale stone. Her fingers could explore almost their whole surface, except for the small section that bound them to the rock. The child wanted to prise the glassy stones free, but they stayed put no matter how hard she wiggled.

Frustrated, arms heavy and weak, she flopped, closing her eyes. Cheese in the sun, she thought, licking her lips at the golden melting cheese that appeared in her mind. Her chest swelled with the crash of the waves below. The seagulls called. Then everything disappeared, except for the warmth and the steady up and down of her chest and the sea.

'Cibelle!'

Chi-bell-eh. Her name woke her, echoing between the rocks. And then the footsteps. They were slow and far away, but she felt them. Faster now, and louder. Suddenly, strong hands grabbed her around the waist and hoisted her into the air. The child opened her eyes, but the world was bleached and blue and too bright to tell her anything, so she shut them again. She didn't need her eyes anyway. The smell of garlic told her this was her papa. He pressed her against his chest and stroked her hair, picking small stones from her curls. Nuzzling into his rough shirt, she inhaled the dry dust he always carried with him. It tickled her nose. Beneath the shirt his chest thumped.

'That woman,' he said. 'I'll bloody kill her.'

Cibelle opened her eyes again and the world was back to normal. When her father carried her she felt like a giant, so tall she could see right across the narrow path that connected their rocky home to the village, then up the hillside to the mountain with the clouds on top. She saw little boats bobbing in the harbour and men mending nets in the sun. Cats asleep on white walls. Turning her head, she saw the green terraces on top of the outcrop where they lived and, below them, the dark windows of their house carved from the cliff face.

The man carried Cibelle up irregular stairs to the wall of stacked stones that surrounded their house. Gate and front door were open. Inside, he checked the three dim rooms dug into the rock, but all were empty.

'Where is she?' he asked, frowning, as he walked outside.

'Don't know,' Cibelle said. Her mother had been sitting at the table when the child took herself back to bed for her afternoon nap. When she woke, the house was deserted. Stretching, still sleepy, Cibelle had opened the gate to look for the woman but, drawn to the waves frothing over the rocks, had wandered to the water's edge instead.

Setting Cibelle down in front of a huge clay pot with a tree in it, her father reached into the glossy green leaves and pulled out an orange. It was almost as big as her head and bright as the setting sun. His fingers peeled back the skin with its white fluffy padding. The pieces made a pile by his knee. He split the fruit into segments, and Cibelle opened her mouth. She bit down hard and sucked, loving the juicy squirt. The strong taste made her screw up her face, but as soon as she'd swallowed the flesh and lost her scowl, her mouth opened for another piece. She was draining the juice from the last segment when her mother walked through the gate, with a red scarf over her curly hair and dirt on her fingers.

Her father stood up. 'Stay here, little one,' he said, following her mother inside. Cibelle leant back against the pot and licked her lips, her fingers, even the insides of her arms where the juice had dribbled.

Louder than usual, harsh, her papa's voice carried. 'Where the hell were you? I found her outside, alone.'

'There was no air in this damn crypt. I couldn't breathe, so I walked up to the terraces. They've been left fallow. No one's touched them in years. I thought I'd grow some herbs, start a garden.'

'And you just left her? She could have fallen off the rocks and drowned . . .'

'She was sleeping. I thought she would be safe. She must have wandered out . . .' Her mother sounded confused, as if she had only just woken from a sleep herself.

'Madonna the pig! She's six, tall enough to reach the latch on the gate now, or haven't you noticed? Most days I think you're only half here.'

Something shattered, and the sound echoed through the house to the orange tree. Cibelle jumped, then slunk round the pot to the other side. She heard her mamma snuffling. Her papa spoke again. This time his voice was softer.

6

'You accepted my proposal. I put my hand on your belly and felt the life kick under your skin. I married you, even though I knew it wasn't mine. One day I thought you'd forget. I thought you'd come to look at me the way you looked at him.'

Cibelle didn't know what the words meant, but they made her belly clench. Her mother's response was only just louder than the waves.

'So did I.'

The house was silent for a long time. Finally, her mother spoke again. 'How could I forget, with that red curl reminding me of him every day?'

Cibelle knew about the red streak. She'd discovered it, tomato bright in the black curls of her reflection, when she'd leant forward and peered into a rockpool for the first time. Her mother had shaken her head when the child asked about it, and looked sadly across the sea to the horizon.

'I never had a chance,' her papa said.

Someone was sweeping. Cibelle heard the rush of the broom and the tinkle and scrape of glass across the floor of the house.

'She's my daughter,' her papa said, 'no matter what anyone says.'

The next morning the family drank milky coffee together as usual. But Cibelle's father shook his head when the child trotted to the gate to wave him off. He hoisted her onto his shoulders. 'You will work with me today.'

Cibelle clamped her legs tightly around his neck as he stepped down the stairs. At the bottom he turned to face the house in the hill. With him, Cibelle watched her mother climb the other stairs, the wooden ones that snaked up around the rock to the terraces on top of the outcrop. Turning, her mother waved, and Cibelle saw she was smiling.

'When did you last smile for me, my love?' her father whispered. Cibelle patted the top of his head, wrestled with his coarse black hair, then reached down to knead his cheeks and pull his lips into a smile like her mother's. She played with his cheeks as he walked across the little stone path to the village. She began to drum, and a hollow sound came out when her papa opened his mouth. It made her laugh.

Cibelle drummed the pair past houses painted white and pink, up cobbled steps to a church on top of the hill. From here she could see the sun sparkling on the ocean, which stretched on forever. She had never been so far from her home. Most days her father rose at first light and walked across the strip of land to the village, while she and her mother stayed close to the house, throwing lines into the sea for fish, and spreading the family's laundry over rocks to dry in the sun. Twice a week Luisa, the fisherman's wife, delivered goats' milk in clay urns, flour and eggs.

Once, Luisa brought one of her own children, a sturdy boy a few years older than Cibelle, who curled his arms around his mother's waist and pushed his face into her belly. Cibelle frowned at their embrace. She longed to crawl into her own mother's lap, wrestle like she did with Papa, but her mother froze when she reached out, pulled away, and the child learnt not to try. Some nights though, long after she had gone to bed, a tickle of warm air on her cheek made her stir. Recognising the scent of herbs and wood smoke, she wanted to open her eyes, to reach out to the cheek so close to her own, but she knew her mother would bolt. So she lay still, inhaling the scent until the change in the air told her she was gone. Almost unbearable, the weight of the woman's gaze and the thin layer of air separating their two bodies, but each night Cibelle lay rigid, hoping, just once, to feel her mother's warm skin against her own.

On this day, high upon her father's shoulders, she squinted into the sun, but she couldn't see the little house in the rock. Her guts churned. Where was it? The child struggled until her father lifted her from his shoulders and stood her on the church wall. He held out his hand and pointed, and Cibelle followed the line of his finger until she noticed the windows in the rock. They were tiny, smaller than her fingernail. From here, the terracotta tiles of the porch looked like the ridged shells she sometimes found on the beach. She saw a red dot on top of the rocky outcrop, attached to a stooped figure. It was her mother working the terraces, but she had shrunk too, right down to a doll. The child's guts still fluttered, and she kept looking to make sure she didn't lose the house or her mother again.

Through the garden of the church, her father skirted crosses and stone women with peaceful faces. Cibelle liked the women. They had flowers scattered around them, pale buds from the orange tree that smelt like home, and others in bright reds and yellows that the child had never seen before. Most of all Cibelle liked the stone women for the babies they carried, plump bundles nuzzling into their necks and breasts. It made her hungry to see them, and sad, so she wrapped her arms around her father's thigh, stood on his foot, and let him swing her with his giant steps.

Cibelle's father walked to a small building littered with rough stones, tools and rolls of paper. There were more of the smiling ladies, but these were trapped in stone blocks, with only their faces peeking out. Cibelle's footsteps disturbed the dust on the floor and she screwed up her nose to sneeze. It was the same dust her father brought home with him, snagged in the fibres of his clothes. She had wondered where he went when he left the house in the mornings; now she knew.

Clearing a place for her at his bench, he unrolled a sheet of blank paper.

'I have to finish a plan,' he said. 'Why don't you draw with me?'

Unsure what to do with the burnt stick her father gave her, Cibelle wrapped plump fingers around it as she saw him do, then watched. Her father's paper quickly filled with the faces of young, smiling women. He worked on one woman's eyes, the lips of a second, then sketched a veil over the shiny curls of another. Cibelle saw the tip of his tongue peek from the corner of his mouth as he worked. It waggled, glistening like a squid tentacle, and made her giggle.

Touching the paper with her charcoal, she copied the flowing movements of her father's hands. She scribbled and coloured and dotted and striped. The lines on the paper didn't look like Papa's at all—they didn't look like anything she had ever seen. Didn't matter, though. She liked the feel of the charcoal stick in her hand and the quiet squeak as it touched the paper. She made up stories about the shapes and talked to the cats and birds and scuttling crabs that appeared between the lines. She kept drawing even after her father stopped. She heard him tap away at a block of stone, but was too interested in the dark lines to stop and see.

Even the church bell didn't rouse the child. Clang-clang-clang.

'Enough to wake the dead,' her father said, but Cibelle wasn't moving. Her father lifted her arms from the page and uncurled her fingers to remove the charcoal, reduced to a stub by her scribbling. Cibelle didn't want this, despite the bite in her belly and her numb bottom. She fought her father's hands, kicked and bit and whined as he lifted her from the bench and carried her outside. He washed her hands in a bucket of water, her arms and her face too, then sat her on the church wall in the sun.

'What a fuss,' he said. 'You can do it again this afternoon. And tomorrow. There's no rush.'

Cibelle kept up her scowl, but she stopped kicking him and even accepted the chunks of smoky cheese and spiced sausage he sliced for her.

'Not much,' he said, 'but now that I've lost your mother to the terraces it's the best I can do.'

Munching on the sausage, the child watched a procession of people climb slowly up the steep path from the village to the church. A man with a beard and a dress and a tall pointed hat met the people at the gate. Cibelle was fascinated by the man's beard. Streaked with white, it hung down over his belly. When the man spoke the beard bobbed up and down.

After the last person passed through, the man walked over to the wall where Cibelle and her father sat.

'Coming in?' he asked. 'The door is always open.'

Cibelle's father shook his head. 'You know me. If I can't see it . . .'

The man with the beard nodded. 'But think about it, for the sake of the child. She's not been baptised yet. Never heard the holy word of God.'

'She'll make that decision herself, when she's ready.'

Her father's eyebrows moved closer together. Something twitched in his cheek, just above the jawbone, as it had yesterday before Cibelle's mother had returned. Stop now, she thought, her body tensing for more shouts, but none came.

The grey beard shook slowly. 'If your father was here . . .'

'He felt the same.' Her papa stood. He lifted the child from the wall and carried her to the gate. The bearded man followed.

'He welcomed the Lord at the end.'

'Only because he was frightened and in pain. Now, excuse us, we both have work to do . . .'

Cibelle was surprised by the words that came from her father's mouth as he carried her back to his workshop. They were harsh words, like thunderclaps in a storm. Madonna the cow, Madonna the pig, Madonna the oh-that-man-frustrates-me. He repeated the words when he returned to his work, cursing as he chipped at the stone.

While her father carved, Cibelle crept out of the workshop and walked to the doors of the church. It was dim inside, lit only with candles. She walked through the door and hid behind a wooden seat. She couldn't see much at first, but she could smell flowers. When her eyes adjusted to the low light, she noticed bunches of orange blossom all over the church and at the feet of the statues, like in the garden. They reminded her of the sea—the bunches of flowers like white spray thrown up on the rocks when the waves hit. The man with the beard was singing at the front of the church, and his song reminded her of the sea too. Not the words, because she couldn't understand them, but the steady rise and fall of his voice, and its rough edge, like the gravelly undertow of the waves. The man's voice made Cibelle sad. She thought of the songs her mother sang, waiting for the fishing line to twitch. She didn't understand those words either, but felt sorrow in their currents. The child climbed up onto the wooden seat, stretched out and let the song send her to sleep.

Cibelle woke in the village, slumped on her father's shoulder. When they reached the house, she made him sit outside with her while the sun set. As the light changed, she watched the patterns flickering on the rocks around her. Sometimes she saw animals, boats or the curves of shells. She followed the shore with her eyes, past the village to another knobbly cliff along the coast. At the end of the outcrop she saw a man's face, side-on, with a large nose and heavy eyebrows. There's a man living in the rock, she thought, watching the giant face shift in the light. At first he seemed happy—she thought she saw him wink at her—but then, as the sun turned orange, he grew sad. He closed his eyes. Cibelle couldn't look any more. She made her father lift her inside. She curled up in bed, stroking the wall beside her until she forgot the sad man's face and fell asleep.

The next day Cibelle's father again carried her to his workshop beside the church. He laid his tools on the bench and named each one. The hammer and the point. Drill, chisel and claw. He showed her how to hold the metal instruments, how to spot the cracks in the stone that invited a clean break. Cibelle stroked the flaws in the ragged stones, poked her fingers in the weak spots, but she couldn't make them shatter the way her father did.

He also showed her how to split rock with wedges of damp wood, saying that this was how his own grandfather had hollowed out their house. In colder places, water could split rock by itself, as it froze and swelled in the cracks. He talked about the rocks they lived in being worn down by rain and sea, turned slowly into sand. Cibelle didn't like that idea. She saw their little house stolen, grain by grain, and imagined waking one day to find the house had washed down into the sea. She put her hands over her ears until her father stopped talking. He kissed her forehead and slid a clean sheet of paper across to her. She drew without speaking until the light turned orange and it was time to return to the house in the rocks.

Every day Cibelle visited the workshop. She named the stones by their colours—grey and green and pink—but her father called them 'tuff'. Cibelle thought it was a silly name, but she liked the feel of it on her tongue. Her father spoke of the rocks' birth from a fiery mountain, when the liquid centre of the world boiled up and bubbled over, bursting a hole in the earth's shell. He said there was one not far away, called Vesuvio. Some of the stones her father worked with came from melted rocks that had flowed down from the spout. The rocks where they lived were formed this way. Others were made from dust and ash that flew up into the air and then fell back to earth, turned to stone by pressure and time.

With his hands he showed her how the rocks were squashed and twisted into the strange shapes she saw in his workshop. He pointed out animal bones trapped within them and twigs turned to stone. Cibelle collected chips from the workshop floor and tucked them in her pockets, fondling the sharp edges with her fingers. She learnt to recognise the rocks outside the workshop and the ones in her house on the outcrop. Sometimes, alone, she explored the rocks behind the church. She never worried about getting lost. Wherever she was, she listened for the steady tapping of her father's chisel against stone and let the sound lead her back to him.

Cibelle kept her eyes closed as she felt herself being lifted. She lolled, grumpy, as gentle hands unwrapped her blanket and slid her floppy limbs into shirt and stockings. She felt cool air against her bare skin, so she snuggled deeper into the warm woolly fabric of her smock.

When she opened her eyes, she was in her papa's arms outside the house in the rocks. He was wearing his good shiny shoes and had a little suitcase at his feet. Her mother was there too, but she was barefoot and still in her nightgown.

'You could come,' Papa said. 'It's only a couple of days. There's a later bus, another ferry. I'll wait.'

The woman shook her head. 'I need to prune,' she said. 'And some of the terraces collapsed in the last storm. I need to shore them up before the next one, or my good soil will be gone.'

Papa didn't speak. He kissed his wife on the cheek and walked down the steps. She waved, and Cibelle raised her arms to wave back. The child knew her mamma would be in her gardening dress and striding up the stairs before she and her father reached the village. Cibelle didn't understand what pulled her mother to the top of the rocks and away from her family, but it must be something special, because she went every day.

'We're going to have an adventure,' her father said when they reached the bottom of the steps. He kissed her forehead. 'I've never been off the island and neither have you. And there are all these discoveries I've been reading about near Napoli. How about it?'

Cibelle didn't know what her father was talking about. She'd never heard of Napoli and didn't know what an island was, but he was warm and she was comfortable snuggled over his shoulder, so she nodded.

They followed the mule track out of the village, then her papa held out his hand for the bus that rattled past. On the winding roads Cibelle's teeth clacked together, and she was glad when the bus skirted the mountain to drop them at the port. There were more boats than she had fingers and toes, large ones that belched black smoke from their funnels and tore up the water behind them.

She waited by the suitcase while her father bought a ticket, then followed him to the water's edge and onto a waiting boat.

A deep sound vibrated through the ship. It was the engines, Papa said, that would move the ship. Cibelle imagined engines to be huge goats that stomped their hooves to make the noise. The rumbling grew louder; she felt it through her feet, gasping as the boat started to move forward. Holding her hand tightly, her father led her to the back of the boat. The wind was cold. It lifted her curls from her face and tugged at her clothes.

'Wave goodbye to the island,' he said.

Cibelle waved to the craggy mountain with its head in the clouds. She waved to the little houses that clustered around the steep sides of the port and to the seagulls swirling above the fishing boats. Then she scratched her head. 'What is an island, Papa?'

'That is,' said her father, pointing back to the mountain. 'Where we live.'

Cibelle screwed up her face. 'But what does it mean?' she whined. 'I don't understand.'

Her father picked her up and stretched his arms to hold her high. Now she could see both ends of the boat and right over the sides too.

'What do you see?' her father asked.

'Water. All around.'

Her father lowered her gently to the boards. 'Exactly,' he said. 'An island is like a big boat, except it is fixed to the earth and doesn't move. It's part of the earth that pokes out through the sea. Here, I'll show you in the atlas.'

He walked with her to a wooden bench and clicked open his suitcase. There were books on top of his clothes, and he pulled out one with a blue cover. Cibelle recognised this one, remembered touching the frail blue spine on the bookshelf at home. She often saw her father poring over the pages at night after work, when he wasn't looking at other books about fossils, carved stone people or buried cities. The pages of this book were blue and green and brown, divided into squares by dark lines. He said the book contained the whole world. The child shook her head. The world was much too big to be squeezed between two tattered covers.

There were black dots on the pages, with words attached. Cibelle knew about words. Papa was teaching her to understand the funny scrawls. She didn't know how to read them yet, but she knew the names of the little letters that made them. She tried to name the letters in the blue book, but her father turned the pages too quickly. His fingers chose a page, and he pointed at a patch of green shaped like a boot.

'This is what we would look like if you peered down from the sky,' he said. 'The blue is the sea. That tiny green dot is our island. This is the mainland. We're on a boat heading from here to here. See?'

Cibelle didn't see. Nothing on the coloured page looked familiar. She looked up from the page to the island, but there was little of that left now. The sea had swallowed it. All she saw was a grey blur in the distance. Mamma, she thought. Where are you? She looked back at the page, then the sea, the page and the sea, until it made her dizzy. The sea was choppy, swirling with foam. It had been smooth in the harbour, but now rows of little mountains rose up ready to swallow the boat. Sooty smoke poured from the boat's chimney. Cibelle couldn't breathe. She wanted to be back in the little house dug out of the cliff, where the ground didn't sink and swoop and send her belly into her shoes, but all she saw was sea.

Feeling a spasm in her stomach, Cibelle tensed, wishing it away, but the spasm moved up to her throat. She was hot and her heart beat fast in her neck. Suddenly her mouth opened. The spasm escaped with a gush of stinking orange liquid.

It spilt over her chin and onto her father's coat. Cibelle didn't know where it came from. She could only hold her belly until she was empty. Her father carried her to a small room with a tap where he wiped the sticky stuff from her mouth and her hair. When she was clean he wiped his coat, scraping dried sick off his cuffs. He couldn't get the smell out, though. Cibelle wrinkled her nose. The smell made her let go again. Her stomach cramped, she gagged, but nothing came up.

The boat soon docked at Napoli. Cibelle knew that was the name, because she spelt it out to her father and he told her how to say the word. He pointed to a large mountain by the bay, with two peaks and snow on the top. It was much bigger than Cibelle's mountain back home.

'Vesuvio,' her papa said. 'The volcano I told you about.'

He scooped Cibelle with one arm, grabbed the suitcase with the other and walked from the port. He asked the first person he met how to get to the station and followed the trail of pointed fingers towards the piazza.

Cibelle didn't like Napoli. It was all right at the port, because she could smell the salt and see the sky. But the further they walked, the less she liked it. The light was fading and the streets were narrow and dark. High buildings either side dwarfed her. They were dirty and ready to fall down. Wet washing strung between the flats dripped on her head. Newspapers collected in gutters with scraps of rotting food. Dogs shivered in doorways. She could see their ribs. Some nipped at rubbish in the gutters and left huge stinking messes on the footpath. Her father had to swerve to avoid them. He swerved to avoid the bicycles too, the donkeys and horses and carts and trams and cars that crowded the cobbled streets, beeping and honking and ringing their bells.

It was even worse at the piazza by the station. Everywhere Cibelle looked there were people, yelling and laughing and waving fish and tomatoes and cigarettes. One man with a pipe in his mouth held a live chicken by its feet. Cibelle flinched from the wings and the squawk. Old men pinched her and clutched at her father's suitcase, and dirty children held out their hands as they walked through the crowd. She felt sick, as she had on the boat, and she was about to heave when her father stepped through a doorway into a stairwell. The stairs stank of tomcats and sweat, but at least it was quiet and they were alone. Cibelle's stomach settled. Her father carried her up the stairs, where a man behind a desk greeted them. He showed Cibelle and her father to a dim room with six metal bunks and gave them a key for the baggage cupboard.

'Use it at your own risk,' he said.

Even with shutters and window closed, Cibelle heard the yelling from the piazza. She hated this noisy, dirty place. She wanted her own bed, where she could stroke rock walls and listen to the sea and not be afraid of faces that lurched and loomed. She wanted her orange tree. She wanted her mother and the paper her father had given her for drawing.

'I hate you,' she yelled at her father, punching his stomach. 'Why did you bring me here?'

'I'm sorry, little one,' he said. 'I didn't know it would be like this. He curled his body around hers, tucked the thread-bare blanket over them both, then cupped his hands over Cibelle's ears. Immediately, the yelling disappeared. It was replaced by a quiet rushing sound, like the ocean on a summer night. The sound merged with the thud of her father's heartbeat knocking on her back.

. . .

The city didn't seem so bad the next day. A cold wind blew through the streets, but the sky was blue and everything looked clean. It had rained in the night, and most of the rubbish in the streets had been washed away. Without the crowds, Cibelle could see the market stalls with their bright fruits and shiny fish. Cibelle's father took her to a street vendor's for breakfast. He gulped down a coffee and bought her a sweet *sfogliatelle*. Biting into its crisp pastry layers, she licked sugar from her lips, then sucked out the creamy lemon filling. The lemon made her lips tingle.

Buttoned up against the wind, they crossed the piazza and walked to the station. Cibelle had to run to keep up. Occasionally, her father's hand pulled her and she swung from it. She flew until her toes touched the ground again. Her father was excited. He kept licking his lips. That morning he'd pulled another book from his suitcase and shown her sketches of a city destroyed by the big volcano.

Cibelle watched the volcano from the train. Her father said it hadn't erupted in years, but she wasn't sure. When they got off the train, the double peaks of the volcano had swapped sides. Somehow the train had taken them behind the peaks, even though it felt as if they were travelling in a straight line. The volcano looked peaceful enough, but she didn't trust it. Part of it was hidden by cloud, and Cibelle knew that behind the cloud the volcano was scowling.

Pulling Cibelle all over the ruined city, her father pointed out paintings and shop signs and grooves in wet flagstones where feet and cart wheels had worn them down.

'I've wanted to see this all my life,' he said to the child. Cibelle couldn't understand why. All the houses looked like they were falling down. Hardly any had roofs. It's cold here, she thought, and wet.

She lost her father a few times. Stopping to pick up a piece of sparkling stone from the path, then a tiny pinecone and a damp leaf, she sat down on a kerb to rest her wobbly legs. Her father dashed into another crumbling house. Minutes later he came back, scolding her for running away. Too tired to say it was he who had run, Cibelle held out her arms.

He carried her to a part of the city crowded with statues. They weren't smooth like the statues her father made for the church garden, but rough, as if they hadn't been finished.

'They're not statues,' her father said. 'They're people who got caught by the volcano.' He told her they had been trapped by clouds of ash. Their bodies rotted and left holes shaped like them. Years later, scientists had poured plaster into the holes, then chipped away the surrounding rock to reveal the people who had died.

Looking back at the bodies, Cibelle cringed. Mothers bent over children. Old couples curled together against the ash. She saw folds in their clothes, even the weave of the fabric itself. A dog twisted on its back at the end of a chain, tongue out, eyes bulging; captured at the moment the clouds choked it. Cibelle saw a round loaf of bread that had been turned into stone. It was divided into eight triangular pieces and, except for its glittering grey colour, looked ready to be broken up for lunch.

'We eat that bread,' she said. The idea troubled her. Her father nodded. He pointed to a woman with shards of a terracotta pot by her feet.

'They had no idea, did they?' he said. 'She must have been cooking. Living so close to the volcano, what chance did they have?'

Cibelle reached for the woman's hand. Her chubby fingers touched cold plaster, and the plaster crumbled; the edges of the hand drifted through the air. She shook her hands to get the dust off, but it clung. It lingered on her skin, greasy when she rubbed her fingertips together. She bent down to wash her fingers in a muddy puddle, but the stickiness remained.

That night Cibelle dreamt of the volcano. She climbed to the rim and stared at the bubbling rocks below, gripping with bare toes to stop herself sliding in. Across the crater her parents stood with their backs to the volcano mouth. Cibelle felt the ground rumble and watched her parents slide backward. They were falling into the volcano and they didn't know it. She woke up screaming. Other people in the room yelled. Her father held her until the screams stopped.

The next day was cold, but without the blue sky. Cibelle shivered, cupping her fingers around a steaming *cioccolata* until they were warm and tingling. It was Sunday, and she heard the bells calling everyone to Mass. The piazza was almost empty, except for a group of men smoking by a big statue and the thin children pulling at their sleeves.

Her father again took them to the station, but this time they travelled in the opposite direction. He said they were going to another ruined city, one surrounded by burning fields. Cibelle didn't like the sound of that.

They stepped out of the train right next to the sea. It seemed ready to rear up over the platform. Cibelle looked around. She couldn't see any burning fields, but there was a faint smell of fire in the air, reminding her of the time she caught a lock of hair in the candle. The hair had crackled and burnt and left behind the same rotten smell.

Walking along a road with pine trees on either side, the child saw fields of vines in the distance and, close up, the black-eyed flowers of bean plants. She scrabbled on the ground, picking out pale seeds from crushed cones and nibbling them. The road had no end. She was tired already.

'Where are we going?' she asked. She hung heavy on her father's hand.

'I told you, to the city of Cuma,' he said. 'I thought we'd go past the lake.'

Cibelle grumbled. Stupid lake. She didn't know what a lake was, but she knew it would be stupid. Her father led her to a stretch of water, like an enclosed sea. Except it was dirty and green and there were dead birds in the reeds. She didn't like it. Too quiet. No birds sang. No animals twitched the grass. Her breathing was loud and close in her ears.

She recognised the source of the burnt hair smell.

'It stinks,' she said, pursing her lips and scowling. Her papa laughed. He lifted her onto his hip and tickled her. 'My grumpy little Bella,' he said, whispering his pet name for her into her ear. 'My beautiful child.'

Coaxed from her tantrum by his voice, Cibelle closed her eyes and rested her head against her father's shoulder. When she opened her eyes again, they were walking under a stone arch. Looking down, she saw a deep trench with three layers of columns and arches carved into the rock. Grass and scrubby plants grew over the stones, and a rabbit leapt across the path as they approached. A family of black dogs wagged their tails and barked a welcome, their yelps echoing through the chambers. With glossy coats and upright tails, they looked healthier than the ones in Napoli.

This city was messier than Pompei, as if giant fingers had pushed over the stone walls and taken the columns apart, but there was interesting stuff everywhere. Buckets and boxes with netting in the bottom and little shovels like her mother carried up to the garden. There were ropes and hammers and chisels leaning against walls. It was a mess.

'Like your workshop,' she said to her father.

'If only,' he sighed. 'I would give anything to work on this dig.'

An important discovery had been made here, he told her, just a few years ago. A cave had been written about in stories, but lost for thousands of years. One man on the site had looked behind a big oven, and there it was. It had been there all along, hidden by a wall of Roman bricks.

He led Cibelle to an opening in the rock shaped like a broken arrowhead. The child peered into a long tunnel, striped with bands of light.

'Here it is,' her father said. 'The Sibyl's cave. We shouldn't touch anything. They're still excavating.'

Cibelle laughed, because the first thing her father did was touch the walls. He stroked the sharp edges of the excavations, marks fresh from chisel and hammer. He squatted on the ground and fossicked through the piles of rocky chips, holding tiny pieces to the light. His tongue poked from his mouth, and Cibelle knew she had lost him to this old city, as she had in Pompei. As he stood to explore the rest of the ruined city, she walked into the tunnel—quietly, so not to disturb him.

The dogs trotted down the tunnel, and Cibelle followed. She heard the sea far below and the rustle of the wind through the trees outside. Somewhere, further on, she heard water dripping. The sounds didn't frighten her. They reminded her of her little house. It was carved from a similar rock too, pale and hard. She was only frightened when her footsteps disturbed a pair of pigeons. They flapped their wings and screamed, and the echoes in the tunnel made her heart flutter.

The walls of the tunnel were roughly cut and open to the sky at regular intervals, so that light split the darkness through the cracks. Every three steps the child passed from dark to light, light to dark. Ahead, the dogs disappeared when they stepped into a band of darkness. In a light patch, Cibelle peered down at the tunnel floor, finding puddles in the sandy soil and curvy oak leaves collected at the edges. More buckets and hammers down here. Squatting like her father, she dug her hands in the sand, letting it trickle through her fingers. She found fragments of shell and even a splinter of fossil bone, which she pocketed. Standing, she stroked the walls, finding green mould and sharp lines scored into the surface. There were cobwebs, too, and holes cut into the walls.

As she walked further into the tunnel she noticed a smell. It wasn't awful like the lake, but strong, and becoming stronger with every step. It reminded her of dogs in the rain. Perhaps the dogs live here, she thought. There was something else in the smell, sour as vinegar or sweat. She thought she heard a slow song, humming with the wind in the tunnel. It was a sad song, but familiar, and she was drawn to it.

The child walked on. The end of the tunnel opened to a high arched ceiling. The dog smell was stronger here. She saw a little room to the left, with two stone benches and rows of melting candles flickering light into the corners. An old woman sat on one bench. Cibelle froze. She hasn't seen me, she thought, holding her breath. She hasn't.

The woman was thin and spiky. Her limbs were too long for her body; she looked like a cricket ready to jump. If she'd uncoiled her legs to stand she would have towered over the child. The woman wore a fisherman's cap, tufts of white hair sprouting from underneath, and a man's coat. Even so, her wrists poked from the sleeves. She bent forward, feeding bread and meat to the dogs, who gobbled the scraps, then licked the woman's fingers and pushed their heads into her hands.

'Want to feed them too?' she asked. The words were hoarse and slow. Cibelle thought of her father's rasp moving across raw stone. The woman turned to face the child and smiled. She was missing her front teeth. 'They won't bite,' the woman said.

Not knowing what else to do, Cibelle accepted the meat the woman offered and held it out to the dogs. They nipped her gently, nuzzling her with wet noses and licking with coarse tongues. The tongues tickled her wrist. Cibelle's giggles echoed in the chamber.

'Not so bad, eh?' the woman said. She leant close and stared at Cibelle. She had more wrinkles than anyone the child had ever seen, and her skin was the colour of the waxed-wood table at home.

'What have you brought me?' she asked.

Cibelle didn't understand. She hadn't known the woman would be here, so how could she bring anything? She shrugged.

'But you're my guest,' the woman said. 'You must have something? A bite to eat. A coin for an old lady . . .'

Reaching into the pocket of her smock, Cibelle groped with her fingers, but there was nothing there, not even a sticky sweet collecting fluff in the corner. She tried the pocket of her coat too, but that was empty. Except for something hard . . . Cibelle pulled it out and found the piece of bone she'd picked up in the tunnel. She offered it to the woman, who peered at it near the candle flame, then tucked it into her own pocket.

'It'll do,' the woman said. She pulled a bottle of clear liquid from the other pocket. There was a pile of empty bottles in the corner of the room. Cibelle hadn't noticed them before because the light was too dim, but now her eyes had adjusted. The woman uncorked her bottle and offered the child some. Thirsty after her walk, Cibelle filled her mouth until her cheeks swelled, then swallowed. The liquid burnt her throat. She spat it out, waggling her tongue in the air to cool it down.

'Don't waste it!' the woman cried, snatching the bottle back. 'I nearly got caught stealing that one.' She offered the child the bottle again. 'Take little drinks.'

After a few sips Cibelle didn't gag. The drink reminded her of the wine she'd drunk with her parents at dinner once, except this was stronger. She found she liked the warmth that trickled down her belly and lasted long after she'd swallowed. The warmth travelled out from her gut and into her arms and legs. Closing her eyes, she remembered lying on rocks in the sun. She heard waves and the sad cries of gulls. Something tapped her on the head, then she felt the wet tongues of the dogs.

'How are you feeling?' the woman asked.

Cibelle blinked, confused by the presence of stone walls where moments before there had only been the sea. She screwed up her face.

'Dizzy,' she said. 'I can't feel my lips.' She bit down on them, but the feeling was gone. The old woman was talking again, but Cibelle couldn't concentrate on the words because the woman was lisping through her empty front gums, and the sound made the child giggle. She laughed until her eyes watered and her stomach hurt, and then, as suddenly as it appeared, the laughing fit vanished.

The old woman took a stick between her knotted fingers and scratched wave patterns in the sandy floor of the chamber.

'Watch the lines,' she said. Her voice was faint. She seemed to speak without moving her lips. Cibelle obeyed. The rhythm of the woman's hand was regular and as soothing as the sea. Cibelle's eyes drooped. Her chin dropped to her collarbone. Suddenly, she was back on the volcano with her father. He was sliding in. She tapped his chest to warn him, but her hand passed straight through his ribs. It was warm inside the cavity of his chest, and wet, and Cibelle pulled her hand back in disgust. Something quivered in her closed fist. She opened her fingers and found her father's heart in her palm, labelled like the diagrams in his anatomy book. Somehow she could read the Latin names of the different chambers, of the veins and arteries sprouting from the organ. She screamed.

When Cibelle opened her eyes she was in the cave again. Her scream echoed along the tunnel, loud as a hundred wailing mouths, and she put her hands over her ears to keep the sound out. Her own heart fluttered. It had risen to her throat, choking her. She couldn't breathe.

The old woman stroked Cibelle's hair, and gradually the child's heart slowed. Her breathing returned to its usual rhythm. She watched the old woman scrape a handful of dry leaves from the edges of the cave, then scatter them over the sand.

'What do you see, little one?' the woman asked.

Cibelle shrugged. She was tired of this game. Her feet stung from the walk, and she was hungry. She wanted to eat now, eat everything. Olives, sweet flaky pastries, camellia petals dipped in sugar, bread fresh from the oven and spread with tomatoes. Triangles of fried polenta. And then she wanted to sleep. She sighed.

'A pile of leaves. Stupid leaves,' she said.

'What do you see in the leaves?'

'Veins. Wrinkles. Holes.' Cibelle felt like saying all the rude words she'd overheard in the piazza, but she didn't. She thought them, though, sent them to this horrid lady who kept asking questions and poking her when her eyes were closed.

'What do they make you think of?' the woman asked.

'An old woman. Like you. Ugly.' Cibelle squinted in the candlelight. 'What am I supposed to see? They're just leaves.' She paused. 'Hang on. I see something. A shape. It's . . .'

Before she could finish her sentence a gust of wind from the tunnel disturbed the leaves. They scattered, scuttling over the sand like crabs at low tide. Only one leaf remained. Cibelle stamped her foot onto it.

'I nearly had it. I saw a face. But it's gone now.'

The old woman pulled the leaf from beneath the child's shoe. The leaf was long and curved. Bending close to examine it, Cibelle thought it smelt of lemon.

'Take this with you when you go,' the old woman said. 'It might help you remember.'

Tucking the leaf in her pocket, Cibelle walked along the tunnel. Her legs trembled and she couldn't walk straight. Her head hurt. She squinted into the light at the other end of the passage and saw a dark figure running towards her.

'Cibelle!'

Her father picked her up and clutched her to his chest. 'Where have you been? I couldn't find you, and then I heard the scream, but I couldn't work out where it came from. I ran all the way up to the acropolis . . .'

'There was a woman,' Cibelle said. She couldn't make the words. They were furry inside her mouth and her lips weren't working. 'She gave me a drink.' She burped, then giggled. Her father sniffed her breath.

'Grappa!' he said. 'Where is she?'

Cibelle pointed. Her father sprinted to the stone room with Cibelle joggling against his chest. The candles had been blown out, leaving trails of smoke in the air, and the woman and her dogs were gone. Her father shook his head.

'I shouldn't have left you alone,' he said, stroking Cibelle's hot cheek. 'I get distracted. Not any more,' he said. 'I won't leave you again.'

That evening in Napoli, Cibelle's father took her away from the piazza by the station. He took her to Santa Lucia, where young couples kissed by the water and bony cats crawled over sea walls. The fishing boats lit their lanterns and headed out for the night. The sun was low and orange. It tinted the sweep of the bay; even the snow on top of the volcano glowed. Cibelle's head still hurt, and she had to squint because of the light, but she decided she didn't mind the city.

Her father led her to a small restaurant overlooking the sea. 'A special meal,' he said, 'for our last night.'

They sat at a table with crisp white cloth napkins and shiny silver forks. Papa said they could only afford antipasto, but when the plates came they were overflowing with mussels and sun-dried tomatoes and spinach and two tiny octopuses. Cibelle chewed and sucked, dribbling oil over herself and the table-cloth.

Once she had cleared her plate, she looked up. Her father had hardly touched his meal. He was staring at a group of people at another table, who were talking loudly and waving their hands in the air. Cibelle didn't know what they were discussing, but it made their foreheads shiny and their cheeks red. She carefully brought her fingers around to steal her father's octopus, but he didn't notice. He was muttering and shaking his head.

'It is so frustrating,' he said. 'Don't they realise?' He bit his lips and clenched his fingers, and Cibelle saw he was going red too. She jumped when he stood up. In a loud voice he told the other table that they were stupid for believing the rubbish they were fed, that they should learn to form their own opinions and not follow blindly.

'Fascist, anti-Fascist, Communist, Catholic—you're as bad as each other!' With that, he sat down. There was a moment of silence, then the people began to clap. They moved their chairs and welcomed him into the circle, filling his glass with wine and urging him to tell them about himself. He put Cibelle on his knee and settled in.

'I'm only a stonemason,' he said, smiling, 'but I have given this some thought . . .'

The people at the table groaned, then urged him to continue. The child watched her father swell with the attention. Soon, he was waving his arms with the rest of them.

Cibelle didn't mind; she liked seeing her father this way. Also, everyone was too interested in talking to care about their food, so she nibbled the leftovers within reach. She tried cheese that tasted like ham, little parcels of spinach pasta and tiny balls of puff pastry stuffed with cream.

Full and sleepy, she looked around the room. Other tables were not as loud as theirs. A man eating alone seemed to be following the conversation. He often looked at her father, then scribbled in a small notebook. She didn't like this man. He stared and made her nervous. She wanted her father to take her back to the island, but he was happy talking. He talked until the waiters coughed and looked at the clock and asked them all to leave.

All the way back to the room by the station, her father talked. He was explaining things to her, the things he had discussed at the table. She didn't understand any of it, only that he was happy. The crowds of men in the piazza stared as he passed, but his voice must have scared them away, because they left them alone.

That night Cibelle didn't sleep well. Her belly bubbled and groaned, bulging with rich food. Her head hurt. She decided she hated the smelly old woman and her grappa, and all the people in the restaurant. Her father was restless beside her, tossing and sweating and muttering to himself. Images and words from the last days swooped in her head. She heard her father's voice, then the old woman, then the laughter of the people at the table. Putting her hands over her ears didn't help, because the voices were inside her head, and she couldn't make the sea noise like her father. She was glad when the bells on the alarm clock jangled her father awake, and they could begin the journey home.

Cibelle had been back on the island for four days. She had counted the pale winter sunrises on her fingers. The family was eating lunch, sardines and pasta and bitter green salad, when a stone came through the window of the house in the rocks. Cibelle screamed. She felt her father's arms lift her from the seat and tuck her under the table. She often played under the table, but today the space below was different. She could only see her parents' feet and part of their legs. The truncated view disturbed her, as if the rest of their bodies had been chopped off or stolen.

'Don't move,' her mother yelled.

No fear. The child was petrified.

Her father walked over shards of glass, and Cibelle heard them crunch beneath his boots. There was a stone on the floor with a sheet of paper wrapped around it. He knelt to unwrap the paper. She saw it was inscribed with only one word.

'Traitor,' he spat. Sighing, he opened the door. 'They're in a boat. Cowards!'

Barefoot, her mother stepped carefully between the glass fragments towards her father. Their feet almost touched—Mamma's toes next to Papa's boots. Cibelle had never looked at her mother's feet before. They were beautiful, the colour of the glazed terracotta bowl she scooped water from in the mornings. Watch out, Cibelle wanted to scream, watch out for the glass, but her mouth wouldn't move.

'What have you done?' her mamma said. She was up on tiptoes.

'I haven't . . .'

'Don't. Don't tell me this was unprovoked. Things like this don't just happen. People make them happen. Who have you upset?'

'No one. I . . .'

Mamma took a step forward, then Papa took one back. They repeated this pattern until Papa's heels touched the wall. Then he bent his knees and slid down the wall to the floor. He put his head in his hands.

'I got talking to a group of people in Napoli. We were having dinner. They were ranting on about what Fascism has done for this country. I . . .'

Her mother tapped her toes. 'And?'

'I didn't say anything. At first. But I . . . I had to . . . I may have complained about them melting down your wedding ring for the invasion. And about Spain. I didn't think that . . .'

Cibelle watched her mother's foot swing to kick her father's shin.

'Stupid man. You don't think at all. You can't say those things any more. Maybe in the village, yes. But Napoli? The Prefect himself might have been standing next to you. They'll cart you away for less. Don't you realise? It's not just about you. What would she do if anything happened to us?'

Cibelle hated them shouting. She put her hands over her ears, but the shouting travelled through her fingers. She climbed out from under the table, kept her hands over her ears, and yelled louder than she thought she could.

'Stop!'

The word bounced off the stone walls, filling the room with its echoes. Cibelle repeated the word quietly. Over and over and over until the words turned into one long hiss. Her father stood. He didn't say anything, just picked her up and rocked her gently.

'I'll go to the port and get another sheet of glass,' he said.

Cibelle's mother knelt and swept the broken glass into a pile.

'There's no point,' she said. 'They'll do it again. When you next forget.'

Her husband shook his head. 'I won't forget.'

Three weeks passed, bringing the bright festivities of Christmas and New Year then, a week later, Cibelle's seventh birthday. That evening, as the family gathered by the fire, her mother put down her glass of wine, opened the atlas and laid it on the table.

'I came from Kythera,' she said. 'I walked to the water and found a boat. It was blue. Had an eye painted on the front.'

The child watched her mother speak. It was rare to see her this way, flushed with wine and talkative. Cibelle wanted to say how beautiful she looked, but she kept her mouth shut, frightened the wrong words would scare her mother away.

'The sailor was waiting for me,' her mamma continued. 'Playing cards with the children. He took me all the way to Piraeus for a basket of grapes.'

Her father laughed. 'You got a good deal.'

Her mother smiled. She traced a line between Greece and Italy with her fingers.

'Later, in another boat, I crossed the Ionian Sea and came through the Strait of Messina. We . . . '

'You're making that up!' Papa interrupted. 'No one attempts the Strait. Experienced sailors go around Sicily rather than risk that shortcut.'

'It's true,' her mother said. 'Although your way might've been better. For my stomach . . . '

She rubbed her belly, then turned to the child. 'In that part of the world they have three huge tides a day, and whirlpools. All foam and bubble. Our captain had to steer between them.'

'Where do they come from, the whirlpools?' Cibelle asked.

'The captain told us a story,' her mother said. 'Underneath the water lives a terrible monster called Charybdis. You'll never see her, but three times a day she sucks in the water, then spews it back out again. She's the one who makes the whirlpools.'

'You know what?' her father asked.

Cibelle smiled. He had that expression again, the one he wore before doing something silly. 'What?'

'She does this if she catches you.'

She squealed as her father lunged, lifting her high into the air. Strong fingers gripped her ribs, then swung her around. The world spun.

'Mamma, help!' she yelled, laughing. 'The monster's got me!'

Cibelle was dizzy when her father put her down. She stumbled and reached for the table to steady herself, but missed. She slid to the floor, her bottom slapping cold stone. Crawling under the table, she felt the room spin.

The room was still spinning when the door opened. Cibelle watched pairs of black boots and black trousers pour into the kitchen, until they blocked out the light, blocked her view of her parents' legs. Everyone was shouting. She heard glass break and her mother scream, cut short by a loud slap. Her father's voice was hoarse. Cibelle curled into a ball on the floor. She yelled too, yelled for the black boots to leave, for them to shut up, for her parents to rescue her. She yelled until her throat hurt, until the muscles in her neck felt ready to snap.

The boots marched out. Cibelle peered from under the table. The room was empty, the floor sullied with muddy footprints and broken glass. Cibelle couldn't find her parents. She heard shouts outside the house, along the beach. Tucking the atlas under her pullover, she jumped down the steps towards the wharf. Her parents struggled in a tangle of black arms, her mother wide-eyed and open-mouthed, her father with a cut on his cheek. Cibelle ran along the promontory, but her parents were already in the boat. She ran to the water's edge, even though her lungs burnt and her heart beat faster than she could count. She watched the green and red lights of the boat disappearing behind the edge of the island. Her parents were gone. There was nothing left of them but the boat's wake, curving into the darkness.

Cibelle looked up. Two men with black boots and shirts stood over her on the wharf. She recognised one as the scribbling man from the restaurant on the mainland. She leapt. For a split second she flew. Then an arm caught her waist and slammed her back to the wharf. She sprawled on the stones, gasping, her tongue stuck out like a dog. She heard her own breathing and the thump of her heart. She couldn't stop shaking.

Then she saw a woman, with wild hair and a shawl over her nightgown, running along the wharf. It was Luisa, the fisherman's wife, who had often carried fresh goats' milk to the house on the promontory.

'What harm can she do?' Luisa asked, panting. 'She's a child.'

The men didn't answer. The fisherman's wife snorted. 'I'll tell the women that the Blackshirts are afraid of a little girl!'

She knelt down and wrapped her shawl around the child. Strong arms scooped Cibelle up, crumpled her against a wobbly breast.

'Don't worry about her,' she heard one of the men say. 'We've got work to do.'

Luisa carried Cibelle across the wharf and up a twisting set of stairs, to a little house with peeling plaster walls and a statue of the Madonna in an alcove. She put Cibelle in front of a fire that crackled and spat. Cibelle stared at the glowing embers, watched the flames flow over the wood like water. She reached out to the flames, felt the hairs on her arms singe, before the fisherman's wife slapped her hand away.

'Drink,' Luisa said, and thrust a glass to the girl's lips. Cibelle swallowed and winced, then swallowed until warmth flooded her throat and eased her tremors. Grappa, she thought. Luisa tried to pull the atlas from Cibelle's arms, but the child gripped tightly. She'd grabbed the book on instinct, couldn't leave it behind, and she wasn't going to give it up now. Wrapping Cibelle in a coarse blanket, Luisa lifted the child onto her lap, rocking her gently.

'Let it out,' she said, stroking Cibelle's cheek. 'They'll bring your parents back soon, I know they will.'

Cibelle stared at the fire. There were no tears. She felt the graze on her knee where she had skidded along the wharf and the bruise where the atlas had dug into her ribs, but inside she felt nothing.

. . .

Cibelle didn't cross the narrow path to the promontory. Keeping her back to the rocky outcrop, she learnt not to look at the smoke scars above the windows or the pile of ashes near the front door where the men from Napoli had burnt her father's books. She shook her head when the fisherman's children invited her to play. Instead, she curled up with the dogs outside their house and pressed her ear to the stone stairs, listening for the steady thud of her father's footsteps. I will hear him coming, she thought. Won't be long now.

One chill morning, alone inside the fisherman's house, Cibelle opened her atlas and stroked the pages. Her father had said the atlas contained the whole world. If she looked hard enough, peered closely at the blue and green pages, she would find her parents in the tiny letters and dark lines that divided the earth.

The fisherman and his wife talked to Cibelle often, but she rarely answered. She didn't know why. They were good people and they cuddled her and fed her bread and sweet buns, but she didn't know what to say to them. After a month, they stopped talking about Cibelle's parents returning. They talked about sending her to a little school close to the port, the one their own children went to, where she could learn to read and write. Cibelle didn't tell them that she already knew how to read or that she was afraid to leave the village in case her parents returned. At the dinner table the couple talked about the war in Spain and next year's grape harvest, chewing over all the local gossip. One day they spoke of a crazy old woman who had come to stay in the village.

'She's back again,' the fisherman said. 'We see her every few years. Stays until someone chucks her out, then finds a new place.'

Luisa laughed. 'Last time she was here we found her talking to an olive tree. She talked to the tree for half an hour, as if there was someone there.'

After lunch that day, Cibelle didn't take her usual nap. She walked down the steps to the wharf and looked for the source of the couple's gossip. It wasn't difficult to find her, slumped against a pile of fishy nets. It was the woman from the cave. She'd lost her cap, and her hair stood up in messy spikes, but she'd brought the dogs. Kneeling, Cibelle held out her hand until the youngest dog licked her.

'Nice place,' the old woman said. 'I wondered where you came from. They turfed me out of the old city, you know. Practically pushed me onto the ferry. No respect for their elders.'

Cibelle sat with the woman, feeling the knots of the nets against her spine, the floats and weights digging into her ribs. They sat together in silence, listening to the waves and the snuffling dogs, until Cibelle began to speak. She was surprised by the muddled words that tumbled from her mouth—she couldn't stop them. She told the woman about her parents and about the men who had taken them from her, about the meal in Napoli and the wake of the boat on the night they were taken. The woman listened, sucking from her bottle and nodding. She pointed at the sun about to slide below the horizon.

'Go home, little Cibelle,' she said. 'They'll be worried.'

Cibelle shook her head. She didn't want to return to the fisherman and his wife.

'What's your name?' she asked. 'You never told me.'

The old woman bared her gums, and it took Cibelle a moment to realise it was a smile.

'Never tell anyone,' the woman said.

'But what do I call you?'

'Up to you.'

Cibelle stamped her foot. 'But that's not fair. You know what I'm called. Why won't you tell me?'

The woman stood and brushed sand and dead leaves from her trousers.

'The power of the first secret,' she said. 'Remember what it feels like.'

'I don't care. I've got a secret of my own,' Cibelle said, thinking of her atlas. 'You don't know what it is.'

The old woman smiled. 'You learn fast.' She bent forward to whisper in Cibelle's ear. 'Your father is coming. Any day now.'

Cibelle ran up the steps to the fisherman's house, past villagers taking their evening walks. Everything she saw was beautiful. Faces glowed in the last rays of the sun. Houses radiated warm pinks. The orange trees had blossomed early and their fragrance hung in the air. They were coming back! Cibelle ran through the house to the little room where she had been sleeping. She filled a bag with her atlas and the clothes Luisa had given her, hand-me-downs from her own children, cut to size. She didn't sleep that night. She listened to the sea and waited for the dawn.

When the sun came up, Cibelle stood with her bag in the piazza by the wharf. The old woman was gone, but that didn't matter. Would they come by boat, or on foot down the mule track? She didn't know, so she looked in both directions, afraid that by turning away she would miss them. All day she looked for the tall man and the woman with curly hair, but they didn't come. Apart from the fishing boats, no one docked at the wharf, and the only person she'd seen come down the mule track was a skinny man with bright orange hair. At dusk she sank to the ground and let the fisherman carry her back to the house.

The man with the orange hair was sitting at the table. He spoke to her, but the words came out crushed, and Cibelle couldn't understand what he said. Luisa knelt beside her and explained that this kind man had come to look after her, he had come to take her back to England with him, and tomorrow they would go on a boat together, and then on a train. Cibelle shook her head. She couldn't leave—she was waiting for her parents. The old lady said they were coming any day now. She kicked and screamed and knocked over the wineglasses, but the fisherman and his wife shook their heads.

The next day Cibelle scrabbled and dragged her heels in the sandy path, until the man with the orange hair picked her up. Cibelle was exhausted when they reached the top of the hill. She went limp, flopping in the man's arms like a doll. The village was far below them now, and tiny.

'I am taking you to England,' the man said.

'My father is coming!' Cibelle yelled, but he kept walking up the winding road.

'I hate you,' Cibelle said quietly. 'I hate you.'

Leaf

New South Wales 1990

Birdsong calls Billie to consciousness, away from a dream of pumice-grey rocks beside a gentle ocean. Sweating with only a sheet over her, yet reluctant to move, she keeps her eyes shut and listens, picturing the bird clearly behind closed lids. A currawong, with glossy black feathers and yellow eyes, its fluid notes a call from another world. Invading her dream, it perches on the rocks, claws scraping the pitted surface, before opening its wings to flap the dream away.

Next, a pair of cackling kookaburras. Oversized dowdy king-fishers, always dishevelled, they're Billie's favourites, with only a tiny patch of blue on the wings to link them to their glamorous European cousins. Two summers back, she left chunks of Italian sausage on the railing of her deck and watched, fascinated, as a kookaburra swooped from the angophora beside her house to snatch the meat. It twisted its head, smashing the sausage against the wood as if it fought a wriggling lizard.

Squawking and squabbling, the lorikeets come next, and Billie imagines the riot of green and red feathers outside her window. They'll be out there when she rises, tame as pets and bold enough to eat sunflower seeds from her cupped palm.

Soon the rising sun will hit the glass, filtered through a canopy of eucalypts, to warm her face and fill her studio with light. Time to get up. She's got to finish a commission for a couple up river, and the Sydney gallery that sells her work wants four of her leaf paintings for an exhibition next month.

Yes, there's work to be done, but she's not quite ready to move. Languid, she stretches her arms back, grazing knuckles on the sandstone wall behind the bed. Striped with rusty sediment lines, the wall was here when she bought the sloping plot, as well as four massive pine poles bored into bedrock. The contrasts appealed to her eye—the horizontals of the neatly stacked blocks, the pine verticals and the chaos of paperbark and fern that claimed the rest of the site. The blocks and poles were relics from the previous owner, who tired of the island even before his house was finished, but she kept them, sweating alongside carpenters to preserve the relics within floors and walls. The striped blocks are the keystone of her studio, supporting two wooden walls squared by a wall of glass.

When Billie finally opens her eyes, she cringes. The bench running beside her window is littered with charcoal sketches, pots of brushes, the paint-streaked pebbles she uses to support her tools, pencil stubs and rolls of butcher's paper, with a small space cleared for work-in-progress. The two wooden walls hide behind a layer of paper: preparation sketches for earlier commissions, watercolours of the river, a pencil drawing of her hand holding a roll-your-own. On wooden planks supported by scavenged bricks, she stores her sketchbooks, a haphazard collection of spines in all colours and sizes, most thumb-stained with ink or paint.

Outsiders would dismiss the mess as the product of a cluttered mind, but Billie knows the location of every scrap and shred. In the chaos, she sees patterns unfurl like fern fiddle-heads. If a gust of wind from the open window rustles the papers, she feels the difference and notes the new locations. Trained to observe, her eyes take in the changes automatically.

For years she's been meaning to organise the studio, sort and archive the old material ready for the next work, but some-how there is never enough time. The days slip away, and the studio never changes. Old procrastinator, she thinks. Of course there is time, but something stops her.

Stan, a painter friend from her Sydney days, often teases her about it. For almost ten years he has inhabited a fibro shed behind her house and, one humid Sunday afternoon last summer, after they had made bottle-shaped holes in Billie's wine cellar, he bailed her up.

'You paint on leaves and sell them as "ephemera",' he had said, marking the word with his fingers, 'but you can't bear to let go of even the smallest slip of paper. Eventually your studio will be full to the gills—what are you going to do then?'

'It's my marketing plan,' she had said, laughing, avoiding his question. 'When the leaves crumble, people will have to come back and buy another.'

It had been a risk, beginning to work with the leaves. At the time Stan told her she was crazy. Why give up a good living? She'd made a niche for herself in the city, painting portraits of wealthy eastern suburbs couples and their children. Satisfied customers referred her to their friends. It was mechanical work, without inspiration, but it paid well, and she did it for years, fulfilled enough by the brush in her hand. Renting the small-est room in Kings Cross, she saved most of her earnings, banked them where other artists in her circle drank them away at the bars on the street. She made few good friends, only Stan really, and ten years quickly passed. At the time, she didn't know why she did it. She just knew she had to.

One blistered March evening, Billie trudged past the strip joints after a preliminary sketch in Vaucluse, burdened with rolls of paper and her tackle box. She looked down at the pavement, air rippling above bitumen, to avoid the dog shit and sick on the path, but kept the edges of her vision sharp, especially when passing alleys rank with piss and rotting garbage. She avoided the sad eyes of junkie prostitutes, stick-insect thin and shadowed in doorways, and walked around the rusty stain near her building's door. A pimp had been stabbed the week before and, until yesterday, the place of his death had been marked by police tape.

She'd put her box down to unlock the door of her building and, bending to retrieve it, she noticed a leaf trapped under one corner. A gum leaf, long and curved. It seemed out of place in Billie's street, lined with flats and without a tree in sight. Intrigued, she picked up the leaf, ravaged by insects, and held it to her nose. It smelt of lemon. In her mind, triggered by the smell, an old woman rasped: 'Take it with you when you go. It will help you remember.'

That evening in her room above Kings Cross, portrait work ignored, she painted a tiny acrylic impression on the leaf. A dead tree on a dry plain, a memory from her first train journey from Melbourne. She held the image to the light bulb and frowned. A quick sketch, badly executed, but, by the tingling in her gut and the nervous flutter of her heart, she knew the rest of her life hinged on the scarred leaf in her hands.

The next week Billie withdrew $600 from her savings and bought a station wagon, a two-tone green FB Holden with chipped paint and dull chrome—twelve years old now and too battered to be worth stealing. She tied thread around the leaf stalk and hung it from the FB's rear-view mirror, so it swayed as she swerved, behind the wheel for the first time in twenty-five years. On the weekends, she locked her flat and drove from the city, directed by the lemon oils of the leaf.

Over the next six months, she came to know the green places at the fringes of the city, north, south and west, where the sprawl fell away. Places with birds and cicadas and fragrant morning air. Until one spring day, September 1975, she found herself on the road to the island.

In the studio, a rustle from the ceiling makes her look up. Above her head, hundreds of dried leaves cluster like bats in a cave. Broad fig blades and elms, eucalypts like inverted tears, hearts from the flame trees and sinuous oaks. Native and imported varieties side by side, each with a tiny image in oil or acrylic, painted with the finest sable.

The leaves overhead, twirling on the ends of their threads, are the ones Billie can't part with, even though she knows the gallery owner who sells her work would snap them up. The first leaf she ever painted hangs there, crumbly as old books and rubbing against the newest, oils still tacky. These she paints for herself, not others. Images from her sketches appear, faces and places she hasn't seen in almost thirty years, not since she disembarked in Port Melbourne, one of the £10 passengers from England. Eddied by river breezes, the painted memories rasp against each other in random patterns, new every day.

Stan is right: she's running out of room, struggling to find a bare patch of ceiling, but she doesn't have the heart to sell any of these leaves. She could take them down and archive them by date, by subject, but it doesn't seem right. They've become an installation. She has grown accustomed to their whispers.

Other leaves, with miniatures of ghost gums or sandstone boulders gazing at their reflections in the river, she mounts on creamy backing card and sends to the gallery in town. The tourists love them, the owner says, buying enough now to cover Billie's food and rates. Overseas visitors, unable to carry the leaves back through customs, pack her watercolour landscapes into their suitcases or fold their clothes around the pen-and-ink coils of grevillea stamens. It wasn't always like that. The first five years on the island, she drove the green FB into town, relying on her portraits to feed her and pay the mortgage. Her leaves, painted between commissions, sold slowly at first, scorned by the abstract expressionists of her old circle for being too realist, too folksy. Over the last years, though, they've found plenty of buyers, and she paints fast to satisfy the gallery's demands.

Suddenly, Billie can no longer lie still. Her fingers fidget, impatient to be working. She folds back the sheet and stands, slipping a loose cotton dress over her head. Barefoot, she pads out of her studio into the hall, floorboards cool against her soles. The house is quiet—as usual she is the first up. Troy, the young bloke who cooks for her in return for a place to stay, was at a party on the mainland last night. Billie heard his tinnie skip across the river only a few hours before dawn. His door is closed, and she doubts she will see him before noon. I might be cooking lunch today, she thinks, smiling at the thought of the young man who answered her advertisement.

She'd placed the ad three years ago, when her leaves really took off, tired of forgetting to eat, or scoffing eggs on toast because there wasn't time for anything else. Four people turned up for interviews, all river dwellers, but three fidgeted and didn't look right in her kitchen. With tanned, scrawny limbs and white-blond dreadlocks, Troy hopped from his tinnie carrying a basket of vegetables and a bream he'd caught that morning. He was eighteen; on the cusp of adulthood, yet with features still touched by the delicate androgyny of adolescence. His eyes drew her, vivid blue and rimmed with white lashes, salt crystalline around a rock pool. I will draw you like an ocean beach, Billie thought, as they walked together up the hill to the house. Turquoise, tan and white.

Stuffing the fish with herbs, Troy pan-fried it for her, filling the kitchen with the smell of hot butter and opening her cupboards as if they were his own to search for plates. He'd been cooking lunch ever since.

'Why do you want the job?' she'd asked, as they sat outside savouring the fish with a Pinot Grigio from Billie's stash.

'I love to cook,' he'd said simply, 'and I can't live at home.'

Afraid he was too young, Billie had been ready to convince him to return to his parents, but then had a sudden memory of herself at that age. At eighteen, she had known she couldn't go home either. She raised her glass.

'Welcome to the island.'

He ferried his belongings over that afternoon. There didn't seem enough, just a bag of clothes, one other bulging with recipe books, and a fishing reel and nets in the tinnie. Months later, Billie discovered it was all he could grab when his parents turfed him out, and that he'd spent the month before the interview bunking on a friend's floor.

In the kitchen, lighting the gas for her first tea of the day and adjusting the knob to keep the flames within the circumference of the kettle, Billie peers out the window towards Stan's fibro shed at the back of the property. It was the first thing to go up when she bought the land, and she'd lived in it as the house grew. Stan moved in after the house was built, when debt collectors kicked him out of his flat because he never had enough buyers to pay his rent.

It was only fair, Billie had thought at the time. Before she'd found her tiny room in Kings Cross, Stan had put her up. She'd met him in a bar on her first night in Sydney and, after hours of drinking, he'd offered her a place to stay until she found her feet. There was more to it than that; she saw it in his eyes. Bet you sleep with every new girl in town, she'd thought. Making it clear she wouldn't be sharing his bed, she accepted. It became a flattering joke between them: Stan propositioning, Billie manoeuvring out of it. Over the next months, Billie's portrait career took off, but Stan's remained on a plateau. When clients invited her to parties, she took Stan along, but few were interested in his paintings. Her income often paid the rent. After six months, needing space, she moved into her own flat, and Stan struggled. During her Kings Cross years she'd bought his work when things got really tight—although not often enough to deflate his pride. Billie was settled in her house on the island when Stan was evicted. Worried that she had left him to founder, she offered him her shed.

Today there's no movement inside the shed or on the little verandah. Like Troy, Stan is a late sleeper, not lifting his brush before the sun is low in the sky and working into the night.

Billie doesn't mind sharing her house with two night owls, because it means the mornings are hers alone. She carries her mug outside and sits on the deck in the new light, inhaling cool morning air and listening to the birds. Lorikeets squawk from the railing, but she shows them her empty palms. Nothing today, she thinks. I've run out.

This time of morning, before any words are spoken, prepares her for the day ahead, distilling fractured images from her dreams into ideas for future paintings. She never smokes before midday, reluctant to sully the air with musty fumes. Later, when others have breathed it in and the air has lost its dawn purity, she will roll her first, but now it is sacrilege.

On this morning, she sips her tea. Strong and hot, with only a dribble of milk and no sugar: rationing-style, as she's had it since she was nine. Exactly as she likes it, yet she frowns, thinking about Stan. Something niggles. Every night for the past month, as she's climbed his sandstone steps to say goodnight, she has not found Stan in his usual spot in front of his easel, Brylcreem hair slicked from his face and shirtsleeves rolled. He's the same age as Billie, but his restless male energy makes him seem a good decade younger. If you didn't look too closely, he could be a suave film star from the sixties, always with a woman nearby. Most of them posed for him. His Muses, he once called them, when Billie teased him about the stream of women through his studio.

'More like a flood,' he'd said, with a wink.

Lately, Billie has found him slumped in front of the television. The night before, she joined him on the sofa, watching images flickering from Kuwait. Perhaps it was the eerie light from the screen, but Billie thought he looked older, suddenly frail, with creased skin and slumped shoulders, hair thinner across his forehead.

The blank canvas in the corner of the shed disturbed her. Normally monumental nudes stared from Stan's canvases, their lines drawn in big, raw strokes, distorted almost to abstraction, then single features, like the glitter in their eyes or the curve of one earlobe, carefully worked in photo-realistic detail. The opposite of Billie's miniatures, but she loves these brash nudes with their crimson lips and nipples. Last night his easel had held a three-foot square of bare canvas. Hoping he would talk, she'd sat with him until her eyes drooped, until she knew she had to stagger to bed or she would end up sleeping on his sofa, but he never once spoke. She'd stood, resting her hand on his knee.

'Good night, my friend.'

He nodded, but didn't look away from the screen. As Billie was about to drift off to sleep, she realised how long it had been since she'd woken to find one of Stan's women smoking on his verandah, face flushed, hair in clumps, clad only in an old shirt.

On the deck, Billie gulps the dregs of her tea, still troubled by Stan's blank canvas. She walks inside to the bathroom, standing under the shower until the cool water rinses off the sweat. The air is beginning to heat up; the morning's clarity replaced by a muggy haze. Another stinker on the way, probably with a storm in the evening, so she doesn't dry herself, but leaves her skin damp before slipping back into her cotton frock.

In front of the mirror, she swirls her wet hair into a loose bun and skewers it in place with a slender paintbrush she finds next to her toothbrush. She must walk out of the studio with paintbrushes in her hand, put them down as she goes to the toilet or makes another cuppa. Last week she found one in the fridge, balanced on a jar of sun-dried tomatoes. She catches her reflection's eyes, taps her temple. Mind's going already, old girl. Decrepitude can't be far off.

I really am sixty, she thinks, staring at the lined face in the glass. Probably more lined, she realises, because her eyes are changing as she gets older, losing the ability to see small details. Her reflection surprises her; in her heart she often imagines herself near thirty, a young woman new in Australia. She hadn't known what to expect; she yearned to be away from the cramped familiarity of England, and Australia was as far away as she could get.

The *North Wind* had dropped her in Melbourne, and she stayed for two years, adjusting slowly to the harsh accents, to Orion's stars in a handstand and the inverted face of the moon. Eventually, chilled by squally winters and cramped, terraced streets too similar to London, she had caught a train and headed north, called by the Mediterranean blue skies and pink frangipanis she'd seen in pictures of Sydney. She had stared out the train window, stunned by the parched land separating the two cities. When her eyes strained with the glare, she shifted their focus to her own reflection in the tinted glass, a sallow ghost superimposed over dry fields.

Billie is slow to accept the face staring back from the bathroom mirror, with cheeks sagging to jowls and permanent creases between her brows. It happens so quickly. She squints, blurs her eyes, and the reflection shows a younger face, but only until she blinks. They're always there, she realises, the earlier selves, layered inside like Russian dolls. You just have to learn to re-focus your eyes.

In her studio, she sits at her desk and snaps on her lamp, needing all the light she can get now. She stares at the messmate leaf pinned to a sheet of board in front of her, the commission for the river couple. It's a big leaf, broad as her spread fingers, unlike the gum-slivers upon which she once painted. The leaves, and the images on them, have grown as her vision changed. Troy found the messmate on top of the island, a eucalypt imported from Victoria, sheltering beside a sandstone boulder. He gathered leaves for her, presented them like a bouquet of flowers, after she told him she was losing the details, pushing her work further away to see what she was painting.

The messmate leaf is stiff and dry, pressed flat for weeks between old newspapers and then primed with oil-based grounds. The layer of white evens the colour, but the epidermis is dimpled, like human skin. Lightly, with a soft pencil, she has sketched the basic shapes of the composition and, over the last few days, has begun to paint oils on the sealed surface. When it is finished, when the oils dry, she will varnish it with beeswax and thinners. She doesn't usually seal her leaves, preferring to let them crack with time and air, but the couple insisted. It was for an anniversary celebration, they said, and it didn't seem right to have something flake and decay. She could have stuck to her guns, but the money made it worthwhile. It's the same with the gallery work, the same as her old portraits. I'm buying time, she thinks, for my island life, for my other leaves. A necessary compromise.

The couple have given Billie a photograph of themselves, smiling from their clinker-built boat, and she works closely with it. Her pupils flex until she no longer sees the couple but patterns of shade and form, which she works to transfer to her leaf.

For the first days of the week she blocked in the basic colours with a wide brush, underpainting with pigment thinned by turpentine, then working in greater detail. Paint mixed with damar glaze and a drop of cobalt drier, oily and dark as she applied it, has dried transparent to seal in the base colours. Yesterday she began with less diluted pigments, blending the base shades of sky and river. Over the next week the paint she uses will thicken, her brush tips narrowing, as the detail becomes finer.

Settling into the chair, tongue tucked in the corner of her mouth, Billie gets to work. The process is a function of her hands, not her conscious mind, and she lets them move, satisfied by slick bristles and the whiff of paint. Liberated from the task, her mind explores other subjects: what she will paint next for herself and the gallery, the brushes and sketchbooks she needs to order, other places on the island she wants to explore in pastels and watercolour.

Lifting her brush from the leaf, Billie shifts in her seat. Her shoulders are hunched, and her fingers cramp around the brush. She looks at the clock. No wonder. Seven hours have passed since she sat at her desk but, engrossed in the strokes of the brush, she has not been aware of the moving hands of the clock. The light in the room has changed but, in the white glow of her lamp, she has not noticed the shifting patterns on the walls as the sun followed its westward arc. Her stomach hasn't even pulled her to the kitchen, or her bladder to the bathroom. She stretches and rolls her shoulders back, rewarded by a pop from her sternum.

Swirling her brush in turps, rinsing it under the tap she had specially plumbed in, she twirls the bristles to a point and rests the brush on a chunk of sandstone on her bench. She opens the drawer underneath and retrieves a small snap-lock bag bulging with dried green mull, courtesy of Troy, who grows a couple of jagged-leaf plants on top of the island. Aware of the bag since she sat at her desk, she has listened to its call but refused, teasing out the anticipation and the pleasure. Now, satisfied with her progress, she rewards herself.

Practised fingers sprinkle green flakes into a tobacco paper and, with a swift movement, roll it into a thin tube. Silver Zippo in hand, she carries the joint to the armchair that inhabits the corner of the room, with bulging arms and carved wooden feet. Her thinking chair, rescued two years ago from a house near the wharf. Awkward to transport in boats, very little furniture ever leaves the island in the Hawkesbury. Instead, cast-off tables and wardrobes appear by the path, waiting for the next owner to resurrect them. Beyond salvage, only split wood and peeling veneer float slowly across the river on the garbage barge. There's life in you yet, she'd thought, stroking the chair's threadbare arms and protruding springs. Troy helped her lug it back up the hill, and they re-covered it in a red velvet curtain from his room.

The velvet is cool against her skin, soft as fur, and Billie snuggles into the chair's embrace. Lighting the joint and inhaling, she holds the harsh smoke in her lungs until her alveoli spit and pop like the seeds in the joint, then blows it slowly out. Breath by breath, as the drug seeps into her blood, the room begins to spin, and she is glad of the chair, solid behind her. Her arms and legs grow heavy. Lethargic, she leans her head back against the padding to stare out the glass.

The window looks towards the front of her property, where the land tumbles steeply to the path and, further, over the roofs of other houses to the wide green river. It's not a clear view, but she glimpses water and moored sloops through eucalypt fringes, the blaze of the Christmas bush and the spiky orbs of grass trees. Above it all, a wide blue sky and ferocious white light.

The light terrified her when she first arrived in Australia, sucking her dry as it drained the desiccated land. Relentless, she called it. Under the glare, the landscape seemed bleached and shrivelled, dull as a line of faded socks. But on the September day she discovered the island, her vision shifted. A slight bulge in the lens, perhaps, or a contraction of the dark brown fibres of her iris, but when she got off the ferry, something changed.

Craning her neck to stare up at gum trees arching over the path, she saw their subtle flecks of green, lilac and grey for the first time. The silver sheen of their trunks. She noticed spring blossoms, bells with white and pale pink filaments, and inhaled air perfumed by other blooms: cascading purple jacarandas, trailing jasmine and the wattle's yellow puffs. It was a revelation. On that day, wandering the island, she found a 'For Sale' sign tipped over and snared in lantana and knew she would live there.

Today there's a strong breeze, hot gusts from the west smelling of dust and a whiff of smoke. Only the tops of the trees move; protected from the westerly by the rise of the hill, the bottom layers barely sway. Exposed, the white-bellied banksia leaves remind her of olive groves. There are currents in the canopies, and she watches, mesmerised by their ebb and flow, and by the sound that accompanies them, a gentle washing like the sea.

The swirling leaves draw a memory of her dream to the surface, and Billie shivers. She loves the process, like the slow surfacing of an idea for a painting. It begins with knowledge of a presence—nothing substantial, but a glimpse, a hint that something is coming. She feels it in her gut, and in the sudden awareness of her heartbeat. It calls her body to attention. She pretends to ignore the presence, concentrates on something else, afraid that her conscious inquiry will abort its growth. She has learnt to wait and see. Slowly, the dream unfolds, shifting from the knowledge of a memory to the memory itself, as immediate as if she had just opened her eyes.

She had been sitting on pale grey rocks, warmed by the sun, looking out to sea as the spray tickled her toes. Someone called her name, and she turned, but the rocks behind were empty. The sound echoed, bouncing, but when she turned her head to follow, she saw nothing. She explored every shadowed nook, but found no one. The echoes faded; the sea the only sound. Where are they?

A knock breaks her reverie. Billie blinks, rubs her eyes, the dream bolting like a startled rabbit. Troy pops his head around the door, blond dreadlocks bound into a pineapple crown on top of his head. His white hair fascinated Billie when she first met him, and its contrast against his tanned skin. She had never seen anyone like him before, with electric-white eyebrows and lashes, and a pale fuzz over his arms. He was a cut-out colour negative brought to life.

'Sorry to disturb you,' Troy says, 'but you've got a call. It's Mary down at the shop.'

He speaks with torso hidden by the door, respecting a house rule laid down when he first arrived: 'No one comes into my studio'. Then she hadn't known him enough to invite him into her sanctum. Now, when he is as familiar as the shelves along the wall, it seems absurd, but she loves his respect for her boundaries.

'A woman's asking for you at the wharf,' he continues. 'Well, she's asking for someone called Sybille Quinn. When she described who she was looking for, Mary said it had to be you. Will you speak to her?'

Stunned, still stoned, Billie's thoughts whirl. On the island she's just called Billie. She doesn't need a surname. No one in Australia knows the other name, except for the officials, and she'd been away from England long enough that only one person alive could use that name and be able to describe her. It's Lorelei, it has to be, but she isn't due for another three weeks. Billie remembers distinctly from her niece's last letter: Lorelei was to have Christmas and New Year with her husband and daughter, then she and the child were flying out early in January. Why is she early? Why hasn't she let her know?

'Billie?'

She blinks. 'Tell Mary I'll be down in ten.'

Troy closes the door behind him. Ten minutes. Time to hot-foot it down the path to the wharf. No time to make the place look special. No time to dust cobwebs and spider husks from the ceilings, to pick up stray mugs and other household clutter. Over the next weeks she'd been planning to give the place a massive clean, make it look like something from a magazine, struck by a desire to impress the niece she hadn't seen since 1962, when Billie climbed aboard the liner at Southampton. A boisterous five year old, she remembers, grabbing her hand and ordering her not to go. She remembers Lorelei's mother, Audrey, watching the display with thin lips and jealous eyes.

Audrey had died almost a year ago, born and buried in the same Norfolk village. The trip to Southampton was the only time she ever left, as far as Billie knows. She never heard from her again, and the letters Billie sent across the oceans were not answered. In January a letter arrived from Lorelei. She'd found the address, she said, as she sifted through her mother's things after the funeral.

The news made Billie quiet, but she found it hard to grieve. In her memories, a red-haired Audrey, woman's face on a girl's skinny body, stood folding washing in an impossibly tidy house. She would have changed, drooped and sagged as Billie had, but her features were as Billie had last seen them, and her body moved in the quick way she always had. From the other side of the globe, her death was impossible to believe. Audrey lives on in Billie's mind, folding wind-dried sheets in an empty Harrowstone house.

Letters passed between Lorelei and Billie in the months after Audrey's death, threads to darn a thirty-year hole, but communicating only the basics. Billie knows the chronology of the missing years—Lorelei's marriage and the birth of her daughter—but there hasn't been time to go beyond this. She has no mental picture of her niece as a grown woman, often imagining the tugging child as the author of the letters. But she is grown, and her child is almost ten, and now they are here. Waiting on the wharf. Waiting.

The thought catapults Billie from her chair. Head spinning from the joint and the quick movement, she stomps out her studio and through the house, ignoring the piles of newspapers on the floor of the lounge and the clean washing draped over the sofa. In the kitchen, Troy is beginning his dinner ritual, crushing garlic cloves with the flat of his knife and chopping the white flesh with neat, assured strokes.

'Would you make enough for two more?' Billie asks, buckling her sandals. 'My niece and her kid. They'll be staying for a while.'

Drawn by gravity, like a pebble down a mountain, Billie bounces towards the wharf. She's watched the island kids do this before, racing for the morning ferry to make it to school on time. She doesn't run like them, but walks fast, almost skips. Any faster and she'd lose control, hurtle to the water's edge. I am unfit, she thinks, seized up and wheezing, as her heart pounds in her ears. The corridor of trees either side of the path blurs, a flickering pattern of dark and light. Suddenly, the trees open out to the little shop and the wharf, the sun sparkling on the water, and she slows her descent, needing to catch her breath.

She sees Lorelei immediately, a thin woman in an olive-green dress standing in the shade by the telephone booth, reading the notices taped there by islanders. She's inherited Audrey's lean build, and the red hair that runs in their family. Beside her, a young girl sips from a lemonade bottle, watching a group of kids her age splash in the shallows by the wharf. Lorelei's hair is neatly combed in a long bob while her child's is unruly, frizzy curls pulled into two ponytails, the fringe held back by a hairclip. Looking up, Lorelei waves and moves out of the shade. The child follows. When the light hits them, Billie gasps. In the sunlight, their hair glows like copper wire.

As the gap between them narrows, Billie is acutely aware of her dishevelled state. She is shiny with sweat, hair loosely pinned, with a stupid paintbrush of all things, and hands and faded frock splattered with pigment. She feels like the wild woman of the island compared to Lorelei, who is so fresh it is hard to believe she has flown for a night and a day to get here. The dark stains under Lorelei's arms and the slight sheen of her skin are the only signs she is even affected by the day's heat. Thin, streamlined and functional, she reminds Billie of a bird, with no bulges to mar the aerodynamics. I am as aerodynamic as a boulder, Billie thinks, feeling bosoms, belly and thighs jiggle beneath her dress. It's mull paranoia talking, she knows it, but she can't shake the flush of disgust at her unruly body.

Lorelei holds out her hand, a strangely formal gesture, as if they were meeting for the first time. 'Aunt Sybille? It's Lorelei, Audrey's daughter.'

The ends of Lorelei's sentences tumble down in the English way, softened at the edges by the Norfolk Broads. Familiar, her accent paralyses Billie, who is suddenly bicycling on a lane through ploughed and frost-rimmed fields. A gnarled tree is silhouetted against the sky, its leafless outline smoothed by an ivy ruff. Her ears ache with cold, and she inhales peaty air through wet nostrils.

'Aunt Sybille?'

Billie blinks, surprised to see eucalypts and the wrinkled trunks of jacarandas. Embarrassed by her lapse, she holds out her own hand.

'Call me Billie. I haven't been Sybille in a long time.'

'Sorry, I know that from your letters. It's just Mother never called you anything but Sybille, ever since I was a child, and it's stuck in my head. You're just as I remember.'

The red-haired woman gently pushes the child forward. 'This is my little girl, Elissa.'

El-iss-ah.

Billie shivers. She hasn't heard that name spoken aloud in over forty years. The three syllables reverberate in her head, an echo in a long tunnel.

El-iss-ah.

The child shrugs her mother's hands from her shoulders to stand alone.

'Mum! I'm nearly ten, okay, not your little girl.' She turns to Billie, pumping her hand like a grown-up.

'I prefer Eli,' she says. 'Rhymes with 'jelly', with a circle over the 'i'. It's what Nana called me.'

She would, Billie realises. The child is as confident as an adult. A miniature adult—Billie's tanned palm dwarfes the child's pale and freckled hand.

Dragging suitcases behind them, the women begin the slow climb back up the hill. The suitcases have wheels, but they are made for plush airport carpets, not the ruts and roots of this bush path, and they topple often. Eli runs ahead, ignoring her mother's calls. She dashes off beside the path, into the narrow trails lined with lantana and ivy that lead to other people's houses.

'Come back,' Lorelei yells. Her voice frays, the first sign that the journey has taken something out of her.

'She'll be okay,' Billie says. 'The path loops back on itself. She can't get lost.'

Lorelei nods, but keeps her eyes on the child's back. 'At home, even in a village like Harrowstone, you have to be careful. You hear such terrible stories. I worry, that's all.'

She walks faster, matching the child's pace, and Billie struggles to follow. Audrey, Lorelei's mother, was the same, she remembers, never letting the infant out without her. In the years before sailing for Australia, Billie offered to take the child to the village green or the old church and let her exhaust herself among the trees. With her husband working in the north of England, Audrey needed the break. She had shadows under her eyes from struggling with her daughter and maintaining her cleaning routine, but she wouldn't let go.

'Then come with me,' Billie had said. 'We'll have a picnic, the three of us. How much dust can fall in a day? The house will survive.'

But Audrey shook her head. Sometimes Billie played with Lorelei while Audrey cleaned, teaching the infant's fingers to hold crayons and ignoring the other woman's watchful eyes. Eventually, Audrey even stopped this, complaining about the scribbles on the walls and the waxy marks on the child's skin. I hope it changed, Billie thinks, I hope she relaxed as you grew, but she doesn't know Lorelei enough to ask these questions.

'Number one-three-seven,' she shouts after the child. 'It's carved on a tree stump.'

Neither woman speaks much on the journey up the hill. They exchange a few words, about the weight of the luggage, the slope of the hill, but none bridge the years since their last meeting. Billie is quiet, without easy phrases to begin the process. Living so long on this island, she thinks, I have forgotten how to relate to people. She talks to Troy and Stan, but they're as familiar to her now as the cigarette scar on her hand, the little white moon of burnt flesh. The islanders often reach out, invite her to barbecues and parties at the island's tiny beach, but she declines, blaming her workload. It isn't that, she knows it and so do they, but she can't explain her reluctance to become part of this small community.

Something else clamps her lips on the journey up the hill. Audrey. Both visitors have mentioned her, and her death lurks behind every phrase Billie can think of, but she cannot broach it. Not yet. Lorelei's quiet stops her. The Englishwoman's words are like surface ripples on a deep lake. Below, she is still, as if she has chosen not to speak on levels other than this. She has put her words away, neat as linen folded in a drawer, and Billie cannot disturb them.

At the base of the steps to the house, they pause for breath, as Eli skips up to them with her little bag. It took Billie ten minutes to reach the wharf, but three times that to lug the suit-case up the hill. Hauling the cases by the handles, the women take the steps slowly and singly. They stagger past the two sand-stone boulders guarding Billie's land, encrusted with lichen and bound with lantana, then beside tall kangaroo paws.

Cresting the hill, Billie spots Troy in his herb garden, chat-ting to Eli. The girl is half his height, but there is symmetry in their hair. Touched by late-afternoon sunlight, Troy's white dreadlocks glow orange like the curls of the girl beside him. Billie calls his name, and Stan's, loud enough to reach the shed.

'Give us a hand with these cases will you? We're knackered.'

After quick introductions, the men carry the suitcases up the remaining stairs to the house, and Lorelei and the child walk with them. Hands on hips, chest heaving, Billie waits out-side. Another joint would be nice, she thinks, to take the edge off, but she doesn't want it enough to go inside. A quiet minute in the garden to catch her breath will have to do.

Alone in her sanctuary, she sees the property through strangers' eyes, remembering why she left the city. Here, black velvet butterflies brush past her face. King parrots swoop overhead, revealing the crimson secrets of their underwings. Native violets open in damp shadows by the overflow pipe, reviving as the sun leaves them. The sprinklers are on, and the last of the day shimmers through spheres of fine mist. She lets the cool water soak her dress and stares at her home.

She loves the clean lines, the roof pitched steep so falling branches and leaves slide to the ground. She often hears them in the night—whoosh! Thought it was possums at first, until she realised there were no native animals bigger than a rat on the island. Windows need a clean, though. And mildew is taking over the verandah. Damn, she thinks, walking slowly up to the door, my knickers are on the line. Big white knickers, flapping for her guests to see.

Roasted garlic wafts to her nostrils as she leaves her sandals on the verandah and walks inside. Troy has outdone himself. In her absence, he has given the place a once-over, picking up the clutter, straightening and ordering. No time for cleaning, but it looks tidy. He has laid a feast on the table: bowls of green salad, home-made herb bread wrapped in foil, jugs of cool water with slices of lemon and lime floating with the ice cubes, a huge bowl of creamy salmon penne, flaked with parmesan, and a plate of hot chips for the child. Appetite stoked by her joint, Billie could devour it all. She should write a letter to his TAFE tutor, tell him what Troy does with his knowledge. On the dresser, a vase of kangaroo paws and native irises from the garden and, beside it, a single citronella candle to keep the mosquitos away. Propped against the candle, a handwritten sign says 'Welcome'.

Smiling, Lorelei and Eli sit on the chairs held out by the men. Troy walks around to do the same for Billie, and she clasps his hand, unable to find words to express her gratitude. He winks, then tucks the chair behind her. Soon, the neat arrangement on the table is demolished. Chip in hand, with the brazen exuberance of a child, Eli chatters at Troy, and he nods and chatters back. Billie can't hear the words, but what he says makes the child giggle. Sometimes she forgets how young he is, closer in age to the child than to Billie. On the other side of the table, Stan talks quietly to Lorelei. He smiles, looking like himself again, not the slouched man she saw yesterday. Observing the two conversations, but not part of either, Billie feels like the benevolent matriarch of a family feast.

As the food disappears and the scrape of cutlery against china quietens, she watches Lorelei and Eli fade with the daylight. Their green eyes have grown heavy, and they blink slowly, as if slightly out of phase with the world. On the boat for six weeks, Billie's body had time to adjust to each new time zone, but their bodies are dislocated, whisked through the stratosphere and dumped at the wrong end of the day.

'Thanks, Troy,' she says, standing and collecting the empty plates. She turns to the sleepy travellers. 'Do you want showers while I sort out your room?'

'It is that obvious?' Lorelei asks, rubbing her eyes.

While she and her child wash away the journey, Billie vacuums the dust and cobwebs from the spare room, opening the window to the cool breeze drifting up from the river. This was meant to be a guestroom but, beside Troy and Stan, no one has ever come to stay, and over the years it has filled with junk. She clears the two single beds of boxes of records, broken umbrellas and old coats, piling them in her studio, then vacuums the bare mattresses. With fresh sheets and frangipanis from the garden, it begins to look more like a bedroom than a storage shed.

As Billie brings empty clothes-hangers to the room, Lorelei walks in from the shower, shiny with moisturiser, wrapped in her dressing gown and hair wound in a towel.

'This looks great,' she says. 'I could sleep forever.'

She clicks opens her suitcase, smoothing creases from carefully folded dresses and shirts and hanging them in the wardrobe.

'I would have done it sooner,' Billie says, 'but I didn't expect you for another three weeks.'

'I know. I'm sorry. I . . . I had to change the plans. I can't believe I forgot to let you know. Is it still okay to have us?'

Billie nods. She watches the woman empty her suitcase, without asking what caused the change. The information belongs in the quiet place, with Audrey's death, but she hopes Lorelei will tell her when the time is right. It was the same with the lorikeets when she first came to the island. She sat on the verandah and watched them learn to trust her, eventually coming close enough to sit on her fingers and split sunflower seeds in her palm. She shivers, remembering the first tickle of their tiny beaks.

'This is for you,' Lorelei says, pulling a red exercise book from her case. 'Mother made me promise to give it back.' The words are quiet, barely above a whisper. Lorelei seems to struggle to stand, to keep her eyes open.

The book's dog-eared covers are suede-smooth to Billie's fingertips. The front cover has a crest, with 'Harrowstone School 1937' inscribed below. Reading the inscription, her stomach contracts, and she realises she needs to be alone to open it.

'Thank you,' she says. 'I'll leave you be. Let you get your head down.'

At her desk, commission pushed to one side, she sits with the book in front of her, listening to the house creak as two new pairs of feet walk to the toilet. She reaches out to stroke the cover and, in tandem, sees her chubby child-hand reaching out, over fifty years ago. Little book, she thinks, I left you behind. How could she have forgotten about it? Why did Audrey hold on to it all these years?

Gently, as if touching a relic from an archaeological dig, she opens the book. Its bindings are loose, the cover ready to tear in her hands. Sketches fill the first pages. Faces, animals, a feather. Windows cut into rocks. The drawings are simple, without depth or perspective, but they stir her gut. Afraid of the stirrings, she wants to close the book, tear it up and scatter it on Troy's compost heap, but she can't. She turns the pages.

At the centre of the book, where it falls open at a cotton-stitched seam, words begin to compete with the sketches for space. On one page the same phrase repeats in pairs: 'My name is Sybille'.

The first line of the pair is written neatly, each version identical, like prints from the same block.

'Copy my words,' she hears her headmaster say. 'You've quite some catching up to do.'

The writing underneath is haphazard, a reflection in a cracked mirror, a misshapen twin. These letters slope at odd angles, weaving above and below the faint blue lines of the page. On later pages, the letters shuffle close and breed, more words to a line, but the angles remain uneven. She fingers their sharp edges, the same as the scribbles in her sketchbooks.

'Nothing changes,' she says to the empty studio.

The exercise book, with thumbprints in the margins and tides of spilt ink, takes Billie to another room, where two young girls complete their homework by gaslight at either ends of a polished kitchen table. One has red hair, the other's is curly and black, but with a red forelock. The headmaster never hit you with a chalk ruler for your writing, did he, Audrey? You never washed its dusty residue from your palms, never held your fingers under icy water to ease the cane's sting. Your perfect copperplate writing, a replica of the headmaster's. All curly capitals and parallel uprights like prison bars. I never did master it.

Inside the back cover of the exercise book is a portrait of a red-haired woman. Childish, not much more than a stick figure, but Billie recognises her. Water spills have blurred some of the lines, but the woman's green eyes stare clearly from the page. Smiling, she could be Lorelei, but for the thirties' hairdo and the name printed in spidery writing.

'El-iss-ah,' Billie whispers.

Released from the red book, shredded memories rustle and swirl like the leaves above her head. Taking her sketchbook and a pen to the bed, she props herself on the pillows and lets ink flow with the images, crowding the other memories she keeps between the covers of her books. Hours later, she looks up. Outside, a new moon has risen, a night bird whistles. Stiff fingers put the pen aside, let the sketchbook fall to the boards beside the bed. She tucks the exercise book under her pillow and sleeps, dreaming of a woman with shining red hair.

Sybille

Norfolk 1937

The girl squinted into the fog. Ahead, a row of windows glowed in the fading light. It looked warm inside the whitewashed houses. The girl shivered. Her nose dribbled and she sniffed. It was cold in this country, a different cold from anything she had ever felt. A damp cold that seeped through her clothes into her bones, making her cheeks numb and her jaw stiff. Heat escaped through her boot leather. Even though the girl wrapped her arms around herself and rubbed, she could not get warm.

The fog stole colour from the world. A dog lifted its leg beside a lamp post and left a yellow trail in the snow, and the girl was glad for the bright dribble. The only other colour she saw came from the man walking beside her. Except for his skin, he was all orange. Hair, eyebrows, eyelashes, moustache. A faint orange down, like the first feathers of a chicken, grew across his cheeks. The girl tugged her hat further down her forehead, hiding her own red forelock under the woollen brim. She knew the clump of orange in her black curls bound her to this man in some mysterious way, but the knowledge made her belly churn, as it had done once when she'd left her morning milk

69

to cool and skin had clung to her lips. Queasy, she hugged her bag to her chest and tried not to look at him.

The man with orange hair led the girl across an open space dusted by a thin layer of snow. Blades of frozen grass poked through the snow and crunched under the girl's boots. Glossy black crows gathered, pecking the grass and scratching in the earth. One had a mouse in its beak.

Stopping to kneel, the orange man put his hands on the girl's shoulders and turned her to face him. He made quick, high sounds, like a dog when a careless foot traps its tail. His lips moved, his Adam's apple bobbed, and he waved his hands as if it might help her understand. I hate you, the girl thought, turning her head away from his sickly skin and pale eyes.

At first, at the beginning of their journey, the man had spoken using words that she knew, though they sounded odd coming from his mouth, strangled. Parts of his sentences were missing, but at least she could understand his meaning. Ferry, she understood. And food. Train. The man had spoken in broken sentences for days, but the girl did not reply. Eventually the man reverted to his strange sounds and the girl liked that better, because she didn't have to listen.

Suddenly the man spoke in her language again. It gave her a start, because she had stopped struggling to find meaning in his babble. The village was called Har-ow-stun, he said. In Nor-fok. The child winced. They were harsh words, sour as an unripe lime.

The orange man stood, brushed the damp knees of his trousers, and began to walk. Their steps took them past a white building with a picture of a deer hanging above the door. In another window the girl saw big blue bottles and a set of brass scales. The man stopped at the next window, and the girl stopped too, relieved to catch her breath. She saw loaves of bread in the window and inhaled yeasty air. The girl had not eaten since they'd caught the train in the big city, and she was hungry.

Signalling for her to follow, the man went into the shop. It was warm inside, and she wanted to unbutton her coat, but she was not sure if they were staying. She took off her hat, though, shaking her head to release her curls. The man with the orange hair talked to an older man whose skin was the same colour as the loaves of unbaked dough sitting in a tray by the counter. A woman dusted her hands on her apron and came to listen. She had the same brassy red hair as the orange man, arranged in neat waves. Their yelping tongue had begun to sound familiar, although it made no sense and the sounds jarred. There was no melody to these sounds, no song.

The girl closed her eyes. She let the sounds surround her and drifted in the warm air, until she heard her name and opened her eyes. All three were looking at her. None seemed happy. The older man rubbed his forehead. The woman had bitten her lips into a thin line and there was a red patch high on each cheek, as if she'd been slapped. Touching the girl's orange forelock, she muttered, then shook her head. She stood next to the girl and bent close.

'SIB-EEL,' the woman said, so loud the child jumped. The word hissed like a snake. The woman's earrings shook as she moved her jaw. Floury fingers tapped the girl's chest. When she looked down, she saw white fingermarks on her coat. The woman repeated the word and pointed at the child. She turned her back and spoke to the men. Then she and the older man left. The man with the orange hair knelt in front of the child.

'We stay here,' he said, in her language.

He held out his hand. She stared at it, hanging in space. It was fish-belly pale and stained with small orange dots, fingernails bitten to the quick. The child looked back at the man. Kidnapper, she thought, immobile. He sighed. In silence, they walked through the bakery and up a flight of steep stairs.

The woman with the thin lips said the snake word often. Sometimes she shouted it. The child didn't know what it meant. At first, because of the hiss, she thought it was a warning, but no matter how quickly she whipped around, she never saw the flicker of a snake in the small rooms. The woman would say the word, then prod the child. Once, the child looked up when she heard the word and waited, tightening her muscles for the prod. But it did not come, so she looked up the next time she heard the word. The child suddenly realised that the snake word was her name in this new place, but she didn't understand. She already had a name—the orange man had even said it to the older couple. How could a person have two names? The child responded to the snake word, but she kept her own name safe and whispered it in her mind so that she would not forget.

It was dark. Sybille sat at a table opposite the orange man. The older man sat at the head of the table, hair slick with grease. He was grey at the temples, as if he had scrubbed the flour from his cheeks but left a sprinkling above his ears. The woman carried a plate of food upstairs before returning to begin her own. Sybille wondered who the extra plate was for. No one spoke. Sybille heard the slimy sounds of chewed food. She looked down at her plate of boiled meat and potatoes and bread smeared with yellow grease, then gagged.

Beside Sybille sat another girl, about her own age and flame-haired like the man. Three orange heads bowed in the gaslight. And me, Sybille thought, disturbed again by the thought that her forelock might connect her to this family of strangers. The other girl scowled and pinched Sybille under the tablecloth, so Sybille stuck out her tongue. Hard against her cheek, the woman's hand surprised her. Sybille covered her burning cheek with her own hand. The orange man stood up. The woman did the same. Their faces were close and they yelped at each other. Sybille looked down at her plate until the noises stopped.

The woman with the thin lips grabbed Sybille and the other girl by the hand. She dragged them from the dining room up more stairs to a small bedroom with two beds. The other girl leapt on one that was already made up. Sybille sat on sheets and blankets piled on the second bed. The woman with the thin lips turned off the light and closed the door.

Unfolding the sheets in the dark, Sybille crawled under the covers. It was cold, and she rubbed her legs. She hadn't been warm since the orange-haired man brought her to this icy place. She longed for sun on her bare skin and a blue sky. The girl in the other bed whispered something in her strange tongue, something sharp and filled with venom, but Sybille pretended to be asleep. She couldn't sleep, though. There were shouts from downstairs, loud enough to travel up through the floor-boards. The voices tantalised the child. Occasionally she heard a ghost of a word she thought she knew, mangled and twisted, but the word was gone too quickly, submerged in the flow of babble. If she had been alone, Sybille would have pressed her ear to the floor and listened. The presence of the other girl in the room stopped her, so she lay still.

When the shouting stopped, Sybille realised something else was wrong. The house was silent. She couldn't hear the sea. The gentle rhythm of the waves was as familiar to her as the rise and fall of her own chest, and she was lost without it. She strained, but all she heard was the faint whistle of the other girl's breathing. Sybille stared into the dark for hours, eyes dry and itchy. Eventually it began to rain. Closing her eyes, Sybille exhaled slowly. It wasn't the sea, but it was similar enough to unwind her coiled muscles. She dreamt of the sun sparkling on warm clear water and a wide blue horizon.

At breakfast, the orange man again talked to the girl in words from her homeland, and she hated him for it. He had stolen the words as he had stolen her. She watched his mouth, repulsed by his fleshy lips and the drops of saliva that landed on her face. She blinked, slowly, while he talked, and stared when he stopped. He seemed to be waiting for her to speak. She counted sixty heartbeats before the man sighed. He stood up.

'Stay,' the man said in the girl's language.

Once the door closed, Sybille ran to the upstairs window. Below, she saw a patch of green. Yesterday's rain had washed the snow from the grassy triangle in the centre of the village. She watched the orange man and the others, stiff in their Sunday clothes, walk to a grey stone building with a cross and a square tower. A church, she realised, but nothing like the one she remembered. Wrinkling her nose at the orange-haired girl skipping between the baker and his wife, Sybille climbed off the windowsill.

Alone in the house for the first time, she explored the downstairs rooms, opening each door in turn. Outside, she sat in the draughty toilet and, with a noisy splash, let out yesterday's dinner. Even her shit was different here. Tiny black balls plopped to the bottom of the white bowl, dried-up olives compared to the great log she had once watched bobbing with the waves after letting go in the sea. Standing on the tips of her toes to flush the chain, Sybille laughed at the rattle and clank of pipes, ready to shake the house apart. In the scullery, she saw piles of clothing and dirty sheets next to two huge tubs, one with the ashes of a fire beneath. She opened cupboard doors in the kitchen, then warmed her hands against the stove, embers still glowing in its belly. In the storeroom behind the bakery, she prodded huge bags of flour and stole a cinnamon bun from the glass cabinet.

Licking sugar from her fingers, Sybille climbed the two sets of stairs to her room. She checked under the mattress; her atlas was safely hidden. She stroked the worn blue covers and returned the book to its hiding place. Sybille walked across to the other bed and scowled at the doll left by the orange brat. She turned the doll around so the sheet covered its head like a shroud and two white china feet poked into the air, then patted the sheet, satisfied.

There was a door next to Sybille's room. She had not noticed it before. For a moment she thought the orange man slept there, before remembering that his room was on the ground floor, with no steps to puff him out. On the long journey between Italy and England, at stations and ferry terminals, he had stopped many times to wheeze and rub his chest. Serves you right, she thought.

Sybille opened the door quickly, expecting an empty room, and was surprised to see the body of a young woman in the bed. Her eyes were closed and she was tucked under the blankets. Why was she in bed so late? Sybille walked closer, quietly, so her feet made no sound on the boards. The pale blue room smelt of flowers, and she inhaled, overwhelmed by a memory of the fragrant purple spears that grew in the garden of the church by the sea.

The woman slept curled on one side, with knees up to her chest and winter sun on her face. She reminded Sybille of a fresco she had once seen, a face pale like this one surrounded by a halo of light. The woman had the same colouring as the orange man and the brat, her copper hair loose on the pillow, but Sybille was not repulsed. She thought of warm milk infused with vanilla beans.

She stretched out her hand to stroke the woman's cheek, to coil a tendril of the bright hair around her finger. The woman turned and opened her eyes, which were green, flecked with yellow like a cat's. Sybille didn't know what to do. She wanted to run away, but her body was frozen. She could only stare into the green orbs until the lids closed over them. Heart hammering, the child crept out and closed the door behind her.

At dinner that night, Sybille watched the woman with the thin lips take a meal upstairs. The child stirred her bowl and brought the liquid to her lips. Cabbage and stringy grey meat floated on the surface. Perhaps the white bits were potato. Sybille wondered whether the woman in the bed disliked the watery soup as much as she did.

Every time Sybille climbed the stairs to her room she looked at the closed door. Often she paused, fingers wrapped around the handle, ready to enter again. But noises from the rest of the house stopped her: a footfall on the stairs; a floorboard creaking on another storey; a cough from the dining room. It wasn't until the family made its next procession to the church that Sybille turned the brass handle and opened the door.

The woman was awake this time, in a chair by the window, with a blanket over her knees and an open book. She took no notice of the child, but turned the pages of her book slowly. On the floor beside the chair were sheets of paper and a box of crayons. Stretching her hand out towards the paper, Sybille fixed her eyes on the woman, feet ready to bolt. The woman kept reading, even as Sybille knelt to stroke the paper. It was rough on one side, but smooth and shiny on the other. The sheets rustled when they touched. She licked her lips.

Her fingers chose the yellow crayon. There was no reaction from the woman. The child drew lemons and grapefruits and the sun. Yellow pigment filled the page and spilt onto the other pages beneath. When the yellow crayon snapped, Sybille picked up the blue. She drew the sky and the sea and fish scales. She scribbled until the blue crayon became a stub, then the green, scribbled until every sheet of paper was a solid tile of colour, and the crayons were shorter than her fingers. Only the black was whole. She stared at the black crayon, then turned the tip to the page, hiding the vivid tiles under a layer of shiny black wax.

The key turned in the lock downstairs, and Sybille jumped; she had forgotten the others, forgotten where and who she was. Only her hands had existed for her, and the line trailing from the crayon. She shoved the coloured pages under the woman's chair and rushed to her own room. When the orange brat came in, Sybille pretended to be asleep.

That night, Sybille's bladder woke her. She reached under the bed for the bucket, then remembered the little room outside with the china bowl and the chain. She walked downstairs in darkness, with outstretched hands and tentative feet. At every step she was afraid that she would trip on the hall runner or knock over the ugly vase on the dresser. When her fingers touched the wood of the back door, she exhaled, not realising until then that she had been holding her breath. She lifted the latch and scurried out to the toilet.

It was a clear night, lit by a new moon. Sybille would have stood still to observe the pearly halo around the moon and the single star hanging below it, but there was frost on the ground, cold enough to burn her bare feet. She skipped across the flagstones to the toilet, then lit the candle that perched next to the bowl. In the flickering light, her hands looked different, as if they were bruised, yet she felt no pain. She held her fingers close to the flame and saw patches of colour on her skin—vivid yellow, blue, red and green. The crayons had seeped under her nails and made ten coloured crescents like the moon overhead. She clambered up to the cold wooden seat and released her bladder, rubbing her stained fingertips over her lips as warm fluid gushed into the bowl below her.

On the next church day, the woman in the blue room greeted Sybille in her own language. The familiar greeting took the child by surprise and she replied without thinking. It was the first time she had spoken since the orange man had taken her. Sybille clapped her hands over her mouth, but stayed in the room, mesmerised by the smile that followed the woman's words.

'Books learn me,' the woman said slowly, from her chair by the window. The words sounded broken and chopped, but the child was not worried. When the orange man spoke in her language, Sybille cringed; she felt a keen intrusion. But she was drawn to this woman's voice.

'Me speak never. Only read.' The woman tapped her book. It had words in the child's language on the cover, and Sybille recognised the title. A book of folk tales.

'Understand?' the woman asked.

Sybille nodded slowly, jumping when the woman clapped her hands together and whooped.

'I Elissa,' the woman said. 'I have twenty-two years. Come.'

She curled her finger and beckoned. Sybille moved closer, until the woman's lips and her warm breath tickled the rim of the child's ear.

'And I know how you call,' she said, whispering the child's discarded name.

It was only a word, a small word of three syllables, but it had the power to stop the child's heart. How had the woman known? Magic radiated from the word to pucker Sybille's skin. When Elissa opened her arms, the child climbed eagerly into her lap to nestle into her warmth. Elissa began to read from the book. Listening to the fractured sentences, Sybille nodded encouragement when Elissa paused. She leant against the woman's chest and felt the steady thud of her heart. Sybille closed her eyes and let the words cast their spell. She smelt garlic and basil and cedar and fruity olive oil and salt and sulphur; in the pauses between the words, she thought she heard the sea.

Footsteps downstairs opened Sybille's eyes. Hearing the orange man call out her new name, then the slow creaks on the stairs, she knew she should move. Elissa was her secret, and she didn't want the others to know she had been in the blue room, but, warm and comfortable, she was lulled by the rhythms of Elissa's body. Nuzzling into the hollow between Elissa's neck and her collarbone, she inhaled soap, talcum powder and lavender, then exhaled three breathy syllables.

'El-iss-ah.'

As Sybille slid from Elissa's lap, she noticed the orange man leaning against the doorframe. Panting, with a shiny forehead and lips tinted blue, he held out his arms to the child.

'My turn,' he said, wheezing.

'Don't touch me!' she said, in her own language, surprised by the fury that boiled in her chest and bubbled into words. Hateful man. She wanted to kick his knees. She wanted to push him down the stairs. Rushing past him into her bedroom, she jumped into bed and pulled the sheet over her head. Then the bed springs creaked, and she felt a weight beside her bow the mattress.

'Come out,' the orange man said, in gentle Italian. 'Please. Talk to me.'

She would not. She hid, rigid, until the weight shifted and she could no longer hear the man's whistling breath. In the dim tent beneath the sheet, she lay still as her heart slowed.

Listening to the yelping voices of the others, Sybille soon learnt their names. The brat was Or-dree. Her name troubled Sybille at first; she confused it with 'ord-n-ree' and received a pinch for her mistake. The orange man's name was Eye-zak. It was lucky she never spoke to him, because her lips didn't like his name at all. The older couple were Ma-tha and Far-tha, but when Sybille called them this the woman went pale. Upstairs, Elissa whispered that perhaps it would be better to call them Mis-ta and Miss-us Kwinn. Trying this, Sybille received solemn nods.

In the blue room, Elissa and the child played a pointing game. Elissa's fingers chose an object. She named the object in English, dismantling the world into single syllables. Sybille repeated the syllables over and over until her lips found the right shape. When the words wouldn't come, Elissa took the child's fingers and put them in her mouth.

'See,' she said. 'This is how your lips should move. Now you try.'

'Tay-bul,' the child said, feeling Elissa's gentle fingers push her lips. 'Win-do. War-drobe. Mi-ra. Kam-i-sole. Nik-ers.'

If Elissa didn't know the word in Italian, Sybille reversed the strategy and taught the woman the same way. Through the week Sybille spoke little, communicating with the family by nods and shrugs, so after Sunday mornings with Elissa her cheeks ached. It was a good ache, one that followed hard work.

On her bed she rubbed her cheeks, rolled her tongue in her mouth and smiled.

Elissa and Sybille traded words until Sybille's English and Elissa's Italian met in the middle.

'Isaac help you now,' Elissa said, in the child's language. 'He know more.'

Sybille shook her head. 'No,' she said, in English. 'No him want.'

'Isaac speak Italian. He ask me if you like to . . .'

'No.' Sybille turned her back and walked to the window. She didn't speak.

'You and me, then,' Elissa said.

Every Sunday they shared grammar and syntax and slang. On a blustery spring Sabbath, they swapped their first profanities.

'Another,' laughed Elissa, her cheeks flushed.

'Not loud,' the child said. 'Write.'

'Imagine if they found it! We'd be for it then. Whisper. Then only my ear hears.'

Sybille leant forward to cup her fingers around Elissa's ear, and the woman giggled. 'What does it mean?'

Another whisper.

'Sybille! Where did you hear such a phrase?'

Her smile fell away. Her belly clenched. 'The village. My papa . . .' She stopped, feeling the woman's fingers touch the orange forelock. As Elissa twirled the hair around her fingers, Sybille felt her belly loosen.

'We won't say that word then, all right? Listen to this.'

She put her lips to Sybille's ear and whispered silly phrases, mixtures of English and Italian words that made no sense in either language. Slowly the child's smile returned.

Sentences behaved differently in this cold country, she realised. They had an odd rhythm, not like the sing-song melody of Sybille's own language. Here, sentences sloped down at the end, with the gravity of a rock thrown down a steep hill to the sea. The child knew about the forces pulling from the centre of the planet. Perhaps these forces worked on language too, affecting the way words came out of people's mouths, pulling them as the moon pulled the tides.

One day, two months after Sybille's arrival, she entered the upstairs room and stood beside Elissa's chair.

'New word,' she said. 'Ka-vor-ting.'

Elissa looked up from her book and raised her eyebrows, keeping her place with a finger. She coughed.

'That's an . . . interesting word. Where did you hear it?'

'Your father. He not know why his son ka-vor-ting . . .' Sybille rolled the 'r', 'ka-vor-ting with Hitalian rubbish.'

Elissa said nothing. Sybille tapped her foot. 'You know not? I use big book.'

'No. I know the word. It means . . . It means . . . playing with.'

'Isaac play with rubbish?'

'Perhaps they were talking about the . . . er . . . souvenirs he brought back from his travels.' Elissa spoke quickly, her voice catching in her throat.

'Soo-ven-eers?'

'Yes,' Elissa continued. 'I'm sure that's it. Mother told him off for bringing home baubles and trinkets and all kinds of useless things. They'd sent him to Italy for the winter after the fever, because of his heart, and said he'd wasted grand-father's inheritance on rubbish. Thought they were pretty, myself.'

She smiled at the child. 'Does that help?'

Sybille nodded. 'And trol-lop?' She pronounced the word haltingly, its two syllables equally weighted and connected by the long 'el' between them.

'Trollop?' Elissa sighed. She pointed downstairs.

Sybille nodded. 'Your mother. She asked if there were not enough trol-lops in England.' Sybille raised her voice. 'TROL-LOP! My lips like this word. TROL-LOP!'

Elissa put her finger to her lips. 'Not so loud. Say it with me, but never outside. It's not a . . . polite word.'

'No? I think it cake. Was going to ask your mother. Some English trol-lop please, Mrs Quinn.'

'Not a good idea,' Elissa said softly.

Sybille thought she looked sad, suddenly. 'What does it mean?'

'A woman who is . . . friendly . . . with men. Too friendly. Something my parents think is bad.'

'Who is trol-lop then?'

Elissa turned her head away from the child to stare through the window at the village green below. 'I don't know.'

'Isaac told me about your atlas,' Elissa said, when the clanging bells called the family to church the next week. She was in bed, wrapped in dressing gown and eiderdown. 'Can I see?'

'No,' Sybille said, stunned that Isaac knew. She didn't want him knowing anything about her, and the fact that he had discovered her secret disturbed her. She'd been so careful on the trains, pulling the book out of her bag only when he'd begun to snore. Perhaps he'd been pretending. Or, worse, perhaps he'd searched her room, pulled the atlas from its niche between mattress and bedsprings. Sybille resolved to find a new hiding place, one he would never discover. Blinking, registering the hurt in the green eyes for the first time, Sybille retrieved her book from her room, then placed it on Elissa's bed.

'Belong to Papa,' she said softly.

When Elissa opened the blue covers a dried leaf fell to her eiderdown. As Elissa reached for the leaf, Sybille slapped her hand.

'No,' the child barked.

'I'm not going to damage it. Look.'

Elissa held the leaf up to the window. Transformed in sunlight, it glowed gold, and every forked vein was visible.

'Just like us,' Elissa said. She held her pale hand to the lamp and Sybille saw the veins there, thin blue snakes beneath the skin, and a blush of blood. The woman seemed lost, focused only on the movements of her hand and the light shining through it.

The pair turned the pages of the book slowly. Sybille put her fingertip to where she was born, the tiny island hidden beneath her nail. She showed Elissa where her mother came from. And her father. Elissa's longer finger pointed to Harrowstone. She showed Sybille the route Isaac took to and from Italy the first time, and the route he took later with the child. That night Sybille dreamt of blue oceans marked by dark lines of longitude and latitude.

As the days lengthened and spring turned to summer, Sybille began to creep into Elissa's room on other days of the week. Immediately she felt Audrey's spite. Her morning milk tasted of fishy oil from the big brown bottle in the kitchen, and she found holly leaves in her clean knickers. At supper, the girls ate quickly, then raced up the stairs. Sybille always won, revelling in her three extra inches of height and the nuggets of muscle in her calves.

'I chased goats,' she said. 'I am stronger than you.'

Triumphant, she barred Audrey from Elissa's bed.

'Downstairs, baby,' she whispered, watching Audrey's lips tremble. 'Or I tell Elissa you wet the bed.'

Sinking to the floor, Audrey sobbed and hiccupped until Elissa snapped her book closed and put her hands over her ears.

'Shut her up,' she said. 'I can't stand her whining. That's all she's done, ever since she was born.'

Pushing the crying child into the hall, Sybille slammed the door, almost trapping Audrey's fingers. On the other side, Audrey thumped the wooden panels and rattled the handle.

'Can I play?' she asked, sobbing. 'Please.'

'No!' Sybille shouted, climbing back on the wooden bed. She grinned, satisfied Elissa was hers alone. Then, remembering Audrey's anguished eyes, she flushed, suddenly ashamed, but she pushed the niggling thought away and tried to ignore the wails coming through the door.

Propping herself on her elbow, Elissa opened her book. She held it in one hand and a cigarette in the other, snug in a tapered holder. Sybille watched the woman smoke, absorbing the graceful arc of cigarette to lips. Sybille stroked the orange locks with a bristly brush. Elissa's hair shone in the lamplight and smelt of lavender and smoke.

'My turn?' Sybille asked, looking at the cigarette.

Elissa laughed. 'You're an early starter. Go on, just a little puff.'

When Elissa passed the cigarette to the child, Sybille cradled the burning tube between her fingers and sucked deeply. The smoke was harsh and hot, but she loved the crackle as she inhaled and the quick flash of embers. Sybille held the smoke in her lungs until it burst out through her nose. Giggling, she leant back against the bedhead and watched the blue walls spin.

That night Sybille and Audrey were quiet while Mrs Quinn tucked them in bed. She blew out the lamp.

'Sleep tight, piglets. Don't let the bedbugs bite.'

Sybille heard Mrs Quinn shut the door and shuffle along the hall in her slippers.

'I'm telling on you,' Audrey whispered in the dark. 'Telling Mother that you smoked. I saw you through the keyhole. Only Father's allowed. He'll smack you. They'll send you back . . .'

Sybille climbed out of bed to stand beside the other girl. 'Elissa hate you, call you cry-baby.'

She reached under Audrey's blankets and pinched the girl's soft belly. Audrey squealed and kicked. Knees connected to ribs, elbows to cheeks. Sybille's fingers found Audrey's curly red hair. She tugged until she had clumps between her fingers, until the smaller child screamed.

When Mr and Mrs Quinn opened the door, Sybille stood over Audrey with a pillow. She heard the door open, tried to stop, but the swing was too strong. As if time had slowed, Sybille watched the pillow complete its arc to connect with Audrey's head. Thump. Audrey cried like a baby. Mr Quinn led the girls downstairs to the parlour and took the cane from the chiffonier.

When oak leaves fluttered across the Green, Sybille started at the village school. On the first morning, Mrs Quinn began the routine she practised every time Sybille went outside the bakehouse, even on the warmest days of the summer months. She parted Sybille's hair on the side and pinned the streak of orange beneath the darker hair, then pushed a felt hat over the curls.

Sybille's scalp prickled, but she endured Mrs Quinn's deter-mined tugs and kept the profanities inside her mouth. She knew instinctively that the bright skein was something to be hidden, understanding also that it was the reason Mrs Quinn sent her back into the house whenever a customer opened the door of the bakery.

The problems began inside the red-brick school, when the teacher, a tightly buttoned lady called Mrs Dyer, told her to remove the hat.

'It is only manners,' she said.

Lifting her hat, Sybille felt the curls escape their pins. She scratched her itchy scalp and did not blush when the other children gasped at the streak. Sybille heard them whisper. She stared through the window at the September fields, inhaling the smell of freshly cut grass.

In the playground at lunchtime Sybille was surrounded by children from her class. Because of her limited English, she had been placed in a class with younger pupils, and her nose cleared the tops of their heads. But she was trapped in their circle, pan-icked by poking fingers and the faces so close to her own.

'Talk,' they commanded.

When she did they laughed at her accent, called her 'for-eigner'. I will keep my lips tight, she thought, like they do. Only open them a crack so the foreign voice will not escape. She listened to their quick words, determined to mimic their dull tones and sacrifice the melody that made her own voice stand out.

The children teased her about her olive skin, asked her if she hadn't learnt to wash yet, even tried to scrub her with soap from the toilet 'to get the dirt off'. Silent, trembling, she looked across to Audrey. The red-haired girl stared blankly, shrugged, then turned to her own friends. With shame, Sybille recalled the girl's sobs when she had banished her from Elissa's room. After that, Audrey had given up trying, instead spending her time with Mrs Quinn in the kitchen and scullery. I am alone, Sybille realised. Her panic turned to rage. Remembering her extra height, she kicked the nearest children, satisfied by the whines produced when her boots connected with bones and soft flesh. Mrs Dyer hauled her through the corridors to the headmaster's office.

'English children don't behave like that,' the master said, before bringing the cane down on her buttocks. 'We're civilised here.'

At the end of Sybille's first day at school she climbed the steps to Elissa's room. There were more than she remembered. She did not cry, but burrowed under Elissa's blankets, inhaling stale sweat.

'Mamma?' the young girl asked. 'Papa?'

Elissa placed her orange head near the girl's black one.

'Listen, little one,' she said. 'I'll look after you. I'll be your mamma.'

She trailed her lips close to the child's ear and whispered her original name, broken down into single syllables in the pattern of their word game.

'Chi-*bell*-eh,' she whispered. 'Now your turn.'

Sybille repeated the name, opening her lips wide to relish the sounds after a day with lips pressed together. She spoke the name slowly, quickly. She changed the rhythms of the name, rolling her tongue to shift its weight. She moved the emphasis from the beginning to the end, *Chi*-bell-eh, Chi-*bell*-eh, Chi-bell-*eh*, until the sounds chased their tails, lost their meanings, found a melody. Satisfied with the song her name had become, she slept.

The next four days were long and bewildering. Teachers barked orders and scolded when she paused to translate the words in her head. They called her a trouble-maker. Sybille's classmates told her she paused because she was stupid. The child spoke only when forced, braced for the laughter or harsh words that followed. She visited the headmaster's office at least once a day and walked out rubbing stinging fingers or bottom, depending on the master's preference.

On the Friday, when Sybille failed a spelling test, the teacher shouted and sent her to the headmaster. Her hands still smarted from the last visit.

'You again,' the headmaster said. He read the teacher's note, then gave Sybille a red exercise book ruled with faint blue lines.

'Write in it every day,' he said. 'You've got a lot of catching up to do. Next time you fail, I'll cane you.'

Had the afternoon continued in this way, Sybille would have bolted through the school gates. She was saved by the appearance of a woman with a green shawl and an unruly mass of grey hair. The woman carried a leather satchel, from which she pulled a red apple, three sprigs of lavender and a twisted branch with leaves still attached. It was an oak branch; Sybille recognised the deep curves of the leaves. She watched the woman arrange her trophies on the desk, then walk through the rows, handing each child sheets of paper and a thick pencil.

'Today we do still life,' she said, in a sing-song voice with a different rhythm to the other teachers. 'The French call it *nature morte*, dead nature, an apt description of most such works. Give yours some zest.'

The woman continued to walk as the children drew.

'Don't think of it as an apple or a branch,' she said. 'See patches of light and shadow. Learn to draw what you see, not what you think you see.'

She swished her skirt and hummed a quiet song. Entranced, Sybille forgot the other students, the pain in her hands, forgot everything except the pencil in her fingers and the arrangement in front of her. There were no words for her to translate, no strange rituals or hostile voices. Just the objects on the table and the smooth pencil between her fingers. Sybille worked on the gleam of light on the apple's skin, the bend in the branch, almost like a human arm. It didn't matter that the shapes on the page hardly resembled the grouped objects, or that her fingers were clumsy and disobedient. The process captured her. Sybille felt a stillness inside herself. Her hands created this calm space. She let them work.

Sybille stopped drawing when the teacher stood behind her, smelling of spices and soap. The child tensed herself for harsh words. Instead, the woman touched her shoulder gently.

'Good,' she said.

Bells marked the end of the day. Since Monday, when Sybille learnt the bells set her free, she had been the first to stand and run, but on this day she lingered. She heard the scrape of chairs and the murmuring as her classmates left the room, but kept drawing until only she and the teacher remained.

'Time to go,' the woman said.

Sybille pretended not to hear. She concentrated on the crinkled leaves, their ragged edges and the smooth curve of their stalks. The teacher took the pencil from Sybille's fingers.

'Enough,' she said.

The woman's voice was stern, but Sybille thought she saw a slight smile on her lips. She gave Sybille the knotted branch and her pencil, then reached into her satchel to pull out a book of clean white paper, bound at the spine with a spiral of wire.

'Homework,' she said. 'Draw it from every angle and bring me the results next Friday.'

Sybille took the branch.

'What do you say?' the teacher asked.

'Thank you.'

'Thank you, Miss Ludorf. Go on, repeat it.'

'Thank you, Miss Ludorf.'

The teacher nodded solemnly. She flicked her hand towards the door. 'Home now, child. I want my dinner.'

Holding the branch high like a torch, Sybille carried it back to the bakehouse. With the bark prickling her palm and the rustle of the leaves, it was easy to forget the harsh days that had gone before. She took the branch straight up to Elissa's room.

Elissa was asleep in her chair by the window, with her head back and mouth open. Sybille laid the branch on the sleeping woman's chest, so leaves brushed her chin. Elissa twitched, rubbed her nose, but didn't wake. Opening the sketchbook, Sybille placed her pencil against the first clean sheet. The pages quickly filled with images of the branch and always, above it, Elissa's face. Open lips and closed eyes. Her ears. Her hair. Sybille drew multiple images on the same page, crowding Elissa's features between the leaves. She stopped only when her fingers cramped.

That night Sybille took her sketchbook to bed. Once she was sure Audrey was asleep, she held the book up to the moonlight and stroked the pictures. They didn't really look like Elissa, but Sybille knew what they were meant to be. She pressed the pencil scribbles against her cheek and inhaled lavender and musty sweat, as if the smells of the woman had permeated the fibres of the page.

The child kept the oak branch beside her bed, heartened by the slow change in the leaves as they lost their moisture and crinkled on the stem. At night the wind rustled the dry leaves and brought the sound of the sea. She slept easier that way, with the sketchbook against her face and the leaves whispering to her. When she felt sleep take her, when her limbs still sensed the bed below but they wouldn't move, the flat images in her book became warm and solid. It was a secret pleasure, as if she had drifted through the wall and nuzzled under Elissa's blankets. On those nights Sybille slept solidly, without the nightmares that woke her, screaming, to a poke from Audrey's elbow. In the mornings Mrs Quinn would rouse the child with a shake, complaining again about the dark lead stains on the sheets and the pillowcase. Sybille was afraid of Mrs Quinn's tongue, but not afraid enough to stop sleeping next to her sketches.

Soon the sketchbook was full. The images of Elissa and the leaves spilt over into the headmaster's exercise book. Other pictures appeared, flashes from the child's dreams: a rocky outcrop by a wide sea, a smouldering volcano, statues of the Madonna.

Two weeks later the headmaster called Sybille into his office. He flipped through the pages of sketches, shaking his head. Six times Sybille felt the whip of the cane across her palms. Six raw welts intersected the creases of her skin. The headmaster uncapped his fountain pen and wrote lines of evenly sloping words across one page, instructing her to copy the words and return the book to him for more words to learn the next day. Sybille watched the man's hand, his knuckles white around the pen as they had been around the cane when he'd whacked her. He breathed heavily as he wrote, breath rank as a cabbage fart. Sybille stuck out her tongue, but the headmaster was bent over the page and didn't notice. At home she copied the headmaster's words quickly, her uneven letters dribbled with ink, hurdling the task as if it was a fence between her and her drawing.

'You know what?' Elissa said to Sybille, one May morning in 1939. She sat in her chair by the window, holding her closed book to her chest. The windows were open to sunlight, fresh air and the sound of children laughing on the Green below. Sybille sat on the windowsill with her sketchbook balanced on her knees. Cursing, she scrubbed at a charcoal line with her finger. Wrong again. If only Elissa would sit still. Normally she was a perfect model, happy to read or doze while the girl sketched. But today she fidgeted, shifting in her seat and jiggling her legs. I give up, Sybille thought. She looked up from her page.

'What?'

'Today I think I shall go downstairs.'

Standing, swaying slightly, Elissa unbuttoned her dressing gown and threw it across the bed.

'Grab me a slip, will you? And a pair of stockings.'

Sybille took an ivory slip and two fine stockings from the drawer. She watched, fascinated, as the woman pulled off her nightdress and wriggled into a suspender belt and the petticoat. It was the first time she had seen Elissa without her bed jacket, and she was shocked by her wasted muscles and the sharp outlines of collarbones and ribs. Swaddled in wool, Elissa's body had always felt soft and comforting, but for the first time Sybille saw the hard lines underneath.

'I've caught spring fever,' Elissa said, laughing as she rolled up her stockings. 'I just want to be out in the sunshine.' She clapped her hands together. 'Now find me something to wear.'

Infected by her mood, Sybille opened the wardrobe, rummaging through the long-neglected clothes to find the right dress for the occasion. She chose a green one with a white pageboy collar. Taken out for the first time in years, the fabric was musty with naphthalene, so Sybille tucked a sprig of lavender in a buttonhole to disguise the smell. In the bottom of the wardrobe she found a pair of shoes, strappy ones with a little button on the side, which shone after a spit and polish with her handkerchief.

While Elissa sat in front of the mirror powdering her cheeks, Sybille picked up the brush and stroked it over Elissa's copper locks, trimmed the week before by Mrs Quinn into a bob. At last, after dabbing her lips with lipstick, Elissa was ready. She stood, walked slowly to the open door, then paused at the threshold. Her feet, for years familiar only with the borders of this blue room, seemed unable to step into the hall. She blinked, as if surprised to find herself by the door.

Sybille ducked past her into the hall and held out her hand.

'Come,' she said gently, sensing Elissa stood on the verge of retreat. 'It just takes one step.'

Their hands touched, and Elissa stepped out of her room. She tackled the stairs slowly, with Sybille's arm in one hand, the banister in the other. Every fourth step she paused for breath.

'I sound like Isaac,' she said.

While Elissa wheezed, Sybille massaged the woman's wasted calf muscles. It took almost half an hour to reach the ground floor. Elissa made it to the back door as her mother and Isaac returned from the asparagus bed. Smiling, Mr Quinn and Audrey came from the bakery, and the family shared a cup of tea in the garden before Mr Quinn carried his eldest daughter back up the stairs.

Over the next months, Sybille hovered at Elissa's elbow while the woman learnt to walk around the house unaided. She smiled, noticing Elissa's thighs bulge and harden. They walked slow circuits of the garden, past the chicken runs and gooseberry bushes. Then, on a clear summer's day, they ventured through the bakery and into the street.

'Good Lord!' a woman exclaimed. 'Elissa Quinn?'

Another stood beside her, and another, until Elissa was surrounded by cheerful inquirers.

'How are you, love?'

'Feeling any better now?'

Elissa rubbed her forehead, looking ready to faint. Sybille took her arm and pulled her from the crowd.

'We must go,' she said to the women. 'Perhaps tomorrow?'

Walking slowly past the Green, Elissa turned her face from the expanse of recently cut grass. When Sybille asked why, Elissa shook her head.

'You wouldn't understand,' she said. 'You're too young.'

They walked in silence. Elissa was pink and shiny with perspiration when they reached the old church, so Sybille led her through the graveyard to the stump of a yew tree hewn into a seat. Crows called, hidden in the dark green canopies of the yews. Elissa's green eyes stared over the gravestones. Sybille followed her gaze out to the lavender fields beyond the village, then turned to follow the droplet that slid across Elissa's cheek. She wondered if it was sweat or a tear. A tendril of hair fell over the pale cheek, and she reached forward to tuck it behind Elissa's ear. The woman flinched.

'I'm sorry,' Sybille said, pulling her hand back. 'I didn't . . .'

'It's all right,' Elissa said softly. 'I was miles away.' She sighed. 'Perhaps you're not too young. Can you keep a secret?'

Sybille nodded, her tingling skin telling her she was about to be initiated into one of Elissa's mysteries. In the two years of their friendship, she had never asked what kept Elissa in her room, afraid her clumsy questions would push the woman away. She had accepted it as a simple fact—Elissa has red hair, Elissa lives in her room—but here, under a wide blue sky, her curiosity grew. She waited, frightened to breathe, until Elissa began to speak.

'Ten years ago,' Elissa said, 'my parents sent Isaac to southern Italy for the winter. He'd caught rheumatic fever as a child, and had another bout, a milder one, when he was eighteen. He had the whole house fussing around him. The doctor suggested a warmer climate might help him convalesce, so they used some of the money our grandfather left. He spent the winter in the sun and I took over his chores.'

She reached out, cupping Sybille's cheeks in her thin fingers.

'This you must never tell,' she whispered. 'Promise.'

Sybille nodded. She could have stayed like that for hours, head in Elissa's hands, but the woman released her, lowering her hands to fidget in her lap.

'While he was away I nearly had a baby. I felt it growing inside me. Mother found out and made me get rid of it. Then, a month on, I noticed her dress wouldn't do up. Her belly had started to bulge. Five months later, she had one of her own. It was a surprise, she said. She'd thought she was past it.

'She gave birth to Audrey on the kitchen table, a mewing red bundle that never shut up. She was always bawling, never gave me a moment's peace. I couldn't stand it. Wherever I was in the house, her screams ripped through the walls. Mother tried to get me to hold her, but I wouldn't. She seemed so fragile, I knew I'd hurt her. My baby wouldn't have been like that, frail and fretful.

'And then I got sick. I was feverish, my joints ached, I couldn't move. My parents thought it was rheumatic fever, like Isaac, but the doctor said he didn't know what was causing it. He suggested bed rest, so my parents put me upstairs. They had Audrey in with them at the time, and the upstairs room was the furthest away from her screams.

'Contrary creature, she seemed to know that I couldn't bear to be near her. As soon as she started to crawl, she tackled the stairs and headed straight up to my room. Mother nearly had a fit the first time it happened. She'd gone into the scullery to boil the copper, and when she came back Audrey had climbed out of her crib. They looked for her for an hour, when all the while she was in my room. She'd crawled under my bed while I was sleeping.'

She shook her head. 'Nine years have passed since I went into my room and, until this summer, it never struck me that I should leave. Suddenly, I just have to be outside.'

Sybille sat in silence, digesting Elissa's words. She understood one mystery now, but the knowledge had spawned others. Where had Elissa's baby come from? Where did it go? Why had she stayed in her room after she recovered? Resisting the urge to bombard Elissa with questions, she clasped the woman's hand and sat with her until the sun hovered low in the sky.

With linked arms, they walked back through the graveyard and beside a row of Georgian houses. Elissa stopped again next to a block of stone outside the post office. She sat on the block, stroking it lightly. Sybille stroked it too, trailing her fingers across the abrasive surface. Warm, the stone radiated heat absorbed from the afternoon sun. A sign on the wall told Sybille that the block had arrived in the village in 1913, sent by the citizens of Harrowstone, Massachusetts. Elissa pressed her ear to the stone.

'Hear it?' she asked.

Sybille shook her head.

'I can,' the woman said. 'It's telling me about the journey. About where it came from.'

Elissa lifted her head abruptly, kicking the rock with the toe of her shoe.

'Damn him!' she said, her voice getting louder. 'And damn them! They had enough for a car for the bakery and a trip for Isaac. Why couldn't I go? No, it was always Isaac. Him and his bloody weak heart. All I got were postcards.'

Grabbing the collar of Sybille's dress, she pulled her close.

'Promise me you'll get out? Promise?' Elissa was shouting now. Villagers in the post office turned to stare. Sybille nodded and felt the pressure round her neck tighten, then release. She coughed. Elissa was stroking the block again. She seemed to have forgotten Sybille was there.

'I shall,' Elissa said quietly. 'One day I'll escape, and they can all go to hell.'

In September 1939, the Quinns listened to the declaration of war on their crackling wireless. They sat in the parlour in a half-circle around the wooden cabinet, except Mr Quinn, who stood with his hand on the cabinet as the Prime Minister spoke. In the silence that followed the announcement, Sybille followed Mr Quinn out to the crowded street. People looked to the skies and shook their heads. No one spoke.

Later that afternoon, when Sybille watched the villagers from the upstairs window, they had almost a festive air. They pinned black cloth around their windows, singing and shouting to their neighbours. She watched the procession leaving the grocer's shop, baskets laden with candles and tins of corned beef and Spam. Women bobbed their scarved heads to each other and smiled, patting the shiny tins.

Weeks later, when Sybille saw the queue of young men, the war became real. They were lined up by the block of stone, signing papers in front of a man in khaki. Sybille recognised the faces. Older boys from the Grammar School who played cricket and rugby on the Green in the evenings, boys with noses and ears too large for their faces. Their voices were as deep as grown men's, but the rest of their bodies lagged behind.

Sybille walked quickly past the queue on her way back from the dairy, a bottle of milk balanced on one hip. The village doctor was in the parlour when she arrived, talking with the family. Sybille smiled at Elissa, then leant against the door-frame to listen.

'We can't send your brother here out to fight, not with his gammy heart.' The doctor patted Isaac's shoulder. 'I'm afraid you wouldn't pass my medical. But you will, Elissa. Now that you're up and about again, I expect you'll do your bit. Those young chaps in the field will need our help.'

The doctor spoke of a munitions factory in Norwich. It could be dangerous, he said, because the city would probably be an enemy target. Sybille felt as if someone had poured icy water down her spine. Goosebumps sprouted on her arms. She inhaled slowly, hearing her own breath and, through it, Elissa's voice.

'Let me, Father,' Elissa said. 'Let me go.'

Later, in the upstairs room, Sybille waited to talk to Elissa, to convince her not to go, but every time she opened her mouth Elissa was already speaking.

'I'm going to explode!' she said, her face flushed as it had been on that first walk into the village. 'Feel this.' Elissa grabbed the girl's hand and placed it just below her collarbone. Sybille felt hot skin, slightly moist, and below it, the rapid palpitations of the woman's heart.

'My own room! I never imagined Mother would agree. They said I'm to take a set of sheets and Father will send an allowance . . .'

Sybille closed her eyes. She listened to Elissa rattle off a list of the clothes and books that she would take with her. She felt tired suddenly, and small. Looking at Elissa was like looking directly at the sun. Sybille turned her head away from the light in the green eyes, from the first smile she had seen crease the skin below them. She went to bed early but lay awake, listening to Elissa sing as she packed.

Soon after Elissa went to Norwich, a military police lorry drove through the village and stopped at Miss Ludorf's house. Sybille was sketching on the Green. She watched uniformed men walk stiffly to the front door. The knock carried on the still air.

'Twenty years I have been here,' Miss Ludorf said, her slight accent amplified by panic. 'Since the Great War.'

One of the men shook his head. 'I'm sorry, ma'am,' he said. 'It's for your protection as well.'

The art teacher was pale. She clutched her leather bag to her chest. Sybille dropped her sketchbook and ran over to the lorry. She would stop them. She would explain. She held out her hand, but Miss Ludorf was staring straight ahead and didn't respond.

When Italy joined the war, Sybille's belly lurched. She hoped everyone had forgotten where she came from, but the children caught her after school.

'You're next!' they chanted.

Sybille learnt to walk carefully through the cobbled streets. Invisible, she thought. I am not here. She avoided the khaki men who patrolled the streets of the village, and those from the nearby airbase. If one spoke to her, even to joke and smile, she pronounced her words in perfect English with a Norfolk lilt, then ran away as soon as possible. The belief that the men would return for her was never out of her thoughts.

With Elissa in Norwich, Sybille didn't know what to draw. She was so used to sketching the red-haired woman that the moment her pencil approached a blank page it began to trace out the familiar features. But the pictures felt wrong. Without Elissa, the images seemed flat, empty. Sybille was beginning to forget what Elissa looked like.

She remembered what Miss Ludorf had said in her last class before the army took her.

'Draw what you see. Not what you think you see. The mind plays tricks.'

Sitting in the dim parlour, its windows shaded with black-out cloth, Sybille began to sketch. She didn't ask the other Quinns to sit for her—it would feel like a betrayal to concentrate on their faces—so she drew the furniture instead. In pen and ink she sketched the shiny chintz sofa and the leather armchair where Mr Quinn sat to smoke his pipe. She drew the curved legs of the dresser and the arched mirror above it. She sketched the shallow perspective lines of the walls and the seams of striped wallpaper.

When Sybille looked at the parlour picture later, she found she had drawn herself reflected in the dresser mirror. With pen in hand, the world was reduced to a collection of patterns. Concentrating on the patterns, Sybille had not noticed her own face among them, and it was odd to see herself caught unawares. Her eyes were distant, her face expressionless. Only her tongue defied the blank face. There it was, peeking from the corner of her mouth, glistening like the snail tracks that criss-crossed the garden path every morning.

Faces in the other sketches also surprised Sybille; somehow, against her will, the Quinns had worked their way into her drawings. Audrey scowled from the armchair, her arms crossed tightly over her body. Mrs Quinn smiled from a sketch of the scullery. That was unusual, because Sybille couldn't remember the tight lips ever relaxing into a smile. In the sketch Mrs Quinn was bent over the dolly tub, turning the handle of the shaft to agitate the linen. Sybille had captured all the details: the box of Reckett's Blue on the shelf; the steam rising from the copper, the wooden tongs ready to lift the washing up to the mangle; even Mrs Quinn's rolled-up sleeves and the sweat on her forehead. But the smile took Sybille by surprise. It was at the absolute centre of the sketch; the scullery seemed to be built around the smile. Sybille picked up her pencil when she noticed the smile and scribbled 'Monday madness' at the edge of the page.

There were no images of Mr Quinn. The girl had drawn the places where he spent most of his time—bakery, parlour, asparagus beds—but Mr Quinn was quick to notice her. She only ever had time to open her book and turn to a fresh page before he disappeared. Once Sybille followed him. She saw him grab a newspaper and stride outside to the toilet. The bolt scraped against its housing. Sybille shrugged. She sat on the ground in front of the toilet and sketched the wooden door until she heard Mr Quinn pull the chain. It was a good door. She enjoyed its splintered panels and peeling paint. She drew a tiny arrow from the edge of the page. 'Occupied' she scribbled next to it.

Isaac surprised her, too, staring from a sketch of the dining room. His head appeared above a newspaper, looking straight at her. She could only see the top half of his head, because the newspaper hid his nose, mouth and chin, but his eyes seemed sad. Sybille found his sad eyes in other sketches, too, staring at her from behind the bakery counter or from a chair in the kitchen while he helped his mother. He was always watching her. Sybille had not noticed the sadness before, or the purple shadows below the eyes. At first she dismissed the sorrow in the ink eyes, as she did Isaac's frequent invitations to spend time together, but she found herself drawn back to the sketches, returning the gaze she resisted in person.

'What do you want from me?' she wondered. Whatever it was, she knew she couldn't give it.

Audrey and Sybille fought to read the letters Elissa sent from the city. Grabbing the first letter from the postman, Sybille read it quickly and revelled in knowing before the other girl. Triumphant, she handed the thin pages to Audrey, but her triumph curdled as Audrey read slowly, teasing out the letter to fill the afternoon. Sybille bit her lips, melancholy and impatient for the next instalment. She learnt to wait. She let Audrey collect the mail, enduring the excruciating noises Audrey made as she read, and the awful feeling that the other girl would relate what was written. Upstairs, she distracted herself by sketching the village roofs and the fields beyond. Somehow, the noise of Audrey's reading carried through the house—the exclamations, the crinkle of a turned page—and Sybille fumed until she had finished.

When it was Sybille's turn to read the letter, she tortured herself and delayed the reading. She carried the letter upstairs, ignoring its call while she tidied her half of the room. She sharpened her pencils and cleaned out her watercolour tray and organised the tubes of oils that Elissa had sent from the city at Christmas. Then, when she could not contain the excitement, she curled under the covers and read the letter slowly. It was hard—her eyes kept leaping ahead to the next line—but she forced the orbs to read the words singly, savouring them like caramels sucked to a sliver.

Finished, Sybille folded the paper and tucked it into the band of her knickers, comforted by the tickle of paper against her skin. As the collection grew, the letters bulged under her tunic. When asked about the strange lump, she said it was where she kept her handkerchief.

It was hard to read the first letters, because they were written with the manic joy that drove Elissa's packing. She wrote about her jovial boss and scribbled verses from the patriotic songs the women sang as they worked. She described one of the machines, nicknamed Preston because all it did was press metal into tubes. In the early letters she wrote about trips to the Odeon after work, before curfew brought everyone home. *Me and My Girl* came to the Royal, and everyone in the audience joined in with 'The Lambeth Walk'. The picture houses closed soon after, the authorities afraid of falling bombs.

Elissa wrote that she had her own gas-mask—everyone did—and she carried it with her all the time. She even had to wear it at work sometimes, practising for gas attacks. At Christmas, she said, tinsel brightened windows dulled by blackout canvas. Barrage balloons floated above the city, and every couple of nights unearthly air-raid sirens sent her scurrying down the street to the bomb shelter. She couldn't sleep in there at first, squashed between her landlady and the neighbour's smelly children, but she got used to it.

One week Elissa sent a satin rosette that the boss had pinned to her chest for being the most productive worker.

'I beat Jean from Hunstanton,' she wrote, 'and the Cromer crew! Four hundred shiny shells in one day, ready for action.'

Then Elissa's letters began to change. Sybille unfolded them and laid them across her bed in date order. The angle of the writing shifted. The first letters were written in a perfect copper-plate hand, with a regular slope and even spaces between them. The words of the most recent letter were ragged, squashed ten across and pressed close to the lines like a sapling bent by a storm. Sybille stroked the uneven gaps between the words and knew something was wrong. In places the ink had smudged, as if water had spilt onto the page. That night Sybille slept with the letters underneath her pillow. She dreamt of the repetitive pounding of the machines. Sad songs wove around the rhythms of the pistons.

No more letters arrived. The postman walked past the bakery for two weeks, until the morning he arrived with a telegram. Standing by the door, Sybille watched Mr Quinn read the slip of paper, watched him rub his chin with one hand. He screwed the paper into a ball, whispered to his wife, then left the bakery. He swung his leg over his bicycle seat and ped-alled across the Green. He'd forgotten to clip back his trouser leg, Sybille saw, and the brown cloth flapped in the wind. She waited until the rest of the house was asleep to retrieve the ball of paper. Smoothing it out, she stroked the wrinkles in the paper before reading the words.

'ELISSA IN ASYLUM,' it said. 'PLEASE COME.'

Mr Quinn returned to the bakery the next evening. Sybille saw him from the upstairs window. She had been waiting all day, watching the road that led to Norwich. She crept down the stairs until she could hear his voice. Mr Quinn was talk-ing about some kind of hysterical condition, a breakdown, about insulin comas and an experimental new therapy from Italy involving electricity. That night Sybille dreamt that Elissa was struck by lightning, that she glowed and sparked as the charge took her.

Currents

New South Wales 1990

Two redheads greet Billie as she walks early into the kitchen. Lorelei and Elissa are showered and dressed, with pink cheeks and damp, combed hair. Sweaty and ruffled with sleep, Billie feels exposed, grubby. Unused to company at this hour, still tangled in her dreams, she blinks, frowning at the activity— eggs sizzling in the pan, the shriek of the kettle, toast popping up. It is as if she has walked into someone else's house.

'Hope we didn't wake you,' Lorelei says. 'It's the jetlag. We were both awake before the sun.'

Wires snake from Eli's ears to a portable cassette player on the table, and the child bobs her head to the tinny melody it produces.

'We're cooking breakfast,' she chirps loudly, speaking over the music. 'Want some?'

'Just tea, please,' Billie says.

She watches Lorelei fill a mug with boiling water, struck by her resemblance to the other Elissa. Yesterday, overwhelmed with their arrival, she hadn't made the connection. Perhaps she hadn't wanted to. But now Elissa's face is fresh in her mind.

Half an hour ago, she was dreaming of Elissa's blue room, of drawing while the rest of the family sat in church. Now Elissa's twin stands in Billie's kitchen pouring tea, a forty-five-year gap closed.

Except they are not twins. There are differences: Lorelei's lips are thinner, more like Audrey's than the full lips of the other two siblings. Her eyes are the family green, but shaped like her father's, Jeremy Fisher. He, Billie and Audrey had been at school together. In her memory he had grown from scruffy child to teenager, but stopped at sixteen. She'd missed their wedding, and Jeremy had been working up north in the years before she left for Australia.

Closing her eyes, Billie tries to salvage Elissa's face from her evaporating dream, but all she sees now is Lorelei. Two people, two lives, but only one face between them. I have no photographs of you, she panics, only the sketches done when I was young, later than the one in the exercise book but before I knew enough of foreshortening and perspective to render you properly. Elissa's face surfaces often in Billie's sketchbooks, and in the painted leaves, but these are drawn from memory, not life. She is suddenly afraid that over the years, in painting and repainting, she has lost Elissa's true face.

'Are you all right?'

Opening her eyes, she sees Lorelei hovering close. A concerned expression, fingers wrapped around a mug. Somehow I've become a dotty maiden aunt, she realises.

'I'm fine,' she says, smiling, accepting the tea. 'Still waking up, that's all.' She blows ripples in the hot liquid and sips. 'How are you feeling this morning?'

'Better now,' Lorelei says. 'A bit dazed. I still can't believe we're really here.'

'Do you want to call Simon, let him know you've arrived?'

Lorelei tucks a strand of hair behind her ear, turns away to flip the eggs. 'No, that's okay,' she says, over her shoulder. 'I'll talk to him later.'

She's gone quiet again, Billie realises. One question about her husband and her eyes become distant. Something's going on, but Billie doesn't push.

'Going to be a scorcher today,' she says. 'If you're up to it, I thought we could walk, explore the island a bit this morning. Maybe go for a paddle at the little beach, before the sun gets too hot. What do you think?'

'A walk sounds nice. Don't know about the beach. I've never been good in the water, and I've read about your wildlife. Jellyfish, sharks, crocs. All the nasty, biting things.'

Eli grabs her mother's arm, tugs hard enough to spill tea on the table. She yanks the tiny headphones from her ears. 'Can we, can we please, Mum? I want to, ever so much, and you promised, you said we could spend the whole time at the beach. I want to learn how to bodysurf. Can we? Please?'

The child, bouncing with eagerness, makes Billie smile. She must have heard over the music. 'There's no surf, I'm afraid. It's only a river.'

'Then we'll swim. Go on, Mum. Please?'

'No,' Lorelei says. 'Maybe another day.'

Eli frowns, tugs harder. 'You always say that.'

'I remember when the roles were reversed, and a certain child was being just the same,' Billie says, winking at Lorelei. 'Must run in the family.'

As her mouth shuts, she cringes, hoping Lorelei won't infer too much from her comment. If Eli is the child Lorelei once was, then Lorelei has become Audrey, hovering, over-protective.

After a pause, Lorelei relents. 'Just for a bit, then. And only if you promise not to go out too far.'

Triumphant, Eli whoops and skips out of the kitchen. She returns in luminous pink bathers, as Lorelei stacks the breakfast dishes on the drainer and fills the sink with hot water. Billie shoos her away.

'I'll do them when we get back,' she says. 'I don't think we can keep Eli waiting.'

The women return to their rooms to change into their bathers, then follow the child outside. It is like an oven. Harsh against Billie's nostrils, the air draws beads of sweat to her upper lip. Even at nine o'clock, it trills with cicadas. On the verandah, Billie taps her sandals against the boards.

'Check your shoes every time,' she says. 'You never know what's crawled in overnight. And don't step on the holes in the path. They're ants' nests.'

Lorelei grimaces, as if the ants are already crawling over her toes. 'I don't think I want to know,' she says. 'Tell me much more and I'll never leave the house.'

Eli leads them down the steps and onto the path encircling the island, her eager pace pulling the women behind her.

'You sound so Australian,' Lorelei says. 'You really do. The way your sentences go up at the end, like a question. I never expected it.'

'Makes sense,' Billie says. 'Been here almost half my life. Longer than any other place. It's bound to have an effect. Although the islanders tell me I sound English.'

'You never thought of coming home?'

Billie shakes her head. 'I left because it didn't feel like home. And things between me and your mother, well, they were never right.'

'She kept all your letters,' Lorelei says, quietly. 'They were filed in date order.'

'But she never replied.'

'No.'

The women walk the rest of the path in silence. In her most recent letter, Lorelei had written that through her childhood her father was hardly ever home, he was off adding his hammer and nails to the building sites of England in the fifties and sixties. Billie imagines Audrey in those years. The long days alone, with Lorelei at school and Jeremy away on another construction project. Audrey collecting milk bottles from the step and leaving empties for the milkman. Audrey stripping the beds every day to wash the sheets. Audrey only leaving the house to buy bread and groceries and to walk Lorelei to and from the school gates.

Remembering the first letters she sent to Audrey, Billie cringes. She'd been deliberately hoisting two fingers at village-bound Audrey, hemmed in by hedges and cobbled lanes. She emphasised her adventurous life: her fellow passengers on the liner, her years in Melbourne, the beginnings of success in Sydney. She never wrote about the days in Kings Cross when she'd hidden in her tiny room from the hubbub of the street below or when the constant scream of sirens at night made her sleep with her pillow over her head. She never said that she missed the crackle of Norfolk's first frost, nor admitted that some days she wished she could visit Audrey's trim house and inhale freshly washed laundry. A year after Billie moved to the Hawkesbury, she stopped writing. She couldn't even fill a crinkly blue aerogramme. On the island, the old letter voice didn't seem right, but she had nothing, no other mode of relationship, to replace it.

The path winds around the island to a narrow corridor of trees that opens to the river. Cooler air, tangy with salt and mud, blows from the water. The beach is an ochre crescent, only three hundred feet long, and running east to west. At the eastern end, an arm of rust-coloured sandstone embraces the river, with a mangrove sprouting at the farthest point, exposed roots like snorkel tubes. In the west, rickety jetties perch over deep green water.

It is low tide, and a line of seaweed and bark fragments marks the reach of the highest water. Worm holes mar the ripples of damp sand revealed as the water receded. With a squeal, Eli drops her towel and bag and sprints across the moist sand to the water. Yelling, Lorelei follows, but the child is beyond her reach. Fully clothed, she wades in to her waist, calling for Eli to return, but the child ignores her.

After a pause, Billie strides out behind, her skirt ballooning around her thighs, but she's unable to match the other woman's speed. Must get moving again, she thinks. When she first came to the island, she made a circuit every morning, walking up a sweat on the slopes then paddling in the shallows. She loved the smooth wet mud between her toes and the cool water, but never went deeper than her thighs. Her feet remained firmly planted in the riverbed, far from the tugging currents in the deepest channel, the green glassy heart of the river. Swimmers lapping the little cove often called to her, but she shook her head, no matter how much they teased. At some point she stopped paddling—she can't remember when or why. Perhaps when her leaves took off. Or perhaps fear had got the better of her.

She never told the islanders why she didn't swim. How could she explain to these river folk, who moved with amphibious ease on land and in water, the panic that grips her as the water level rises towards her face? The primal reaction that makes her spasm and squeal if a rogue wave splashes. The fear that if she lifts her feet from the mud, she will be carried away. Bred on the water, their blood courses with the river's solution of salt and silty fresh water. They immerse themselves, learning how to breathe and see below the meniscus, happily surrendering to the pull. But Billie cannot.

'It's all right,' she says, when she reaches Lorelei, standing waist-deep in the river. 'The water's shallow. She'll be okay.'

'But look how fast the current's flowing,' Lorelei says. 'She'll be swept away.'

'Not if she stays this side of the mangrove.'

Pointing to the arm of sandstone, using her own tanned arm as a model, Billie explains how the outcrop of rock protects the beach from the pull of the river.

'Here,' she says, 'the water is calm and safe.'

The words are a mantra, as she feels the pull on her own flesh. Gentle, but enough to remind her of stronger currents. She yells the information to the child who, obeying commands other than her mother's, paddles back towards the adults. Closer, but not close enough for Lorelei to reach out and haul her back to land.

I envy you, Billie thinks, watching the young girl twirling and splashing, holding her head below the surface to blow bubbles, even swirling to churn a whirlpool. Billie wishes she could float, let the water take her weight. She knows the feeling in her dreams, when she glides with luminous fish, but, grounded by fear, never in reality.

'Little water baby,' she murmurs.

'She learnt at school,' Lorelei says. 'And her father takes her to the pool on weekends. He's like a fish, too. Grew up in Gibraltar and spent most of his teens in the water. Wish I was like that. Mother never took me near the sea. She hated it.'

She pauses, eyes squinting across the water, where the river slides around the last headlands of the Hawkesbury valley to the ocean.

Billie remembers Audrey's face, shocked and pale, when the infant school announced it was going to take the little ones on a trip to Yarmouth beach. Audrey refused to sign the consent form, and Lorelei had remained at school while the rest of her class boarded a bus to the water. Billie had been at the Harrowstone house when Audrey dragged a tearful Lorelei through the front door. The girl related the others' tales of squealing on the helter-skelter and eating candyfloss until they almost threw up on the bus home. Billie had taken the child's side in the argument, unable or unwilling to share with Audrey her own fear of the water. Why couldn't I tell her I understood? How were things so fraught between us? How did it get so bad?

Tell me about Audrey's death, Billie begs silently. Please. Tell me how you felt at the time. Tell me how you are feeling now. But Lorelei doesn't speak of it, and still Billie cannot ask.

'I bet you're over that very English incompetency by now,' Lorelei says, and for an instant Billie thinks that she has read her mind and means the reserve that keeps the subject of Audrey's death below the surface. Then she twigs.

'Sadly, no,' Billie says. 'Thirty years in this country and I still can't swim to save myself. Can't dog-paddle. Can't even float. But Eli's paddling in water that wouldn't reach our chest. We can wade out and get her if you like.'

The words are a bluff. If she had to, Billie would wade further, but she's having enough trouble with the water at her hips. She breathes steadily to slow her heart and to quieten the little voice that calls her back to shore.

'No,' says Lorelei. 'She'd probably end up rescuing me, and I'd never hear the end of it.' She looks around at the beach, crowded with families and toddlers in floaties. 'There are enough people around. I just worry. What if I'm on my own and something happens?'

'Why don't you learn? Tell you what, we could learn to-gether. Get Eli to teach us.'

Another bluff. Part of Billie knows Lorelei will not agree.

'Can you imagine? I have enough of a discipline problem now. She's been an absolute horror lately. Fights for the sake of it.'

'Probably her hormones. She'll be a teenager soon enough.'

'Lord, save me.' Lorelei shakes her head. 'No. She's been like that since . . . since Mum died. Mum played with her, in a way she never did with me. I think she finally relaxed enough to enjoy children, rather than spending all her time worrying.'

'I'm here,' Billie says, finally finding the words. 'If you ever need to talk, about your mum . . .'

Lorelei turns and smiles. A small smile, one that doesn't shift the faraway focus of her eyes. 'Cheers. It's been a tough year. But I'm all right. I'm getting better.'

The women stare at the child's skinny white legs, poking to the sky as she does a handstand on the riverbed. The legs topple and, giggling, Eli breaks the surface.

'Look at us, standing here in our clothes,' Lorelei says. She turns to look back at the people on the beach. 'Must think we're mad.'

'They expect it from me now,' Billie says. 'Troy told me I have a reputation for being a bit odd. Chances are they're wondering about the redheads.'

'Only been here five minutes.'

'Enough time to begin a good story.'

'Thought I'd escaped that when I left the village.'

'Not a chance. The village is the village the world over.'

Puffing, Eli paddles back to the adults, ducking from her mother's hands, and past them towards the shore, kicking her legs to splash the pair of women. She chuckles at their squeals, and paddles even faster as they follow. Scampering up the beach, she wraps herself in her towel and shivers.

At the top of the beach, the women peel off their wet clothes, drape them to dry over the sandstone boulders and sit on towels in their bathers. Lorelei wears a bikini with little shorts, like bathers from another era. Freckled, flecked with blue veins, her skin glows white in the sun.

'You'll burn if you're not careful,' Billie says. She rummages in her bag, offers a battered hat to Lorelei and a bottle of sunscreen, but the Englishwoman declines.

'No one will believe I've been here unless I go back with a tan.'

Remembering the stubborn child at Southampton, Billie puts the sunscreen away. She balances the crumpled hat on her own head to shield her eyes from the glare, aware of how frumpy she must look.

At the western end of the beach, children tumble in the shallows, with sun-bleached hair and tanned limbs and squeals that carry along the sand. They are led by a boy about Eli's age, who is taller than the others and distinguished by a plaster cast on his arm. Mark, the ferryman's son. While the others swim, he plays with a scruffy blue heeler at the river's edge, throwing a twist of driftwood for the dog and kicking crystal arcs with his toes. When the dog launches into the water after the stick, Mark scowls on the sand and hugs his plaster to his chest.

Billie pulls her sketchbook from her bag and drafts the kids' lines on her page. Quick strokes to capture the movements, and more detailed drawings of the boy with the cast. Glancing sideways, she notices Eli also watches the children.

'Mum, can I play with the others?' the child asks.

Lorelei stares at the group before shaking her head. 'Stay here with us, little one. Where I can keep my eye on you.'

Scowling, Eli worries the sand at her feet, scooping handfuls over her toes then lifting her feet to drain it through the gaps. 'But I'm bored.'

'We haven't come twelve thousand miles for you to be bored. Think of something constructive to do. Build a sandcastle.'

'Sandcastles are for babies,' the child mutters. 'Wish I'd brought my Walkman.'

Billie passes Eli a sketchbook, but she shakes her head. Sulking, she lies on her side, pony-tailed head propped on her hand, ridged spine to her mother, watching the children play.

Wedged between them, Billie concentrates on the view across the river. She sketches the lines of the escarpment and the yachts at their moorings. Ducks bobbing on the water and a sea-eagle soaring in the blue sky. Tinnies and canoes dragged up past the high-tide mark. The neat curves of a clinker-built rowboat. She's sketched the view so often she could do it without looking, but each time she notices something different, a variation in colour depending on the light, or a shift in the composition as boats moor and depart.

In the quiet, lulled by the lap of the river and the occasional buzz of a powerboat in the distance, Billie's calves tingle. It's the water, she realises, evaporating from my skin, leaving behind a sparkling salt crust, but she marvels at the sensation. Her legs hum, raw and stinging, remembering the cool slide of water over her thighs, the squelch of mud between her toes. I am all skin and exposed nerves, she thinks, pulsing like a lover. For the last few years her body has been pure function, practical, forgotten until an aching knee or vertebra reminded her. My body is waking up, she realises. I'll have to begin paddling again. Chip away the calcium building up on my joints, to slow the creeping ossification of my limbs.

Pencil and sketchbook discarded, she has forgotten about the others, but then she hears a small snuffle to her left. Sprawled on her back, arm flung behind her head, Lorelei sleeps, snoring quietly with limbs twitching. On Billie's right, Eli curls like a woodlouse, knees to chest and wrapped in the damp towel. The sun is directly overhead, and Lorelei's exposed belly and the tops of her feet are already pink. Damn, Billie thinks. I should have been more careful.

Reaching out, she gently presses Lorelei's shoulder, and her fingertips make white circles in the pink. At the touch, the Englishwoman inhales sharply and opens her eyes. She stares at Billie, forehead-creased and confused, then looks around.

'I was dreaming,' she says, rubbing her eyes. 'Of Mum. She was showing me her garden, which is stupid, because she never had a proper garden. Just a concrete yard she could hose down.' She blinks. 'I wasn't sure where I was when I woke up.'

'We should get you back to the house,' Billie says. 'You've copped some sun.'

Standing, Lorelei brushes the sand from her pink belly and winces. 'At least I'll go home tanned and triumphant.'

Not likely, Billie thinks. You'll blister and peel, but she doesn't have the heart to say this.

Lorelei wakes Eli, and the three walk up to the house. With the sun overhead, the path is exposed, unshaded, and, away from the river breeze, the air is too hot to breathe. Billie drags her feet, gasping. It's like walking through treacle. Even Eli seems crushed by the heat, with none of the exuberance of her trip down. They meet no one on the path, and no one stoops to yank lantana or pittosporum in the gardens. Even the birds are quiet.

Lorelei and Eli's faces are beetroot red when they reach the house, slick with sweat, and Billie knows hers is the same. She staggers into the dim house, too puffed to do more than wave at Troy, head bent over his books at the kitchen table. Opening the fridge, she pours water into glasses of ice cubes and lime and passes them to the others. Three glasses empty and are filled again. No words, just clinking ice cubes and slowing breath. Lorelei and her daughter walk to the bathroom for a shower, and Billie listens to the water rattle through the pipes.

When her breathing returns to normal, she wanders barefoot to Troy. On holiday from his TAFE hospitality course, he pores over books of cooking techniques and presentation for his next semester.

'How's it going?'

The white-haired man looks up and grins. 'Excellent! Can't wait to get back into it. We've got silver-service coming up. Our lunches will be a whole lot classier.'

'Does that mean I'll have to get dressed up?' Billie asks. 'I'm sure I've got a posh frock in the wardrobe somewhere. Although I think it's paisley. I've not been to a party since 1980, and it wasn't new then.'

Ten years and I haven't been off the island, she realises. She remembers that last party, thrown by one of her final portrait clients. A swanky affair in Paddington, and she'd driven the FB towards the city. Hiding her rough painter's hands, with pigment under blunt nails, she'd stayed as long as she could bear in the company of the glittering women, who gulped champagne and laughed raucously. I have nothing to say to you, she thought.

When she arrived back at the island, cheeks sore from smiling, it was past midnight. A dense fog had rolled down the valley to settle on the river and the damp air penetrated her thin dress. She shouldn't have taken the boat out, she should have banged on the door of the pub to wake the manager and bunked on the mainland, but she was tired and cold, and wanted to sleep in her own sheets. Past the oyster beds and into the channel, she motored out into the fog.

In open water, the fog reflected her floodlight, cutting visibility to a metre. Beyond that, a shroud of dense grey. At full throttle, moored yachts loomed at her bow, and she swerved to avoid them. Dropping the revs to four knots, she steered around the moorings, but the tide ran faster than the engine, and her little tin boat drifted. Billie lost the green and red markers of the safe channels. She lost the magnesium-white lights of the marina. She heard masts clanking, unable to pinpoint the sounds. She was adrift, she knew it, about to be washed out to sea. It should have taken ten minutes to get to the island, but Billie was on the river for hours, steering in circles, before the splintered turpentine poles of the island's wharf emerged from the fog.

Never again, she swore, as she clambered out of the tinnie, heart pounding in her ears. The next week she sold the FB to one of the young blokes from across the river, who said he was going to do it up. She told Stan he could use the boat whenever he wanted, and he had, skipping across to the mainland to pick up groceries or his latest date. Had it really been ten years since she'd left the island?

'You might have to pass the dress on to my mother, then,' Troy says. 'She still has a penchant for paisley.'

Troy rarely speaks of his parents, or the little sister he hasn't seen in three years. Billie's knowledge of his history has grown slowly, with the small but significant fragments he's shared since his arrival. He is a lovely young man, the kind of son she'd have hoped for if she'd ever had a child, yet his parents won't see him. Originally named 'Tomorrow', he was born on a river commune, home-schooled with the other ragged offspring of the group. When the politics of the place became too compli-cated, the family moved to a boatshed downriver. Troy changed his name, he once told Billie, on his first day in a proper school, when the other children teased him. In the last month of high school, when he told his parents he'd fallen in love with another boy, they chucked him out. 'Make love not war' and 'Free love' his parents chanted, but they wouldn't accept him.

'She's welcome to the dress,' Billie says, 'if the moths haven't got to it.'

She squeezes his thin shoulder. It's all right, she wants to say, they will reach out to you, but she is afraid they never will, that he will have to accept the distance between them.

'Would you mind mixing a batch of your sunburn balm for Lorelei? She's terribly burnt.'

Nodding, Troy pushes back his chair and walks into the garden. He returns with five aloe tentacles and a bunch of lavender and chamomile flowers. In the kitchen, he drops the flowers into a small saucepan of water and lights the gas. Moving like a dancer, with precise, hydraulic ease, his muscles remember the tai-chi patterns Billie knows he learnt in the commune. She clears the benches around him and washes the morning's dishes while he works.

As the water boils, he slices the aloe lengthways and scrapes the clear flesh into a bowl, then sprinkles lavender oil from a brown glass bottle into the gel. When the water in the saucepan has bubbled down to a muddy solution, he takes it off the boil and stirs it through the aloe, adding some chilled water from the fridge and a handful of ice cubes.

'Thought we'd have *bruschetta* tonight,' he says. 'Using the oven will heat the house too much.'

Wiping the bench and piling the green aloe husks into the compost pail, he chops cherry tomatoes picked from his vine.

Eli, wet hair loose over her shoulders, walks in from the bathroom and perches on a stool by the bench. 'Can I turn on the radio? The batteries are flat in my Walkman.'

When Troy nods, the girl twiddles the dial, moving through static until she finds a station with a repetitive dance beat.

'What's your favourite band?' she asks him, twisting one of her curls around her finger.

'I've got lots,' Troy says, reeling off a list of names unfamiliar to Billie. It sounds like he is speaking another language. She takes the bowl from the bench and leaves the pair to chat.

Balancing the bowl in one hand, Billie knocks on Lorelei's door. 'Troy's made you a balm,' she says through the wood, 'to help the burn.'

No answer from inside. 'You there, Lorelei?'

This time the door opens. Lorelei wipes her eyes, which are red-rimmed and bloodshot. She blows her nose into a tissue and sniffs.

'I'm sorry,' Billie says, unsure what to do. 'Are you okay? I'll go, if you want me to.'

'No, come in. I'm just having a funny five minutes, that's all. Don't know what came over me. Probably pre-menstrual. The balm sounds great. I thought the shower would take the heat out of it, but it's really stinging.'

Lorelei sits on the bed, wearing knickers and her bra. 'Excuse my underwear,' she says. 'Anything more hurts too much.'

The outline of her bikini top is pale against the sunburnt skin. It looks worse than it did outside. Even her thighs glow. 'Would you rub some on my shoulders and back? I can reach the rest myself.'

She inhales sharply as Billie applies the cool balm. Under Billie's fingers, goosebumps pucker her skin. 'Lavender?' she says. 'It's lovely. Mum couldn't stand it. God knows how she managed to live in Norfolk, with acres of the stuff in all directions. Someone gave her a plant once, and she chucked it straight in the bin.'

I know, Billie thinks. She remembers when Audrey's aversion to the purple blooms began, but she won't talk about it with Lorelei. Not yet.

Over the next days, Lorelei uses the balm often, and the fragrance lingers in the house. The purple fields of Norfolk return to Billie's mind. Unearthly, they appear in her sketchbook, regular rows of lavender parcelled between hedgerows.

El-iss-ah, Billie thinks, when she smells the lavender.

El-iss-ah.

Sybille

Norfolk 1945

It was May 1945. V.E. Day had come and gone. Sybille Quinn was fifteen and she had plans. She had directions scribbled on her arm, underneath her sleeve where Mrs Quinn couldn't see them. She stole a shilling from the purse on the mantelpiece while Mrs Quinn hung out the washing. Tucked it in her shoe. The coin lodged under the arch of her foot like a smooth pebble.

While Mr Quinn was busy with a customer in the bakery, Sybille stole a fresh penny bun, plump with mock cream, and tucked it in her satchel. It was Mr Quinn's first batch of cakes in years—through the war he'd baked only the regulation wheat loaf. Rationing was still strict, but these yeasty buns, miracles of hoarded flour and currants, hinted at better days ahead.

Sybille took the bicycle from the shed at the usual time and rode along the lane to school. At the last turn, where the lane forked, she went left instead of right. She rode away from the voices screaming in the playground and on towards the station. A poster on the flint wall of the station asked her if her journey was necessary. Sybille nodded and pedalled faster, over the tracks and out of the village.

It was a blue-sky travelling day. Nearly harvest time. Open fields beckoned, gentle curves with the sky wide above them. The hills didn't look steep, but Sybille felt the slope in her thighs. She pedalled hard, until her cheeks burnt and sweat stuck her tunic to her back. She had to stop at the top of one deceptive hill to catch her breath.

Sybille leant over a hedgerow. The fields had been stripped of their lavender when the war started, given over to food crops, but hardy lavender bushes sprouted beside the hedgerow, defying the sugar beets and turnips. Sybille bent forward to touch the delicate flowers. Dodging hovering bees, she snapped off three sprigs. She wove them through the buttonhole of her pinafore, then sniffed her fragrant fingers.

On the down slope, Sybille stuck out her legs. She let the pedals spin freely, only touching the brakes at the bottom of the long hill, at another fork. I could go anywhere with this bike, Sybille thought, and chose the road that would carry her to the asylum. Ten miles to Norwich, the sign said. Sybille wasn't sure she could cycle that far. Her legs wobbled like the brawn Mrs Quinn made from the gammon joint. But she pushed against the pedals and forced them on.

When the road brought Sybille to Norwich, she braked and jumped off her bike. The surface was cracked and littered with bricks and splintered planks. Sybille wheeled her bike behind a hedge and covered it with leaves. She walked into the city through piles of rubble. She had read about the damage in Elissa's letters and seen the reports in the papers, but she never imagined it this way. There were blackened gaps between neat brick terraces, empty spaces spanned by charred wood skeletons. Sometimes the bombs had only taken the front of the houses, leaving fireplaces and baths and open doors hanging in the air. One door still had a dressing-gown on the brass hook. The houses looked naked, exposed.

The city bustled. Men in overalls and hard hats cleared paths through the debris and piled broken bricks into wheelbarrows, whistling as Sybille passed. Four army men balanced an unexploded bomb on their shoulders. She wrinkled her nose. The city smelt like bonfire ash after rain has put out the flames. In the village they'd been lucky. Sprinting to the shelter when the sirens wailed, with her gas-mask case banging against her thigh, Sybille had seen the bombers overhead and waited for the explosions. But not one bomb had fallen. They must have been saving them for the city. Dodging the work groups, Sybille walked faster. She wanted to run from the ruins, back to the village with its windows and walls intact, but, remembering Elissa, she pressed on.

Pushing up her sleeve to look at the map on her arm, she followed Heigham Road, keeping the crumbling castle to her right. She passed a church that had been gutted by fire. Pigeons nested in the tower, the only part of the church to survive. On a wooden footbridge over the river Wensum, she nibbled the penny bun she'd stolen from the bakery. When she'd eaten the bun and licked the sugar from her fingers, she wished she'd stolen another.

The cramped terraces near the asylum were undamaged, but Sybille noticed a large crater a few streets ahead. She thought of Elissa in the asylum, hearing the houses explode. Did they have a special shelter inside, she wondered, or did the inmates tremble in bed, listening to the bombs and wondering if they would be next?

The asylum itself was locked behind iron gates. Sybille peered through the bars at a second fence inside the compound, partially hidden by a row of horse-chestnut trees. She saw a red-brick building through the trees and followed the outer fence to the gatehouse.

Sybille didn't know what to expect inside, or even what Elissa would be like. She had listened to Mr Quinn relate the doctors' reports, but found it difficult to link the person they described with her friend. Could Elissa have changed so much in four years, or was she like that all along, and I didn't notice? I have changed, Sybille thought, suddenly frightened Elissa wouldn't recognise her. While Audrey had stayed as scrawny as she had been in childhood, Sybille's body had swelled into women's curves.

A year after Elissa went away, Sybille had bled for the first time. Frightened by the brown stain in her knickers, thinking she'd cut herself, she told Mrs Quinn. In a curt whisper, the woman said she would bleed again the next month, and the next. She handed Sybille a wad of cloth and a complicated belt arrangement, telling her never to speak of it. Sybille missed Elissa more than ever that day, wishing she was there to rub her aching belly and explain what the blood meant.

At the gatehouse, the guard eyed Sybille's curves so closely she thought he was going to reach out and touch them. The attention disturbed her, because she didn't know what to do if he did. Winking as he opened the visitors' gate, the guard walked her through a second gate to the women's building. Sybille strode away, ignoring the man, who slowly licked his lips as she passed.

Terracotta pots bright with red poppies stood by the front door. Ivy claimed the bottom floor, with stands of bamboo and a trellis of wild pink roses. There were bars on all the windows. At the door, Sybille met two nurses wearing stiff white pinafores with black blouses underneath. They led her through dim corridors to the walled airing court, where tendrils of honey-suckle softened the harsh lines of the walls. Women in identical cotton dresses walked aimlessly, talking to themselves. A few squatted or knelt by vegetable beds, scratching in the soil with their fingers. One woman pulled flowers from the creeper, hold-ing out her skirt to collect the blooms. Sybille saw the woman's petticoat, then looked away. One nurse asked Sybille to wait in the garden while she fetched Elissa. The other stayed to watch over the inmates.

Sybille sat on a bench, nerves churning her belly. She dan-gled her feet and watched the women. There were children here too. They were skipping, singing a nursery rhyme. Sybille closed her eyes and let their voices soothe her. None of them look mad, she thought. I wonder why they're here?

When Sybille opened her eyes again, the nurse was walk-ing Elissa across the garden to the bench. Elissa moved like an old lady. Her head was shaven to the skin, with only tufts of orange hair remaining, and scabs like port-wine birthmarks over her scalp. The pale dome shone in the sunlight. Sybille looked away until Elissa sat beside her.

Neither spoke. They sat on the bench and watched the after-noon sunlight stretch their shadows over grass.

'Chi . . . bell . . . eh?' Elissa asked.

Her voice was so slow that at first Sybille didn't understand the sounds. They seemed to come from underwater. Sybille heard the ebb and flow of the current in the woman's voice.

'Cig-a-rettes?' Elissa asked.

Sybille imagined the word moving through the chambers of Elissa's brain. She pulled a crumpled packet from the pocket of her school uniform, struck a match to light the tube, then inhaled deeply. Exhaling, she held it out across the bench.

Elissa reached for the cigarette. She sucked the cigarette until dents appeared in her cheeks. 'No . . . visit,' she said. 'Why?'

Sybille shook her head slowly. 'The war,' she began. 'Travel is restricted . . .' but Elissa interrupted.

'War . . . is . . . over . . .'

'In Europe,' Sybille said, 'but we're still waiting for Japan. Should be any day.'

'Any day . . .' Elissa repeated.

'I brought you these,' Sybille said, pulling the lavender from her tunic and pressing it to Elissa's nostrils. The stems had wilted, but the fragrance hung in the air between them. Sybille inhaled the two fragrances, lavender and smoke, both as familiar as the smell of her own skin. Elissa smiled at the purple blooms, a slow, sad smile.

'Where . . . Why aren't . . . they here?'

Three heartbeats passed before Sybille could answer. 'They're busy. They send love. They . . .'

'Liar.' Elissa sighed. 'They don't know . . . you're here. Doesn't matter.'

The syllables came with difficulty. Sybille held her breath when Elissa paused, never sure if the sentence would continue or drift off into the sky.

'I dream . . . of skinned . . . rats,' Elissa said softly. 'I hear . . . the bombs . . . scream.'

Scuffing the ground with her feet, Sybille didn't know what to say. Elissa's eyes were empty. She seemed to be speaking to herself. Then Elissa blinked and returned to the garden.

'My hair . . . You haven't said . . . anything . . .'

Sybille looked at Elissa's bald head, at the scabs and stubble. 'I . . .'

'It's the rage . . . here . . . darling. All us shockers . . . It'll . . . grow.'

Reaching out slowly, afraid a quick movement would startle Elissa, Sybille placed her palm on the woman's scalp. The orange stubble tickled her skin. She avoided the crusts of dried blood.

'You look like a baby,' she said.

When Elissa had smoked half her cigarette she pushed the burning end into her arm. She made no sound. It was the sulphur crackle of burning hair that warned Sybille.

'Jesus, Elissa! What are you doing?'

Knocking the cigarette from Elissa's fingers, Sybille examined the raw red circlet. She kissed the skin next to the wound. Crushed the lavender stems until they released their juices and rubbed them into the wound.

'Sit down,' Elissa said. 'You'll bring . . . the nurse. They'll send you away.'

She smiled. The burn seemed to have woken her up, because her words flowed more easily. She put her free hand to Sybille's cheek.

'Don't worry, little one. It'll heal. I just needed something . . . to keep. Everything gets lost here. Or taken . . . If I kept your flowers under my pillow, someone would steal them. And the rats! They even eat our underwear . . . But not this. No one can take this.'

Sybille chewed her lip. She lit another cigarette. Keeping her eyes on Elissa, she pressed the cigarette into the back of her own hand. Elissa didn't stop her. She wrapped her fingers around Sybille's hands, made a skin cocoon for the burning flesh. They sat like that, even after the cigarette had gone out, until the nurses came for Elissa.

Afterwards, Sybille told Mrs Quinn she'd burnt her hand at school; she was surprised at how convincing the lie sounded. How easily it came out. As soon as the wound scabbed Sybille locked herself in the toilet. She prised the edges of the scab from the new skin beneath. The sharp pain and the rush of blood to the wound were secret pleasures. Sybille picked the scab so many times that when the burn finally healed she was left with a circle of pure white skin on the back of her tanned hand.

The next time Sybille visited the asylum she showed Elissa the scar. They sat on the bench in the sunshine and compared wounds. A circle of cigarette butts grew around their feet. Elissa talked fluently this time; she said it had been weeks since her last treatment. She seemed calm, even steady, except for her foot. In a black leather shoe with a single strap, Elissa's foot pivoted at the ankle and flapped as she talked. The calf muscle quivered, as if a stray bolt of electricity from the treatment had lodged in her foot and continued to work its spastic magic.

Sybille let Elissa talk. She moved only when her bottom went numb, sliding down to the ground next to Elissa's flapping foot and the cigarette butts. She buried the butts in the dry earth and excavated chips of red brick from the soil.

One by one, Elissa told the stories of the other women in the garden. The old girl on her knees in the lettuce patch, she said, was here because she'd forgotten who her family was. And see the one with the brassy hair? Matron caught her with her knickers round one ankle and her legs through the bars of the men's section, while a male inmate strained on the other side. The rocking girl in the corner never spoke. Her brother had brought her in. She'd been raped, but the brother wouldn't say by whom, and the girl wasn't talking. Elissa pointed to the far side of the garden, where a woman with a belly like a giant egg lowered herself to a bench.

'Her parents committed her because she's got a bun in the oven, but no husband.' Elissa sighed. 'Mother was right,' she said.

When Sybille asked what she meant, Elissa shook her head and spoke no more that day.

On Sybille's next visit Elissa talked again. No one in the asylum listened, she said. They were crackers, only interested in themselves. She pulled Sybille close and whispered about the man she used to watch from the window of her bedroom. She watched him cross the Green on his way home from work and cross it again to the White Hart in the evenings.

'I followed him one night,' Elissa said. 'Spoke to him in the lane. He told me his wife was pregnant. That she was no fun after dark. So I met him every night. He got us wine from the pub and we drank from the bottle, under the trees. I was fifteen.'

Elissa's face glowed. Her eyes were wide open. Sybille saw the full circles of the irises, like green marbles. She longed for her sketchbook. She had left it with the matron, who had forbidden her to bring sharp objects into the asylum. Even charcoal, she'd said. Sybille couldn't understand why the sketchbook had to stay too. They didn't seem to worry about her matches. Sybille thought they could do more damage, but there it was. She stared hard instead, inscribing the image on her memory. Networks of green and gold fibres surrounded the void of Elissa's pupil. Sybille was close enough to see the threads of coloured muscle expand and contract like the muscles in her own arms, and the shift in the size of the pupil when the threads moved.

While Elissa whispered, Sybille rubbed her lips. She loved the woman's soft voice and the way her breath tickled the tiny hairs in her ears. Her limbs tingled, and she shifted in her seat. She crossed her legs, inhaled deeply, and felt a delicious warmth between her legs. She had not heard this part of the story before, but she knew it would take her closer to Elissa's mysteries.

'It got cold,' Elissa said, 'so we went into the bakery. The relief baker walked in. I tried to bribe him with a pound from the till, but he took the money and told Father anyway. And the rest of the village. By the next morning everyone knew about Elissa Quinn, the red-haired hussy, caught with her knickers around her knees.'

Elissa's sigh whirled through the corridors of Sybille's ear. 'Father wouldn't look at me. And Mother? I've never seen her so pale. Not until Isaac told them about his own adventures . . .'

The woman paused. 'Father never knew about the baby. Mother caught me throwing up one morning. Said she would have me committed if I had the child. There were places for girls like me. Looks like she was right.'

Elissa laughed, a shrill laugh that made Sybille wince. 'Mother lied to Father, said we needed some new trays for the oven, then took me to Norwich. She had heard of a doctor. Never breathe a word, she said. It was between me and the devil. But I want you to know.'

Whispered and frantic, unstoppered after so many years, the words poured into Sybille's ear. Images flickered behind her eyelids. Mrs Quinn staring from across the train carriage on the way to the city, her lips white with fury. The surgery in a cobbled lane off the main street. The doctor shaking his head. Fifteen, he tutted. Shiny silver instruments. Afterwards, Elissa stumbling through the streets to the station, weak with blood loss and ether. Staring at her pale reflection in the train window. Elissa, in the months that followed, clamping her lips shut on the secret and the sorrow as she watched Mrs Quinn's own belly bulge with Audrey.

When the whispering stopped, Sybille opened her eyes, gutted. Elissa sat with her knees up, like the silent girl in the corner of the yard. She looked young, confused.

'I know in my heart it was a girl,' she said. 'She would have been your age.'

Sybille opened her arms. She pressed the shorn head to her chest and felt Elissa's tears soak her tunic.

'I was fifteen,' Elissa sobbed. 'Nobody told me how it happened.'

Sybille kissed the top of Elissa's scalp and felt tufts of regrown hair prickle her lip.

'It's all right,' she whispered. 'I'm here now.'

Late in the summer of 1945 Sybille and the Quinns caught the Norwich train together. They had suitcases and sunhats and tickets that would take them to Elissa, then shunt them on to the sea. Mr Quinn had booked a terrace in Great Yarmouth for a week, but he wouldn't come with them.

'People need their bread,' he said. 'You'll have more fun without me there anyway.'

The family took the train from Harrowstone to Norwich. Sybille elbowed past Audrey for the window seat.

'Mine,' Audrey whispered. 'Or I'll tell Mother you've been bunking off.'

Screwing up her nose, Sybille gave up her seat. It didn't matter, because she could see past Audrey's skinny shoulders to the fields beyond. The train tracks followed the gentle curve of the hills, and Sybille looked down on the familiar lanes below.

The family took a taxi from the station to the asylum. All except Sybille gasped at the bombsites and burnt-out buildings. Sybille stared at the landmarks, nodding when Mrs Quinn pointed out the cathedral and the castle. They've got no idea, she thought.

A man was waiting at the front door of the asylum. He had a bushy moustache, and curly hair slicked down with grease. 'You here for the Quinn girl?'

Mrs Quinn nodded.

'Looks like she's out for good,' the man said. 'The Super says we need the beds for our boys. Just sign for her.'

With a shaky signature, Mrs Quinn took possession of her daughter.

'She's groggy. Only had her last treatment yesterday. Gets worse before it gets better, so we've found. A few days and she'll be right as rain.'

Two attendants walked Elissa through the doors of the asylum. She was a mannequin, her arms and legs working separately. The attendants held her shoulders as she swayed between them, butting against their hands until she could stand alone. She stared over the attendants' shoulders. Sybille waved, but Elissa didn't respond. Her green eyes were focused on a vanishing point somewhere to the left of Sybille's head.

Elissa was thinner than when Sybille had last seen her. She wore her own clothes, but somehow they were wrong. Sybille recognised the burgundy mohair cardigan, remembered its soft fibres against her cheek and the soapy smell of the wool. Today the cardigan bagged at the elbows and hung down past Elissa's waist. Her stockings wrinkled about her ankles. The dress looked twisted, back to front. There was enough space for another person to crawl up the skirt and into the gusty space between the fabric and Elissa's body.

Elissa's head was newly shaven. Sybille knew the contours of the bald head, but the rest of the family stared. Mrs Quinn put her hand to her mouth. Isaac coughed. Audrey seemed frozen. No one spoke. Mrs Quinn put a sunhat on her daughter's head. Elissa leant on Isaac. They walked slowly to the taxi.

Sybille held Elissa's hand for the journey to the station. She squeezed, but the hand didn't squeeze back. It lay like a lump of dough waiting to be kneaded. She turned the hand over and

the fingers curled ragged nails into the palm. They curled further, until the tendons strained. Sybille cupped the hand in her
own, gently, the way she cupped a fresh hen's egg at home.
It was a tiny child's fist, so fragile that if Sybille squeezed hard
every bone would snap and crumble. I am half your age, she
thought. But today you are my child.

The train to Yarmouth was waiting at the platform. The
second-class section was already crowded, but the guard looked
at Elissa, then walked the family to an empty first-class carriage.

'There was an accident up the line,' the guard said. 'A right
mess. Shouldn't be long now, though.'

Isaac lowered Elissa into a window seat and sat beside her.
Audrey and Sybille took the seats opposite, elbowing again for
the other window seat. This time Sybille won. Mrs Quinn
unpacked her knitting. She waved a crumpled paper bag.

'Humbug?' she asked.

Isaac, Audrey and Sybille shook their heads. Elissa did not
respond.

'Mind yourselves,' the guard said, as the train began to shunt
away. 'I'm leaving the door open a little today, ladies. A treat,
especially for you.' He winked at Elissa. 'Lets the fresh air in.
Get some bloom in your cheeks.' The guard tipped his cap and
shrilled a silver whistle.

The open door was an anomaly in the carriage. Everything
else fitted: the glass lampshades with frilled edges like the moist
skirts of snails; the black-and-white photographs of Norwich
tucked behind cracked glass; the sign threatening to fine smok-
ers £1 for the joy of exhaling out the window. Even the other
sign made sense, the one lecturing that Projecting Part of the
Person out of a Carriage Window or Door is Forbidden and
the Department will not Accept Liability for Anyone Injured
by so Doing. But the open door was as shocking as a wound.

It was an invitation. It enticed the eye out into the air and under the train, to the steel space between wheel and track where sparks jumped and metal screamed.

As the train swept into a tight corner one of the boiled sweets rolled from the crumpled bag and out the door. It spun in the sunlight, the sugar glaze glistening like a fishing fly over water. Elissa followed the arc. She leant into the dusty window, forehead to forehead with her reflection.

'Sometimes I wonder,' she said, in a barely audible voice, 'what it would be like to let go.'

Sybille listened, transfixed. No one else had heard. Audrey had fallen asleep against her mother, and Isaac was talking cricket with the guard. Elissa's lips had barely moved, just enough to let the words escape. Plump red lips, chapped and bleeding lipstick from the cracks. Whoever applied the lipstick was unfamiliar with the shape of these lips. They didn't know the two ocean peaks below her nose and the dive between them, and lipstick had spilt over the edges.

'So easy,' Elissa whispered. 'Put your toes to the edge. Only one step and it'd be done.'

Leaning forward, Sybille peered into the green eyes. They were smudged with blue eye shadow and spider-leg mascara. Someone had really tarted her up. In the dark pupils, Sybille saw her own reflection in miniature. There was no contraction of the pupil, no wrinkle between the eyebrows to signal recognition. Just an empty stare that pierced through Sybille, and out along the railway track towards the sea.

It hurt Sybille to see Elissa this way. She wanted to stretch across the open door to her, to bridge the distance between them, but the thin arms were crossed over Elissa's body, hands tucked out of reach. Sybille followed her stare out the smeared window to the birch woods beside the tracks. Through the trees, the Broads reflected the sun. She watched boats glide silently, rippling the shimmering surface. Ducks skimmed across the water, chased by squawking coots. The train whizzed past thatched cottages and over arched brick bridges, past bicycles and cars stopped at white gates. Sybille saw an owl perched on a fence post. Out there it seemed so calm. Hard to imagine there had ever been a war.

The Quinn family arrived in Great Yarmouth three days after a bomb had turned Hiroshima to ash. There were banners celebrating the victory and tables in the streets piled high with scrounged rations. Union Jacks fluttered from lampposts. The whole town wore paper hats, blew whistles and ignored the holes where bombs had gutted the houses. Marine Parade was crammed with people, as if everyone in Norfolk had decided to take a holiday at once. Yanks and farmers did the congo down the street. Harry Roy's Tiger Ragamuffins played at the Winter Garden Ballroom for midnight dancing, and the Empire and the Coliseum screened films to full houses.

The ends of the piers were still barricaded by barbed wire. Only a small stretch of sand had been cleared of mines, and this was crowded from first light until dusk. Mrs Quinn didn't fancy being squashed on the sand without even a deckchair, so the family spent sunny days at the bathing pool. With none of them able to swim, they avoided the deep end and paddled in the shallows. Mrs Quinn and Elissa sunned themselves in light cotton frocks, the girls wore new woollen swimming costumes, and even Isaac bought a pair of trunks, baring his ribcage to the sun.

On the last morning in Great Yarmouth, Sybille sat on the tiles at the edge of the baths with her feet in the water. Days in the sun had quickly browned her skin, ripening it to match the polished walnut dresser in the hall at Harrowstone. Beside

Sybille, Elissa sat with skirt pulled up around her knees. A straw hat shaded her face, and light bounced from the water to flicker over her institution-pale skin. With a hat and loose blouse, Elissa had avoided sunburn, but the other Quinns had burnt and blistered over the week, the skin flaking from Isaac's nose and Audrey's shoulders.

The pair sat in silence. Sybille was content beside Elissa, watching the patterns the woman's toes made in the water. The world shrank, containing only Elissa and the sparkling liquid at her feet. Scooping water into her palm, Sybille dribbled it onto Elissa's ankle and watched the droplets glide over the bony contours of her foot, following the blue veins beneath the surface.

Unexpectedly, Elissa began to speak. In a quiet voice she described a memory from the asylum. The shock treatment had razed her brain, she said, and her time there was like a half-grasped dream, but sometimes images surfaced through the confusion. She remembered an injection of cold liquid that flowed up her arm to paralyse her, stopping her chest mid-breath while her eyes stared across at the humming machine with dials and glass bubbles. Immobile, she'd watched the doctor prepare the electrodes, gauze-wrapped callipers that gripped her temples.

'I couldn't breathe,' she whispered, rubbing the skin between her collarbones. 'Crushed under my own chest.'

While Elissa spoke, Audrey waded over to the pair, churning the still water with her steps. Elissa's words lost their momentum and stumbled into silence. Scowling, Audrey tugged at the knitted costume that clung to her just-developing body. 'What you talking about, then?'

'Nothing,' Sybille said. She was unwilling to share Elissa's memory with the awkward girl, unmoved by Audrey's familiar hurt expression.

Audrey slapped the water with her hand, spraying the pair on the edge.

'You always keep secrets from me,' she hissed. She turned and splashed back to her mother. 'Damn you. Damn you both.'

That afternoon the family went to the seafront and walked barefoot along Marine Parade. They bought pickled cockles and winkles in cones of waxed paper. Sybille winced as the molluscs squirted sour vinegar into her mouth. The family walked along Wellington Pier until barricades of thorny wire stopped them. A Department of Defence sign warned of submerged mines, but Sybille saw no dark shapes beneath the water.

There was a summer storm on the horizon. Lightning flickered in thunderhead clouds, but the storm was too far out to sea for the sound to reach the shore. The smell of fish and chips drew the family from the pier. Stalked by elongated shadows, they passed the Ballroom with shoes in hands, watching the strings of lights between the lampposts click on in the fading light.

The storm was nearer now. Sybille walked beside Elissa. She kept close, the distance between them never more than a couple of feet. Elissa didn't seem to mind. She often reached for Sybille's hand, absently stroking the girl's skin like kitten fur. When Elissa reached out, Sybille didn't move or talk; she was afraid the slightest movement might scare Elissa away.

'Damn,' Elissa said, stopping. Sybille paused with her. The rest of the family walked ahead, unaware that Elissa and Sybille no longer followed. The three of them laughed together, more relaxed than Sybille had ever seen them.

Elissa dropped Sybille's hand, which swung in space awkwardly. Sybille clenched her hand into a fist, then crossed her arms. It was easier to hide the limb's confusion that way.

Elissa sighed. 'I left my shoes behind on the pier. New ones too. Well, not new. Newly painted. As good as new.'

'I'll get them,' Sybille said.

'No, it's all right, little one. I want to buy some postcards too. Take my hat for me, though. I don't want to lose that as well. I'll leave my head behind if I'm not careful. Memory's shot to pieces.'

'I'll come with you.'

'No.' Elissa gripped the girl's chin with her fingers. Sybille felt them slide along her jawbone. 'Meet me back at the house.'

Sybille stared. Elissa's face blocked out the world. Her green eyes were so close that Sybille found it hard to focus. The eyes were lit from inside, bright like an empty wine bottle with sun shining through the glass. It was the same light Sybille had seen the day Elissa left for Norwich.

Sybille nodded slowly, against her will, her chin guided by Elissa's fingers. She wanted to shout 'No, I am coming too', but her feet betrayed her. At the corner of Marine Parade, she turned to watch Elissa and her long shadow walk towards the pier. Turn around, she thought, wave, beckon and I will follow, but the figure walked on. From the corner, Sybille watched until Elissa was swallowed by the evening crowds, the men in uniform and heavily made-up women who hit the streets as the sun set.

Mrs Quinn looked up when Sybille walked into the boarding-house. She was laying the table, setting up plates to hold the fish and chips bundled in newspaper in the centre of the table. 'Where is she?'

'Right behind me,' Sybille said. 'She left her shoes on the pier. She said . . .'

'You left her alone? Christ!' Mrs Quinn muttered. 'Please God, no. Not this time.'

Her face changed from pink to pale. She pressed her lips together so they disappeared, leaving only a wrinkled slit in the flesh of her face.

'Isaac!' she yelled.

When Isaac poked his head around the doorframe, she grabbed her handbag and pushed the man out the door.

'Wait here,' she said to Sybille and Audrey.

Sybille sat at the window with her cheek against the glass, waiting for Mrs Quinn and Isaac to return. It should still have been light at this hour, but the storm blocked the sun. The wind blew rain against the window at an angle, smearing the glass so Sybille saw nothing but blurred blobs of colour as people walked by. They reminded her of dollops of paint on her palette. Still carrying Elissa's hat, her fingers clenched and unclenched, curling the straw brim into a ragged edge. Away from Elissa's head, the hat seemed deflated, crushed.

Audrey ripped the corner of the newspaper bundle and ate chip after slow chip, chewing like a cow in the fields. There was no joy in her eating. Sybille turned her head further towards the window until she stared at her own sallow reflection, but she could do nothing about the sticky sounds. It was too much.

Walking into the dark parlour, Sybille stubbed her toes in the unfamiliar room, but didn't turn on the light. Her fingers found the upholstered armchair and she curled up in it, her face pressed against its prickly arms, clutching Elissa's crumpled hat. She tried to sleep, but the rain was noisy on the roof. It wouldn't stop. There was enough rain to drown them all.

When Sybille heard the front door open she looked at the pale face of the clock. Two in the morning and still raining. Isaac and Mrs Quinn were paler than the clock face, even in the warm light of the dining-room lamp. Sybille didn't think they could see her hidden in the darkness of the parlour, so she watched through the doorway. Isaac brought in a pot of tea, lifting the lid to pour the entire contents of his silver hip flask through the steam and into the pot. Mrs Quinn sat at the table with her hands over her mouth. She rubbed her lips, pausing as if about to speak, then returned to the rubbing. As Isaac stirred sugar into the tea, she winced at the clank of the spoon against china, winced again as she sipped the steaming liquid. The pair drank in silence.

Sybille watched a moth flutter around the dining-room lamp. The moth was huge, dark brown with white circles on its wings. It flew directly to the light, pinging when its body hit the glass bulb. Bouncing between the lampshade and the glass, it scraped its wings against the stretched fabric of the shade. The intervals between each impact shrank as panic set in. Mrs Quinn slapped both hands against the table. The cups rattled in their saucers.

'Get it out!' she screamed. 'I can't stand it!'

Sybille jumped. Her heart beat quickly. She watched Isaac cup the moth in his hands and open the casement with his elbow. It will drown in the rain, Sybille thought, imagining sodden wings and blurred patterns, but she could not open her mouth to yell. Isaac brushed his fingers together and closed the window. He sighed.

'I'll tell Father,' he said quietly.

Mrs Quinn nodded. Standing, she scraped the chair under the table and stared at her son, hands squeezed into fists by her side. Isaac reached for one fist, wrapped his fingers around it. The pair stood, eyes locked, hands linked, until Mrs Quinn pulled away.

'Turn the light off when you're done,' she said, and left the room.

Draining his cup, Isaac poured another, and another. He grimaced with the first mouthful, but eagerly gulped down the next. Repulsed, Sybille watched his Adam's apple bob. When only a few amber drops trickled from the teapot, he walked unsteadily to the parlour. Sybille closed her eyes, pretending to be asleep, as Isaac lowered himself into the armchair opposite her.

'I know you're awake,' he said.

Sybille lay still. The clock ticked. Isaac reached out to tuck one of Sybille's curls behind her ear, and she willed herself not to pull away from his touch.

'It should have been me,' he said, his voice faint. 'I wasn't meant to live past twenty. Everyone fussed over me. But it was Elissa . . .'

He stopped, the clock measuring the silence after his words. Sybille counted fifteen beats until he spoke again, the words barely louder than the rain on the windows.

'She tried once before, Mother told me. When I was abroad. Threw herself in the water tank at the bottom of the garden after they caught her with a married man. They pulled her out just in time.'

Sybille's belly coiled and uncoiled, as her fingers had done on the hat. She remembered the green light in Elissa's eyes before the woman returned to the pier. I didn't know, she thought, queasy. You didn't tell me.

After Isaac walked slowly up the stairs, Sybille gazed into the darkness until luminous patterns danced in front of her eyes. She stared, forgetting to blink. The light in the room changed; she could see faint outlines of the armchairs. These mundane objects seemed suddenly wrong, like a familiar word written repeatedly until it becomes peculiar. The chairs' plump curves were obscene in the morning light. Troubled by the poor, battered hat, she hid it under one of the cushions.

Unable to sit still, Sybille crept out of the house before the sun was fully up. She walked along the seafront, past drunken couples slumped over benches and against walls. One woman had fallen asleep straddling a sailor, her skirt hitched over her knees. Sybille saw the puckered flesh of the woman's thigh, and the red welt where her suspender belt had scarred her skin.

Sybille walked without destination or purpose. She walked because she could not sit. She turned away from the cusp of the sun on a sparkling horizon, from the milkman and his cheerful wave. She made a circuit of the Winter Gardens, puzzled by a trail of blood marking her earlier steps. She had not realised that she had left the house without shoes, nor that somewhere on the walk she had been cut.

Surprised when her bare feet carried her to the pier's barbed-wire barrier, Sybille blinked, disoriented, then reached for the wire. The sea air had attacked the metal, and the wire was red with rust. She hadn't noticed the corrosion the last time she was here.

There were fine threads of wool caught on the barbs. Sybille carefully lifted the threads from the wire and held them to the light. They were burgundy, the same colour as Elissa's cardigan. They smelt like her. Sybille pressed the threads to her nostrils, inhaled and closed her eyes. She saw Elissa standing on the pier next to her forgotten shoes. She saw the woman unbutton her cardigan, then hang it from the wire. Her summer dress came next, draped beside the cardigan. Sybille saw Elissa stand on the pier in her slip, the ivory-coloured one with the lace bodice. She watched her pull the slip over her head, then unhook her bra and pull down the big knickers that stretched over her belly. Sybille saw lines where the seams had dug into Elissa's skin. The barbed wire looked like a washing line with Elissa's underthings fluttering in the breeze. Sybille tried to open her eyes, but they stayed shut, forcing her to watch as Elissa parted the wire with her fingers and slid through the gap, only scratching one thigh. They forced her to watch Elissa walk steadily to the end of the pier then, without pausing, walk straight off into the water. There was no struggle, Sybille saw, just a slow slide below the surface.

When Sybille opened her eyes, she was surrounded by upside-down legs. She was lying on the pier, her fingers tightly curled around the threads of burgundy wool. Someone helped her up. A man scooped his arms behind her knees. She pressed her face into his rough shirt, trying to block out the arc of Elissa's descent.

On the morning of the funeral, Sybille wanted to see Elissa before the earth claimed her. She took her sketchbook upstairs and, like the first time, hesitated with fingers on the door handle before twisting the knob.

The first thing Sybille noticed was the smell. Someone had rubbed Elissa's body with lavender oil, and the scent of the crushed flowers was overpowering. The bed was scattered with flowers, and tightly bound bunches filled vases on the mantelpiece and the windowsill. The lavender smelt sharp, almost antiseptic, but there was another smell, like sour milk or rotten food. Sybille concentrated on the smell of the flowers and tried to forget what was underneath.

Elissa's hands had been crossed over her chest. Sybille chose three blooms and prised apart the stiff fingers to tuck the small posy between them. The body didn't feel like a person at all, more like a wax model that looked like Elissa but had no relation to the real woman. The mouth was smiling, cheeks bright with rouge. Sybille was glad the form on the bed wore a wig, ready for the viewing. If she'd had to see that poor shaved head with its tufts of hair and unhealed scabs she might have recognised the body. But the wig prevented that. It was the right colour, but the style was wrong, parted on the opposite side, and dead straight, where Elissa's had a slight kink. The wig was not Elissa, and somehow it made the rest of the body not Elissa as well.

Out of habit, Sybille opened her sketchbook and the tea tin in which she carried her pastels. She drew the top half of the woman's body in three-quarters profile. Mostly she drew what she saw, but her fingers rebelled at the wig. Instead, they sketched the hair as Sybille remembered it, loose and falling across the pillow in waves. The artificial brightness of the rouge became a flush of excitement, of life. In the picture Elissa looked like a young woman sleeping the night before her wedding.

She stroked the patches of light and dark in the sketch, expecting the image to summon the swell of Elissa's body and the soapy smell of her skin, but her fingertips felt only the coarse grain of the paper. Sybille smelt lavender and the slow salty sorrow of the sea.

During the funeral the lavender permeated the tiny church. It was as if Elissa's body oozed it from her pores. The smell was inescapable. Part way through the service, a few villagers left the church with handkerchiefs over their noses.

Sybille didn't cry at the funeral. Neither did the Quinns. They sat straight up in church and watched the ceremony with dry eyes. Sybille ignored the pointing and the stares, the whispers about suicide and unsanctified ground. She kept her eyes on the coffin. When a fly crawled into the white tube of one of the lilies on top of the coffin and explored the yellow stamen, Sybille got up to scare it away, but Mrs Quinn clamped a hand on Sybille's thigh.

'Sit still,' she said, the first words she had spoken to Sybille since that day on the pier.

The vicar's voice was high-pitched and thick, as if his nose was permanently blocked. He never knew Elissa, so why was he up there talking as if she had been his friend? Sybille turned from the vicar in his black-and-white robes and looked towards the west window. Afternoon light touched the stained-glass panels. Sybille concentrated on the lozenges of radiant glass, storing the luminous patterns in her memory to draw later. She ignored the larger picture of the dying Christ and his grieving followers; it was too much.

'It's your fault,' Audrey said to Sybille on the way back from the church. 'You should have stayed with her. You knew what she was like. Why didn't you?'

Sybille shook her head, but kept quiet. There was nothing she could say.

Cave

New South Wales 1990

Suffocating, Billie struggles. I can't breathe, she thinks. I'm drowning, tangled in a fisherman's net. Something presses over her mouth and nostrils, sucking closer when she inhales, and she claws at it. The sheet, it's over my face, she realises as she wakes. Somehow, in the night, she has wound herself in it, but the knowledge doesn't ease the panic. Gasping, she squirms until her mouth is free.

No lounging in bed today. She kicks the sheets away and stands, breathing quick and harsh. Her studio seems small, the walls too close, so she slips on yesterday's dress and walks quickly into the hall. Got to be outside, she thinks. Got to see the sky.

Lorelei's door is open, so she peers around the jamb. Eli curls in bed, hair frizzed over the pillow, but Lorelei's bed is empty. On her way through the house, Billie checks the bathroom and the kitchen, but can't find the Englishwoman. It is only as she kneels on the verandah, fastening her sandals, that she hears the familiar Norfolk voice. Drawn, she follows it through the ghost gums, up the steps to Stan's shed, to hover outside the door.

Lorelei's voice is distinct through the wood. More words than she has spoken to Billie in her stay so far, and their sounds, their rhythms, mesmerise Billie. A flow of words, sentence after sentence, like torrents released by summer storms. Gradually, she begins to listen to the words themselves, to understand their meaning. Lorelei is talking about Simon, telling Stan about a rough patch they've been through. You are just like your mother, Simon had shouted, an overwound spring, and I am tired of trying to make you let go. You don't trust me enough, he said, to just let go, to relax a little. After all these years, you never will.

'And then,' Billie hears Lorelei say, 'and then, he . . .'

The words stop. Silence for four heartbeats, then a quiet mewing seeps through the door. It increases in volume, ragged inhalations turning to sobs. Stan speaks now. Billie hears his comforting bass tone, but the wood and fibro absorb his words. Lorelei's sobs grow: guttural, discordant, primal. The sound of a creature yanked by pain into a realm where language cannot exist. Billie absorbs the pain, feels it touch something buried inside, a fingertip probing the raw flesh below a scab.

Unable to listen, she clamps her hands over her ears. Running from Lorelei's cries, her feet follow the dusty track down the hill. But the sounds pursue her, entangling her like the morning's sheet. She runs to the beach, where the high tide has left only a sliver of sand above the waterline, but even here, where the land ends, she hears Lorelei's pain. Dress on, sandals on, she enters the shallows, limbs slowing as water slides over her thighs. Waist, breast, shoulders. She walks until the water laps at her up-stretched chin, and she has to wedge the soles of her sandals into the mud to stop the momentum carrying her further into the river.

Here, with the undertow tugging at her dress and her body swaying in the current, she closes her eyes. She is at the boundary of the safe harbour. One more step and she'll be out of the reach of the rusty sandstone arm that protects the beach. She'd be dragged into the deepest channels of the river, whipped around the headlands and into the Pacific before anyone notices her absence. One more step.

The current wants her. Insistent. Seductive. Let go, it whispers. Give in. She lifts one foot, feels the water trickle between her callused sole and her sandal, pulling river slime and grains of sand towards the open sea.

One more step.

She lifts her heel, balances on her toes.

One more step.

'Billie? What the bloody hell are you doing?'

The voice pulls her back. She blinks open her eyelids, squinting at the bleached day, at the light glinting on the water. Shielding her eyes from the glare, she anchors her floating foot to the river bed and turns awkwardly to the shore. She had drifted further than she realised.

Barry the ferryman stands knee-deep in water, his face wrinkled with concern. Beside him, his son, Mark, with the broken arm. Both beckon. I am in the river, she thinks. How did I get here? She wades back through the green water, lets them take her hands and lead her up the sand. Released from the current, unable to find her balance on land, she staggers.

'Jeez, you gave us a scare, Billie,' Barry says, holding her arm. 'We were scraping oysters off the rocks when I saw you. What were you doing out there?'

'I don't know,' she whispers.

'Let's get you home,' Barry says.

The ferryman and his son walk beside her on the path. Barry keeps hold of her arm, and his son carries the bucket of crenulated oyster shells. They don't say much, but she knows what they are thinking. Dotty old bird, about to get carried away by the tide. And they're right. She really didn't know what she was doing in the water. In her flight from Lorelei's pain, her body had acted on impulse. The ferryman's broad Australian vowels had roused her from a dangerous dream.

At the house, Barry quietly explains what happened to Troy and Stan. Troy rushes to bring her tea and towels. He wraps one around her, then wipes her muddy feet with the other. She lets him fuss, too tired now to assert her independence. No sign of Lorelei. Relieved, Billie relaxes. After this morning, how can she look at Lorelei and not give away that she knows?

Stan pours a beer for the ferryman, a cordial for Mark, and another cordial for Eli, who rubs her eyes as she walks into the kitchen. It is still early, Billie realises. Not even eleven, yet to her it feels as if the sun should be setting.

'Want to play Sega?' Eli says to Mark. 'Troy's got loads of games.'

The boy nods, and the pair carry their cordial towards the console snaking from the television.

Quiet, still, Billie is soothed by the electronic bleeps from the television and by the murmur of men's talk as they sip their beer. None of it seems quite real. Barry kneels beside her.

'Can Mark stay for a bit?' he asks. 'I've got to start my shift, and he's caught up in a game.'

'Of course,' Billie says. 'I'll send him home later. And thank you, for before. I don't know what . . .'

The ferryman smiles. 'No worries. Just promise you'll be more careful.'

As Barry leaves, she realises that he is the first islander to step inside her house. Can she really have lived here all these years and never had anyone over? Others visited once, when the house was first finished, with bottles of wine to christen the new building. But it had been summer, and they had sat on the verandah overlooking the wild garden. Until recently, Stan's women came and went, and Troy often ferries his boyfriend Jason across from the mainland with him. They met at TAFE early in the year, and Billie enjoys seeing them together. Clad in black, silver-studded, he is Troy's opposite in appearance, but shares the same gentle centre. I have never invited anyone of my own across the threshold, Billie thinks. I really am a silly old bird.

As the door closes, she looks up at Stan. 'You're up early,' she says. There's a sarcastic edge to the words, which she didn't expect or intend.

'Haven't been to bed at all, actually,' he says. If he noticed the sarcasm, he has chosen to ignore it. 'Lorelei couldn't sleep last night. She came in for a chat, and we ended up talking all night. She's gone for a kip now. Think I might do the same. I'm knackered.'

Frowning, Billie stares at her friend. Even after a night without sleep, in crumpled white shirt and brown cords, hair slicked to the side, he seems more attractive than she remembers. Ruddy and vital, while she feels drained. Old. She doesn't know why, but she is angry with him, seething with irritation for the first time since they met. She's grumbled before, when they'd seen too much of each other, or in the quiet, talked-out times, but nothing like this.

'I know you've not had any of your lady friends over for a while,' she says archly, watching Stan flinch. 'But don't play games with my niece. She's had a rough trot lately.'

Stan shakes his head. 'I can't believe I'm hearing this. She just needed someone to talk to.'

She could have talked to me, Billie thinks, but keeps the thought inside. Stan grabs another cold beer from the fridge and walks to the back door.

'Speak to me when you're in a better mood,' he says. 'It's too hot to fight.'

His exit deflates Billie. Part of her hoped he'd snap back, so she could release the anger that had suddenly flared. Instead, she stifles it, squashes it into a hard knot in her belly.

'What was that all about?' Troy says, pouring her a fresh tea. 'You were horrible to him.'

'I know.'

Billie can't explain. She is gripped by fury, like she used to be in the days just before her period or in the angry flushes of her menopause, as her bleeding slowed. The hormone spikes stopped long ago, but this morning she rages like a teenager.

The two almost-teenagers sit cross-legged in front of the television, eyes on rally cars on the screen, fingers twitching joysticks. Billie and Troy walk closer to watch them race. Tyres squeal as the cars take the corners, wheel to wheel, but eventually Eli's crosses the line first. Grinning, she shakes Mark's unplastered hand.

'I did have an advantage,' she says. 'Troy's been teaching me shortcuts. And your cast doesn't help.'

'Come on,' Billie says, bending to turn off the game. 'It's not good for you to be cooped up inside. Let's explore for a bit, while your mum gets some sleep.'

Still draped in her towel, she leads the pair into the sunlit garden. Troy follows, with secateurs and a basket, snipping withered leaves from his herbs and securing the tomato stalks to their supports. While the children crash through the scrub, duelling with slender branches and hiding behind the rough red trunks of the angophoras, Billie perches on a sun-warmed slab of sandstone. The land falls away sharply below, and, on her rocky outcrop, she could be a figurehead at the prow of a great ship. Sprinting down the steps, the children ferret in the bracken at the base of the rocks. The island's wandering blue heeler has joined their game, and they shriek as the dog jumps to lick their faces.

Inhaling, exhaling, listening to the children yell, she feels her anger fade. It had started without her realising, like small cumulonimbus clouds building at the morning horizon, but quickly became a bristling thunderhead. Gone now, dispersed by sunlight and children's laughter. It seems absurd. Why was she angry with Stan? Later, she will talk to him, apologise, but she senses it is best to leave him be for the moment.

She wrings her damp skirt, fans it out over the rock to absorb the sun. Trickling water darkens the sandstone from yellow ochre to burnt sienna. A tiny skink, disturbed by her movement, scuttles to another part of the rock. The end of its tail is missing, and the stump waggles as the lizard moves. On the power line, a kookaburra turns its head to watch the lizard's movement. Don't you dare, Billie thinks, protective of the injured creature. It's been through enough. She claps her hands, and the kookaburra opens its wings to fly away.

'Billie! You've got to see this!'

Waving, Eli and Mark stand at the bottom of the rocks. She slides off her boulder, conscious of the large stain left by her wet buttocks and the yellow dust on the back of her skirt. The children meet her halfway down the steps, tugging her to the bottom two at a time.

'You'll never believe what we found,' Eli says, jumping with excitement. 'A cave, a real cave! I'll bet it has pirates' treasure and everything!'

A cave? Hard to believe, Billie thinks. Her sandstone is porous and water-eroded, but the geological survey told her she was building on solid bedrock. Yet the children squeeze her between two boulders, then make her kneel and shuffle through a curtain of prickly lantana, until, sure enough, they're inside a cave.

It is dim, lit only by a ray of sunlight through a fissure at the far end, and Billie blinks, waiting for her eyes to adjust. Mark and Eli scamper ahead. Slowly she begins to make out the dimensions of the cave. Perhaps three metres long, and wide enough for an adult to lie down. Her head almost touches the roof. A network of dusty grey webs covers the rock above, and small creatures scuttle at the edge of her vision, triggering a reflex spasm and a tickle at the back of her neck. Just huntsmen, as far as she can see, not funnel-webs or the elongated wolf spiders that make flesh shrivel and die.

'Kids,' she whispers. It seems wrong to talk loudly in here, as if she were in a church or a sacred grotto. 'Look up, and be careful.'

Eli and Mark glance at the ceiling, but shrug, too engrossed in something else to worry about the spiders. Still kneeling, Billie shuffles across the sandy floor towards them. In the circle of light from the opening, they sift the sand, letting it fall through their fingers.

'Looking for treasure,' Eli says.

Mimicking their movement, Billie is astounded by the softness of the grains and the way they cloud in the air before settling.

'More like ash,' she says.

The sandstone in the cave is pale yellow, or red where mineral veins have bled with the rain. But here in the patch of light, the rock is darker, almost black, and stains the tips of her fingers as she rubs the walls.

'It is ash. Ancient ash. This is where they would have had their fire. Makes sense. The smoke would have been sucked straight through the hole.'

'Who?' Eli says, still sifting. 'Who lived here?'

'The first people,' Billie says. 'Here for thousands of years before the white folks came.'

From the ash, Eli pulls a ridged shell, bleached to the colour of bone. Blowing off the dust, she passes it to Mark.

'It's an oyster,' he says. 'An old one, like on the midden.'

Billie knows the midden. Beside the sandstone arm of the beach, it is revealed only at the river's lowest ebb. A plain of shells, worn to brittle translucency by the tug of the tides. Once there were mounds of shells, left by the river tribes. So many shells that the white settlers came in their boats to gather them and grind them to lime for the new city.

'But so far from the water?' Eli asks.

The mystery of the shell silences them. They stare at the pale relic Eli turns in her hands.

'Must have carried it up here to cook in the fire,' Mark says, 'then left the shell behind. I've heard that one of the caves on the island has a stencil of a girl's hand, from a long time ago. She's missing the smallest finger of her left hand. It made it easier to wind the fishing nets.'

'Gross!' Eli whispers, eyes wide. 'Where?'

The boy shrugs. 'We could explore the other caves, see if we can find it.'

Billie turns in the sand and crawls back towards the entrance. 'Maybe another day. We should head back to the house before your mother wakes up, Eli. She'll go spare if she can't find you.'

Outside, Billie checks the children for spiders, and all three brush ash from their clothes. Mark jogs down the steps, turning at the path to shout up the hill.

'Can I come and play again?'

Billie looks at Eli, who nods.

'Of course,' Billie yells back. 'As long as it's okay with your papa.'

Inside, Lorelei waits for them, pale, with red-rimmed and puffy eyes.

'Where have you been?' she asks. 'I was worried.' She reaches out to pluck cobwebs and grit from the child's hair.

'We found a cave, Mum, and it was crawling with spiders and there's a picture of a girl with her little finger cut off and I found treasure!'

She holds the oyster shell out to her mother, who looks at it quickly, but is distracted, biting her lips into a thin line.

'Go and have a shower, Elissa,' Lorelei says, sharply. 'You're filthy.'

Recognising Audrey's expression on Lorelei's face, and the tone, Billie knows what to expect.

'Why didn't you ask me, Billie? I don't want her running around without me, especially not over here. Anything could happen.'

'You were asleep,' Billie says, hearing herself make excuses. 'Stan said you'd been up all night. I didn't want to wake you. We were just down in the garden.'

Lorelei bites her lips even thinner. She wants to say more, Billie knows, but politeness keeps the words unspoken. If she was Audrey, Billie thinks, I'd be lectured for an hour. Even in my own house.

'Just be careful, okay? And don't fill her head with gruesome stories. The world is a hard place, I know, but I want to protect her as long as I can.'

She's growing more quickly than you'll let her, Billie thinks. No wonder she's fighting. What will you do in five years' time, when Eli is enough of a woman to begin to make her own decisions? But she keeps her questions to herself.

In her studio that night, Billie sketches the cave in charcoal and brown ink, smudging the shades with her fingertips. She draws the cave without the children, just smoky walls, the circle of light from above and the shadows beyond the light. Fascinated by the quiet, empty space upon which her house is built, she wonders if others scallop the rock below the foundations.

The cave fills the last page of her journal, so she reaches across to her bookshelf, scanning the spines for one of her new sketchbooks, for a ream of blank pages. Her hands hover over the shelves, then stop. Something has changed. The tessellation of the spines, her mosaic of odd tiles, has shifted since she was last in the studio. Not by much, just a couple of misplaced volumes. Others might not notice, but to Billie it's obvious.

Someone has been in here, she thinks. Someone has been reading my memories.

Queenie

London 1946

The young woman stepped off the train at Victoria Station. Under the great metal frame spanning the platforms, she put down her suitcases and adjusted her hat. It was a new cloth hat, a travelling hat, with narrow brim and wide band, and the young woman tugged it over her forehead. Earlier, as the train chugged past the battered terraces and bombsites of outer London, she had checked her reflection in the carriage window, noticing a faint black tidemark across her forehead, residue from the sludgy dye she'd used to stain her orange forelock.

Standing still on the platform by her suitcases, she was overwhelmed by streams of passengers swirling around her. Pushed and jostled, she felt like a lost child, the crowds threatening to knock her to the tiles. I am drowning, she thought. I cannot breathe. She longed for her quiet village, where there was space enough for the entire population to stand in the main street without touching. The memory of the village brought other spaces to mind—the long pauses between words in the house and the empty room at the top of the stairs—and she shook her head. No, she would not return. She pulled her shoulders back. I am sixteen, but I have a woman's body, and that is what they will see. A woman, not a frightened child. Clutching that thought, she ignored the nervous whispers inside her head.

The young woman wrapped her fingers around the handles of her suitcases and let the stream of people drag her along the platform towards the station's atrium. The suitcases were heavy, and she had to stop often, letting the complaints of the person behind wash over her.

One suitcase held the girl's few books, her entire wardrobe and her comfortable shoes. She was ready to open this suitcase and change shoes on the platform, because her good shoes pinched her toes, but she was afraid she would never be able to get the case shut again. She wished she hadn't brought so much stuff. She also wished she'd worn something lighter than her woollen dress, but she'd been fooled by the hint of autumn in the air that morning.

The second suitcase bulged with sketchbooks, paints and brushes. It also carried an acceptance letter from the College of Art in Chelsea, pressed carefully between the covers of the sturdiest sketchbook. One night last October, after the family had gone to bed, she had filled out the application. Please know, she thought, from my precise capital letters and the even spaces between them, how much I need to get in. In the months after the funeral, pressing pencil to paper had been an automatic reflex. Moving her hands held other thoughts at bay. Through the numb winter, she had traipsed over frozen fields to draw the railway line tapering towards the city. She had hunched against the wind to sketch the village green and the pub. A pile of images grew under her bed. In the spring, with the first crocus buds sprouting beside the bakery path, the postman delivered an envelope embossed with a Chelsea postmark and the school's crest. For two days it lay unopened on the hallstand.

What if they said no? But there it was, requesting her presence for an interview. The family never mentioned the letter, or her late return one evening after lugging her folio to London and back. In late May, over dinner, she told them about her acceptance.

'Come August I'm leaving,' she had said, the first words spoken at the table since the funeral. 'To study art.'

The family held their cutlery still to look at her, but no one responded. She slid her plate aside. Only three more months, she had thought, climbing the stairs.

When the young woman arrived at the left-luggage counter, she had aching shoulders and blisters on the palms of her hands. A young boy with a fuzz of down above his lip guarded the desk. She gave him a penny and a smile and left him to stow her cases, then ordered a cup of tea at the cafeteria. The tea was weak, but hot and sweet, and the first she'd had since sunrise. Swilling the last of it, even the dregs with the floating leaves, she walked across to the newspaper seller.

On the wall next to the papers was a board pinned with handwritten 'To Let' notices. There wasn't much on offer, and everything was pricey. The young woman remembered the bombsites. London had been badly damaged, and there were more people without homes than she could imagine. Sighing, she pulled a pen from her handbag and scribbled the numbers on her hand. May as well have a go. She walked to the red telephone booth and dialled the first number.

'Hello,' she said. 'My name is Quinn, Sybille Quinn . . .'

She stopped, remembering her plan to lose herself in the city. 'Queenie,' she said. 'My name is Queenie.'

She played with the name in her head and found it sat well. Queenie, she thought. A name for a grown woman. A new name for a new city.

But the city was not yet ready to welcome her. The bakelite phone ate her coins. Harsh voices on the other end asked about references and demanded a month's rent in advance. Doing the figures in her head, she realised the thin fold of paper tucked into her handbag would only last a month, maybe two. It had taken almost a year to earn that money, selling watercolours at the village market and painting portraits of local dignitaries. A month!

She stormed out of the booth and slumped on a wooden bench. Maybe she could sell more work. There were a few good pieces left. But she still needed a place to stay. Maybe she could trade her work for a room? She shook her head. The landlords she spoke to wanted cash up-front, and lots of it. She couldn't see them accepting her sketches. Her thoughts whirled in circles. She was ready to chew on her hat in frustration.

'I give up,' she said aloud, leaning back into the bench and clutching her forehead.

'Cheer up, love,' a man said. 'Can't be that bad.'

Queenie turned her head. The man sat beside her on the bench. She hadn't noticed him before. He smiled. It was a nice smile, crinkling the skin around his eyes. He was older, she noticed, with grey flecks in his hair and salt-and-pepper stubble on his cheeks. He lit a cigarette and held it out to her, then lit another and asked what the problem was. At first she was hesitant, but the man spoke kindly, and he was the first person to smile at her, so she told him. She hadn't expected to talk, not to a stranger, but the story tumbled from her mouth, of Elissa's death and her own flight from the village. He nodded as she spoke, sucking on his cigarette.

'How old are you?' he asked when she'd finished.

She paused before speaking. 'Twenty, at least.'

'Oh, at least,' he said, smiling. The man moved closer. He laid his hand on her knee, and she felt his warmth through her skirt. His hand moved up her thigh. He leant forward to whisper. 'Some men pay good money to touch a pretty girl.'

The man's breath tickled her ear. He smelt of kippers. Her skin crawled and she shook her head.

'No!' She tried to stand, but the man dug his fingers into her thigh and pinned her to the bench.

'I'll give you a half crown,' he whispered. 'That'll get you a room for a few days.'

Frozen, Queenie felt the man's hand creeping up her thigh to press between her legs. He was breathing heavily. He stuck his tongue in her ear, then whispered again.

'Some men wouldn't be so polite. They would just take what they want. Ask yourself which is worse.'

She dropped her cigarette. The station bustle faded; she could only hear his breath. Her own came in gasps, and her heart strained in her chest.

'You pig!' she said, wrenching her thigh free. She stared, repulsed, ear wet from his probing tongue. A quick turn, and she fled across the atrium towards the exit. Buffeted again by the crowds, she made slow headway, and behind her the man laughed.

'Good luck!' he yelled. 'You'll need it.'

The street outside was bright after the station's gloom. Queenie squinted into the sun, staring at the intersection ahead. Roads split off in different directions, but she didn't know where any led. Afraid the man had followed her, she chose the closest to her right, and walked hard. 'Vauxhall Bridge Rd', the sign said. A whistling matelot, trim in blue serge, slung his arm around her, but she shrugged it off without slowing, ignoring his entreaties. She strode faster, aware that other men stared.

One winked as she passed, and another groped her buttocks at a crowded omnibus stop. All sorts looked, in suits or overalls, bowlers or bobbies' peaks. When their eyes met, she turned her head away.

To avoid the eyes, she ducked off the pavement into a café, ordering tea and a chip butty from the menu on the wall, then sitting at a table by the window. Here, in a grimy glass bubble, she could be the watcher. By the time the waitress brought her order, teacup tinkling in its saucer, Queenie's breathing had slowed. The butty disappeared quickly, left a greasy smear around her mouth, but she dragged out the tea, sipping lukewarm dregs before ordering another. And another. Late in the afternoon, returning from the dank toilet in the alley behind the café, she found the chairs upside-down on the tables.

'Time to leave,' the waitress said, untying her apron. 'I'm closing up.'

'But where will I go?' Queenie asked.

'Sorry, love.'

On the pavement, she watched the waitress walk away, the woman's heels clicking briskly at every step. The street was empty now; the sky mauve over inky buildings. Lampposts flickered further down the street, but here it was dark. Alone, she hugged herself. Her cardigan was back at the station, jammed in one suitcase, but she didn't want to return. The man might still be there. So she continued along Vauxhall Bridge Rd. Her heels chafed, and fluid trickled into the tight shoes. The strap dug in below her ankles. My feet, she thought, are bloated chunks of meat.

As her eyes adjusted to the light, she realised the street wasn't empty. The commuters and shopkeepers had been pulled to the fuggy entrances of the Underground, but other figures moved in the shadows.

'Got a fag?' one asked. 'Spare some shrapnel for a meal?'

She shook her head and walked on, past bottle-blonde women with glossy crimson mouths and men in shapeless overcoats who spread newspapers in doorways reeking of urine. They're preparing for the night, she realised. Bedding down. Up since before dawn, she was aware of gravity's pull on her limbs. She wanted to fall onto crisp white sheets with pillows plump behind her head, to close her eyes and inhale fresh linen and lavender. A hotel? Perhaps one of the inns she'd passed near the station? The slim sheaf of notes in her purse said no. A doorway then, a mattress of yesterday's headlines, but each alcove she passed was already claimed by men with wild eyes and clumps of matted hair.

Afraid she would stride out of the city before she found a place to kip, she turned left into a narrow street, drawn to a bombed-out spire by glints of fire at its base. In the rubble around the church, groups clustered beside ten-gallon drums, where embers burnt orange inside. Drawing closer, she watched men's silhouettes drag planks from the debris and hoist them into the fire. Aching to warm herself in the glow, she walked towards one drum, but the circle around it waved her away.

'Sod off!' a man yelled. 'Build your own fire.'

Too tired for one more step, she found a stone ledge, the remains of a flying buttress thrown to earth when the bomb exploded. Shoes on, handbag under her head, she curled, staring into the flames until her eyes closed. She drifted, but didn't sleep, too aware of the raucous crowd to let go. Just before dawn, the noise dropped off. Queenie opened her eyes and saw most of the crowd had collapsed, slumped round the smouldering drums. Finally, I can sleep, she thought, but then a policeman began moving through the crowd, poking snoring bodies with his truncheon.

'Move along now,' he said. 'This is no place to sleep.'

Her body creaked as she stood, stiff and grubby with dust. She tried to ease her feet out of her shoes, but the blisters had wept, and the shoes were stuck tight. A sharp wrench and off they came; her heels were raw. Barefoot, with shoes in one hand and bag in the other, she walked slowly back to the station. Even at this hour it was busy, and the swirling commuters made her dizzy. Exhausted, she flopped on the nearest bench. What was she going to do?

'Cheer up, love,' a familiar voice said, close to her ear. 'It can't be that bad.'

The man. His hand on her knee again. 'My offer still stands.'

Queenie closed her eyes. She tried to block out the clammy feel of the man's hand on her leg, his voice in her ear. She couldn't go back to the village. The thought made her want to scream. She needed to be part of this city, bomb-blasted and dirty as it was. Term started in a month, and she had to be settled. She couldn't keep sleeping rough. Would it be so bad? The man looked clean. Except for gripping her thigh tightly, he had been kind enough.

Yet alongside this calm voice, another screamed in fear and disgust: the child's voice that had panicked on the platform yesterday. Don't let him touch you, it said. Run. Find another way. But there was no other way. I am Queenie now, she thought, a woman, not a child, and I will do what needs to be done. In her mind she shoved the screaming child into a rocky nook, then trapped her behind a wall of terracotta bricks, trying to ignore the muffled screams. She opened her eyes.

'Let's go,' she said quietly.

She followed the man to a boarding house in a narrow alley beside the station. The room smelt damp, its floor littered with mugs and dirty clothes. The man sat her on the bed. She felt like a doll. She didn't move as he unbuttoned her dress. She didn't even flinch when he grabbed her breast and squeezed hard, his fingernails cutting her soft flesh.

'It's the first time, isn't it?' the man asked.

She looked at him, but said nothing. He licked his lips, then grinned. 'I knew it. I've wanted this since they shipped us back, but the women I got were all used up. They stank of other men.'

The man pushed her back onto the bed and dragged off her knickers. He dug two fingers inside her, then shoved the rest of himself in. It felt like he would rip her in two, but she bit her lips and didn't scream. I am Queenie, she thought, a woman. I am Queenie. On the ceiling above her was a patch of green mould, and she focused on the mould while the man shook her with his spasms. Suddenly, he was limp. His weight crushed her ribs. She slid out from under him, burning between her legs and deep inside. Fluid trickled down her leg. She wiped herself with her handkerchief and dressed slowly. She picked up her shoes. I will carry them, she thought, unwilling to let him watch her buckle them with shaking hands.

'Half a crown,' she said, struggling to keep her voice steady. Unable to look at him, she stared at the door. 'You promised.'

The man opened his wallet and held out a silver coin. Grabbing it, and her bag and shoes, Queenie ran from the room. She ran until she reached the station, shut herself in a toilet cubicle and wrapped her arms around her shivering body.

'I am Queenie,' she whispered, over and over. She took deep breaths, and slowly the tremors eased.

She held the coin to the light, turning it to see the King's face. The coin glittered. She brought it to her lips and kissed it. Unexpectedly, she giggled. The giggle made her cheeks ache and gave her a stitch in her belly. Her eyes watered, but she couldn't stop. Hearing the laughter's ragged edge, she knew the giggles could turn to sobs faster than she could blink, but she also knew she wouldn't let them. Mid-hiccup, the laughter disappeared. She wiped her eyes.

It was the coin. She owned it. She held a fragment of the city in her moist palm. She'd had one of its inhabitants inside her, and she knew that he had needed her. His eyes told her. I want you, they had said. Like the other men's eyes. The pain between her legs faded.

Unlocking the cubicle door, she walked to the basin and stood with hands gripping cold porcelain. I can stay, she thought, staring at her face in the mirror. Under the running tap she rinsed her handkerchief, using the damp cloth to wipe last night's dust from her cheeks, to scrub again at her sticky thighs. She combed her hair with her fingers and pulled her hat from her bag. To look at me, she thought, no one would know what has just happened. Gingerly she dabbed her heels with the handkerchief, then slid her feet into the shoes, wincing as stiff leather pressed into raw flesh. With shoulders back and a straight spine, Queenie walked out of the station.

In the street she heard sounds of industry from every direction. Metal against stone, metal against metal, metal against wood. Underneath it all was the repetitive boom of a machine pounding the ground. Queenie couldn't see it, but the bass rhythm travelled through the thin soles of her shoes. The sounds didn't frighten her; she felt England rebuilding herself with single bricks and planks, repairing the damage done by incendiary bombs and fire.

Striding in time with the heartbeat of the invisible machine, she walked along Victoria Street to the Houses of Parliament, then continued up Whitehall until it met the Strand. She stared at the smoke-stained landmarks around her, pinched toes forgotten. Her rhythm faltered when she came to St Paul's Cathedral. She saw the dome from Fleet Street, hovering like a giant egg above the other buildings. It had survived the Blitz, but the area around it was flattened. The dome seemed even taller in the flat landscape. Avoiding the holes, Queenie picked her way through the rubble. Some had been removed to make paths, and there were low walls around the deepest pits.

Queenie's good shoes carried her down Threadneedle Street past the Bank of England. During the air raids a bomb had landed between the bank and the Royal Exchange, ripping a huge crater in the road. At the splintered edge of the pit she stopped and looked down. The explosion had gone through to the tube station below, and she saw the station's signs and strips of tangled girders. She was looking into the core of the earth, expecting rivers of red lava to erupt from the pit. Dizzy, she stepped back from the edge.

Outside the bank, men in shirts and braces clustered to smoke. There were women, too, at the edge of the groups, older women with heavily rouged cheeks and stains on their skirts. They laughed and called out, but the men shook their heads. Fingering the coin in her pocket, Queenie knew what she had to do. She approached one of the youngest men, moving slowly, smooth as a snake. With a cigarette between her lips, she asked the man for a light. The other men watched. She knew they were holding their breath. She bent close to the man's ear and asked him if he wanted some fun, surprised by her steady voice and the wink that ended her offer. Surprised, too, by how quickly he agreed to follow her into a quiet lane.

For a shilling, she let the man fumble beneath her dress and snap her knicker elastic. The man held out two more coins and winked. She shook her head, demanded half a crown. The man gave her the coin, then lifted her up, shoulders to the wall, and bounced her against his hips. Staring over his shoulder, she felt bricks graze her back. It hurt less than the first time, and she found she even liked the spurt of warm fluid that the man released inside her. The man buttoned up his trousers, leaving her in the alley to wipe her thighs and tuck the coins in her purse.

Back to the bank, Queenie approached another man. This time she asked for more money, and the man agreed. He didn't even try to bargain with her, just checked his watch and nodded. This man laid her on the ground in the lane and pressed himself on top of her. Watching clouds drift across the blue sky between the buildings, she repeated the routine until her back was raw and her thighs burnt. Each time, she upped the price, grinning when the last man handed her a crisp pound note.

At the end of the day, Queenie counted her money. There was enough to get a room and pay two months' rent in advance, at least. Leftovers, too. The fold of money could stay in her bag for emergencies. She looked up at the stone edifice of the bank. Perhaps I should open an account, she thought, now that I'm Miss Money Bags.

The omnibus carried her back to Victoria Station, where she dropped more coins into the telephone. With no references but plenty of money, Queenie quickly secured a room above a pub in Battersea. She collected her suitcases, then caught the tube to Vauxhall and flagged another bus. Pinned between her suitcases and other passengers, staring at cramped Clapham streets through a smeared window, her exhilaration evaporated. Suddenly, she felt tired. When the driver yelled 'Battersea Park', she pulled the cord and lugged her suitcases towards the Bold Forester.

The pub clung to the fringes of the terraced sprawl, across the road from a green park and the wide river. The knobbled spine of roofs and chimney pots continued on the other embankment, yet here were trees and the glint of sun on water. Something quickened inside. Queenie realised she missed Norfolk's gentle horizons and its big skies, even after just one day. The crowds and narrow streets in this part of the city blocked out the sky and made her hold her breath with nerves. People seemed small and hunched, and the curves that had drawn the bankers to her were now lumbering and awkward. She felt huge, as if she took up too much space. I will fit, she thought. I will make this my home.

At the bar of the pub, Queenie traded her pound note for a key with '4' scratched on it. She dragged her cases up the stairs and opened the door. The room was small, furnished only with a narrow bed, a dressing-table and a patched armchair. In the corner she spotted a tiny sink and a single gas ring. Blackout curtains still covered the window. It was bare, but it was hers.

Stepping through the door, she wrinkled her nose. The room smelt stale and sweaty, and the smell remained even after she pulled back the curtains and propped the bottom sash open with a cup from the dressing-table. It's me, she thought, I smell of all those men, but she was too tired to care. Taking off her shoes, she stretched out on the bed and let sleep take her.

Before term started in September, Queenie crossed the murky river at Albert Bridge and walked to Chelsea. It was a short walk, but she was struck by the change in the houses. On the Battersea side of the Thames, the terraces were small and dirty, with lines of washing hanging from the windows and skinny children playing in the bombsites. The Chelsea terraces were taller, each with its own nameplate by the front door. There were umbrella stands and leadlight windows and plump cats on the windowsills.

The walk took her past the Physic Garden to the college. She stood at the gates and looked up at its undamaged façade. The doors were locked, so she paced the grounds. 'I belong here,' she whispered to herself. When the gardeners raised their eyebrows or yelled 'Oi!', she tapped her sketchbook, her passport to this new country.

At the back of the building she sketched the college's private face—the smaller windows and doors without porticos hidden from the street. A pigeon groomed itself on the crumbling statue of Venus, and she drew that too. She wished she'd brought her pastels to capture the glossy purple bulge of the pigeon's throat. One of the gardeners winked at her. When Queenie asked him to pose, he held his rake like a staff, sweat drying on his tanned skin.

The first weeks of term passed in a blur of excitement. Bouncing from class to class, inhaling turpentine and linseed oil, Queenie absorbed details of different grades of paper, types of ink and brush techniques. She no longer dreaded the bells signalling the end of class, as she had done at school in Norfolk, for here there was always another art session: life drawing, watercolour, oils, pen and ink, lithography. In the third week, during a break, she leant against a wall and closed her eyes, etching what she had learnt into her memory. She clutched her sketchbook to her chest, tantalised by the promise of the three years ahead.

It was weeks before she noticed her fellow students. Focused only on the instructors and the easel, she had ignored the faces in her peripheral vision. Gradually, details emerged—blue eyes, green eyes, little round glasses, a cigarette held in gesticulating and nicotine-stained hands, a gaudy tie—and she began to recognise familiar faces in the cafeteria. Yet she never joined the animated discussions around the tables. Groups had formed while Queenie had been distracted, and, afraid of their casual familiarity, she chose to sit alone.

One face appeared in many of her classes. His olive skin and blue-black hair set him apart from the sandy blondes and mouse browns of the other students, and Queenie felt her eyes drawn to his face. With faint lines under his eyes, he seemed older than the others. Twenty-five, she guessed, or a young thirty. He smiled at her when their eyes met. Although no words passed between them, his recognition was comforting. He notices me, she thought. I really am here.

Life drawing gave Queenie another way to make money with her body. Not much, not enough to pay the rent, but it all helped. On mornings when she had no classes, Queenie took off her clothes in front of full rooms of students. Under a bare yellow globe she untied her dressing-gown, positioning her body in a serpentine curve and extending her arms in the Venus pose. In her first session Queenie avoided the eyes of the first-year students who still tittered and blushed. She stared over the tops of the easels to the wall behind, watching the hands of the clock mark the length of the pose. A couple of short poses to warm the class up. A longer one. Watching the minute hand rotate, she felt the blood drain into her shoulders and congeal. Her arms trembled until the tutor ordered a change.

The man with the black hair came to all of the classes that Queenie modelled for. He stood near the front and smiled when she looked away from the clock and caught his eye.

'Piètro,' the man said one morning when the other students had left. 'You are my favourite. Such lovely curves.'

The rhythm of the man's words caught Queenie off-guard. Hearing his name, she'd expected him to be Italian, but she didn't expect the effect of his intonations upon her. The sentences were in correct English, but they were pronounced with an Italian rhythm, as if the man's lips still obeyed the commands of his mother-tongue. Like static electricity, his inflections raised the hairs on her arms. I could tell him everything, she thought, my real name, where I came from, and he would understand. But she didn't. One day, perhaps.

'I'm Queenie,' she said, in the perfect English accent she'd mimicked since infant school. 'Would you like some tea?'

In the cafeteria Piètro pulled a drawing from his folio and passed it across the table. It was from one of Queenie's modelling sessions. The charcoal sketch was touched with ochre pastel, so her thighs gleamed like polished cypress against a background of summer sunshine yellow. Absurdly pleased by the gift, Queenie took the sketch back to her room above the pub. She stuck the sketch on the speckled mirror of her dressing-table and smiled at it as she made up her face in the mornings.

One day late in September, Queenie stood at her locker, sorting through paints and thinners for the next class, when Piètro flickered into the corner of her vision. Other students stared as he passed, and huddled to whisper.

'Filthy Eye-tie,' hissed one girl.

'Master's boy!' yelled another.

'Give over!' Queenie yelled back, surprised by the volume of her voice and its echo in the corridor. The dark-haired man walked towards her with a firm step and straight shoulders, but his cheeks were unusually flushed. Shoving the paints back into her locker, she grabbed her bag and rushed to his side, sliding her arm under his.

'Word gets around,' Piètro said, quietly. 'Perhaps they will arrest me.'

'Tell them we're lovers.' Queenie looked up at him. 'Is what they're saying true?'

'Guilty as charged, I am afraid. Yes, I was born in Italy and yes, I am on . . .' he coughed, 'intimate terms with the etching master.'

'They're just jealous,' Queenie said.

'So they should be!'

'Although,' she said, steering him through a fire escape, 'I can't picture you with old Geoffreys. He's twice your age!'

'Like a fine wine,' Piètro said, with a wink.

'Come, deviant fellow,' Queenie said, smiling. 'Enough school today. I'll show you my private sketching place.'

It struck Queenie, as they walked over the bridge and through the park, still dug into vegetable allotments, that some of her men were old enough to be her father, even her grandfather. She couldn't picture that either; in her mind the encounters seemed to happen to someone else.

She led Piètro to a slight rise she'd discovered the week before, with the river and embankment spread below them. Cross-legged on the grass, sketchbooks on knees, they talked until Piètro's cheeks cooled. First, he spoke about the master, then about the camp where he'd been interned after Italy joined the war. He'd been the cook, sketching the English guards between meals.

'One in particular,' he said. 'Profile of an emperor.'

At war's end his officer wrote a letter of recommendation to the college.

The sun set and, quietly, in the twilight, Piètro told her about his journey from Italy and the family he left behind. About the Blackshirts.

Lulled by the rhythm of his voice, Queenie listened, nodding but never speaking, still unable to tell him her own story. She had trained herself not to speak of it outside the blue room in the Norfolk house, to keep secret the memories that would define her as alien; now it was impossible to tell him she understood. On another day she would tell him about the house carved into the rocks, and about her men in the alleys, but not now.

When Piètro stopped talking, the pair sat in silence. Queenie watched the reflections of streetlamps ripple on the river. She felt his hand, warm and large, cup her fingers.

'Thank you,' he whispered.

As October turned to November and the days lost their warmth, Queenie gave up alleys and brought men back to her room. Except for the bankers, of course. She made an exception for them. One afternoon a week, she left her classes to travel across town and wait on the stone steps. Sometimes she crossed the road to the Royal Exchange and approached brokers beneath the huge triangular pediment. She learnt to carry a thick cardigan with her and would lay it on the ground before the men clambered on top of her.

After the bank closed, she walked down St Michael's Lane to the Jampot, a wood-lined pub where bankers gathered. They loosened ties and slurped pints and willingly followed her outside. Between the back of the pub and the church was a tiny patch of grass. Leading the men there, she spread out her cardigan. She collected their pound notes once a week, every week, except for the days her body was fertile. During one visit to the asylum, Elissa had whispered about the eggs women's bodies produce halfway between monthly bleedings, and the journey of the man's seed.

'That's where the baby came from,' she had said. She pointed to the pregnant woman in the garden. 'She told me. Never knew either, until it was too late.'

Queenie's bleeding was as regular as Big Ben. Remembering Elissa's visit to the Norwich doctor, Queenie used this regularity to protect herself. She kept a calendar on her wall and monitored the cycle of her bleeding carefully. She counted days and marked the expected date of her ovulation with a big red cross. Every month on the knocker a sharp pain in her side, like a stitch, coincided with the pencil cross. She imagined the little egg beginning its journey, expectant and full of hope. No men came to the room on that day, or the days around it, and she did not visit the bank.

Bess, the landlady, was horrified by this method. Perched in Queenie's armchair with a cup of tea and a cigarette, as had become her Saturday morning habit, she'd asked about the calendar. When Queenie explained, the landlady nearly spilt her tea.

'I don't mind the men,' she said, in a broad London accent. 'Most of the rooms here belong to girls in your situation. You've been damned lucky so far, but your body won't always behave like a machine. You just can't risk it. Jesus!'

Leaving her tea behind, she rushed downstairs, returning with a round tin, which she handed to Queenie. A small sponge nestled inside, wrapped in net and with a long string attached.

'I always keep a couple around,' Bess said. 'You'll need to organise it before your company arrives. Chemists will sell you a special powder on the quiet, but I've used vinegar and lemon juice to soak it when I'm strapped.'

Grateful for the landlady's advice, and for her own luck so far, Queenie boiled the sponge clean in a saucepan on the gas ring every night, after her last customer left. She watched the blue flames and the bubbling water, calmed by the cleansing ritual, then left the sponge to soak overnight in acid fluids.

Queenie kept her coins in a shoebox under her bed. When there were enough, she gathered them into her purse and walked to an art suppliers on King's Road, opposite the Town Hall. She inhaled fresh paint and thinners until she was giddy, and staggered out of the shop laden with sharp new pencils and canvases to stretch. Sometimes, when a client thrashed on top of her, she imagined she was in the little shop. She was the only customer and she browsed slowly, in peace. By the time her customer had juddered into stillness and buttoned up his trousers, she knew exactly how she would spend his money. She didn't spend the bankers' notes, but pressed them between the pages of her old atlas. They came in green and brown and war-issue blue and mauve. The pressure of the countries above the notes slowly ironed the creases from them until, apart from the men's greasy fingerprints, the money could have come fresh from the Mint.

When one of Queenie's customers fell asleep she didn't wake him with a sharp elbow, as she knew the other girls in the pub did. Instead she reached under the bed, quietly retrieved her sketchbook and drew the man as he slept. Sleep turned men into children, and the change fascinated her. The adult mantle fell away to reveal the face of a small boy, smiling. She sketched the smiles, like those seen on corpses' faces.

'What are you smiling at?' she whispered. 'I could slip a knife into your throat and you'd never know.'

She also sketched the frowns that flickered across the men's faces when nightmares gripped them. Veterans, she guessed.

They'd end up with the old blokes in red coats who sat outside the hospital. The men never said, but their nightmares gave them away. Her sketches couldn't contain the noises the men made, the whimpers escaping as sleep twitched their bodies, but she listened while her hands moved. If the tutors at the college wondered about the portraits in her book, the ones of so many different men connected only by their closed eyes, they never said.

Some veterans didn't want to have sex with her. They watched her undress and stroked her naked thighs, but it never stirred them. She groped under their trousers, grabbed and squeezed, but they stayed limp. They gave her money to lie next to them and listen, saying they needed the warmth of her body. Some had come back and found their wives with other men. Others returned to faithful wives, but couldn't slot back into their old lives. One man cried into her belly.

'I thought it would be better,' he sobbed. 'Once the war ended.'

She stroked the man's hair until he fell asleep.

'No sex,' she told the landlady the next morning. 'Can you believe it? Cushy money.'

'Careful, love,' said Bess. 'I've seen them turn nasty. Watch out for yourself.'

Three nights later, a new customer, a veteran, pulled a leather case from his pocket.

'A special treat,' he said. He took a steel and glass syringe from the case, but Queenie shook her head. The veteran stood and brushed the creases from his trousers. He put on his hat.

'I hate doing it alone,' he said. 'I'll take my business else-where, then.'

Queenie couldn't afford to lose this one. Her rent was due the next day and the bankers seemed to be tiring of her. She saw them too often to play the virgin any more, and had started spending more time smoking out the front of the bank with the tired-looking women than in the alley. What harm could it do? She lifted her slip and presented a dimpled buttock.

'Will this do?'

The man smiled. 'Your arm is fine.'

The needle hurt. It was the first time Queenie's veins had been pierced and she didn't expect the sharp pain or the chill of metal and clear liquid. But then the warmth came, and she forgot about the pain. It was gradual, like sliding into a deep bath. The warmth melted her muscles. She slumped on the bed, closed her eyes, and surrendered to the opium tide.

The man frequently came to her room with his needle. Other men did too, especially those who limped or held their arms stiffly. They brought their needles even after the wounds had healed, and they all liked to share.

She didn't mind the morphine or the warm bodies in her bed. Never knew quite what would happen each time. Some nights she fell asleep immediately. On other nights she would lie awake staring at patterns on her wallpaper. She saw faces and animals in the shadows. Sometimes, when she squinted, the walls turned to stone. Reaching out to stroke the coarse surface, her fingers only ever found blistered paper.

Once, for a week, no veterans brought their needles to her room. She found she missed them. Well, her body did. It ached. Every day she listened for footsteps on the stairs and a knock on her door. When the footsteps finally came, she'd rolled up her sleeve before the man had hung up his hat and unbuttoned his coat. She watched him sterilise the needle with alcohol and flick the phial of clear liquid with his fingers, feeling the muscles contract between her crossed legs and spurt fluid into her knickers. Until that moment she'd felt nothing for her clients.

Her body was so dry she'd often had to use her margarine rations to convince the men she was aroused. Suddenly her body had released some of its own precious rations. She wanted the man to prick her with the needle, then empty himself inside her while the opium warmed the rest of her body. But she knew he wasn't interested.

Some of the men left phials of clear liquid instead of money. She came to love the way the injection slowed the world, was happy to spend days without clients, lying on her bed and listening to the ebb and flow of the traffic.

'Like the ocean,' she said to the empty room. She smiled as the gentle sound rocked her to sleep.

Dreams were vivid when Queenie put a needle in her arm, but she awoke hung over and flat. The dreams left few memories, only the knowledge that there had been magnificence, a visit from an angel. Her mouth tasted of old cheese and something metallic, like blood. In the mirror, she saw a sour woman with a creased forehead and blue circles under her eyes. When Bess grabbed her bruised arm and told her it was time to stop, Queenie pulled away, infuriated by the landlady's concern.

Often, she performed the ritual alone. She cleaned the silver needle with alcohol and laid the shiny instrument on her bed. Her own. A gift from a regular. The cool glass tube made her shiver with anticipation. She raked the point of the needle across her skin. She held the phial.

'Half a grain.' At least, that's what she thought the man had said.

The grains multiplied. Half became one. Became two. Four. One day she gripped the phial between two hands and pressed it to her forehead. She couldn't remember.

'Today I have,' she said. 'Today I have . . .'

When the needle found her vein and her fingers found the plunger, she didn't care how many grains of morphine she'd held in her hand. Sliding her fingers between her legs, she cared only for the poppy's warmth and the slippery satisfaction of her own desires.

Every day Queenie injected and chased the bright dreams. She ignored demands from her clients and stopped attending her art classes. The life drawing teacher sacked her. He said the bruises upset the students. She had no money for dye, so a streak of bright orange sprouted at the front of her hair as the chemicals faded. It didn't matter, anyway. Not any more. She stopped washing. She forgot to eat. Her life contracted to hold only the needle and the doctors she bribed to sell her morphine.

Queenie emptied her shoebox, then used the emergency fold of money from her handbag. She opened the atlas, taking pound notes from the pages until, no matter how hard she shook the book, no more leaves marked with Britannia fell onto her bed.

Driftwood

New South Wales 1990

On the verandah, Billie blows pastel dust from the page and sighs. The landscape is meant to be a gift for Lorelei: a little piece of the island to pack flat into her suitcase back to England. But it is ruined now. Marred by another small sketch that appeared in the white space of the page as Billie drew, intruding on the green shimmer of the garden. Almost a cartoon—a stick-figure curled on a bed, shadowed eyes taking up most of the face, head too large for the scrawny body. Her joints throb, remembering. Silly little girl, Billie thinks. So far under.

'Have you seen my handbag?' Lorelei asks, stepping out onto the verandah. 'Got to be on the ferry in fifteen.'

Billie looks up from her sketchbook, shielding her page with her hand. 'On the table, last time I saw it. Where are you going?'

'Into town. Only a week until Christmas, and I haven't got anything for Eli. All these blue skies. I'd forgotten about it completely. Doesn't feel right.'

She's made up, Billie notices. Face powdered and lips slick with colour, her eyes kohl-ringed. She looks pretty, but fragile, a porcelain-pale doll.

'Would it be okay if she stays here with you?' Lorelei asks. 'I wouldn't normally leave her, but I can't really go secret shopping if she's at my elbow. She's playing video games with Troy.'

'Fine.'

'You ready?' Stan calls from inside the house. Billie turns her head to look through the window at him. He's smartly dressed, in an ironed shirt that she hasn't seen before and his grey formal trousers. He seems younger every day.

'He's going, too?' Billie asks.

A nod from Lorelei. 'Said he'd show me the sights if we get a chance. Hope so. Can't come all this way and not see the Opera House. Though I'll have to take Eli into the city before we go home, so she can see them, too.'

Some host, Billie thinks. It never crossed my mind to take them exploring. I didn't think beyond the watery boundaries of my island. She hears the steady chug of the ferry skirting the island, revving its engines in reverse as it approaches the wharf. Too late to make up for it now, to suggest they all travel together.

'Better get moving, then,' she says. 'Last ferry back is at half seven.'

Stan and Lorelei skip from the house like teenagers on their way to a dance. And me the fuddy-duddy, Billie thinks. She closes her sketchbook and walks into the lounge, where Eli sits on the floor in front of the screen. Perched on the sofa beside her, Troy plaits the orange curls, binding each thin braid with green ribbon.

'Your mum's going out for the day,' she says to Eli's back, winking at Troy. 'She's got a few errands to do.'

'Hope she buys something good,' Eli says, eyes on the screen, fingers quick on the joystick. 'Last year I got stupid dolls.'

Amazed, Billie stares at Troy, who shrugs. 'What can you do?' says his expression.

'You mean . . .' Billie says. She is unwilling to finish the sentence.

'Grown-ups must think we're silly,' Eli says. 'Mum never thought I'd recognise her handwriting on the presents. Haven't the heart to tell her.'

The child presses a button and pauses the game. 'Can we explore more caves? Find the girl's hand?'

'I don't think so. You mother gave me a serve last time.'

'What about the beach? We could swim.'

'No. That'd go down like a lead balloon as well.'

'Chicken. You're afraid Mummy will shout at you.'

I am afraid, Billie thinks. But not of your mother. Last time, if it hadn't been for the ferryman, she would have let the water take her.

'No. Because I can't swim. I wouldn't be able to help you if anything happened.'

'Then I'll teach you. I'm very good, you know. I've got my gold badge from the swimming club.'

'What if something happened while I was learning?'

The child looks at Troy. 'You could come, couldn't you? Watch out for Billie, rescue her if she starts to drown?'

'I meant if something happened to you,' Billie says.

'Nothing would happen. I'm the best swimmer in the school squad.'

'Sounds good,' Troy says. 'I've got a couple of hours before meeting Jase. I'll come to the beach with you for a bit, then head off when you're finished.'

But I don't want to learn to swim, Billie thinks. I need my feet in the mud. But somehow, the child's enthusiastic logic has manoeuvred her to a point she has deliberately avoided, and she cannot say no. In her studio, she changes into her bathers, then follows the others to the beach, towel over her shoulder. Once they reach the sand, her heart beats quickly. I can't do it, she thinks. As Troy and Eli run towards the water, she shakes out her towel, weighs it with her bag, and plonks down her buttocks. Out comes her sketchbook, a movement as habitual and comforting as rolling a joint.

'It's all right,' she says, when they turn and beckon. 'You go in. I'll sketch for a while.'

Shaking her head, Eli stomps up the sand. 'You've done enough sketching,' she says, in a stern teacher's voice. 'That's all you do. Today we're teaching you to swim.'

'But I don't want to. Not today,' says Billie, aware she is whining. 'Another day.'

The child squats. She peels the sketchbook from Billie's hand, puts it down and passes the hand to Troy, then holds the other, pats it like a frightened puppy's paw.

'We will be careful with you,' she says softly. 'Trust us. We won't hurt you. And you can come out any time. Just give it a try. Think how good you'll feel when you don't have to be afraid of the river.'

Billie stares at the small face, level with her own. When did children become so knowing? She nods, chest heaving, then lets the pair guide her slowly into the water. Usually, she doesn't panic when she wades, because she knows how far she will go. But today, she imagines herself swimming, imagines the water over her face, her body at the mercy of the current. Run, her muscles say. Run now.

But the pair tightly clasp her hands and lead her into the calm river. She lets the waves lap her ankles, her calves, her knees—a lumbering Venus born in reverse.

'You swim for a bit,' she tells Troy. 'I'll call if I need you.'

'You're the boss,' Troy says, smiling as he slides into an easy freestyle and deeper water.

'First, we're going to run,' Eli orders. She sprints in the shallows, leaping like an old-fashioned athlete.

'Lift those legs!' she orders.

It is an absurd sight, and Billie begins to chuckle, laughing hard enough to give herself a stitch. The laughter chases away the fear and, still laughing, she pursues the girl. Eli's scrawny limbs hardly cause a ripple, but Billie's thighs throw up a great wave of water with each step. A giant next to a fairy, she thinks, laughing harder. Thank God for an empty shore.

At the other end of the beach, Eli turns. 'Stop!' she yells.

'Yes, sir!' Billie salutes, watching the girl struggle to keep her composure. Her heart thuds in her chest, but she feels exhilarated. She should run more often.

'Next,' Eli says, 'we're going to sit down.'

She plops into the river and suddenly the water is at her neck. Billie follows, feeling the soft mud of the riverbed on the backs of her thighs. Disturbed by their feet, the river clouds with silt.

'Now breathe in and lie back,' Eli says. One long inhalation and her skinny white limbs bob at the surface. She floats in the water with hands and feet poking out.

'See?'

Billie inhales until her lungs are ready to tear, but nothing happens. Her buttocks remain firmly planted in the mud.

'I'm too heavy,' she says.

'Nothing to do with weight,' Eli says. 'Try lifting your legs and breathing in.'

Obeying, Billie lifts her legs, but she loses her balance and tips backwards. Green water closes over her head and shoots up her nostrils. It burns. She tastes mud. Panic. Got to get out. She squirms and claws, floundering for the surface, but hitting the bottom. Two hands grab her shoulders and pull her head above water. Billie wipes her streaming nose and rubs her stinging eyes. Above her, Eli stands with arms crossed. She is laughing.

'Chicken,' she says. 'Thought I'd have to call Troy over. I've got another idea. Sit down again.'

She squats beside Billie, putting one hand on her shoulder blade and the other low on her spine. Thin digits dig into Billie's flesh.

'Now lean back,' Eli says. 'Don't worry, I've got you.'

I'm not so sure, Billie thinks. I am three times your weight. How can your stick limbs hold me? But she leans anyway. Eli scoops her hands further under and pushes, grunting as she shoves Billie's torso upwards. Billie's head is above the water, but she isn't floating. She is a plank, hanging at forty-five degrees with heels dug firmly in the mud. Her body is rigid. The tendons in her neck are steel cords, and her fingers clench into fists. She feels Eli's arms tremble.

'Lift your legs!' Eli yells.

Billie tries, but each time they sink back to the mud.

'Fill your lungs!'

She obeys this order, too. Her heels feel lighter, but they do not lift.

'I can't,' she says, frustrated by her stubborn body. She sits back in the water, ready to go home, but Eli won't let her.

'We are going to do this,' the girl says. 'Give it another go.'

Again, Billie leans against the skinny arms. One of Eli's hands goes to the base of Billie's spine. A quick push, and her heels rise. She is so surprised she almost drops them straight back. She is still rigid, but at least on the same plane as the river.

'See?' Eli says. Knots of muscle in the girl's arms look like hard-boiled eggs. Looking up, Billie sees Eli grinning. She grins back. Eli moves Billie's body through the water slowly, so the waves don't break over her face.

'Relax,' Eli says. 'Close your eyes. Let the river take your weight.'

She understands, Billie thinks. This child understands. The water laps at the edges of Billie's limbs. It covers her ears, so all she hears is the rush of the water and her own steady breathing. Tension ebbs as the girl swirls her in slow figure eights. I could lie here forever, she thinks.

'If I take my hands away,' Eli says, 'you should float. Ready?'

Filtered through water, the child's voice is strange and distant. Billie nods—a minimal movement, afraid anything more will upset her tenuous balance. Eli withdraws her fingers and, for an instant, Billie floats. It is exactly like her dreams. But the buoyancy lasts only a second. She opens her eyes. A glimpse of blue sky, then her body remembers its own weight and sinks.

Eli's splayed fingers catch Billie before the river smothers her.

'You nearly had it,' Eli says. 'But you turned into a rock. You've got to learn to let go.'

The child holds out her hand and helps Billie to her feet. She rubs her arms and her teeth chatter. 'Can we go back now? I'm cold.'

The sun is low. We've been in the water for hours, Billie thinks, and I didn't notice. No wonder she is cold.

Out of the water, she wraps her towel around Eli and waves at Troy, still patrolling the little harbour in laps.

'Fitness freak!' she yells.

Even in the sun, Eli shivers. Billie shivers, too, but not with cold. Her skin buzzes, as it had earlier, like blood returning to a numb limb. She shakes her head, invigorated by water drying on her skin and her rapid heartbeat. Every tingling cell tells her something important is about to happen, but she doesn't yet know what. Wait and see, her instincts say.

'Need more meat on you,' Billie says, turning to the shivering child and squeezing her scrawny shoulder.

Eli nods, and Billie marvels at the strength of her bony arms. They carried my entire body, she thinks. Her thoughts return to the moment Eli took her hands away, to the instant she floated, unsupported and untethered.

'I floated,' she yells to Troy, emerging from the water. 'I did it!'

'I saw,' he says, grinning. 'Well done!'

Billie and Eli walk Troy to the wharf, where their long shadows stretch over the weathered planks. Troy unties his tinnie and motors out, water rippling like molten gold. A ferry docks as they wave, disgorges its passengers, but Stan and Lorelei are not on it. It's getting late, Billie thinks. Where are they?

Damp towels around shoulders, they walk slowly back up the hill. With plaits plastered against her forehead, tired, Eli looks younger. More like a child than a girl on the verge of adolescence. She scuffs her flip-flops on the path.

'I wish Daddy was here. He could have helped you. That's how he taught me.'

'You miss him.'

Eli nods. 'It's not fair. Just because he and Mum have split . . .' She stops, hands over mouth. 'I wasn't supposed to say anything.'

'It's okay,' Billie says. 'I know.'

'She told you?'

She can't tell this child that she found out by cavesdropping. A lie is better.

'I guessed. Had to be something to make your mum leave early. How are you holding up?'

'It's horrible. Mum and Dad fought for ages, then Dad leaves. I didn't see him before we caught the plane. Mum changed the tickets, took me out of school before the end of term, called Dad from the airport to tell him.'

'They'll sort it out when you get back.'

'Hope so. Or maybe he could look after me. Mum's been a right cow since he left. I can't do anything right. If I knock a glass over, or don't clean up my room, she shouts like I've burnt the house down. I'm sick of it.'

Reaching out, Billie tousles the wet plaits. 'What will cheer you up?'

The child purses her lips. 'Anything?'

A nod.

'Well, Dad used to make me pancakes.'

'Pancakes it is. They won't be as good as your dad's, but I'll do my best.'

In the kitchen, Billie prepares the batter while Eli washes the river salt from her skin. Two eggs into a mound of flour, a teaspoon of caster sugar and a dribble of vanilla essence, then, slowly, she beats in the milk. After years away from the stove, the wooden spoon in her hand and the slop of the batter satisfies. Oil sizzles and smokes as she ladles batter into the hot pan. When Eli emerges from the bathroom, a stack of pancakes, dimpled like the surface of the moon and crusted with sugar and lemon juice, waits for her on a plate.

On the verandah, the child fits four pancakes into her belly, more than it seems possible for her tiny frame to hold. In fading light, Billie stares down the steps to the path, alert for the others coming home. The only movement comes from the lorikeets, who whirr and cheep on the rail. Eli offers the sugary scraps to them, squealing as the birds clamber over her hand.

Afterwards, full, they loll on the couch. Remote control in hand, Eli flicks through two channels of Christmas carols before settling on a movie, a re-run of *The Wizard of Oz*.

'Is this okay?' she asks. 'I love this film.'

Billie watches the minutes pass on the LCD panel of the video. Above the television, she listens for the chug of the last ferry. It comes and goes, but no one walks up the path. Where could they be? Water taxis zip across the channel between the island and the mainland until eight, when even they stop. Why haven't they called?

Through the film, the child's eyes droop. By the time Dorothy falls in the poppy field, Eli is asleep.

'Time for bed, little one.'

Eli struggles awake. 'No,' she says, petulant. 'Not until Mummy comes. I want her to tuck me in.'

'Look, I've got some work to do. Why don't you have a nap while I paint? I promise I'll wake you up when they come in.'

'Promise?'

Billie nods. She leads the child up the corridor to the guest-room, folds back the sheet and tucks her in. Within a minute, Eli's breath whistles regularly and she murmurs. Her limbs twitch. When I was young, Billie wonders, did I sleep like that? Now she sleeps like the birds, lids cracked a fraction and ears pitched for the slightest sound.

In her studio, Billie prepares paints for her commission, but each stroke feels wrong, out of place, and she eventually pushes the leaf aside, afraid she will ruin it. She listens to the night island: the buzz of a runabout, the gentle sound of the waves.

In the quiet, images flicker through her head—Stan and Lorelei knocked over by a car or mugged in the city. All the worst possibilities. Any minute, the phone will ring, she knows it. The police will tell her they've found two bodies washed up in the river. Nothing to worry about, she tells herself. Stan has probably looked up his old friends from the Cross and has taken Lorelei out for a drink or three, but she can't shake the dread.

She lets her hands concentrate on simple tasks, something they can't ruin. From the drawer, they pull out blunt pencils and her penknife, whittling wood and graphite until the points are sharp when she tests them in the soft flesh of her fingertips. She scoops the shavings into her hand, sprinkles them out her window. Her reflection stares back from the glass.

Midnight. Still no call. She peers out into the darkness, up at the sky. No moon tonight. There's the spill of the Milky Way, the arc of the constellations. Orion is already at the zenith; soon he will begin his descent. In the bright city, she never saw the stars clearly. She never knew directions either, but living on the island she has learnt to orient herself. She knows the path of the moon and where the sun will rise, but she blinks in surprise when the sky changes colour. A change so subtle she thinks she has stared too long into darkness and her eyes are playing tricks. Almost imperceptible, just a slightly paler shade of blue above the silhouette of the wooded hills. She knows the morning colour changes as intimately as she knows the shade made by blending two pigments. But this dawn is unlike the ones Billie knows, fresh from sleep. Its hues are pale watercolours, washed with sorrow. Where are they?

At ten o'clock, Lorelei and Stan stagger up the path. Billie watches them from the lounge. They look as shabby as she feels. Inside, sweat and cigarette smoke leech from yesterday's clothing.

'Where the hell have you been?' Billie says furiously. At dawn, Eli woke, saw the empty bed beside her and panicked. For hours, Billie has tried to comfort her, but nothing worked. The child wouldn't go back to bed, wouldn't eat, wouldn't watch television. Arms crossed over chest, she has sat on the sofa, staring out the window at the path.

'You could have called,' Billie says.

Lorelei nods. 'I know. But can we talk later? I'm shattered.'

Before Billie answers, Eli rushes past and throws herself at her mother, hugging and hitting her, crying.

'I thought you'd left me, too,' she sobbed. 'I thought you'd gone.'

'No, little one,' Lorelei says, kneeling beside the child. 'I'll never leave you. We bumped into some friends of Stan's and got talking. I couldn't get to a phone, but I knew you'd be safe with Billie. Come on, Mummy's tired. Why don't you curl up with me for a while?'

Wiping her eyes, Eli nods. Lorelei bends forward to lift the child and, as she does, her shirt collar falls open. On the pale skin where her neck meets her shoulder is a dark red bruise. For a second Billie doesn't register. A love bite? It takes her breath away. Takes her words away. Silent, she watches Lorelei carry her daughter up the corridor. Stan walks away as well, towards the door, but at the frame he pauses. A broad smile, a wink, then he is back out the door and up the steps to his shed.

Fuming, Billie stands alone in her lounge room. So angry she doesn't know what to do with herself. She wants to fight, but there is no one left to fight with. Frustrated, she stomps back to her studio, pulls the drawer under the desk so hard that the pencils rattle. There it is. Her little bag of green comfort. With rapid fingers and hammering heart, she rolls joint after joint, then sprawls out on her bed to smoke them one after the other. She smokes until her throat burns, until the room spins, until her anger seeps away. Limbs heavy, bed lurching, she gives in to sleep.

Queenie

London 1947

Shaking. Out of money and out of energy. The only thing left for Queenie was to drag her bones to bed and pull the sheet over her head. Cramps locked her muscles and, when the spasms came, she lost control of her bowel. Bladder. Fluids trickled between her buttocks to crust on her thighs. There was vomit on her chin. In her hair. Dust in her eyes. Scratch and blink, scratch and blink. Get it out, she thought, but the grit had slipped under her eyelids. Tiny hard grains that ground lines in the milky flesh of her eyeballs.

'Got to get it out,' she said aloud. 'Get out . . .'

She rubbed until the skin around her eyes was raw, but the dust still gouged.

Someone was knocking on Queenie's skull. They'd been knocking for hours now, on and off, knocking for as long as she could remember. Knock. Knock. Knock. The sounds were so familiar that she thought she'd heard them since the day she was born. An image of herself as a child appeared in the space behind her eyes and, there it was, the knocking. Shouting. So loud that the ground underneath the child trembled. Trees quivered. Tiny puffs of earth rose into the air. She wrapped her arms around her head, but the knocking continued.

'Living so close to the volcano,' she heard someone say, 'what chance did they have?'

She tried to work out what was shaking the earth and why it wouldn't stop, but when the thought had a shape of its own the tremors came again and she watched the thought dissipate. She crawled further under the sheet, away from the thumping, but the vibrations travelled through the floorboards and up through the bedframe into her limbs.

A key rattled in Queenie's lock. Then she heard the land-lady's voice, shrill with concern. A man swearing in Italian. Something like 'Madonna! The pig!'. Footsteps. Giants stalked the room, but if she kept her eyes closed maybe they wouldn't find her. Glass imploded. She heard each fragment grind into the carpet. Slowly, as if time itself had shattered. She remembered the empty phials scattered around her bed. Flicking open her eyes for a second, she peered out at two black boots crushing the phials to shards.

'Egg shells,' Queenie thought. 'Earthquake. Volcano. They're coming.'

A man stomped towards her. Huge hands pulled back the sheet. She screwed up her eyes, burrowed deeper, but the hands had her.

'QUEENIE. QUEENIE. LISTEN. IT IS PIÈTRO. YOU REMEM-BER, FROM COLLEGE.'

The voice was loud and slow. She blinked without recognition. The vibrations came again, strong enough now to roll her whole body.

'Drowning,' she thought, realising her lips had moved and she'd spoken the word aloud.

The slap, when it hit her face, snatched her from the water and dumped her back in the bed. She gasped. Her eyes watered. She held her breath, stroking her cheek. The face above her was too close to focus on all at once, so she stared at pieces. There was a hair growing from a nostril. Dark stubble on his cheeks and a white-head, ripe for squeezing, in the chin cleft. She laughed. The laugh came from outside her body, someone else's, laughing at her. It vibrated in her eardrums, and she put her hands over her ears.

'Stop,' she thought. 'Stop.'

'PIÈTRO. YOUR FRIEND. REMEMBER?'

Struggling, she screwed up her eyebrows and covered her face, but before she could remember anything the spasms returned and she gagged. The landlady screamed. Suddenly, there was a tin bucket in front of her; the man must have brought it with him. She spat rank bile. Simultaneously, the muscles in her arse relaxed, and warm shit slid down her thighs.

While Queenie's body cramped, part of her mind observed the process with detachment. She registered her burning throat and the taste of sick in her mouth. She noticed the vivid yellow of her vomit and its harsh smell, amazed that fragments of her stomach lining weren't floating in the fluid. I am empty, she thought. How can there be anything left?

She felt the man's warm hand across her forehead, supporting her head so she didn't fall into the bucket and, sometimes, a damp cloth wiping her mouth. The man began to speak again, gently this time. His words were soft and lilting, and they penetrated the bands of tight muscle in her belly. She sagged against the man's hand, let it take her weight until the convulsions eased.

Queenie's body had no life of its own. She lay on the stinking bed. She felt the man roll her in the sheet and scoop his arms underneath her. She curled close to the muscles of his chest, bobbing with his steps. He smelt of garlic. There was a draught now, chill on her skin, and whispers. They must be in the passageway. Even with her eyes closed, she could picture the other boarders staring from their doorways. It had been that way when Elsie died. Everyone had clustered to watch the police carry the body down the stairs, drawn to the shape under the patched grey blanket.

Soon she heard water running. A splash, then hot water surrounded her body. Her limbs bobbed. Even her ears were covered. She heard sounds in the water, gushing from the tap, her heartbeat in her ears, but most curious were the voices from downstairs. Transmitted through plaster and pipe, the conversations in the pub were clear, as if the punters were yabbering right next to her.

Something tickled her skin, prickly like sponge or pumice or an old flannel. It scrubbed every inch of her body, between her thighs, under her arms. Strong fingers massaged her scalp. All the while the man's hand supported the back of her head. Bess was there, too, tipping more warm water from a jug. Queenie heard the stream cascade and, filtered through the water, the landlady humming quietly. Her body, clenched as a fist, slowly began to uncurl.

Baptise me, she thought, surrendering to the buoyancy of the water. Christen me.

Too soon, the chain rattled. Suddenly, the water squealed and dropped its level. She felt a tug from the plughole, imagining herself swirling down into the sewers with the bath water. She lost the underwater conversations once the water level fell below her ears. The plug stopped screaming, then the faucet opened again and fresh water rinsed her body. When the faucet was turned off Queenie stayed in the bath, absorbing heat from the still-warm metal. She couldn't have moved even if she'd wanted to. She let the man rub her with a rough towel. Her skin stung. Between the bath and the towel, she'd lost the top layers of her skin, left them behind in the scummy water. Gentle fingers stroked her face.

'Rest now,' the man said.

Queenie woke in her narrow bed, in crisp clean sheets with something bulky, like a nappy, wrapped around her middle. She felt another spasm coming, so she leant over the side to the bucket. Her chest heaved, her throat strained to eject more fluid, but nothing came up. She shivered. The air in her room was cold enough to make her breath cloud, so she fell back against her pillow and snuggled into her warm cocoon. Someone had drained her veins of blood and replaced it with lead. It hurt to breathe. Even her eyes moved with difficulty. She slid them from side to side and felt them grind against their sockets.

The room looked different. It took Queenie and her slow eyes time to find the reason. The windows were bare, the glass fogged. Normally she kept the curtains closed. It began when she first brought clients to her room, but continued after the morphine sent the men away, because even the watery winter sunlight hurt her eyes. The curtains were heavy fabric, regulation blackout twill left over from the war, and they let in no light. But now there was moonlight, and yellow light from the street lamps. Where had the curtains gone? She saw the shapes of her furniture and a man slumped over the armchair with a blanket tucked around him. What was he doing there? Vague memories teased her; she recalled his voice and a strong smell of garlic, but her brain was foggy. It was like looking through her steamed-up window. She squinted, but let the thoughts be; she was too tired to chase them.

The room looked dreary in the pale light. When had the damp risen above the sink? When had the wallpaper started to bubble and peel away from the wall? When had she last dusted? She didn't know. She sighed. She felt wrung out, a rag squeezed through the mangle. There was an ache in her chest and her belly, different to the sharp pain of the cramps. It was a sad, low longing, a grieving, but she wasn't sure what for. The cold, shabby room made her want to cry, and so did the shouts from the street outside. '*Mirror*. Getcha *Mirror* here, gents.' 'Little runts! Shut yer bleeding trap, will yuh? Some of us are still sleeping . . .' But no tears came. Dawn couldn't be far off, she thought. Dry-eyed, she watched the sky through her curtainless window and listened to the sparrows.

As the light increased, she made out the features of the man on the chair. His black hair was cut short and shorn above the ears, but the length left on top curled like sheep's wool. Tanned skin. Like mine, she thought. She slowly pulled her hand from the blankets to look at her skin, but didn't recognise its colour. It was pale, not the rich hue she remembered. She slid her arm back under the covers and looked again at the man. He wasn't one of her clients, she knew that, but his features were familiar. She had the knowledge hidden somewhere, but retrieving it was a delicate process; there were big holes in her memory. Then an image came, the two of them talking in the college cafeteria where the man worked, rushing off later to their classes. It seemed so long ago. It was like being at the pictures; difficult to recognise that excited girl as herself.

'Piètro,' she breathed.

The man on the chair responded to his name. He shifted position, threw one arm behind his head, yawned, then opened his eyes.

'Welcome to the land of the living,' he said, and smiled. She smiled back, comforted by the familiarity of his accent. His voice triggered another memory: the autumn afternoon they'd spent sketching the river and the embankment from Battersea Park.

'Morning,' she said, then grimaced. It hurt to talk. Her voice was gravelly, and her breath stank. Wrapped in his blanket, Piètro sat on the bed next to her and held a glass of water to her lips.

'Four days it has been,' he said. 'But you have come back.'

Queenie sipped slowly. The water, icy from the tap, trickled down her gullet to her empty belly. The muscles reacted quickly, jumping to spasm again, but she held her breath until the tremors eased.

Piètro reached under the bed and pulled out an orange. Its dimpled skin glistened in the morning light; a miniature sun in his hands. Queenie watched him carefully peel it, so the rind came off in one piece. He split the fruit with his fingers and peeled the pith from the centre before offering her a segment. She opened her mouth, sucked, then winced. Bile had burnt her mouth and the tart liquid stung. She shook her head.

'Hurts,' she said.

'I know. But you will heal more quickly. One more suck, eh? I hocked my watch for these. First I have seen since the war.'

Piètro spoke like a parent to a petulant child.

She sighed. She opened her mouth for the orange segment and grimaced before sucking it dry. Piètro removed the desiccated husk.

'Where did you . . .' Queenie's sentence trailed off. She did not have the energy to finish it.

'The grocer's boy in Clapham. "From the sarfa France and rare as jewels, guv", that is what he said.'

Queenie smiled at the Cockney accent. 'You do that well.'

'He gave me these, too,' Piètro said, opening his shirt collar to reveal a row of round red bruises. 'Took me under the Albert Bridge.'

'You be careful.'

She lifted her head to sip more water. The mirror opposite the bed shocked her. The woman in the glass was tiny, shrunk to the proportions of a child, but crone-haggard. Her head was too big for her body; it looked as if it might tip over and fall off. She sighed.

'I feel old,' she said. 'Empty.'

She extended her arms over the sheet and they trembled. Her forehead creased. Her head fell back into the pillow. She looked again at the bare window.

'What happened to my curtains?'

Piètro rubbed his mouth before speaking. 'You will kill me, but I had to use them.' He tapped the cloth around her bony hips. 'I needed something to keep you clean. Bess had no more sheets to spare, so . . .' He shrugged.

Queenie stared. 'Why did you come for me?'

Piètro let the silence unravel between them, then passed his sketchbook to her. The charcoal figures at the beginning were huge; girls with wide hips and solid thighs that sprawled over the pages. Smaller figures began to squeeze in the gaps. Skinny girls with empty ink-blot eyes took over the last page, limbs tangled. Queenie saw muscle threads and the sharp corners of bone.

'I thought you would vanish,' Piètro said. 'When you got thin enough for the wind to snatch you, you did.'

He tucked his finger into the space behind her collarbone. 'My mamma would be ashamed to see you this way. Yours too.'

Queenie shook her head. 'I don't have a mother.'

'Then I shall be your mamma,' he said, smiling. 'Now eat.'

She nibbled a slice of dry bread. At first her body rejected the solid food. She brought it straight back up, mixed with orange pulp and water and bile. Finally, the retching stopped, and she rubbed the hollow between her breasts where the craving lived.

'I'm hungry,' she said.

Piètro pooled their ration books and, locking the door behind him, left for Clapham Junction. He is afraid I will search for more morphine, Queenie realised. He was right to worry. Had she the strength to move, she would have slipped back to the world where her heartbeat didn't echo in the cavern behind her ribs, where emptiness didn't whistle through each word formed by her lips. Instead, saved by frailty, she lay still, eyes on the second hand of the clock, ears straining to hear snippets of pub life or the world outside, anything to distract her from the ache.

Piètro returned with bread, dried egg powder, margarine, tins of spaghetti, a paper twist of dried herbs and a tiny square of chocolate. He opened the cans and perched them on the gas ring until the spaghetti juices bubbled. The flames brought a little heat into the room. Rolling the food over her tongue, Queenie let each tastebud absorb the juices, and aromatic herbs quickly replaced the metallic tang left by the morphine. She ate until her stomach bulged.

Drowsy after the meal, she curled on her side and slept until she heard the key turn in the lock. It was dark outside again; she had lost another day. She watched Piètro lock the door behind him. He unwound his scarf, then hung the key around his neck. Queenie let him tiptoe across the room before she coughed.

'It's all right. I'm awake now.'

He unpacked a pot of stew and half a loaf of bread, leftovers from his shift at the cafeteria. A jam jar followed, filled with golden oil, then two cloves of fresh garlic and a sprig of green basil that Piètro potted and placed on the window sill.

'How do you do it?' she asked. 'The rest of London barely eats but you come home with . . . with . . .'

He smiled. Raised one eyebrow.

'Tricks of the trade, me luv,' he said, and they both laughed at the landlady's voice emanating from Piètro's mouth. 'I'll tell you a secret. Stole the herbs from the greenhouse in the Physic Garden.'

One morning Piètro left the room before light and didn't return until dusk, bringing with him the smell of leaf mould and winter woods.

'I caught the train,' he said, rubbing his hands together and blowing on his fingers. 'I hid in the toilet all the way to Kent.'

From his bag he pulled a limp rabbit carcass and two eggs still marked with manure. Queenie watched in silence as Piètro sliced the rabbit along its belly. The cut was not deep enough to release the organs, but it separated skin from muscle. His hands were quick and sure, and within fifteen minutes the flayed rabbit lay next to its fur.

'You've done this before.'

Piètro nodded. His fingers delved into the marbled flesh to remove the bones.

'Although not many times. I watched my father. He used to bring home four at a time. He tied their back legs together and carried them on a stick.'

A pile of bones grew beside the rabbit.

'My father caught and skinned the rabbit, and my mother cooked it. Today I will do both for you.'

Piètro sliced the meat. He dipped each slice in flour, then egg, then in stale breadcrumbs he'd scrounged from the baker.

'I cannot remember my family,' he said. 'Their faces are gone. But when I make this rabbit I see them all. Papa is out in the fields, waiting for his trap to fall. Mamma is in the kitchen, feeding me the tender bits of meat that cook first, because I am the boy and that is tradition. And my sisters say "Piètro, Piètro, pass the rabbit", because they are too small to reach over the table.'

Striking a match, Piètro ignited the tiny gas ring, dribbled oil into a saucepan, then laid the fillets in the sizzling oil. When the breadcrumbs turned gold he lifted them from the pan and dropped them onto newspaper. Compelled by the smell of the frying meat, Queenie ate the rabbit immediately, even though the crispy meat burnt her lips. The pair ate in silence, reaching for the next morsel while the last still rolled over their tongues. That night they slept with unwashed fingers and rabbit grease drying on their chins.

It was a week after Bess and Piètro had opened the door to the room, and someone was prodding Queenie in the ribs. She grumbled and burrowed under the sheet.

'Come on, little girl,' Piètro said. 'Time to work.'

The prodding continued. She sighed, then poked her head out of the tangle of sheets. The clock said seven. In the morning? Already? It wasn't even properly light outside.

'What are you trying to do?'

'You must work.'

'I must sleep. I'm weak.'

He shook his head. 'Too weak to hold a pencil? Too many days in bed already. Too many more and there will be nothing to crawl out for. Remember? I told you. They are going to chuck you out of school.'

Queenie flicked her wrist. 'See if I care. Can't draw. Anyway, I make a great whore. More lucrative than drawing.'

'Our great hero is afraid even to get out of bed.'

She looked at Piètro.

'I am afraid,' she said, closing her eyes. 'Of so many things. Of never seeing the sea again. Of being stuck in London. Of dying alone.'

The words rushed out in one breath. When they stopped, her mouth opened and closed, as if there was more to come but the words had been lost. Piètro stroked her face.

'Do they go away when you sleep?' he asked softly. 'When you take the needle?'

She shook her head. 'I just don't have to do anything about them.'

He took his hands away. 'You are lazy as well as afraid.'

'If you want to martyr yourself by cleaning up my shit, fine. But I will sort this out alone.'

Piètro pulled the blankets from Queenie's body. Her limbs hardly dented the mattress.

'You spent weeks getting poison from your body. Did it alone. Nearly starved to death. There are harder bits to come, but you push me away.'

He touched the orange forelock. 'I am your friend. I want nothing, except for you to draw again. Trust me?'

Queenie bit her lip. She didn't speak.

'Try?' Piètro asked. He smiled and tucked the blankets back around her body.

She was still too weak to move, so Piètro brought her sketchbook to her bed. Her drawings began as clusters of fine lines that grew more solid as she did. She crawled across the room to the chair one morning and sketched a different view of her room. She sketched Piètro cooking, Piètro in a towel, pink after a scalding bath, Piètro sleeping.

When he was evicted from his own room, because his wages went on food and the pound notes he gave to Bess to cover Queenie's rent, she asked him to share hers. He arrived with a bundle of canvases, a small suitcase and a shy expression that made her laugh. When he wasn't working in the evenings, he slept in the armchair, head bent on an awkward angle and long legs dangling over one frayed arm. It was wrong to see him like that, huddled against the cold, so one night she patted the sheet next to her, smiling as he curled his body around hers. There was just enough room for the two of them. She felt his heart beating through her back. His breathing slowed; she knew he was asleep. Comforted by Piètro's warmth along her spine, and by the absence of desire between them, Queenie slept more deeply than she had since arriving in London.

Another morning she woke early, fidgeting until Piètro stirred beside her. He rubbed his eyes.

'What is the matter?'

She lit a cigarette. Inhaled, then exhaled a smoky sigh. 'I miss it.'

Piètro didn't ask what she was talking about.

'My dreams seem flat now. Everything does. If I could paint in those colours. Capture it somehow . . .'

The sentence drifted. She flicked ash into an empty baked-bean tin. Folded the butt until the flame died.

'It gets me here.' She touched the bottom of her ribcage, rubbed the soft belly below, then thumped the bones between her breasts. 'I want it so much. Will it ever go?'

Piètro shrugged. 'You either learn to live with it, or give in. And you should give up those cigarettes.'

'One thing at a time,' Queenie said.

At night it was harder to ignore the cravings, so he locked the door and slept with the key around his neck. Sometimes he sang to Queenie. They were ancient songs from his village, passed down from one generation to the next. She closed her eyes and caught her friend's sorrow in the cup of her ear. She didn't understand the words, but the melodies sneaked in through her pores, until she felt she had known them all her life.

Piètro sang his songs every night, and they infiltrated her dreams. In one, she was a child and her father was the singer. His voice came from behind, but when she turned her father was gone. Her mother, too. She couldn't remember their faces. She woke smelling rock dust and the sea.

'You talk in your sleep,' Piètro said the next morning as he boiled the kettle for their tea.

'What do I say?'

'I am usually half asleep, too. I recognise the language. Some of it, I think, is a southern dialect. But you speak in Italian.'

Queenie brought her eyebrows together, surprised by the revelation. She hadn't spoken the language in years, and in her mind it felt rusty and seized, like a bicycle left out in the rain. Her English was perfect, regulated by the harsh Norfolk reactions when she'd slipped. She thought she had pushed the Italian down, suppressed it, but it had bubbled over in her sleep. She reached for Piètro's hand.

'There's something I have to tell you,' she said quietly. 'I should have told you sooner, but I couldn't.'

She told him about the night the men came to her house in the rock. He was silent while she talked, drawing gentle circles on her knuckles with his fingertips. When her words trailed off, he rolled her on her side and curled around her, stroking her cheek and hair while he sang another of his songs, a slow lament about the tears of Christ. She felt Piètro's tears trickle through her hair and slide down her neck, but her own remained unshed.

Opening a cupboard, Piètro discovered bulging tubes of oils. 'I am surprised you did not sell them.'

Queenie smiled. 'I would have, if I'd remembered where they were. I even forgot my own birthday. I'm seventeen now.'

Her friend brought home a small bottle of mineral turpentine and a tin of whitewash that he had stolen from one of the art rooms. They painted over Queenie's old canvases and leant them against the wall to dry. Acrid fumes drifted out the window.

With charcoal poised over a dry canvas, Queenie hesitated, reluctant to mar the fresh gesso. But then the curve of Piètro's neck compelled her, bent close to the dressing-table mirror as he shaved, and she began with a single, smooth line. Another followed, and another, until her fingers were sooty and the canvas scored with lines. She drew him with the back of his head towards her and his face reflected in the glass. His mirror face stared back from the canvas, cheeks smeared with soap, framed by the cut-throat razor in one hand and a glass of sudsy water beside him.

The oils were tough to open; the paint around the cap had dried to a seal. Queenie forced the caps, satisfied by the spurt of colour that escaped as the cap twisted, and the bright powder that crumbled onto her fingers. She had forgotten the slick feel of oils beneath the brush and the flex of the palette knife. It pulled her in. Throughout that afternoon, and the days that followed, Piètro spoke, but she never thought to answer. Canvas after canvas, she painted until her body ached, returning to the early ones after they'd dried and painting over them again when she spotted misplaced strokes or awkward compositions.

When June came, Queenie and Piètro walked to the assessment session together. It was the first time she had been outside in months. Her legs dragged and she wanted to go back to their room, but Piètro shook his head. As they crossed Albert Bridge, she squinted at sunlight reflected from the Thames. Walking slowly along the embankment, she tripped on the ragged edge of a bombsite and grazed her knee on broken concrete. Piètro tied her canvases to his while she spat triple-barrelled obscenities at her frail legs.

'Fishwife,' Piètro said. 'Where did you learn to swear like that?'

Queenie didn't laugh.

'Give it time,' he said. 'Let your body heal the way it wants to.'

At the college gates she paused. Inhaling, she felt the breath tickle the lowest regions of her belly. She wound her hair into a bun and secured it with twine, then held out her arms for the canvases.

'A goddess,' Piètro said, smiling. They walked through the portico together.

Queenie's legs swayed as she opened the door of her assessment room. Draped in their honour robes, the panel of black-clad masters reminded her of crows, with sharp beaks poised to tear her and her paintings apart. She wanted to crawl under the long table. You are posing for a class, she thought, or these men are your customers. She tilted her chin a couple of degrees and stepped over the threshold.

The masters said little through the examination. They let Queenie hang each painting on the easel and explain the processes she had used and the decisions she had made through its creation and execution. They scribbled quick notes on their jotting pads. She would have preferred them to speak; the dry scratching of their nibs made her nervous. She strained to read what the masters had written, but the notes were too far away and upside-down. She talked until her throat hurt and she had discussed every painting. The masters nodded in unison. She retied her canvases in silence and quickly left the room.

Waiting outside, Pietro slumped against a column, scuffing the flagstones with the toe of one boot. 'They said nothing. They looked and scribbled. No questions, nothing.'

He seemed more cheerful when Queenie spoke of her own experience.

'Perhaps that is how they do it,' he said.

She shrugged. 'Wait and see, I guess.'

Pietro had solicited a pound from his favourite master after the session and he hailed the first black cab that drove past the college, but Queenie touched his arm.

'No,' she said.

'What is it?'

She felt a quiver in her limbs. Her skin tingled. 'Walk with me.' She held her arm out to the side, twirling fingers and thumb in the morning air.

Pietro waved the cab on and walked slowly, holding Queenie's canvases.

'Do you feel it?' she said.

She looked at the summer street. Sunlight bounced off windows and windscreens. The brass balls above the pawnshop sparkled. Even the blue medicine bottles at the chemist's glimmered.

She smiled. 'Someone's washed it. Thrown a bucket over us and rinsed the grime away.'

She led Piètro back across the bridge and stood at the railing, staring at the water below. The river, normally murky as mud and stinking of effluent, glistened like liquid gold. Swans slid with the current, arching long necks to preen the fanned plumage of their tails.

The pair walked the embankment to Battersea Park and followed winding paths through the gardens, pausing to examine the vegetable beds in the allotments. The shining white towers of the power station poked above the trees, and Queenie used them to get her bearings. At the fountain in the centre of the gardens, she dunked her hands in the water and shrieked as sparkling liquid gushed over her forearms.

'Didn't think . . . it would . . . be . . . so cold,' she gasped.

She sprinkled icy drops over Piètro, who sprinted off too fast for her wasted legs. Soon he returned, still laughing.

Reaching for the bright bushes lining the path, Queenie lingered at each flower, moved slowly from sunflower to dahlia, geranium to marigold, as if she'd gone blind and needed to touch every petal. The flower beds were lined with dark grey stones, and she fell on her knees beside them. The rocks were warmed by the sun and she stroked their rough surface. Tiny specks of quartz in the matrix glittered. She dug her fingers into the cool soil and lifted one of the stones. Shaped like a giant egg, it took two hands to hold it. Wiping off the earth with her skirt, she began to walk home with it, but the park inspector spotted her.

'Vandals,' he yelled. 'Bloody 'ooligans.'

He blew his whistle. Queenie dropped the stone. She made Churchill's Victory sign with two fingers, then reversed it.

'Up yours!'

Piètro grabbed her hand and pulled her to an awkward run. Luckily the inspector was ancient, and frailer than Queenie. The laughing vandals were out of the park and on a bus before he could hobble past the gate.

'I'll remember your faces,' he yelled. 'Don't bother coming back.'

The bus pulled away. She watched his red face until they turned a corner. Still laughing two stops later, she pulled the cord and jumped out in front of the pub.

It was July 1949. A summer evening, light even at nine o'clock. In the room above the pub the fumes of turpentine and oil paint had been replaced by cigarette smoke, sweat and cheap cologne. It was hard to hear the telephone in the hall above the voices and the brass boom of the gramophone. Queenie let Piètro take the call. She waited in the room, pressing her ear to the closed door so she could hear his response.

'Hello? Sorry. I cannot hear. Speak louder please. Who? Sybille Quinn? There is no one of that name here. What? Who lives here? None of your business! Hanging up now. Got a party to attend to.'

Queenie opened the door of the room. 'Who was that?'

'Wrong number. No need to worry.'

'Who were they looking for?'

'Sybille someone. King? Quinn, I think. Never heard of her. Have you?'

She shook her head. 'No.'

'Sad, though. The woman sounded upset.'

The next morning Queenie left the pub while Piètro slept off the effects of his wine. She walked past the pillar box to the red telephone booth at the end of the street. Shutting the door on the traffic, she slid a coin into the slot and dialled a number from memory. The telephone rang out. She dialled again.

'Hello?'

A woman's voice. Norfolk accent and a blocked nose. Queenie didn't answer.

'Hello?'

Silence.

'Isaac, they're not answering. You take it. I can't deal with this now.'

The words were muffled, the receiver covered by a hand, or pressed to a chest.

'Hello? What's your game?'

Isaac paused. The gruffness left his voice. Queenie heard crying in the background.

'Why don't you speak?' he asked softly.

Silence.

'Is that you, Sybille? Please don't hang up. There's something important I have to tell you. Our parents . . .'

Queenie's fingers severed the connection. She kept the receiver to her ear until the dial tone replaced the harsh beeps of a broken line. She walked to the baker's, then returned to the room.

Piètro surprised her. He was waiting when she returned.

'Where have you been?'

She had an excuse tucked under her arm, a loaf of bread wrapped in paper.

'I went to get bread,' she said. 'We'd run out.'

'Liar. I watched you from the window.'

'I didn't want to wake you.'

'By using the phone in the hall? Come on! Who did you call?'

'It doesn't matter.'

Piètro grabbed her shoulders. 'If you are back on the morphine, after all we have been through, I will goddamn skin you alive.'

The expletive jarred. It upset the rhythm of Piètro's voice, usually so melodic. Queenie turned away.

'Don't, Piètro. I'm tired. Let me sleep a little. Then we'll talk.'

He pushed her gently to a chair. 'We do it now. Tell me. Who did you call?'

Sullen, Queenie lit a cigarette.

'A woman in Norfolk,' she said. 'My sister.'

'You told me your family was dead.'

'They are.'

'I am confused,' Piètro said, rubbing his forehead. 'Then this sister . . .'

'The Quinns took me in. When I, when my . . .'

Piètro grabbed her shoulders. 'Why not tell them you were in trouble? They are family. Family! They could have helped.'

'They're not family. I told you. My family is dead. These are just people.'

She didn't tell him about the red hair that bound them together, or her repulsion when she looked in the mirror and saw the forelock.

'People who you grew up with. They must worry. At least they know where you are now.'

Queenie shook her head. Watched her cigarette smoke drift out the open window.

'I saw you,' Piètro said.

'No. I dialled the number. Listened. Hung up.'

'Why not speak?'

She shrugged.

'If I had family here,' Piètro said, 'blood or otherwise...' He sighed. 'I have no choice. You do, but you stay away.'

Queenie said nothing. She scratched a fleck of paint from beneath her nail and looked out the window.

'How long does it take you to get ready?' Piètro yelled from the street below. 'We have a long way to go.'

Lugging her suitcase from the empty room, Queenie met Bess on the landing. She handed the landlady her key, prolonging the contact to tightly press the woman's hands. They stood with linked hands, ignoring the horn blasts from downstairs.

'Thank you,' Queenie said, willing her gratitude to travel through their skins. Bess nodded, freeing one hand to touch Queenie's cheek.

'Good luck.'

Piètro's van, a green Fordson bought cheap from the owner of the cafeteria, carried the pair and their paintings south through London on hoarded petrol coupons. For months after their graduation, Queenie had watched her friend plan the round of exhibitions, waiting for acceptance letters from gallery or hall owners, then sprawling on the floor to circle another destination on their map. None of the big London galleries accepted their proposal—few even bothered to reply—but Queenie was pleased at the number of small towns and villages eager to welcome them. She'd left that side of it to him, happy to make posters for the tour while he plotted their course.

Piètro persuaded his boss to give Queenie a job, and she scrubbed greasy dishes while he readied the food for the cafeteria. They worked days, nights, double shifts, until Queenie's hands were permanently pink from scalding water, but eventually they had hoarded enough money to begin their tour.

Her heart quickened as they drove through the mess of the city. It was good to leave the bombsites behind, the crowded tube and queues of sullen people. She wanted to see green fields, to breathe clean air. The mechanical sounds of the city faded as they left, and at first she felt lost without the steady rhythm.

Their tour began like a holiday. They drove down to Brighton to play slot machines on the pier and walk along the pebbly beach beside a violent sea. Pietro took them to the chalk edifice of Beachy Head, and Queenie crawled over the grass on her belly to stare at the waves below. She had to dig her fingers into the soil to stop herself jumping. Rosy-cheeked from the sea breeze, they followed the coast past Portsmouth and stopped to eat lunch beside a stone marker that read '60 miles to London'.

The pair developed a routine. Once their paintings were hung in church halls and tiny galleries, they counted their remaining money, divided it by the number of days left on the road. Usually they had only enough for meals, so they slept in the van. In Salisbury, after three quick sales, they could afford a hotel. They flashed the cheap rings bought to silence the gossips and signed into a room as a married couple.

'Electroplated,' Pietro said, laughing. 'Nothing but the best for my girl.'

When the exhibition closed in Salisbury, they drove through the Vale of the White Horse to Uffington. Queenie stared at the simple design carved into the chalk hillside thousands of years before. She wanted to stop the car, to stomp through muddy fields and touch the stone horse, connect with the hands that had carved it, but they were overdue in Bath.

The green van drove them from Bath to Bristol. It took them into north Wales, then across to Manchester and Sheffield. On the quiet winding roads connecting the galleries, Queenie learnt to drive. The vibrations of the steering wheel made her palms tingle, but she didn't want to stop, entranced by the vanishing point ahead of her, always out of reach.

As Piètro's maps carried the pair back south, Queenie began to shift in her seat. She recognised the slow curves of Norfolk fields and the ivy-cloaked oak trees that shook their branches beside the road. Outside Norwich, she turned to look at the asylum and nearly drove the van into a ditch. She didn't say anything, just bit her lips and turned the starter key. When Piètro directed her into a narrow lane curving between fields of lavender, Queenie switched off the engine and stopped the van in the middle of the lane.

'Bastard,' she said.

'What?'

'Don't pretend you don't know. I can't believe you. The last thing I wanted to do was take a detour through here. I said I'd never come back.'

'This is the right way.'

'You mean you've booked us here? We're exhibiting? Christ!'

Piètro nodded. 'You did not read our itinerary?'

'You're joking? You can exhibit but you'll be doing it alone. I'll find my own way back to London.'

'But they are looking forward to seeing you. At the opening. Your family.'

She looked at Piètro but said nothing. Spiteful words formed in her mouth, but her lips refused to let them out.

'How . . . how did you find them?'

Piètro did not look at her. His voice, when it came, was quiet. 'I steamed open the letter. The one for Sybille Quinn.'

She had wondered about the blurred ink and crinkled edges of the envelope as she returned it, unopened, to the post office. But she never thought that Piètro . . .

In a second, she was out of the van and walking back towards the main road. She heard Piètro swear and scramble across to the driver's seat, but ignored the reversing van.

'Come on,' Piètro said. 'Give them a chance. Isaac seemed . . .'

Stopping, Queenie glared into the van. 'Don't you dare, dare try to tell me how he seemed! What would you know?'

'Why not go back, just for an afternoon? It helps, sometimes, to go full circle, to go back where you . . .'

'So when are you going to Italy, huh? When will you make the mythic trek?'

Piètro took his foot off the accelerator. The van slowed.

'I . . . Well, now look here . . .' He paused. Frowned. 'There is nothing for me to go back to.'

Piètro spoke softly. He turned his face away. Queenie thought she had him, thought she'd scratched his smooth veneer. For a second. Until he looked back. The uncertainty was gone, smiling mask in place once again.

'Less of the bastard, hey? I know my papa.'

So do I, Queenie thought. She tried to keep her scowl but Piètro's smile, even forced, knew how to tempt her mouth to smile in return, and she climbed back into the van. But their smiles did not last for long.

'When I spoke with Isaac he told me something,' Piètro said. 'He said . . . Mr and Mrs Quinn had died. I wanted to tell you earlier, but . . .'

'It would ruin your secret?' She held up her hands. 'I know. Isaac tried to tell me when I called, but I hung up. I guessed it was that.'

'But you chose not to go back for the funeral?'

She shook her head. Pìetro didn't understand, but for once she didn't care. She didn't want to explain.

When the van arrived in Harrowstone, she turned her head to look at the Green.

'Let me out,' she said. 'I'm going for a walk.'

Drawn to the dark green outlines of the yew trees, Queenie walked towards the church, then through the churchyard, to stand at the foot of two new graves. It had been months now, but the earth was still bare, barren of grass. She wanted to walk to another part of the graveyard, to visit another Quinn headstone, but something stopped her. Instead, she crossed the churchyard and stood next to the post office, in front of the block of stone. She stroked the dusty stone, ran her fingers over its crumbling surface.

'I got out,' she said. 'So did you. We kept our promises.'

Rubbing her hands together, she swept the dust to the ground, then walked back to Pìetro's van. Together they went to the bakery. As Queenie's hand pushed open the door, the bell tinkled, and a waft of yeasty air sliced twelve years from her life. She was a small child again, with numb fingers and cheeks, entering the bakery for the first time. She shivered, then shook her head, pulling her spine straight. I am a woman now, she thought, a woman.

The others were standing beside the counter. Pìetro's eyes flicked from Queenie's forelock to the two red heads, and she could see he had made the connection she had tried to avoid. She looked away, back to Isaac, shocked by the change in him. It was only three years since she had left, but he was gaunt, aged. While living at the house, she had discounted his weak heart, ignoring his wheezing breath and the afternoons spent in bed, but now his heart's struggle was evident. His lips were tinged blue, and there were circles under his eyes. Audrey, skinny as ever and wearing the same auburn plaits as when Queenie had left, looked like a taller version of the girl she remembered.

'Isaac. Audrey. This is Pìetro.'

Isaac held out his hand. 'We've spoken on the telephone. Come in.'

The four sat on leather lounges in the dim parlour. Queenie stared at the grandfather clock. With each steady tock she watched the second hand, convinced that it would quiver eternally but never move on to the next moment. She'd done the same as a child. I might never have left, she thought.

Audrey stood, smoothed her dress, and walked to the kitchen. She returned with a tray, laying four cups onto the table. No one spoke as the amber stream from the teapot filled them. Queenie flicked out a cigarette.

'Mind if I . . . ?'

Audrey answered before Queenie had finished her sentence.

'I do, actually, Sybille. We had the vicar over last month and he lit his pipe in here. Mother would have been horrified. The smoke got right into the curtains. Filthy. Couldn't get rid of it. I've washed them three times but I can still smell it.'

Audrey shuddered. 'Anyway, you should've given it up ages ago.'

Queenie slid the cigarette back into its packet. Tucked her matches into her bag. Coughed.

'It's Queenie now,' she said. 'Didn't expect you'd still be living here. I thought you'd have moved.'

'This is our home.' Audrey paused. 'I've never left Norfolk and I've no desire to. Not like some people.'

Isaac frowned. 'Audrey! I told you, none of that.'

Audrey picked at her skirt. Isaac continued.

'When Mum and Dad died we . . . Piètro, you did tell her?'

Queenie nodded. 'I visited the graves this morning.'

'We couldn't sell the house,' Isaac said. 'Where would we go? I thought it best we stay put. We sold the business, though. Never did learn how to bake. Dad got someone else in before he died.'

'How did they die?'

The question was addressed to both siblings, but neither spoke. Audrey broke the silence, her voice quieter than before.

'They faded. Elissa's death hit them hard. And then you left.'

Queenie didn't know what to say. 'I . . .'

'Oh, it's old ground now. I won't dredge it up. They were crossing the road, up by the dairy. The driver of the milk cart said they came out of nowhere. In his blind spot. They were so frail. Mother died then, Father in hospital. They were buried together. We thought you might see the announcement in the papers. I've got the notice.'

She reached into the bookcase and removed a brown leather-bound book, opening it for Queenie. The Quinns' death notices had been cut out with pinking shears. The newspaper squares reminded Queenie of dead skin, yellow and crisp.

'The whole town came out. The church wasn't big enough. I tried to call you in London. We got a number from one of your tutors, but it was wrong. I sent a letter, but it came back. They'd have liked for you to be there.'

Queenie flicked to the beginning of the book. She stroked the death notice at the top of the first page, the paper fibres soft against her callused fingertips.

'Elissa Quinn,' it said. 'Taken suddenly.'

The pages separating Elissa's death notice from her parents' were filled with other notices and unfamiliar names. Each one was neatly cut out and glued to the page; a collection of other people's deaths. Audrey's even copperplate writing dated the death and named the newspaper in which she'd found it. Queenie closed the book, passed it quickly to Audrey, and suppressed the tremor that gripped her body.

She helped Audrey stack the teacups. Her lipstick had left a red mark on the edge of her cup, and Audrey's eyes returned to the red mark as the pair walked to the kitchen. She put her fingers to her own pale lips.

'Mother never let me wear make-up,' she said quietly.

'It's funny,' Queenie said, unsure how to continue after the admission. 'I've never had tea in the parlour before. I feel like a visitor.'

Audrey's hand fell to her side. 'You are. Or don't tell me you're staying?'

Queenie shook her head. 'We're booked in Colchester straight after the exhibition here. I don't think there's time to . . .'

'No. Thought not.'

Neither spoke. Queenie looked out onto the garden as she rinsed the teacups under the tap. It wasn't as she remembered. Mrs Quinn's flowerbeds, once overflowing with peonies and dahlias, were empty. Through the war the flowers had been replaced with potatoes and turnips, but even those were gone. There were no blooms, no green vegetable heads, only sticks in dry ground. The soil in the asparagus bed was untilled, its surface cracked by summer sun. Even the leaves of the trees had withered. Only the stinging nettles seemed unaffected. They clustered at the edge of the garden, along a fence that leant inwards.

'Your garden needs water,' she said.

Audrey nodded. 'I haven't had the energy since . . . Too much to do in the house. Isaac doesn't care how the place looks, but I do.'

Queenie wiped the lipstick stain with her fingers. Outside fourteen white sheets and fourteen white pillowcases gusted on the line.

'That'd keep the neighbourhood in sheets for a month!' she said.

Audrey turned to pick up a tea-towel. 'Yes. I . . . It's washing day. I've been putting it off.' She had her back to Queenie and her voice was muffled.

'Looks like it.' The more Queenie rubbed the cup the more the lipstick smeared over the translucent china.

'Don't,' Audrey said. 'I'll do it later.'

'No. I insist.'

'Go back into the other room.' Audrey's voice was hard. 'I said I'll do it later. Leave it.'

Queenie left the unwashed cup in the sink. 'Whatever you say.'

'It's good you've married,' Audrey said, her voice softer now. She passed a tea-towel to the other woman. 'Keeps you company.'

Confused, Queenie frowned, then looked down at her left hand. She was still wearing the ring they had bought in Salisbury. She should have corrected Audrey, but she didn't. She shrugged.

'How did you meet?'

'Art school. We . . . worked well together.' Queenie coughed. 'What about you, any special young men?'

Audrey looked at Queenie before speaking. Their eyes met for the first time, and Queenie noticed how empty Audrey's were. Weary. Old eyes in a girl's body. The green irises had dulled almost to brown. Audrey sighed.

'Have you forgotten what it was like? This was not a house you brought boys into. Or friends. There was no laughter. No conversation. No one talked about it. No one talked at all. I don't even think they spoke to each other. Did you know they took me out of school after you left? Mother was convinced I'd end up like Elissa. I was sixteen. I didn't leave the house for two years, except to go to church. And all the while you were cavorting about London. I should've left too.'

Audrey's expression changed. She smiled slightly, blushing. 'There was one boy. Jeremy, from our class. Do you remember him?'

Queenie nodded. She pictured him clearly, a freckled boy with brown hair who once sat behind Audrey, tying her plaits to the seats and dipping their ends in the ink pot. He'd lost his older brother in the war, came to classes pale and quiet in the months that followed.

'He used to walk me home from school,' Audrey said. 'Once, he came right to the house. He asked Mother and Father if he could take me dancing.'

Audrey stared out the window. 'But Mother said no. She stopped him walking with me.'

It was difficult to hear Audrey talk like this. Through their childhoods Queenie had pushed the other girl away so often, ignoring her pleas for inclusion and her hurt cries, that it was impossible to offer her friendship. She didn't know how.

'I'm sorry,' she said, unable to listen any longer. She tucked the tea-towel over the rail. 'I'm going outside for a cigarette. All right with you?'

'Make sure you put the stub in the bin. I can't stand the sight of them.'

Audrey walked to the parlour and shut the door behind her, but Queenie didn't go outside. Instead, she climbed the stairs to Elissa's pale blue room. It hadn't changed. A crisp sprig of lavender was tucked into the bedhead and a recipe for Christmas pudding, written in copperplate, was taped to the mirror. The reflective backing was peeling and she saw mahogany through the patina.

On her knees, she opened the wardrobe. Crocheted bags of dried lavender hung over each coathanger's neck. Breathing deeply, she stroked the sleeves of a velvet jacket. Touched the sheer fabric of a knee-length skirt. In a drawer she found pairs of clean knickers, big ones that used to billow on the Quinn washing line.

'You called them elephant knickers,' she said. She sighed, then pressed them to her face. 'They smell like you.'

She sat on the bed and lit a cigarette, reached over to the dresser and found the ashtray hidden where she expected it to be. She watched the cigarette burn to a column of ash before flicking it away. Next to the bed she found Elissa's holiday suitcase. The leather travelling straps were still tightly buckled, but the stickers announcing her destinations peeled at the edges.

'Can't bring myself to unpack it.' Audrey was leaning against the doorframe. 'Even now.' She said nothing about the cigarette.

'Could have happened yesterday,' Queenie said. 'It's all so clean.'

'I dust. Every Wednesday. Put everything back where it came from. Their room too. Isaac thinks I'm barmy, but . . .'

She laughed, a nervous laugh, frail as a leaf in winter. Put her hand over her mouth. 'I didn't know what else to do.'

Dinner was unbearable. Queenie chomped through the dry meat and pale vegetables. Her tongue had become used to

Piètro's delicate flavours and the joy with which he cooked. This food had no joy in it, as if all sensuous pleasure had been sucked out.

'Different to London fare, eh?' Audrey said. 'I hear rationing is still strict in town.'

Queenie tried not to choke on her potato. She nodded at Audrey, then winked at the dark-haired man opposite her.

Piètro cleared the plates, then went out to the garden with Audrey, leaving Isaac and Queenie at the table. Isaac poured them both a port. The bottle was half empty.

'Audrey doesn't like to see me drink,' Isaac said. 'She worries about my heart. She's learnt to be elsewhere when I fancy a tipple.'

He ran a fingertip around the edge of his glass. In the silent room, the sound was shrill, unearthly.

'Why did you change your name?' he said. 'I can't think of you as anything but Sybille.'

Queenie stared at Isaac before responding, surprised by the venom he released in her. She'd thought it would fade with time, but she still struggled with the urge to strike his freckled face, split his full lips. 'You would, wouldn't you? That's what you called me.'

'It was Mother's choice.'

'But you never stood up for me. You could've said, Mother, wait. The little girl already has a name. But you didn't. You dragged me halfway around the world and then you let them steal my name.'

Isaac filled up his glass. 'You look like your mother.'

Shut up, Queenie thought. His words made her skin crawl.

'She smiled more than you do. I remember the sun on her face. She laughed like an angel. One day . . .'

Queenie didn't want to hear him talk like this, didn't want to see the gentle smile on his lips. She seethed with the desire to hurt him.

'I don't remember her laughing,' she said.

Isaac's smile slid away. His green eyes caught her gaze. They were Elissa's eyes, she realised, noticing again the sorrow they held. It was unbearable; she looked away.

'What do you remember?' he asked, quietly.

Queenie sipped her port, closing her eyes so she didn't have to look at him.

'A house carved in a rock above the sea. Fishing. I remember working with my father. He used to lift me onto his shoulders.'

She opened her eyes to stare across the table, wanting to see how the words affected him. The urge to hurt him shamed her, but she couldn't stop. 'Did you know my father?'

Isaac paused. 'I heard she married a carpenter.'

'He was a mason.' Queenie blinked, slowly. 'What was my mother's name?'

Isaac coughed. 'Pardon?'

'Her name. What was it?'

'Don't, Sybille. Queenie. Whatever the hell you're calling yourself. Don't tease it out like this.' Isaac rubbed his temple. 'If you've got something to say . . . I should never have left her behind, but I was young. I didn't think . . . Don't make me dredge up the past to . . .'

'Isaac. It's a simple question.' She spoke quietly. Her lips hardly moved. 'I just want to know her name.'

'How can you not know your own mother's name?'

'Don't you remember? I was seven when you took me away. Seven!'

She was shouting now, her rage boiling over. She slammed her glass onto the table. The stem snapped, and the glass bell rolled on the tabletop, spilling the port. She grabbed the stem, ready to hurt Isaac with it. She wanted to poke out his eyes. She wanted to kill this orange-haired man with flabby fingers and pale skin.

'I never knew them as anything but Mamma and Papa. I found my father's name in his atlas. Cristofano Salvatore. At least I think that was him. It could just as easily be the person he bought the book from. But my mother? How else am I supposed to find out?'

Queenie whispered her last question, more for herself than for Isaac. Her anger drained away. Emptied, she felt flat and tired. Her hand, still holding the broken stem, trembled.

Isaac sighed. Reaching out, he pressed her hand for a second, before taking the stem from her. He picked up another glass from the dresser, filled it to the brim and slid it to her past the glittering fragments. She accepted it without a word. Neither spoke as they sipped the port.

When Audrey and Piètro returned, Queenie stood up to leave.

'Her name was Afrodite,' Isaac said, quietly, as Queenie walked away. She didn't respond, and Isaac didn't repeat the name.

A week later, Piètro and Queenie removed the canvases from the church hall.

'Not so bad, was it?' Piètro asked. 'Why all the fuss?'

Queenie shrugged her shoulders. 'Hard to put into words. I needed to go forward, not look back. Pillar of salt, that sort of thing.'

'Never picked you as superstitious. You have never really left a place until you can comfortably return. Otherwise it has a hold on you. Part of you stays behind.'

'It's not part of me. She's still here, the little girl. All of her. She never left. I thought I saw her yesterday, silly sad-eyed creature with her stupid red forelock, fending off the other children.'

She looked across to Piètro. 'Isaac and Audrey didn't come to the exhibition.'

'No. But Audrey bought the Elissa picture,' Piètro said. 'The blue oil. She sent the baker's boy over for it. Paid in cash.'

'Did she?'

'He said she hardly ever leaves the house now. By the way, did you see Isaac's study?'

Queenie shook her head. Even as a child she had avoided that room, unwilling to enter the orange-haired man's private space.

'Audrey took me in to fetch a road atlas,' Piètro said. 'Incredible—books everywhere, all about other countries. One wall just for books on Italy and Greece, and a map with journeys plotted in red. Audrey said it was where he hoped to travel one day, if his heart was up to it.'

As they drove away in the van, Queenie watched the village shrink in the rear-view mirror. The last thing she saw was the church spire with its square turrets. Distorted by the curve of the glass, it didn't look real. She looked away from the mirror to the vanishing point ahead, where hedges either side of the lane converged with tarmac. While Piètro drove, she watched the road through the windscreen and tried to ignore the images flickering in the rear-view mirror.

'To Colchester, then,' she said.

Flame

New South Wales 1990

At her desk as the sun rises, Billie reads the last lines in her workbook. They encircle a sketch of a young man with dark curly hair. You'd like it here, Pìetro, she thinks. We could sit at the beach and sketch together. You'd like Troy, too. The pair of you could cook up a storm in my kitchen. Sometimes he reminds me of you.

On a clean sheet of paper ripped from the workbook, she begins a letter to her old friend. Gets as far as the date and his name before she remembers. No letters have crossed the oceans between them in the four years since his death. Yet each time Billie collects her mail from the little shop by the wharf, she still expects his handwriting on an envelope.

The final letter broke her heart. Pages of wobbly writing and a photograph of skin stretched over bones. Pìetro's smile was as she remembered, but it was too big for his wasted face. She hardly recognised him. With scrawny arms and sagging neck, eyes huge in his head and collarbones protruding from his hospital gown, he had been shrunk to a small boy by the virus that left his system defenceless.

As she read his last letter, Billie stubbed out her cigarette.

Today I will do as you asked, so many years ago, she thought. I'll give up the ciggies.

Taking her tobacco pouch into the garden, she had scattered the fragrant strands over the soil, vowing never to buy another packet. And she hadn't. Mull was different, she told herself later, when she first rolled joints of pure green.

After reading his letter, she called the hospital in London. It would be late there, but she had to speak to him.

'I'm sorry,' the night-nurse said, in a faint voice. Static on the line. 'We lost him last week.'

Pneumonia had got him in the end. He had died alone, with only the nurses to ease his final hours, to watch the slow cessation of his breath. In the studio, Billie closes her workbook.

The cicada chorus begins at nine. The air is hot, dry, all moisture sucked away and acrid with smoke. Some idiot's cranked their barbecue, she thinks, on a total fire-ban day, too. She peers out the window to find the culprit's smoke plume, but there's nothing, just a blue haze settled over the valley and an orange sun. Hope it's back-burning, she thinks, not a fire gutting the hills and gullies of the river catchment.

There's been no fire on the island in twenty-five years, according to the locals, but it has come close, scorching the back fences of the little township on the mainland. Picking up her mail one day when she was new to the island, Billie said to the shopkeeper that she thought they'd be safe in the Hawkesbury's salty embrace, but Mary shook her head.

'It's the embers you've got to watch,' she said. 'The wind carries them ahead of the fire. They could jump the river easy. A few of those in the dry scrub, and we'd be in trouble.'

The house has sprinklers now, with a diesel water pump, and shallow gutters that don't hold the leaves, but the thought of flying embers troubles Billie. She imagines them, disaster's avant-garde, set down by the wind and smouldering. In her mind, fallen leaves crackle: volatile eucalypts and she-oak needles. One ember and everything could be lost.

Shaking the blackened trunks from her mind, she returns to her desk. With visitors in the house, she hasn't had much productive time, and the river couple's commission is due in a week. She lifts her brush, but there's a knock at her door before she can touch the leaf.

Expecting Troy, she looks up, but the face that peers around the door is smaller, and lower.

'Santa's been,' Eli says, with a wink. 'Are you going to come and open your presents?'

I completely forgot, Billie thinks. Troy dragged the tree up from the wharf yesterday: a wilted she-oak, the only one left. All the lush pine trees, resin smelling like Christmas, had already been sold. He and Eli decorated it in the evening, with tinsel and homemade silver stars. She puts her work aside and follows the child through the house to where the other three adults wait in the lounge room, in their nightclothes, red-eyed, half-awake. Eli has been their alarm clock too, she guesses.

Rummaging under the tree, the child distributes foil-wrapped presents, then begins on her pile. The adults wait with parcels on their laps while Eli opens hers. None of Santa's presents enthral; these she opens and discards. But Troy's gift she hugs: a tiny make-up kit, with an eye-shadow palette and five miniature lipsticks. Stan's is even better. Eli unfurls a wing of orange and pink fabric, with struts as long as her arm.

'A kite!' she yells, and kisses Stan on the cheek.

Billie gets a kiss for her gift, too, but her watercolour pencils look small and dull beside the kite's neon splendour.

'Your turn,' Eli orders, and one by one the adults open their gifts. Troy has made chocolates for the others, but for Billie he bought a large magnifying glass on a stand.

'So you can look through it and paint,' he says. 'There's even a light. I thought it might help.'

She embraces his skinny body. He is as chuffed with her presents to him, a knife of Japanese steel and an old English herbal book, yellowed by the fingers of its many previous owners, but his eyes stray under the tree. Billie knows what he looks for; it's not there. Nothing from his parents, but there is a surprise. She collected it from the shop yesterday. A small box with childish handwriting. Inside, a handmade card and a school photo in a frame. It's his little sister, the same age as Eli. She has Troy's toothy smile, his white hair and sun-brown skin.

Standing the photo-frame on the dresser, Troy serves Christmas breakfast: mince pies and chocolates and coffee, with a special milky one for Eli. Later, when everyone is dressed and showered, he lays platters of freshly shucked river oysters and prawns from the fish market on the table. There are bowls of walnuts and cashews, candles and crackers. Bonbons, Troy calls them. Billie has never got used to that one. Eli waves a prawn in front of her mother, tickling her nose with the feelers, but Lorelei pushes it away.

'Behave,' she says.

'Humbug,' Eli replies.

The others snap prawn tails with gusto and slurp oysters from their shells, but Lorelei moves the shellfish around her plate, arranging them like pieces of a puzzle. She seems flat, Billie thinks, dull. Her eyes are still red-rimmed.

'More for me,' Eli says, raiding her mother's plate.

Oyster shells pile on the table, and the conversation lulls as bellies fill. Willing her body to move—she'll fall asleep if she doesn't—Billie scrapes the shells into a bucket and gathers the dirty plates. Stan returns to his studio to sleep off lunch, and Troy walks Elissa to the top of the island to fly the kite. Kneeling beside the Christmas tree, Lorelei folds the wrapping paper. Her hands move, but her eyes are distant.

'For next year,' she says. 'An old habit of Mum's.'

She fingers the tinsel and the fronds of the wilting she-oak. 'The decorations look wrong in this light. Do you ever get used to it?'

'Not really,' Billie says. 'And I've been here almost thirty years. It's the spray-on snow that gets me. Always on top of the window pane, defying gravity.'

Lorelei nods, but doesn't seem to have heard the words. 'Last year Mum and I danced outside,' she says. 'Don't know what came over her. Simon took a photo of us in our Christmas frocks, clear blue sky, frost on the ground. There was a waltz on the radio, and we danced.'

She sighs. 'You feel them, at times like this. The absences.'

I know, Billie thinks. 'The first year is always the hardest.'

Lorelei looks up, eyes brimming. 'I might go back to bed for a while,' she says. She runs through the house to her bedroom, shutting the door. Two steps behind, Billie pauses at the closed door, hearing sobs through the wood. She lifts her palm to stroke the grain, but cannot open the door. Banished from the woman's grief, she walks slowly back to her studio, positioning herself in front of her leaf commission.

'Back to work as usual,' she sighs.

The week before New Year's Eve broils, and Billie spends most of it in her studio. Outside, the December sun glares, and it is too hot to stray from the shade of the house. Draughts through the windows tang with smoke. The air is dry, without the usual tropical humidity of Sydney summers. In the garden, undergrowth shrivels and burns. Even the native trees look parched, scorched by the sun. The ground cracks. The island is a tinderbox.

Confined to the house and unable to sleep properly, the rest of the household seems dazed. They trip over each other on the way to the toilet and squabble over midday television programs. In the mornings, Billie walks into the shower fully dressed and drips water through the house as she dries. Troy keeps Eli amused, borrowing board games from a neighbour for breaks between video racing. Mark visits often, and the three play together. Lorelei is quieter than usual. She spends most of the time with Stan in his shed, or on the verandah, staring over the garden with a box of tissues beside her. Billie carries out cups of tea, but they cool, undrunk, beside Lorelei's chair.

'What can I do?' Billie asks, tipping another cold mug on the tree ferns. It is heartbreaking to see her like this. 'How can I help?'

'I'm all right,' Lorelei says, smiling, but the words are hollow. Billie thinks of the window she leaves open in winter, just a crack, and the sad howl as the wind blows through it.

Pockets of Lorelei's grief hang in the air of the house. Billie walks through them, cold in dry summer air. She recognises the gravity of the grief, its siren call. Sleep, it whispers. Drink. Smoke. It will be better then. It will go away. But Billie shakes it off. I will fight this time, she thinks. Fight. She concentrates on the leaf commission, determined to finish it before the year's end. On New Year's Eve she puts her brush down and pushes the leaf aside to dry. Closing her eyes, she exhales deeply, releasing the composition held by her eyes for so many days. Let it go. Make room for the next.

As she breathes, another image dominates the space behind her eyes. It's a memory from the day Lorelei fell asleep in the sun and fried herself. She sees the Englishwoman on the bed in her underwear, as she was when Billie brought in the lavender balm. Compelled, Billie stares at the snapshot from her memory. Her eyes are drawn to the white stripes where Lorelei's bathers protected her. To the pink curve of her burnt breast as it slides into her bra. A brown mole on the inside of Lorelei's thigh. The white brand label on her black knickers. The bulge where her bra strap digs in under her arm. Billie hadn't realised her eyes had taken in so much.

As if she had just stepped from the water, her skin tingles. Her epidermis amplifies and absorbs sensation: air currents swaying the fine hairs of her arm, the coarse weave of her dress, curls moist with sweat at the nape of her neck.

Shocked, Billie opens her eyes to blink, but the picture of Lorelei in her underwear is etched on her retina, an afterimage, like when she's stared at the sun too long. Everywhere she looks, she sees Lorelei's burnt body.

To escape the vision, she scurries from her studio to the kitchen. Troy stands beside the stove, stirring a bubbling pan. It smells peculiar, medicinal, and Billie peers to examine it. In the saucepan, leaves and flowers float in a white brew. She focuses her eyes on Troy to distract her from Lorelei's pink and white limbs.

'For the party tonight, at Nadine's place up river,' Troy says. 'Went down a treat last year.'

He pours the bubbling liquid through a strainer into a flask, scraping the mesh with a spoon to extract the juices. 'But forgot to sieve it last time,' he says. 'Half the party wandered around like zombies, with leaves coming out of their mouths. Not a good look.'

'You coming down to the beach first?' Billie asks.

'For a bit. Might stay for the kids' fireworks. Then I'm meeting Jason on the mainland.'

As the celebrations draw near, Troy calls Eli into the lounge and re-plaits her hair, weaving red and silver beads though the strands. He binds his dreadlocks into a white crown on top of his head, standing warrior-like in loose black pants and no shirt. At the hallway mirror together, he and Eli smear glitter-paint over their cheekbones, trail it through their hair and over their shoulders, until they both sparkle.

While they complete their preparations, Billie wanders through the house looking for Lorelei. The bedroom is empty, with no sign of her on the verandah. Running water draws Billie to the bathroom. She approaches the door, hearing zips and the clatter of a buckle on the floor. Hand to the door knob, she is about to knock, to call and see if Lorelei is all right, but the vision returns, of Lorelei in her knickers. It stays her hand. Instead of knocking, and horrified by her own actions, she bends until her eye reaches the keyhole. Peering through the tiny opening, she glimpses a lean, pink thigh, a flash of bone-white buttock. The world shrinks to contain only this view. Her heart beats fast, and there is a tension between her thighs, a warmth. She is holding her breath.

The cough surprises her. It is quiet, but close. She feels faint, as if all the blood in her body has rushed to her feet. Standing, rigid, she turns around.

Stan. Raised eyebrows and a little smile.

'What are you doing?' he asks.

Where are Billie's words? Why won't her tongue work?

'I . . . I just wanted to check . . . that she was all right . . .' she stammers.

Stan shakes his head. 'No,' he says softly. 'Don't play the concerned relative with me. I've seen how you look at her.

And it's not how an aunt looks at her niece. Jesus, Billie. You're disgusting.'

He shakes his head, then walks away.

Billie's stiff posture collapses. She leans against the wall and slides to the floor. Covers her mouth with her hands. Frozen, she replays the last few minutes in her mind. With each repetition her flush grows hotter. She is ready to curl into a ball and sink through the floorboards when she hears the water squeal in the plughole and a splash. Lorelei is getting out.

Standing, using the wall for support, Billie scuttles to her studio. She grabs her workbook and begins to sketch. The detritus on her desk. The view from the window. Her hand holding a joint. Another joint. Anything, as long as it cools her cheeks and distances her from the memory of Stan's broad smirk as he turned away.

A knock on her door. 'It's time, Billie,' Troy says. 'We're heading down to the beach. You coming?'

'Just a sec.'

I can't do it, Billie thinks. I can't face him. But she has to. To refuse the invitation would raise more questions. She sucks her joint until her cheeks hollow, then stubs it out. Resolved, she stands, grabbing her sketchbook for moral support.

As the sun slides towards the west, Billie follows the household down the hill. Everything is normal, she tells herself. Normal. Burdened by an esky of ice and wine, Troy chats to Eli, who brandishes a breadstick like a sword. Stan and Lorelei walk together, carrying bags of dips and fruit. Billie struggles to catch their words, but they talk too quietly. Please don't tell her, she thinks, squirming.

At the shore, islanders mimic the curve of the river in a line of self-contained groups, connected by laughter and loud words and the regular hiss and spit of opened beer cans. Children tear between the groups, engrossed in a game of tag. Mark, arm still encased in plaster, directs their activity.

'You're it!' he yells, touching another boy's shoulder with his good arm.

Troy's bare feet reach the sand first. He chooses a spot above the high-tide line and the others follow, fanning the blankets in a rough circle. One by one they sit, graceful as a ring of collapsing dominoes. Only Eli stands.

Lorelei pats the blanket beside her. 'Sit down, Eli. By Mamma.'

The girl shakes her plaited head. She fingers the temporary tattoo on her upper arm, a pair of lips pursed for a kiss. She'd found it in a Christmas cracker, Billie remembers, asked Troy to put it on.

'Stop treating me like a kid.'

Opening her sketchbook, Billie transfers the girl's sullen lips to the page with a 2B pencil, while Troy opens the first bottle of wine.

'I'm going to play,' Eli says. Her mother shakes her head, but the child scurries away before Lorelei can grab her ankle.

'She'll be okay,' Billie says. 'We can keep an eye out from here.'

She watches Eli join the game. Normally the children would build a bonfire before the fireworks, a great pyre of driftwood and kindling to light as the sun fades, but Billie heard on the radio that today is another fire-ban day. She's surprised the fireworks haven't been called off, imagining how easily the island would ignite if a rocket strayed into the crisp undergrowth.

On the blankets in front of her, Stan and Lorelei talk in low voices, their faces close. Stan fiddles with his hair. In a new silk shirt, he looks younger again tonight, handsome, with cigarette and side-swept hair. Lorelei skols the dregs in her wineglass and licks her lips, holding the glass out to Stan to refill. The wine has coloured her cheeks and loosened her limbs, and she laughs at one of Stan's comments. Their glasses touch.

On the edge of their conversation, Billie feels small, insignificant. She turns to Troy instead, sketches his profile as he tells her his ideas for the future. One day when his course is finished, he says, he's going to open a restaurant on the river with Jason.

'We're developing our business plan,' he says, tracing spirals in the sand with his fingers. 'Working on the details.'

The day pales, and more wine bottles empty. Flushed, Lorelei lies on the blanket next to Stan, head propped on one arm. They share a cigarette. Lorelei fingers the straps of her top. The points of her nipples are visible under the cloth. Billie bites her lips and looks away.

By eight-thirty, the river is dark. Conversations carry from yachts moored in the channel, with premature renditions of 'Auld Lang Syne'. The first fireworks display of the night comes at nine, bright explosions from a barge in the river. The crowd cheers and applauds each fiery bloom. When the fireworks end, leaving trails of sulphurous smoke, Troy stands, brushing the sand from his trousers.

'Happy New Year,' he says, bending to kiss Billie's cheek. 'You don't mind if I head off to pick up Jason?'

'Not at all. Have fun.'

Troy winks. 'Always.'

As the families collect their children and leave the beach, Eli creeps across the sand to sit next to Billie.

'You missed the fireworks,' Billie says. 'Where have you been?'

'With Mark,' Eli whispers. 'He gave me this.'

She opens her hand. Nestled in her palm is a shard of green glass, sharp edges smoothed by water. She holds the glass up and it glimmers, an emerald.

'Treasure,' she says.

At the child's voice, Lorelei turns her head. 'Bedtime, little one,' she says, adjusting the straps of her top. She and Stan gather blankets and bags, draping them over their arms while Billie collects the empty bottles.

Up at the house, Stan and Billie wait in the kitchen while Lorelei tucks in the child. Stan doesn't speak, but Billie knows what he is thinking. How can he not? She is mortified by her behaviour, by the thought he may have told Lorelei. How can I explain it? No answer comes.

When Lorelei returns, the three move to the verandah and uncork another bottle. Billie holds out her glass, even though she has had too many already. Her head spins from the joints she smoked earlier. It spins harder when she watches Lorelei and Stan, engrossed in conversation. She slurps her wine quickly, sees the others match her pace. After another glass, she stares at the Milky Way overhead to distract her from Stan and Lorelei, flirting like teenagers.

Before midnight, no longer able to bear it, Billie stands. 'I'm turning in,' she says, too loudly, over the top of the others' words. They stop talking.

'Okay,' Lorelei says, after a pause. 'Happy New Year. See you in the morning?'

Billie nods, unable to speak. Her anger simmers. The conversation continues as she walks away, trying not to stumble as the wine upsets her balance. Fuming, she listens to them laugh. On the outer again, she thinks.

In her studio she reaches for the small plastic bag in her drawer and rolls a joint. I do this every time, she thinks, to get me through, even as I tell myself I won't. She feels weak, surrendering to the craving, but she will not refuse.

By the time the crackling fireworks and the horns blaring from the river announce the new year, Billie has reduced two joints to ash and damp paper roaches. The mull tames her anger, transforms it to listlessness. She lies on her bed, spread-eagled under a spinning ceiling, watching the shapes in the shadows thrown by the candle on her dresser and the fluttering leaves on her ceiling.

Closing her eyes, the green tinge behind her lids reminds her of the Hawkesbury on a sunny day. She remembers plunging her feet into the river, ankles tickled by foam. The skin of her calves crawls, as it did when the water evaporated to a salty crust. Slow tickles tease the downy hairs of her knees and stroke upwards to her thighs. Languid, breathing slow, her ribs rise and fall, as if her bed is the river and she a moored runabout, bobbing in the water. Her heart pumps pleasure from the extremities of her limbs to her core; exquisite waves break over her body. Moist between her legs, she throbs with her pulse. How long since she felt this anticipation?

After Elissa's death she had bound these stirrings, tight as the laced boots she wore as a child in England. Yes, she shared her body with London men and, later, with Kings Cross lovers fumbling at her bra-strap, but none made her flop to the pillow as they did, faces slack with release. There had been glimpses, while she was caught in morphine's drift and once, long ago, on fragrant nights far from British shores, but something held her back. What am I afraid of? Too stoned now to cling to the shore, she thinks. Loosen the moorings. Tonight I am adrift. She slides her hand under her skirt. Let the river take me. Let fluid wash my dusty spaces.

A quiet click close by sends her hand scuttling back to the sheet. She straightens her skirt and opens her eyes, vision adjusting slowly to the shift. In the open doorway, Lorelei stands on the threshold of the studio.

'Stan's passed out,' she says. 'Can I sleep in your bed tonight?'

Bella

Campania 1954

She wasn't sick on the boat, but she came close enough to hunch over the railing, ready to eject a stream of bile into the swell. She found a flight of steps below deck and crouched there, trying to ignore the rolling sea, until the boat docked at the island port. On the rattling bus from the port, her gut lurched with her luggage. She was glad to stumble out of the bus and walk the slow curve down into the fishing village of San Michele. Scuffing the dusty path with her sandals, the earth shifted as the boat had done.

The land beside the path was divided into uneven parcels. Supported by banks of round stones, every terrace was cramped with useful plants. Olive trees grew next to chilli pods wrinkling on the bush. Tomatoes and oregano skirted orchards of orange and lemon trees. There were spindly grapevines wherever she looked, with lettuce and cauliflower sprouting in the rows between them, and spikes of rosemary and lavender.

When her legs buckled, still wobbly from the sea passage, she sat on a low wall of pale grey tuff, absorbing the stone's warmth through her thighs. Dry grass and succulents grew from cracks in the rock to cascade over the edge. Below, waves foamed over a shelf of rock. The water was bright blue, almost glacial and, even though the spring sun shone, she shivered. Standing, she let gravity pull her down to the rocky promontory.

I never said goodbye, she thought, remembering how she'd struggled against the man with orange hair. You never let me. Her guts churned. I am struggling still. She walked on, eyes on the white-washed walls and cobbled streets below. Bells clanged on the hillside above, and a line of villagers hurried up the steps to the church. Breathing deeply, she gripped her bag, then entered the village. An old couple put their heads close to whisper as she passed. One of them pointed, and she touched her hair self-consciously. Damn. She'd forgotten to dye it, and she knew the forelock must be glowing in the sun. Not even a scarf to cover it. To begin her search in secret she had booked into the hotel under a new name: Bella, her papa's pet name for her. So much for my disguise, she thought. But she decided to keep the name anyway, having grown attached to it while preparing for the visit. In the *albergo* in Santa Lucia, the day before the ferry sailed to the island, she'd played at introducing herself in the mirror. Each time she said the new name, she heard an echo in her head, spoken in her father's voice.

Scuttling across the piazza to the hotel with the peeling façade, she looked ahead. The corners of her eyes noted the stone wharf and the fishing boats at their moorings. Nets heaped on the wharf, and cats curled among the floats. She recognised the striped awning of the waterfront *alimentari*, but the fabric was sun-bleached, paler than she remembered. Turning too far left, she saw the path across to the rocky outcrop and windows cut into the stone. She turned her head, fighting the urge to lie down on the flagstones and gag.

The hotel's name didn't sound familiar when Bella made her booking, but her instincts had brought her straight to it. It hadn't changed at all. She tugged the frayed rope beside the door and heard a faint bell inside. A lined face peered around the door. You were taller, she thought, smiling. Nearly twenty years and run by the same man. She collected her key and climbed the stairs to her room.

In front of Bella's door was a wooden crate covered with cloth. Lifting one corner, she saw lemons and mandarins and a grapefruit almost as big as her head. She found a jar of citrus marmalade, thick with peel, and the tight buds of an orange blossom nestled among glossy green leaves. A bottle of island *rosso*.

'Thank you,' she said to the empty corridor.

Inside, unpacking her bag, she laid her clothes in drawers that smelt of camphor. The room faced south, overlooking the sea and the narrow strip of grey sand leading to the rocky outcrop, but she avoided the doors opening onto the balcony. Pouring water from the ceramic jug into a wide blue bowl, she scrubbed dust from the crevices of her face. She dug her thumb into a mandarin and peeled back the skin, sucking the juice from each tart segment. She sighed. It was impossible to ignore the jagged outline of the promontory; it invaded the view no matter where she stood.

Opening the wine, she walked out to the balcony, sitting on a wicker chair to look across the water. She'd thought that she would want to kick and fight, like the screaming child she remembered, but instead she felt calm. Quiet. Knees to her chest, she stared. Pale green bushes, tinted with yellow, grew on the eastern flank of the rock. She remembered the tiny flowers. *Ginestre*, she thought. In the fading afternoon light the rock was light brown with chocolate-coloured shadows. In her memory it was grey.

The sun turned orange and sank towards the west. Fishermen untangled their nets and prepared the lamps for a night out at sea. Villagers gathered at the bar and strolled in pairs across to the outcrop. She couldn't hear their words, but she watched their expressive hands, punctuated by bursts of laughter.

The sea washed against the foundations of the hotel. It reminded Bella of a heartbeat, with a pause between the crash of one wave and the surge of the next. Sometimes they hit with a solid thunk, shaking the foundations and splashing high. So much activity and power, yet soothing. Not like the city she had left. She breathed in time with the waves, filling her lungs then holding her breath and waiting for the next crash to exhale. The pattern was natural, as if her body had always moved to this rhythm.

It was almost dark. A gibbous moon rose in the east, partially obscured by cloud. Seagulls flocked to the rocks to find a place to roost for the night. A fishing boat motored out to sea, lanterns lit. She looked again at the outcrop. Its colour shifted with the changing light. Now the rock seemed green, split with black shadows. The sun vanished. The rock and its shadows merged, revealing no depth, only an ink-coloured silhouette.

As Bella stared, a light appeared on the outcrop. She jumped. It wasn't on the rock—it was inside. She could clearly see the shape of a window. Someone was living there. It's them, she thought, they're home! She wanted to scramble up the stone steps and through the gate, plucking an orange from the tree in the big terracotta pot. She wanted to knock on the door and hold out her arms for her father to pick her up and hoist her to his shoulders. She wanted to be inside, down by the fire in the snug rooms she knew so well. She wanted to fall asleep in front of the flames, listening to her parents talk. But she stayed put. It wasn't them, she knew it in her heart.

Looking at the glowing square, she felt a keen ache, deep between her breasts, but sitting on the balcony staring wouldn't help. She wrinkled her nose. Smoke. Kitchen fires were being stoked in the village. She imagined pasta and bread, soup thick with vegetables, and her stomach growled in response. Apart from the mandarin, she hadn't eaten since breakfast. She left her room and walked barefoot downstairs, following the smell of wood smoke. I am always hungry, she thought.

The dining room was empty, and dark but for a bank of candles flickering by the open window. Leaning against the doorframe, she watched a woman lay knives and forks next to white plates, ready for tomorrow's breakfast. The woman polished each set with her apron and aligned the silver carefully before laying it down. Bella watched in silence, but something made the woman turn. She smiled.

'I'm sorry,' Bella said, in English. 'I didn't mean to disturb you. I thought the kitchen was open late.'

'My kitchen never closes,' the woman said. 'Sit. I'll see what I can find.'

The woman returned with a tray. On the white cloth she placed slices of toasted bread, bowls of salt and squid and olives and sun-dried tomato, a peeled garlic clove, a jar of oil and a bottle of white wine.

'For you,' the woman said. She scattered fresh basil leaves over the table and poured two glasses of wine.

'They call this one *Làcrima Christi*. The tear of Christ. It comes from the mainland near Napoli. They say when Lucifer was banished he snatched a piece of Paradise and flew to live among our volcanos. Even this heaven on earth he corrupted with sinful desires, and Christ was heartbroken by the change. His tear fell to the ground and, by some miracle, a vine grew.'

Bella smiled. 'What if I don't believe in God?'

The woman shrugged. 'Neither me. But the story makes me shiver, just the same. My name is Didóne. Allow me.'

Didóne reached for two slices of bread. Against the white cloth, her tanned arms glowed.

'This is an important process,' she said. 'Watch.'

She scraped the garlic over the surface of the bread, leaving trails of white flesh. A sprinkle of salt. Oil. A layer of basil.

'I saw you arrive,' she said. 'You haven't been out of your room all afternoon, not even to the thermal baths. That's the first thing people do.'

'No,' Bella said. 'I just sat on my balcony.'

She looked across the table at the other woman. 'I found a box of oranges by my door. Do you know who . . .'

Didóne nodded. 'The owner. A lovely man. Always welcomes his guests that way. Would do anything for you. Not like the manager.' She sighed. 'Stay away from him.'

The squid lay on the bread, green olives tucked between its tentacles. Didóne slid the plate across the table. 'Eat.'

Bella lifted the *bruschetta* to her lips and bit down. It was crisp and chewy, fishy, sweet and salty. Oil dribbled over her fingers and down her arm. She swallowed the first mouthful quickly, her stomach demanding the next one. Both *bruschette* were soon devoured, then she swirled a slice of plain toast around the plate to mop the spills.

Didóne passed her a napkin. 'A woman of appetite,' she said, smiling. 'What I like to see.'

It only occurred to Bella later that night, as she curled under crisp white sheets listening to the waves below, that Didóne had spoken to her in Italian and she had replied in the same language. She had been in the village one day, and she'd switched from English to Italian with no awareness of the transition.

The next night Bella waited until the other travellers had left before entering the dining room. She ate with Didóne again, and together they set the tables for the next day. It soon became a habit.

One warm night the pair sat out on the hotel balcony sipping Christ's tears. The lights of the Italian coast were hidden by the eastern tip of the island, and the balcony looked out onto darkness.

'It's easy to imagine this is the end of the world,' Didóne said.

Bella nodded.

That night Didóne told Bella stories of the village and the island and of the volcanos that ringed the mainland. The burning fields, she called them. Bella didn't know if the stories were history or myth, but she let Didóne's deep voice wash over her. Didóne savoured her words as a child savours ripe purple grapes. She told Bella about a nearby convent where the nuns were placed on stone seats and left to rot when they died. She spoke of the Greeks who settled seven hundred years before Christ was born, and the ancient sibyl who hid on the island after prophesying the divine birth.

Another evening, Bella listened as Didóne described the time that the archangel Michele visited the island and graced the village with his name. Didóne told the story as if she was there, on the beach, watching the manifestation of the bright angel.

'I know that story,' Bella said. 'I've known it all my life.'

While Didóne talked, Bella shut her eyes. Behind closed eyelids the stories merged with her dreams. She woke slowly, hearing the woman's voice before she opened her eyes, amazed to find Didóne awake and still talking. Didóne talked so long that the pair waved at the fishing trawlers returning from the sea with their catch glittering in pure morning light.

Bella reached for Didóne's arm. 'There's one story in particular I want to hear.'

'Thought so. No one listens that long without a reason.'

'Tell me about Afrodite.'

Didóne leant back in her chair. 'It's a long story. She was the goddess of love, born from the surf that foams around Kythera, and it is said she bathed in the thermal waters here.'

Bella shook her head. 'No. There was a woman in this village called Afrodite. A real woman.'

'Never heard tell of her.'

'You would've been a child. Before the war. She married a mason called Cristofano.'

'No idea,' Didóne said. 'Leave it with me, though. There's an old woman who helps me in the kitchen. She might remember something.'

Didóne stood. She walked behind Bella and lifted her black locks. Her lips tickled Bella's neck.

'You can't evoke my favourite goddess without consequences,' she whispered. 'Come.'

Bella followed the woman to a room smelling of jasmine and orange blossom. She let Didóne undress her, surprised by the waves of gentle pleasure that pulsed through her body as each garment fell. Naked, she tingled from her fingertips to the moist warmth between her legs. The moisture surprised Bella, too. She'd been dry for so long, dusty as a pile of dead leaves.

The hotel manager didn't bother to knock.

'It's eight o'clock,' he said. 'I've got ten angry Germans and a Frenchman swearing because you haven't prepared breakfast.'

He tugged off the sheet and whistled. 'Tasty.'

Bella nuzzled into Didóne's shoulder. Sleepy and warm, she trailed her fingers across the woman's belly and felt her shiver.

'Unbelievable,' the manager said. He slapped Didóne's exposed thigh hard, leaving a red weal. 'I won't warn you again, slut. Now, get up.'

In the dining room, still sleepy, Bella watched Didóne serve breakfast. The woman concentrated on her work, giving huge portions to the guests. Occasionally she looked up and caught Bella staring. Didóne licked her lips slowly, then returned to her platters with a smile.

When the guests were finished and their plates washed and stacked in the kitchen, Didóne took Bella to the market. The fishermen's catches glistened, submerged in bowls filled with water and chunks of lemon. Bella dipped her hand into one bowl, exploring silver sardines and ribbed clam shells with her fingertips. Even after her skin dried, it retained the scent of fish oil and citrus. Didóne haggled for a flounder and a large crayfish. She grinned when one fisherman showed her eight dead rabbits his daughter had trapped in the terraces above the village.

'Excellent!' she said. 'Tonight we'll have stew.' She moved closer to whisper in Bella's ear. 'People watch you.'

Nodding, Bella looked around. At every stall, someone stared. As she walked past, old men bowed their heads and hid their eyes, and old women turned away. She didn't know where to look, or whether she should acknowledge the attention or ignore it.

'I dream about this place,' Bella said quietly. 'I tried to sketch it, but I could never get it right.' She pointed. 'When I walk round that corner and know how the cobbles will curve up the hill, or know that the water from the springs will taste like blood before I sip, it's like I have walked into that dream.'

When Didóne returned to the kitchen, Bella took her sketchbook to the beach, following the line of seaweed, sponge and worn shells left by the tide. She explored the wharf, then turned to her back on the sea to face the mountain. She drew the jagged peak wreathed in cloud. East wind brings the clouds, she thought. The mountain seemed smaller now, less daunting.

Steeling herself, she tucked her sketchbook under her arm and walked across the narrow path to the outcrop. She climbed the stairs carved into the rock, noticing for the first time that each stair was worn into a smooth semi-circle. How many have come this way before me? She walked up to the gate and peered over. The house in the rock wasn't as she remembered at all. The fruit trees were gone. The terracotta-tiled porch had been replaced by a solid wooden framework woven with vines. Under the vines, a woman combed a young girl's hair, singing as she untangled the knots.

At the gate, Bella stood and watched the woman and the child until she heard a man's voice calling from inside. She jumped, then scurried further around the rocks. Silly to run, she thought, but she didn't want to be caught peering over the wall. Hidden by a shelf of splintered rock, she sat, waiting for her heart's pace to return to normal.

The rock here sloped steeply, plunging vertical to the sea. She was amazed she hadn't fallen into the water as a child. Little mountain goat, she thought. It would have been the end of me. As a child, she had splashed in the sea, wet up to her waist, but had never learnt to swim. While the family had scrubbed their bodies and their clothes in the salty water, she couldn't remember ever having seen her mother or father swimming. She wondered if other villagers had learnt the secret of buoyancy, or if they would sink like stones, as she would. The fishermen chose not to learn, she knew, to ensure a quick death if they fell over the side. Imagining brine filling her lungs, she grimaced, chest suddenly tight. Not that quick.

There were stripes of black pebbles in the pale stone, and she traced the flow pattern of the lava with her fingers. The lines twisted where seismic movements had buckled the rock. She felt the movement, as if the lava was still fluid. Any minute, she thought. A tremor, a rumble from below the surface, and the cliff could slide. It would take the little house with it, the village, too.

She continued to stroke the rock, abrasive as the pumice stone she used to grind yellow rinds from her feet. The surface was slippery with loose scree, waiting for the next rain to wash it away. As a child she didn't believe her father when he told her water could erode stone. It made no sense. But now she saw the narrow valleys where the flow of rain had worn channels, sluicing the scree into the water and taking a layer of stone with it. She ran her fingers along the channels, soothed by the friction.

The sunlight faded to twilight. She had come to the peninsula with fingers itching to sketch but, once there, they had resisted the task. They were hungry to learn the contours of the rock directly, not mediated through her eyes.

She walked slowly back to the hotel, creeping into the kitchen before dinner, to peel cloves of garlic while Didóne prepared the rabbit. An old woman sat with them at the table, pulling strings from runner beans with her head turned to the window. Her hands moved quickly, knowing their task well enough to work without vision. Bella tried to catch the woman's gaze, but the woman would not face her. Bella continued to stare.

'What?' the woman asked suddenly. Her hands maintained their quick rhythm. 'Have you nothing better to do?'

Blushing, Bella said nothing.

'It's okay, Luisa,' Didóne said. 'She just wants to ask you something. Go on,' she said, when Bella shook her head. 'Ask.'

Bella paused before speaking. She had waited so long to ask these questions, but now that the moment had arrived, she was unable to voice them. Perhaps it would be better not to know. The questions waited behind her teeth until she forced her lips open.

'Do you remember a woman called Afrodite? She used to live here. And Cristofano. Cristofano Salvatore, her husband.'

The old woman shook her head, the movement of her hands unaffected. 'My memory isn't what it was. Now let me be. I've got work to do.'

'Don't fib,' Didóne said. 'Yesterday you told me you knew a story about every person who's lived in this village from the time you were five years old.'

Her voice was gentle, wheedling.

'Some stories are best never told,' Luisa said, quietly.

Kneeling before the old woman, Bella stopped the quick hands and placed them on her cheeks, holding them there even though they struggled.

'I remember you,' she whispered. 'You are the fisherman's wife. You fed me. I stayed at your house. You had dogs.'

Luisa's saggy throat contracted as she swallowed, but she did not speak. Frustrated, Bella let the hands go and turned to leave the kitchen, but the old woman grabbed her skirt.

'If you're here for revenge,' she said quietly, 'there's no point. The Prefect and his mates waved their Fascist flags and got caught when Napoli was liberated. Serves them right. They're old men now, frail or senile.'

She sighed. 'After the war it was a mess. Everyone tried to forget . . . We never talked about it. No one does.'

Bella shook her head. 'I just want to know what happened. Did they come back? Did you ever hear from them?'

The old woman's eye sockets quivered and filled, then spilt over onto her papery cheeks. Bella dug her fingernails into her palms, concentrating on the pain so her own eyes wouldn't betray her. Turning away from Luisa's tears, she watched Didóne, busy in another part of the kitchen, soothed by the woman's smooth, economical movements as she quartered tomatoes for the stew.

'Even now,' Luisa said, wiping her eyes. She sniffed. 'No, they never came back. A guy from the mainland said something about an internment camp up north, but I don't know for sure.'

Bella wanted details. If they were alive, she wanted an address. If not, she wanted to know where they were buried, so she could trace their names on the headstone and plant a hardy shrub of rosemary or lavender.

'I used to make up stories about them,' she said, 'but that's all they were. Stories. I need to know. Tell me what you remember.'

Luisa bit her lip. She closed her eyes and kept them closed for five full minutes. Bella thought the woman had fallen asleep, but then she spoke.

'Your mother couldn't speak a word of Italian when she arrived, and we spoke no Greek. We didn't know what to make of her. She wasn't like the others who came for the thermal waters.'

The woman's words seeped out like wine from a cracked barrel.

'Your mother was a mystery. She hopped off that mule as a visitor, but chose to stay. She was the first stranger to settle in twenty years.'

Luisa smiled. 'She used to cook in the ashes of the fire. Bread and fish and tomatoes, all in little pans, with the lid on and ashes heaped over them. I tried to tell her there were other ways, that she could cook in the hot sands around the headland, but she was stubborn. Said her mother had taught her and that one day she would teach her child.'

'And my father?' Bella asked.

She listened as Luisa described Cristofano watching Afrodite at the bar where she worked, how he had taken his books there during lunch to be near the woman.

'He was like a shy boy,' Luisa said. 'I don't think he'd even talked to a woman before. Always had his head stuck in books about science and mythology.'

Bella heard how the gentle mason courted the Greek girl. She heard about his elaborate preparations for the marriage, smiling at how Cristofano's laughter had infected the village that day.

'We didn't see much of your mother after they married,' Luisa said. 'He carried her across the isthmus and that was that. She rarely came into the village. Cristofano bought fish in the mornings and fresh meat from the farmers.'

'And the other,' Bella whispered. 'My real father. The Englishman. What happened before he came for me?'

'Leave it. There's nothing that can be done now.'

'Tell me.'

Luisa's sigh came from deep in her chest. 'Just like your mother. Have your story, then. It's given me heartburn for years.'

She leant back in her chair and rubbed the hollow between her sagging breasts. 'The Englishman came for the winter and stayed until April. It wasn't unusual. What was unusual was that he caught Afrodite's eye. Must've been that red hair. You could spot him a mile off. She'd been here for a year and had most of the men in the village after her. She had smiles for everyone, but gave herself to none. Except him.

'He was a young man, barely twenty, and we were surprised to see him here alone. His family couldn't afford a chaperone, he said, there was just enough to send him out here. He was frail in the beginning, looked like a ghost when he slid off the donkey, but he grew stronger. He spent his days in the thermal baths, then came to the bar in the evenings. That's where they met.

'You could see why she liked him. Even sickly, before the waters did their work, he was a beacon. His enthusiasm drew you in. He asked about everything, even at the beginning, with his schoolboy Italian. And his accent! Diabolical! But he persisted. At the bar, absorbing the chatter and jokes, he'd laugh ten seconds after everyone else, slowly translating punch lines in his head. One morning he bought a squid from my husband without a clue how to prepare it. I cooked it up at my place to show him and, between mouthfuls, he quizzed my husband about the island's tides. Our daily routines were revelations to him. He said this was his first time away from England and he was drunk on new air.

'When the Englishman left, we all felt her pain. But we laughed. "Slut," we said to ourselves. "Serves her right." We were jealous of our husbands' desires for her, and our husbands were jealous of the Englishman's success.

'Cristofano watched Afrodite and the Englishman. He had watched her since she arrived, even taught himself Greek from a dictionary so he could speak to her in her own language, but he was rarely brave enough to actually talk.'

Luisa looked at Bella. 'After the Englishman left, Cristofano trailed behind Afrodite. Wherever she was, he wasn't far away, leaving small stone carvings at the bar for her. We called them the lost soul and her shadow. She ignored him for months, but eventually, after her belly started to show, I saw them talking. Not long after, they married and went to live in the house in the rock.'

The old woman reached for Bella's hand. Her skin felt dry. 'His grandfather was the first to hollow out the tuff. Cristofano would have wanted you to live there,' she said. 'It's been empty for years. A family from Napoli moved in only recently. Wouldn't stand a chance if you took it to the courts.'

Shaking her head, Bella knew she would never be able to live there. On the journey to the island, she had thought she was going home, thought she would slip back in where she'd left. But the hole left by the little girl was too small for her grown body, and she knew she could not stay. My gift, she thought, remembering the woman brushing the girl's hair.

'What happened?' Bella said out loud. 'I remember them being taken. I remember a fire. Why?'

Luisa shook her head. 'I can't,' she said, quietly. 'Ask someone else.'

Bella grabbed the old woman's shoulders. 'Everyone looks away,' she said. 'I need to know. Don't you understand?'

She stared at the woman, close enough to see the beginning of a milky cataract forming over one eye and the twitch in her left eyelid. Luisa returned the stare, blinked, then nodded.

'Have it your way,' she said. 'We don't know for sure, but someone heard he got up the nose of the boss in Napoli. He was like a child sometimes, never knowing when to shut his mouth. Someone, I don't know who, told the authorities that he was speaking against *Il Duce*. The Blackshirts came. They took them both away.'

Luisa sighed. 'I wrote letters,' she said, 'after the war. The replies came back quickly but with no information. "Regrettably, we have no records to answer your inquiry." They suggested I try different places, but I found nothing. I'm sorry.'

Luisa talked through dinner. She talked until Didóne had washed all the plates and stacked them on the shelves. When Didóne blew out the candles, Bella blinked. She hadn't been in the kitchen at all. She had been staring at the shrinking faces of her parents as the boat took them from the island.

'More,' Bella demanded, but the old woman shook her head. 'Tomorrow.'

Bella carried Luisa's stories with her. That night she pulled away from Didóne's embrace, returning to her own bed to be alone with the words. She dreamt of men with shiny black boots and woke with a rapid heartbeat.

The next day, Luisa passed her a bundle of letters, bound with a faded blue ribbon. Unable to read them in the kitchen with the other women, Bella returned to her room, sitting on the bed to untie the ribbon and lay the pages on her bedspread. The letters were typed on crinkled paper so fine she could see her hand through it, with official crests at the top of each page. They were from internment camps in the north, all denying knowledge of her parents. She stroked the pages. Where are you? Where can you be?

'How did Isaac know to come for me?' she asked, the next morning in the kitchen. Today Luisa was scaling fish, scraping a metal tool over the silver bodies until the air around her shimmered with translucent flakes. She slid the fish into a bucket of water for Bella to gut.

'I tracked him down,' Luisa said. 'Through the *pensione* he stayed in. They had a record of his home address. I thought it would be best for you. When I wrote to tell him what had happened, he borrowed money against his share in the bakery to return to the island. Until then he didn't know you existed. I should have thought of it sooner. Your mother could have told him about you herself. It might have been easier for her if she had written to him.'

Pausing, Luisa wiped her forehead with her arm. 'She was in a terrible state when he left. They were only together for a few months, but she never got over it. She had no one here, no family to run to. She said she could never go home, but she never told me why. I tried to make it better, but it wasn't the same. I never felt like I really got through to her.'

I know, Bella thought, struck suddenly by a memory of her mother. She remembered standing beside Afrodite in the house in the stone, with a picture drawn in the workshop by the church.

'Look, Mamma,' she had said, tugging on her mother's skirt. 'Look what I made.'

But her mother didn't respond. She stared out the open door of the house, over the rocks to the horizon. The child tugged and tugged, until Afrodite looked down, frowning slightly, as if surprised by the child at her feet. The expression was familiar; Afrodite never seemed fully present, always looking beyond the village at something the child couldn't see.

'I told Isaac I'd write again,' Luisa said, 'as soon as they came back. But they never did.'

Luisa's first letter, the one calling him back to Italy, Bella imagined Isaac reading in his study, the room Piètro had described as they left Harrowstone. Book-lined with accounts of other places, and a map of journeys untaken. You never wanted to be a baker, she realised. You wanted to explore. In her mind she saw him clearly, natty in a white suit among Delphic or Trojan ruins, another excited young man on a grand tour. Yet you hocked yourself to the teeth to fetch me, and you became tied to the business you never wanted. With the war and Elissa's death, Isaac's dreams had shrivelled like cut blooms. She recalled the times he had held his pale hand out to her and she had let it hang. She remembered his sad eyes. I'll write to him soon, she thought. Ask him to tell me how he met my mother. About the places he'd one day like to see.

Luisa's stories changed the village. Wherever Bella looked, she saw her family. She saw Afrodite brewing coffee. She heard the mutterings of the village women, afraid the pretty stranger would tempt their husbands from their homes. Isaac stood by the counter and Cristofano scowled from a table. For the first time, Isaac appeared as Afrodite might have seen him: excitement as bright as his hair. You're more like Elissa than I recognised, she thought. She watched the couple walk slowly up the hill to the terraces behind the village, pausing as Isaac wheezed. Then, Afrodite at the end of the wharf, cooling her bare feet in the water and watching the horizon. Afrodite and Cristofano outside the church, a flutter of camellia petals in the air. Cristofano grinned, his hand on Afrodite's distended belly. She heard the taunts as Cristofano carried his pregnant bride across the path to the house in the rocks.

The visions felt like Bella's own memories. But they couldn't be. In most, she hadn't been conceived. In others, she would have been a pea lodged in her mother's womb. These were false memories, spawned by Luisa's stories, but it didn't matter.

The visions brought others. Cristofano's callused hands, rough as the stone he worked with. The undertow at her ankles as Cristofano walked her along the water's edge. Sharp, sweet basil in her mother's hand. Is that how it happened? She didn't know. I've made up so many stories about my life, she thought, that it is impossible to tell. Real or not, she thought, they're mine.

The visions overwhelmed her. The village existed in three times at once: before her birth, when she was a child and now. She covered her eyes with her hands. It was too much. Run. Go somewhere you have never been before.

She filled a basket with bread, dates and a salty paste made from ground olives. Wrapping a bottle of red wine in a cloth, she tucked it in the basket with her sketchbook, then followed the headland to a great cleft in the rock. Here the stone rose in tall pinnacles, stained with violet stripes. Water trickled in the ravine, but she couldn't see the source. The bottom of the cleft was hidden by grass and spiky aloe vera. She scrambled up a steep path until she reached terraced fields overlooking the sea, panting with mouth open like a dog.

With the mountain behind her and the slow curve of the beach below, Bella stretched out and began scribbling Luisa's stories into her sketchbook. She interspersed the words with quick drawings. Perhaps if she stored them on paper, they wouldn't crowd her head.

Below, the village of San Michele performed its afternoon rituals in silence. A balding donkey pulled its load up the cobbled path. Children danced at the end of the wharf, waiting for the fishing boats to leave. Bella watched a sailing boat skirt the peninsula. She scribbled until the light faded, then clambered slowly down from the hill, muscles stiff and aching from the climb.

Her feet led her up the steps to Luisa's door. The old woman welcomed her with a nod, then poured a coffee, black and laced with grappa. Bella winced, but drank the coffee in one quick swig. After groping in her pocket, Luisa slid something shiny across the table.

'You left it behind,' she said. 'I found it under your mattress.'

It was a small silver coin on a loop of leather. There were patterns on the surface, but Bella couldn't see what they were. She picked up the coin and peered close. On one side it looked like a tripod. The other had a woman's face in profile, with an elaborate coiled hairstyle. Instinctively, Bella rubbed the coin between her fingertips, and the movement triggered a memory. Her father had unearthed the coin at the ruined city. He had shown it to her on the boat home.

'I found it on the dig,' he'd said. 'Don't tell anyone.'

On the island, he had made the coin into a necklace for her. Stretching out the thongs, Bella lifted the coin to her neck, but the ends were too short to tie. Or my neck is too big, she thought. She wrapped the leather around her wrist instead, then held out her hand to Luisa.

'Thank you,' she said, as the old woman tied a double knot.

When Bella returned to her room she found a note on her bed.

'You missed dinner,' it said. 'I missed you.'

She folded the note carefully and tucked it between the pages of her sketchbook, ignoring the call of the woman and her bed. Alone, she thought.

Her sketchbooks were filling rapidly. She had brought five with her to the island and they were crowded with quick draw-ings, watercolours and Luisa's stories. There would be no more books until Bella returned to Napoli, so she turned them upside down to use the backs of the pages. She sharpened her pencil and began to draw, from memory, an image of Cristofano's face.

The next day Luisa told Bella the story of her birth. 'I knew the midwife,' she said. 'She was my neighbour.'

Luisa described how the midwife gasped when Afrodite's child had crowned. The child gushed out of her mother's womb with a red forelock, a bright bolt of copper among black wire. The midwife crossed herself when she saw it.

'An omen,' she told Luisa. 'The sins of the mother, there for all the world to see.'

'And your eyes,' Luisa said. 'You didn't blink or cry. Never fretted like other babies. You looked like an old woman shrunk into a baby's body. It was creepy. If you'd been a boy, those eyes would've got you taken to some monastery in Rome or Assisi.'

She sipped her coffee. 'Perhaps not, without a scrap of holiness between them. The wedding was the only time I saw your mother in church. And Cristofano only went because he carved the statues.'

Luisa looked at Bella. 'Have you been up to the church? Have you looked at the little infants? Some of them have your face.'

Bella closed her eyes. Tomorrow she would climb the winding path to the church and find the statues. She'd stroke their smooth contours and see if Luisa was right. But now she needed to listen.

'Your mother wasn't well after the birth,' Luisa continued. 'Most women, as soon as the baby plops out, lift it straight to their chest, gore and all. But your mamma was different. She didn't want to hold you. She had no milk for you, so I used to carry goats' milk over for Cristofano to feed you. She never said, but I think it was that forelock. It reminded her of what she'd lost.'

The old woman rubbed her eyes. Bella helped her to bed for her afternoon nap, then walked through the empty village. She looked up at the church. Cristofano would be there carving solemn Marias to guard the graves. She would see him tomorrow. Crossing the promontory, she climbed Afrodite's wooden stairs to the terraces above.

The boards were damp and splintered, and she trod carefully, afraid she'd put her foot through a rotten piece and tumble to the rocks below. At the top of the stairs, the rocks gave way to narrow terraces of soil supported by walls of small stones. She'd expected it to be windy up here, but the southern face of the outcrop continued upwards and sheltered her from the gusts.

The terraces were overgrown with tall grass and ivy, but Bella saw their regular pattern clearly. Other plants grew wild beside the ivy, self-seeded oregano, mint and rosemary, untouched for almost twenty years yet still thriving. Uneven rows of stakes, bleached by the elements and with scraps of twine still tied around them, would once have supported beans and tomatoes. Gathering a bunch of wild herbs for Didóne, she resolved to tell her about the garden hidden on top of the rocks. It pleased her to imagine the plants responding to the woman's deft, brown hands.

One terrace had collapsed, and precious soil spilt over the stones. Squatting, she picked up a stone the size of a grapefruit and wedged it back into the broken wall. She grabbed another, jiggling until it fitted snugly. She enjoyed the weight of the stones in her hand, the rich, dark grit that stuck under her nails. Her tongue tickled the corner of her mouth.

There were shards of terracotta pottery in the soil. Lifting them out and wiping them with stained fingers, she blew soil from the cracks. Some of the shards were marked with geometric patterns: zigzags and spirals and stripes. Others had jagged lines on them. Peering closely, she recognised letters from the Greek alphabet. Didóne had told her about the island's earliest settlers. Did they begin these terraces all those years ago? She remembered her mother's slow, sad songs, in a language she didn't understand, drifting down from the garden. It was Greece, she thought. You were building a new Greece.

When Bella had fixed the break in the terrace wall, she cupped her hands and returned the spilt earth, patting the soil heavily, so rain wouldn't carry it away. Pleased by the smooth line of rock and soil, she smiled. She stood quickly, swaying, then steadied herself on a broken stake.

Water glittered on both sides of the outcrop. The horizon stretched as far as she could see. Below, seagulls flocked above dark flecks in the water. It was breathtaking. She saw her mother standing closer to the edge, staring out to sea with arms crossed over her body.

'Why did you never bring me with you?' Bella asked out loud, but her mother didn't answer.

A telegram from Piètro waited at the front desk of the hotel.

'SAD NEWS,' it said. 'ISAAC'S HEART GONE. CREMATION TOMORROW. WILL GO FOR YOU. P.'

Walking out to the dining-room balcony, Bella stared at the evening horizon. She watched the sparkling lights of the fishing boats and the vibrant orange and mauve sky towards Africa. Slick with water, the rocks below reflected the colours of the sky.

'It's not going anywhere,' Didóne said, smiling. It was a sad smile, the smile of a child holding back tears.

'I know,' Bella said. 'That's why I like it.'

Didóne touched her face. 'You didn't have to seduce me to talk to Luisa. I'd have asked her anyway.'

Bella shook her head. 'If I remember rightly, you seduced me.' She held out her hand. 'Come to bed.'

Bella and Didóne made love with a gentleness that surprised them both. Their kisses were tentative, their fingers infinitely curious. They teased each other, delaying their climaxes as if to delay the morning. Neither spoke, but Bella knew it was a farewell. Nose to nose, breathing the same air, she watched Didóne sleep.

Untangling herself from Didóne's limbs before dawn, Bella walked out to the balcony. She stared at the sky lightening in the east. Untouched by sun, the air was chill, and she rubbed her arms. The breeze rippled the sea and the canvas covers of boats pulled up on the sand. Seagulls swirled overhead, squawking. I have nothing for you, she thought, showing them her empty hands. She watched the sun rise to glitter near the horizon and illuminate the shallows of the harbour. Time to go.

Returning to the room, she packed her bag. Five bulging sketchbooks and a pile of dirty clothes. Crushed letters from internment camps. She thought Didóne was asleep until she turned to leave and saw the other woman watching her from the bed.

'Not going to say goodbye?' Didóne asked.

Bella was ready to lie, to say yes, of course, I was about to wake you, when she saw Didóne's expression.

'I can't stay,' she said. 'Not any more. It's not that I don't . . . I mean, you are . . .'

Didóne held up her hands to stop the words. 'I know,' she said. 'I've known from the beginning. Your eyes, they've always looked through me. When I met you, I thought you were just hungry. But no matter how much I fed you, you still looked empty.' She smiled, the same sad smile Bella had seen the day before. 'This place isn't a destination for you. It's somewhere you pass through.'

Didóne paused. 'Your body has changed since you've been here. When you first came you were like sea-mist. You hardly touched the ground. But look at you now.'

In the mirror, Bella's reflection curved gently, soft at the hips. Didóne climbed out of bed to stand behind her, wrapping her arms around Bella's waist and resting her chin on her shoulder. They watched each other in the glass.

'Come with me,' Bella said.

Didóne shook her head. 'This is my home. I thought if I distracted you with my stories you'd forget you had to leave.'

'There was only one story I wanted to hear,' Bella said, rubbing her cheek against the other woman's ear. 'I didn't realise until I heard it. I'm sorry.'

'It wasn't even one of mine, was it?'

'No.'

Didóne sighed and took her arms from Bella's waist. She pulled a bulging leather pouch from her bag, then held it out.

'I gathered them,' she said. 'For when you left.'

Bella felt the sudden weight in her palm. She untied the bindings and tipped the contents of the pouch on the bed. Small stones spilt over the sheet. She knew the names before Didóne could tell her. She heard Cristofano's voice in her head. There were pebbles of tuff in grey, green and yellow, even a pink one that she recognised from the ravine near the village. There was a lozenge of volcanic black glass and a chunk of pumice smoothed by the sea. She touched each one with her fingertips.

'Thank you,' she said. 'I . . '

'Go,' Didóne said.

Leaving Didóne sitting on the bed, Bella walked up the mule track to the road and waited for the bus. From the back seat, she watched the village shrink. The fishermen unloading their catch on the wharf were small dolls. The village was a row of brightly painted boxes. A plume of smoke rose from the hotel's chimney. Seven o'clock, by her watch. Breakfast time. She imagined Didóne in the kitchen, baking the morning's bread.

'Goodbye,' she said.

From the port, Bella caught the first ferry to the mainland. Standing at the stern of the boat, she watched the port shrink as the village had. Cloud obscured the peak of the mountain. She walked towards the bow. The boat crested the big waves and flew, before splashing back down and wetting her face with salty spray. At the top of the wave the boat paused in mid-air, unsure whether to fall back to the sea or continue the motion straight up. Her heart paused too. The motion turned her stomach and she walked quickly to the rail.

The sensation was familiar. As a child, too small to see over the side of the boat, she'd balanced on an enormous metal cleat, one the sailors used later to secure the boat to the wharf. On her tiptoes she had leant with the rail digging into her gut, ready to release her breakfast to the foam. Isaac had grabbed her around the middle and pushed her into a seat.

'What are you trying to do?' he had yelled in Italian. 'Kill yourself?'

The child stared. Forcing her lips together, she'd trapped the hot gush of bile inside her mouth. Swallowed. The foul taste clung for days. Bella winced at the memory, then shuddered as the bile rose again. Over the side. She spat, wiping her mouth with her hand.

In three hours, the ferry would drop her at the Stazione Marittima in Napoli. Then a train north, through Roma and Firenze, to the prison camps named in her sheaf of letters. There wasn't much left of them now, they were abandoned after the liberation, but she might be able to track down people who worked in them. I know you're out there, she thought, staring over the waves to the horizon, the only stable thing in the shifting sea.

And then what? Standing at the prow, the ferry's figurehead with face to the spray, Bella knew the island was lost to the earth's curve. She wouldn't return there; she knew that already. Back to London, then, to carve out a career with Pièrro, to huddle together in the watery light of the flat they had shared, or one just like it, painting with numb fingers. She shook her head. That wasn't right either, not now, not for good. There were loose ends to tie, but none that bound her to the grey grids of the British Isles. She needed somewhere new and entirely her own, another island in her archipelago, with blue skies and clear light.

I know you're out there, she thought again, licking her salty lips.

River

New South Wales 1991

'Can I sleep in your bed tonight?'

Lorelei is still there, Billie thinks. She's been there hours, it seems, swaying against the doorframe, scuffing her bare feet, although the second hand of Billie's clock has clicked only thirty times. Thirty seconds since Lorelei opened the door without knocking, since she leant against the doorframe in her cotton slip, one strap falling from peeling shoulders.

This is it, Billie thinks. All it would take is a slight movement, an arm extended to brush her skin. Billie doesn't move, but she cannot look away. She knows that if those peach lips pressed against her own, she would surrender. With inhibitions smoked to stubs in the ashtray, there is no moral dilemma, only desire. Stan was right, she realises. I want her.

As Lorelei sways, Billie watches it unfold in her mind. She sees Lorelei release the other strap, let her petticoat fall to the ground. No bra, just a pair of black knickers. She sees Lorelei standing on the boundary of her studio, on the threshold, sees the white skin where her bikini top protected her from the blistering sun. Her freckles returning as the burnt skin peels and fades. She sees Lorelei walk towards her, arms outstretched. She wants me, too, Billie thinks.

As the clock ticks, she sees all this, then blinks. Petticoat still on, Lorelei sways in the doorway.

'Can I sleep in your bed?' she asks again. Her words slur. She's as drunk as I am, Billie realises. It wouldn't take much. I could pull her to the bed and we could tumble in my sheets, explore each other until dawn. But something stops her.

Lorelei seems smaller tonight, like a little girl in her nightdress. She looks up, and Billie catches her breath. There's no desire in the green orbs. They're not the eyes of a woman looking for a lover. Glimmering, ready to spill over, they belong to a child who has strayed too far from her parents and been swept away by the crowds. To a child who is lost and sees no way home. Her question, Billie realises, is not a sexual invitation. It is a cry for comfort, a craving for the human warmth of another.

She wants to hit herself. What was I thinking? In this world, she realises, you and your child are all I've got. We three are bound by blood. Pulsing moments before, her desire evaporates.

Walking unsteadily to Lorelei, she grasps her hand and pulls her gently to the bed. Her brown arms encircle and protect, like the sandstone isthmus guarding the little beach. Lorelei burrows into the embrace, resting her head on the soft flesh of Billie's breasts. As they touch, skin to skin, Lorelei shudders. Her tears spill, soaking Billie's dress, and she sobs. The same ragged spasms Billie heard through Stan's door.

'Simon's left me,' Lorelei whispers. 'Mum's gone. I have no one.'

'Not true,' Billie says. 'You've got Eli. And me. And Simon's still there. You two just have to sort things out.'

Squeezing tighter, she says nothing more as the tears flow. She holds the sobbing woman, strokes her hair from her face and wipes the mascara trails with the hem of her dress.

Eventually, the spasms ease. Lorelei slowly relaxes, head heavy on Billie's breast. Her breathing changes, begins to whistle and snuffle. Billie pulls the sheet over her thin body.

'Sleep now,' she whispers. 'I'll watch over you.'

She strokes Lorelei's hair until the sky begins to lighten. Again, she greets the dawn with no sleep, but this morning is different, pink in the pale eastern sky. Red sky in the morning, she thinks absently, sailor's warning. There'll be a storm tonight.

As daylight seeps into the room, Billie looks down at Lorelei's head on her chest, inhaling lavender and the harsh smoke of Stan's tobacco. Red hair fans across her shoulder. Close for the first time, she sees a fuzz of new hairs along the parting, not yet long enough to obey gravity. In the watery light, the strands shine. Escaped from its bun, her own hair cascades, the forelock the same copper colour. Entangled, it is difficult to tell them apart, except that Billie's hair falls in tight curls. Such a delicate link, she thinks. But it is all I have.

The morning's first bird isn't the currawong or the kookaburra, but the channel-billed cuckoo. Billie watches it through her window. Hatched from an egg deposited in a currawong's nest, the chick has quickly grown to match the foster parents' size. For weeks, Billie has watched the exhausted currawongs fetch slender lizards and fish to feed their monstrous offspring. Now, hungry, it opens its beak. Raucous and loud, its shriek travels through the garden.

Against Billie's chest, Lorelei stirs. She nuzzles, grinds her knuckles in her eye sockets, then blinks open her eyes. A frown.

'I'm in your bed,' she says. A statement, not a question. 'And I feel like death warmed up.'

'Too much vino will do that to you,' Billie says, smiling. 'I doubt there's any wine left in my cellar.'

'I haven't drunk like that in years,' Lorelei says, her voice husky. 'Not since I turned eighteen. Mum found me down at the White Hart, chatting up half the village. I didn't drink after that until I left home, and even then never more than half a glass.'

'I'm dressed,' she says, lifting the sheet. 'Well, half-dressed.' She rubs her furrowed forehead until the skin reddens. 'I hope . . . I mean, I didn't do anything awful, did I?'

'No,' Billie says. But I almost did. 'You just needed a cuddle.'

Shifting to the right, she pats the space beside her. They lie side by side, heads resting on the pillows.

The sun is higher now, its light moving across the floorboards of her studio to the bed. The sunlight illuminates the dusty nooks where spider webs and moth husks gather and the dirt on the outside of the windows. In the path of the light, everyday objects become clear-edged, hyper-real. Hypnotised, senses acute after a night without sleep, Billie watches the rays creep over the sheet, transfixed by the folds and shadows of the cotton, by the cross-weave of the fabric and the flaw where a thread has snagged.

'Sorry about Simon,' she says quietly.

'I blabbed about him? Jesus!'

I could lie, Billie thinks. Say she told me everything in a drunken stupor, but, on this first day of the new year, basking in pure light from the window, she knows it is wrong.

'No,' she says. 'I confess. I overheard you telling Stan a couple of weeks back. Why didn't you tell me?'

There it is, like a bindi-eye in the sole of her foot.

On her back, Lorelei stares at the ceiling, worries the seam of the sheet with her fingers. 'It was Mum and Dad all over again,' she sighs. 'I saw it happening. Watched myself turn into her. Over-protective. Over-wound. Pushing Simon away. But I couldn't stop it. When Mum died, it got worse.'

Her eyes, still veined from the night before, brim again. 'Somehow it was easier to tell Stan. He wouldn't see the pattern. But you'd see straight away. I couldn't bear you knowing.'

Her tears trickle slowly from the corner of her eyes to her ears, without the violence of the night before, but steady, relentless.

'When he left,' she says, sniffing, 'I just had to get away. It was unbearable in the village, in the same network of streets I'd known all my life. I took my holiday leave all at once and ran.'

Opening the drawer in her bedside cupboard, Billie rummages until she finds a box of tissues. She hands them to Lorelei, who sits up to wipe her eyes and blow her nose.

'He's still there,' Billie says. 'Probably holed up in a dingy flat in Norwich, waiting for you to ask him back.'

'No,' Lorelei says sadly. 'He made it clear. The only contact he wanted with me was about Eli.'

'Why don't you try? Tell him what you told me. Tell him about your trip. Your mum would never have done that.' She smiles. 'The furthest she got was Southampton.'

Nodding, Lorelei manages a half smile. 'And even that was too much. I don't remember leaving the village after that.'

Billie pushes herself upright until her head is level with Lorelei's. She reaches out to tuck a strand of Lorelei's hair behind her ear. 'Promise you'll call him?'

'Maybe.'

With the sun on her face, she turns to Billie. 'I have a confession, too. I've been reading your sketchbooks.'

'I know,' Billie says. 'You put them back in the wrong places.'

When she first realised someone had been in her studio, rifling through her pages, she was furious. But now, warmed by the morning light, there is no anger. If only it was always like this, she thinks.

'Mum never spoke about Elissa,' Lorelei says. 'The first one, I mean. I found out by accident. On that binge on my eighteenth, one of the old blokes at the pub touched my knee and said I was her spitting image. Mum froze when I told her and, later, nearly had a fit when she found out what we'd decided to call the baby. Even then, she wouldn't say it. Eli was her compromise.'

She pauses. 'I thought you were adopted. That's what Mum told me. I didn't realise . . . '

It is Billie's turn to half-smile. 'Neither did I, not for a long time. At least, I didn't want to. On some level, I've always known. Have to call myself your cousin now, not your aunt.'

Lorelei reaches for Billie's hand, clasps it tight. 'Did you ever find them? Afrodite and Cristofano?'

Billie shakes her head. She shuffles to the edge of the bed, to pull another sketchbook from the shelf, but the other woman's hand grips her hard, stops her rolling from the sunlit bed.

'No you don't,' Lorelei says softly. 'In my head I've got a patchwork of stories, pieced together from the words and sketches in your books. But you're all I've got. My only link. Will you tell me in your own voice? Tell me about Italy and Isaac, about Elissa, about my mum. Please.'

Leaning back against the pillow, Billie is connected to Lorelei by their joined hands, where hips and ankles touch, and by the strands of red hair splayed over the pillows. She begins to talk. At first the words are slow, hesitant, but soon they gather momentum. As the sun moves across the bed, she talks until her throat is hoarse. When the light leaves the bed to warm the floorboards, the stories stop.

'I am talked out,' she says. She squeezes Lorelei's hand. 'Now it's your turn. Tell me about Stan. He's a lovely man, but twenty years older than you. What on earth do you see in him?'

'That's a change in tone,' Lorelei laughs. 'You don't see it because he's your friend. He makes me feel sexy, something I haven't felt since Simon left.'

'You slept with him then?'

Arching her eyebrows, Lorelei elbows Billie's ribs. 'Have you no shame?'

'I'm not the journal reader, am I?'

'If you must know, yes. Well, sort of.'

'The night you stayed in town.'

Lorelei nods. 'We slept together. In the same bed, at least.'

'What do you mean?'

'Promise you won't say anything?' Lorelei leans forward. 'We tried. But he couldn't. Not for months now, apparently.'

The blank canvas. It makes sense now. Aching, she feels Stan's humiliation, his frustration. Women and painting had been the two pillars of his life, but to be without either . . .

While Billie digests the information, something peculiar happens. A giggle begins low in her gut. It's no laughing matter, and she doesn't understand the laughter, but she cannot suppress it. She clamps her hands over her mouth, but the giggle escapes. It's cruel and inappropriate, but she cannot help it. She doesn't know where the laughter comes from, but the thought of Stan and his poor limp penis sets her off. Hysterical laughter, shrill and infectious. It snares Lorelei, and soon both women convulse.

'That'll teach him,' Billie gasps, between spasms, 'to sow wild oats. Now there's nothing left.'

'Stop it,' Lorelei says, wiping her eyes. 'I've got a stitch.'

Troy's voice calls from the corridor outside. 'You in there, Billie? It's a beautiful day. Thought I'd take Lorelei and Eli out on the river in my boat, but they're not in their room. Have you seen them?'

He pokes his head around the open door. Still sparkling, eyes kohl-smudged from the night before. 'Oh,' he says to the giggling women, 'there you are.'

He is silent for a moment. Billie quietens her laughter, but it bubbles below the surface, threatening to boil over again. One snort from Lorelei and she'll lose it.

'Where's Eli, then?' Troy asks. 'I figured she'd be with you.'

Immediately, the urge to giggle dies, replaced by a crawling dread in Billie's gut.

'She not in our room?' Lorelei says. 'Not playing that damn video game?'

Troy shakes his head. 'Been through the whole house, and I couldn't find her anywhere. No sign since I got back this morning.'

'Christ!' Lorelei rushes from the bed, dragging the sheet with her. 'Where the hell is she? If anything has happened . . .'

'Nothing has happened,' Billie says. 'She'll be fine.'

Inside, the panic has her, and she is not as confident as her words. She sees Eli lying crumpled below the lookout. She sees her floating face-down in the river or cold and stiff from a funnel-web bite. Crushed by falling rocks while hunting for the hand painting. It will be my fault, she thinks. Again.

The three check the house one more time, just in case, but there is no sign of the red-haired child. Outside, Billie leaps the steps to Stan's shed, bangs on his door.

'Give us a hand, Stan? We can't find Eli.'

'She's not in here,' he shouts, muffled through the closed door. 'Just leave me alone, will you?'

'Grumpy old man!' Billie yells. 'We need your help.'

But there's no time to argue, so she turns, following Lorelei and Troy down the steps. The Englishwoman is still in her slip, Billie notices. They call Eli's name as they descend, words echoing through the canopy to startle magpies from the telephone lines. The pied birds circle overhead, and Billie envies their keen eyes, their aerial perspective. The island is only a kilometre long, but cleft with overgrown gullies and steep fissures. If she's fallen into one of those, they'll never find her.

On the path, they make one full circuit of the island. Their calls flush out crested wood pigeons and lizards basking in the sun, but do not bring Eli crashing from the undergrowth.

'She's got to be here somewhere,' Billie says. She leads the trio down the hill to the little beach, standing on the edges of the sand to scan the crowded shoreline. Toddlers squat in the shallows and excavate with plastic spades, while older children dive from a rowing boat into deeper water. Scruffy blond and shaggy brown mops, but no curly redheads.

'Let's try the wharf,' Troy says, but Lorelei strides along the sand, peering at the family groups.

'I have to look properly,' she says, frantic.

Together, they check every cluster of crumpled towels and pink limbs, but with no success. Scurrying back along the beach, they clamber over the sandstone arm, slippery with green weed, to the exposed midden. It is empty.

'Eli!' Lorelei yells. 'Where are you?'

She is crying now, wiping her nose on the skirt of her slip, and looks ready to collapse.

'We'll try the shop,' Billie says.

'And the reserve behind the house,' Troy says. 'The first place I should have looked. I'll head there now, ask the neighbours.'

'Meet you back at the house?'

Troy nods, then turns to jog up the steep path.

When Billie and Lorelei ask in the shop, Mary shakes her head. Heaps of kids in today, she tells them, buying iceblocks to eat on the wharf, but not Lorelei's child.

'I'll keep my eye out,' Mary says. 'Send her on home.'

Lorelei pulls Billie on another circuit of the island, this time exploring the narrow tracks to each house on the flat, dodging the wheelbarrows and the kids' pushbikes, thrown aside and lantana-snared. She strides, swift as a power walker, and Billie struggles to match her pace. Behind the beach, Billie points out the cross-country shortcut the islanders call the goat track, and they climb, gripping sandstone boulders and rough sapling trunks to scale the slippery incline. Among the trees they see deflated tennis balls and a discarded sneaker, but no clue to finding Eli.

Clambering back onto the path, with mud-stained knees and chafed palms, Billie stands, hands on hips, chest heaving. Lorelei's eyes are open wide, revealing the full circle of the orb.

'She can't be far away,' Billie says, forcing the panic from her voice. 'We'll check with Troy, see if he's searched the reserve.'

At the bottom of the stairs to the house, Lorelei pauses. Looking up the steep hill, her shoulders slump, and the manic energy that has driven her around the island seems to dissipate.

'Where is she?' she says quietly.

She takes the steps slowly, and Billie plods behind, breath catching in her throat. There are more steps than she remembers.

The women's feet move in time, and Billie is aware of their solid thump, like the heavy gait of pallbearers. They stomp over leaf litter and the fallen petals of the Christmas bush, over twigs and swarming ants' nests.

Other footsteps, quick and light, pull her eyes from the ground to the path ahead, but it is Mark, the ferryman's son, not Eli, who leaps down the steps. He takes them three at a time, stumbling on the uneven surfaces. Lorelei holds out her arms to catch him.

'She's hurt,' he says, puffing. 'In the cave. Cut, on an oyster shell.'

He leads the women up the remaining stairs to the sand-stone boulders. By the narrow crevice that leads to the cave, Eli squats on the ground in knickers and singlet. Her skirt is wrapped around one foot, and tears streak her dusty cheeks. She looks up.

'It hurts,' she says, shaking.

While Lorelei strokes the girl's face, Billie kneels and unwinds the bloodstained cloth. She gasps, puts one hand over her mouth. Blood seeps from a jagged cut longer than her index finger.

'Troy!' she yells, loud enough to carry across the reserve. 'Found her. Give us a hand, will you?'

Quickly, she rebinds the foot, applies pressure to slow the blood. 'You're going to need stitches, little one. I'll get Troy to take us to the hospital.'

Troy sprints down the steps, scoops Eli in his arms. With the women and Mark behind him, he carries the child to the wharf, tucks a life jacket over her head as Billie helps Lorelei into the silver tinnie. Mark stands sadly on the wharf, cradling his plaster cast.

While Lorelei settles the child, Troy pulls up the anchor chain.

'Take the tiller, Billie?' he asks. With a nod, she claims the driver's seat in front of the engine. 'Hold tight,' she says, turning the key.

The boat skips across the waves, propelled by the urgency of the girl's tears. The wind blows Billie's hair from her face. Salty wash splashes her cheeks. It was a surprise, she remembers, the river's tang. She'd expected it to be fresh. Gripping the tiller, she fights the river's resistance, steers the little boat towards the mainland. She turns her head briefly to see the wide curve of the wake and the shrinking island.

Halfway across the channel, Billie realises what she is doing. It's great, she thinks. Not one wave of nausea. She should be scared, frightened of being adrift, but she isn't. After the fog, she'd forgotten the joy of being on the river, with the power of fifty horses in her hands. Eli grins, too, her pain seemingly forgotten.

'It's like a ride,' she says, and Billie nods.

As the boat approaches the marina, Billie slows the revs to four knots. Troy clambers to the bow, balances with the mooring rope in his hands. When the boat touches, he leaps to the wharf and loops the rope around the cleat. Lorelei passes the child to him, and he carries her to his car, a faded green Saab from the seventies.

'It's safety green,' he says, smiling. 'And no comments, or you'll be hitching along the freeway.'

The car park at Hornsby hospital is crowded, but Troy finds an empty space near the casualty entrance, and within five minutes they have bundled the child through the glass doors. Billie sits with Troy in the waiting room while Eli and Lorelei see the doctor. The man beside them holds a bloody tea-towel over his nose.

'Fight,' he says through the fabric. 'Some bastard head-butted me.'

Opposite, a teenage girl in silver trousers and a skimpy top shivers, her head resting close to a bucket. Mascara smudges her eyes. The boy with his arm around her shoulders mimics drinking, then shakes his head as the girl retches. A young woman ushers the teenagers into a cubicle, looking barely old enough to be out of school herself. She smiles at Billie.

'New Year is our busiest time,' she says. 'But don't worry. Your little friend will be out soon.'

New Year, Billie thinks. I'd forgotten. She looks at the television bracketed to the ceiling. It is on mute, showing the highlights of last night's fireworks over the city. The crackle of the explosions is replaced by wails from the cubicles and static bursts from the hospital intercom.

Later, Eli hobbles down the corridor on wooden crutches. She holds her bandaged foot off the ground.

'Six stitches!' she says, as they walk to the car. 'Six! The doctor said I'll have a scar. Cool!'

She rubs her upper arm. Below the peeling tattoo lips, the skin is red and swollen.

'Tetanus,' she says. 'Doctor said I'd get lockjaw without it. You should've seen the size of the needle. And I didn't cry, did I, Mum?'

'Not once.'

Billie strokes the child's tight braids. 'Not once? Brave girl.'

She remembers another child who never cried. She had curly hair, too, but it was black, not red, except for one streak at the front.

The journey back to the boat is quiet. In the front, Billie sits next to Troy, turning occasionally to check on Eli. The girl rests her head on her mother's lap.

'Asleep?' Billie whispers.

Lorelei nods.

In the quiet, Billie watches the highway ahead, taking in the steep sandstone escarpments either side. Like a cathedral. Last time I took this road they were new, she thinks. They'd only just put the freeway in, and the stone was raw, fresh. Now it's streaked with rusty stains where water has cascaded over the years.

Air shimmers on hot bitumen as the road curves down towards the great drowned valley of the Hawkesbury. There's a blue haze over the forests, and the river sparkles. Low tide reveals brown mud flats through shallow water. Barnacles cluster on the exposed pillars of channel markers.

The cliffs glow orange in the late afternoon sun. Caught without her sketchbook, Billie watches the transformation of the rocks. Her hands fidget, lost without something between her fingers. She folds them together and rests them in her lap. Watch, she thinks, but do not capture. Let this one be.

It is dark as they climb the steps to the house. Lorelei carries the sleeping child to bed, and Troy goes to his room to catch up on lost sleep.

The corridor reeks of paint and thinners, and Billie knows something is wrong before she reaches her studio. She flicks on the light and blinks in the electric glare. Her workbench is overturned, the easels on their sides with legs snapped. Her sketches have been pulled from the wall, and most of the leaves plucked from the ceiling. The painted faces are ripped and scattered over the floorboards, lips and eyes separated. Miniature vistas shuffle in the breeze from the open window. The bookshelves are empty. Overturned paint tins dribble onto ripped pages. Red. Green. Blue.

'Like a Pollock,' Billie says. She stands at the edge of the chaos and stares. She cannot move.

'I've tucked her in,' Lorelei says, stopping beside Billie in the doorway. 'My God,' she gasps, putting her hand to her lips. 'What the hell happened? Why would anyone do this?' She walks into the studio, stepping carefully over the mounds of paper to tread on bare floor. 'We should have locked the door when we left. I didn't even think.' Kneeling, she picks up a torn shred, turns it over in her fingers. 'I can't believe it, all your work. But Stan was here. He might have noticed something. I'll go get him.'

Stan. Billie knows it was him. She remembers her cruel laughter that morning and knows, with certainty, that he heard. She also knows that there has been a theft. Her blue atlas is missing. She feels its absence in the cage of her ribs, as if her heart has dropped into her stomach and beats a rapid tattoo on her diaphragm. She kicks the debris on the floor and fragments scatter. Stupid, she thinks. Cruel.

'Don't worry about it,' Billie says quietly, taking the paper from Lorelei's hands. 'I'll talk to Stan, then sort this out.'

'You sure?'

Billie nods. Once Lorelei has left the room, Billie stomps through the house to Stan's studio.

In the fibro cabin, Stan sprawls across his bed, shirt undone, with a half-drunk bottle of scotch on the pillow.

'Knew you'd come.' The alcohol in Stan's blood changes his voice. His words are slow. Slurred. 'Saw you two this morning. Didn't even close the door. Sluts. Came to raid your cellar, and I heard you sharing your secrets.'

On the last word, he screws his face into a sneer, then props himself on one elbow. 'But we all have secrets. Guess what mine is. Aren't you curious, just a little? Give you a clue. It's old, it's travelled a long way, and I believe it belonged to your father.'

From under his pillow, he pulls the blue atlas, flicking through the pages of maps. He takes one crisp page between his fingers and laughs as Billie moves towards him.

'What if I do this?' Stan tugs at the page, and Billie jumps. 'Like a trained dog,' he says. 'Jump, you bitch.'

The third time Stan tugs, the page comes away in his hand. The stitches in the spine are strong, but the paper is fragile. The ripping sound mesmerises Billie. Stan holds the atlas in one hand, the page in the other.

'I've got your worthless paper heart in my hand,' he says. His laughter is as dry as the atlas paper. Grabbing more pages, he tugs hard. They come away together. He closes his fist and the pages crumble. He rips again, and again, and there is a vein in his neck that pulses, and one in his temple, and he murmurs to himself.

'Teach you to laugh behind my back, you two-faced bitch. I'll bet you've been laughing since I moved in, seeing me go nowhere while you make it. You slut, fucking dyke . . .'

As Stan disembowels the atlas, Billie doesn't move. She watches his hands and the blur of paper around them. Letting Stan's abuse flow over her, she sees countries torn in half and oceans divided, lines of longitude and latitude split.

The scream surprises her. A chamber of her mind wonders where the sound comes from. It is atonal. Continuous. Disembodied. Only the soreness in Billie's throat tells her that the sound originates in her own body.

The scream releases Billie from her fugue. She falls to her knees in a blizzard of torn paper, snatching at the fragments in the air. Gusts from her hand push them away. One piece nestles in her palm but, as she closes her fingers, it flutters away. Chasing butterflies, she thinks.

She lets the shredded paper fall to the floor. When the pieces settle, she picks up a blue and green fragment. It is dry in her hand. Fragile. Other fragments crumble. She holds out her skirt like a basket and carefully collects them. Damn you, she thinks.

'I want you out by morning,' she says quietly.

In her studio, she rights her workbench and scatters the atlas fragments over it, ignoring the mess on the floor. She sorts neat piles of countries, trying to match paper shreds as if they are pieces of a jigsaw puzzle. But it can't be done; there are too many countries and too much sea. It would take all the years Billie has left, all the years she's already had then one thousand more. But still she sorts. She reads the place names on both sides, using Troy's magnifying glass for the smallest type, but the place she looks for eludes her.

I cannot find the island of my birth, she thinks.

Hours pass. Billie stares at the torn paper. Her neat piles won't remake the atlas, no matter how much she wants it. Pulling an empty shoebox from under her bed, she gently lays green and blue shreds inside. She sorts through the fragments on the floor, discarding those sticky with wet paint. Into the box go torn leaves with tiny faces and the corners of charcoal sketches. Pages of spiky writing and the ripped commission for the river couple.

Scooping hands through the scraps, she watches them flutter to the bench. Again. The movement is compulsive. As the fragments land, Billie sees the hint of a pattern, shreds that seem to belong together. Something stirs in her gut.

Collage, she thinks. Montage. I've never tried that.

Clambering onto her desk, she pulls the few intact leaves from the ceiling. Been there too long anyway. Maybe I can sell them, she thinks. Get that curator off my back.

Feet back on the floor, Billie looks at her studio. Without the rustling leaves, she clearly hears the wind in the trees outside and the river lapping at the beach. The room seems brighter, cleaner, with no sign of Stan's whirlwind. She has reduced the chaos to a shoebox. A bulging shoebox, she thinks, with a length of taut string to keep the lid on. Only faint stains show where paint spilt. I should be upset, Billie thinks, but I'm not. She is oddly comforted by the tidy room, invigorated by the clear work space. Everything is in order, ready for the next project.

Closing the door of her neat studio, she walks down the corridor. By the telephone, Lorelei sits on the floor, with spine to the wall and one knee pulled to her chest. As she speaks, she knots the cord around her fingers. Billie walks on to the kitchen, strikes a match under the kettle. Above the hissing gas, she hears the murmur of Lorelei's voice. Then the click of the receiver being replaced on the handset.

'You okay?' Lorelei asks, coming into the kitchen and sliding onto a chair. 'Do you want me to call the police?'

'No,' Billie says. 'All sorted. It was Stan. I've asked him to leave.'

'Stan?' Lorelei says, rubbing her forehead. She looks tired, as if the events of the last twenty-four hours have caught up with her. 'God, did he hear us laugh?'

'Yeah. But I don't think it was just that. Living here all these years, depending on me, it's not been good for him. He must resent it on some level. I guess it bubbled over.'

The women stare at the table in front of them. I feel heavy, Billie thinks, and suddenly drained.

'You don't mind me using the phone?' Lorelei asks. 'I had to tell Simon about today.'

'It's certainly been a cracker,' Billie says. 'Tea?'

'No thanks.' Lorelei stares down at her nails, worrying a jagged edge with her thumb. 'Please don't be offended, but I've decided to go home early. We've only been here a few weeks, I know, and Eli's already made a friend, but I need to talk to Simon. Face-to-face. Hammer out some kind of future.'

Filling a mug, Billie nods. She dunks the teabag until the water darkens. 'Thought you might.'

'Could we come back, once things are sorted? Stay longer?'

'Of course.'

'Thanks.' Lorelei stands, brushing wrinkles from her trousers. 'Best ring the airlines if I'm going to change that flight.'

In the empty kitchen, Billie blows on her tea to cool it. She could protest, tempt them to stay, but she won't. She knows they will return to the island. She can see it, clear as her hand holding the mug, clear as the white scar on her tanned skin. In her mind Lorelei steps from the ferry, carrying less luggage this time, suitcase replaced by a compact duffle bag. Eli sprouts on successive journeys, girl to lanky teen, until she boards the plane for Australia alone, her crumpled backpack sewn with cloth badges of Paris and Prague and Istanbul.

The next morning, she walks through her house. She senses the change already, the growing pockets of empty space. Out the back, Stan's studio is deserted. His easel is gone. The only traces of his presence are the rusty paint tins left by the door, the bottles of thinner and dirty rags. Lorelei and Eli's room is empty, too. Their suitcases are packed. The red-haired English-woman waits on the verandah.

'Have you seen Eli?' she asks. 'I can't find her, and I'm frightened she's hurt herself again.'

'Leave it to me,' Billie says. Following a hunch, she walks down the stone steps. Eli squats by the entrance to the cave.

Her crutches lean against the sandstone and the bandage around her foot is already scuffed and dirty.

'Be careful,' Billie says, pointing to the oyster blades poking through sandy soil. 'You'll end up with another row of stitches.'

As she kneels to pick up the bleached shells, she notes the girl's sullen expression. 'I didn't mean to disturb you. If you want me to go...'

Eli shakes her head. 'S'okay. I'm having a ceremony. You can help.'

Following the child into the cave, Billie watches her heap a mound of ash around an oyster shell. Billie recognises it— the shell that Eli found when they discovered the cave.

'I was going to take it home,' Eli says, 'make a necklace out of it, but Mark said I shouldn't, because it belonged to the little girl without her finger.'

She is downcast, unwilling. Billie remembers her bracelet. She's worn it since Luisa first bound it to her wrist, only taking it off to replace the strap when the leather wore thin and snapped. She tugs the knot with her teeth, leather dry and salty against her lips, until the knot creaks and releases, then dangles the silver coin before Eli.

'Mark's right. But you could take this home instead. It belonged to a little girl, too.'

Eli looks up, her eyes on the glittering circlet. 'Isn't that the same thing? I'd be taking it from someone.'

Billie shakes her head. 'This little girl wants you to have it. On one condition. That when you don't need it any more, you pass it on to another child who does. All right?'

Eli nods. She bends her thin neck forward for Billie to tie the leather in a bow, fingering the relief on the silver. 'Thanks, Billie. You're ace.'

Reaching into her pocket, she brings out the lozenge of smooth, green glass. 'Would you give this to Mark? There won't be time to see him before we leave.'

'Of course. Now come. Your mum's packed and ready. You'll miss the ferry.'

Troy carries the suitcases down the steps, then loads them into two wheelbarrows. 'I'll take it down for you.'

'It's okay,' Billie says. 'We can do it.'

He waves as Billie and Lorelei push the barrows down the hill. Eli hobbles beside them on her crutches, weeping.

'It's not fair,' she wails. 'Why do we have to go? I was just starting to enjoy myself.'

'I've got to sort stuff out with your father,' Lorelei says, gently. 'But we can come back.'

Eli looks at Billie. 'Can we?

'Already settled.'

At the wharf, the three wait for the ferry without talking. Billie hears the boat before she sees it, the steady chug familiar as her heartbeat. Children bob in the water near the wharf, but slide out as the *Hawkesbury Sun* comes into view. They sprint away, glistening like newborn pups, splashing Billie with cold drops from the river.

Lorelei stands close to Billie. She holds out her arms and the women hug stiffly, yesterday's familiarity gone.

'Can we write?' Lorelei asks.

'I'd like that.'

As the ferry approaches, Lorelei pushes her daughter back from the edge of the wharf.

'Stay there,' she says. She walks carefully down the wooden steps until her feet rest on the last step above the water. The river licks her sandals. The distance between the ferry and the wharf shrinks, four metres, three, two . . . Then, to Billie's surprise, Lorelei leaps the green gulf to the boat.

Holding her breath, Billie expects Lorelei to slam into the hull and slide unconscious into the water. She rushes to grab her, but Lorelei glides across to the ferry, laughing as the ferryman waggles his finger and curses irresponsible tourists. A ripple of applause from the waiting passengers on the wharf, which Lorelei accepts with a smile. She takes Eli's crutches and stows them on a seat by the window, then lifts her daughter onto the boat.

'You know there might be others,' she says, as she lugs the suitcases onto the ferry.

'What do you mean?' Billie says.

'Other family. Cousins of cousins from generations back, strewn across the globe. Of your parents, too. We should look for them.'

Billie nods. 'Maybe.'

From the wharf, she listens to the engines rev, watches the maelstrom as the ferry pulls away. She waves at the two faces pressed against the window. Lorelei is smiling, the broadest smile that Billie has seen since the Englishwoman arrived. Lorelei's mouth moves, she is laughing, she is saying something, but the wind steals her words. Billie knows it is goodbye, but she laughs too.

The island children sprint back along the wharf. No diving, commands the sign by the steps. Irregular tides. But the children dive in anyway, straight into the ferry's foaming wake, bobbing like corks.

Billie walks down the slimy steps. She keeps walking until the water rises over her ankles. Up to her knees. Her skirt floats like a jellyfish crown. At the bottom step, she pauses with the water at her breasts. Here we go, she thinks, then leaps.

The wave she makes is huge, and the children laugh. She sinks like a stone. Panicking, she scrabbles for the steps, until she hears a faint voice. It is Eli, calling from the ferry.

'Fill your lungs!' the girl yells. 'Fill your lungs!'

Time for one long mouthful of air before the green water closes over Billie's head. As her lungs swell, her body rises slowly. Her head breaks the surface. Across the river, Eli waves from the ferry door.

'I'm floating!' Billie yells at the top of her voice, waving back.

As her lungs empty and fill, she bobs. Lying back, she lets the cool fluid play with her hair and tickle her scalp. Her toes poke from the water. I could float like this forever, she thinks. The current tugs towards the open sea, but today her body is strong. The steps are only a stroke or two away, and she is not afraid.

One of the boys in the water points. 'Look,' he says. 'She's still dressed.'

A younger girl pipes up. 'She's crazy, I reckon.'

Perhaps I am, Billie thinks. The children laugh, and she laughs with them at the splinters of driftwood and dead leaves in her hair and at her clothes ballooning around her. She laughs until her side aches, but cannot stop. Her chest heaves and her eyes water. Suddenly, she is crying too, alternating between tears and laughter.

'I am Billie,' she says to the children. 'I am Bella. Queenie. Sybille. I am Cibelle. I am . . .'

Rolling forward, she slowly lowers her face into the water, feels it close over her mouth and nostrils. Over her eyes. The rest of her sentence floats away. The tide steals Billie's tears, sliding them downstream to merge with the pounding Pacific.

With eyes closed, she blows bubbles until her lungs scream, then lifts her head to gasp air. Now, compelled, she dives below the surface with eyes open, exhaling a stream of bubbles as her body sinks into the blurred green world. Sunlight filters through the water, gilding the silt that floats with her. Silver bream glimmer among glossy weeds. Like my dreams, she thinks, remembering weightlessness.

In the calm below the meniscus, she feels the mechanical heartbeat of the ferry, and her own heart, steady, strong. She hears the slow clank of an anchor chain pulled to the surface, link by link.

Below the water, the faces return to her—Cristofano, Afrodite, Elissa, Piètro, Isaac, Audrey—and they smile. You're here with me, she realises. All of you. You have always been here, but I never knew where to look. I was afraid. Emptied of air, her lungs contract. Not yet, Billie thinks. I am not ready. But the faces smile on. We will always be here, they say.

Sobbing, Billie surfaces. She stays in the water until she feels the throb of the next ferry, crawling up the steps to shake herself like a dog, sending arcs of water across the planks. Her skin puckers. Her limbs quiver. She is still crying.

Out of the water, the tingling returns. After her night with Lorelei, she thought it would have gone, but the top layer of her skin feels alive, blood hot and pulsing below. My body is awake, she thinks. I will swim every day, she vows, learn to stay under for longer and let the river smooth my rough edges.

Blowing her nose on her wet skirt, Billie walks to the shop by the wharf.

'You're a mess,' Mary says. 'What happened?'

'Perhaps another day,' Billie says, shaking her head. 'But tell me, did Stan leave a forwarding address? I need to sort something out.'

Mary leans over the counter. 'What happened up at the house? He was on the first ferry with his gear, absolutely ropable.'

'That's between him and me,' Billie says.

'Spoilsport.'

The shopkeeper frowns, leafs through a stack of cards, then scribbles a number on a paper bag. 'Can't give you the address, but call him.'

She takes an envelope from a pigeon-hole behind the counter. 'Almost forgot. This came for you yesterday. The girls would never forgive me.'

As she leaves the shop, Billie opens the envelope. It is an invitation to a post-New Year feast from two women who live round the corner, handwritten on fine-grained paper. Water from Billie's wet fingers makes the ink bleed into the fibres of the paper. Instinctively she crushes the invitation in her hand, her fingers familiar with the action. She raises her arm to throw the paper ball into a bin beside the path, then stops, arm frozen at the zenith of its arc. Unfurling the sheet, she smooths the tracery of wrinkles with her fingers.

'Who knows?' she says, to the kookaburra on the telephone wire above her head. 'Perhaps I will go. Perhaps I'll even throw a party for my birthday.'

Startled by the words, the bird wiggles its tail, distinctive laughter shaking its body. Billie smiles at the sound. The smile becomes a laugh, and the woman with the orange forelock laughs all the way to her house perched on sandstone at the top of the island.

Acknowledgements

This novel was written as the fiction component of a PhD in Professional Writing at Deakin University.

I would like to thank: Annette Barlow, Christa Munns, Colette Vella and Jane Gleeson-White at Allen & Unwin for their inspired suggestions; Lyn Tranter of Australian Literary Management for her support and enthusiasm; Jenny Lee, a dedicated supervisor always willing to read the next draft; Kevin Brophy, Christina Hill and Alex Miller for their comments on the earliest manifestations of the novel; Deakin staff and students for their valuable workshop comments; Peter Bishop at the Varuna Writers' Centre for his frank comments on 'Cibelle'; the many friends and family members who read chapters or entire drafts of the novel; the four interviewees who graciously shared their experiences of migration; my family in Australia and Britain for telling stories of times before my birth; Maria D'Amico of Eataliano for teaching me to make *bruschetta*; Liz Minns for letting me watch an artist at work; and Hendrikus van Hasselt for allowing me to spend three months in his island home on the Hawkesbury.

I am grateful to the Australian Government for giving me an Australian Postgraduate Award and the opportunity to devote all my time to this project; to Deakin University for its generous financial assistance, including a travel grant to visit the settings for my novel and research the Sibyls; to the off-campus library staff at Deakin for their willingness to send books by courier; to the staff at the State Library of New South Wales for their help in my Sibylline quest; to the staff at the Biblioteca Nazionale in Naples for allowing me to view their manuscript of Virgil's *Aeneid*; to Bruno D'Agostino for discussing the excavations at Cumae; to Salvatore Iacono of the Appartamenti 'Le Pleiadi', Ischia, for his kind hospitality; to the staff of the Norfolk Records Office in Norwich for showing me the archives of Heigham Hall; to the staff at Great Yarmouth Library who let me rummage through their extensive photographic archive; and to the kind staff of the Bank of England Museum for telling me which London pubs survived the war.

Most of all, I'd like to thank Matthew van Hasselt and our families for their support.

I would also like to acknowledge the many texts that have helped me create this novel. While not quoted directly, the following works have offered historical, geographical and cultural details vital to the imaginative construction of the narrative.

I relied on *A Guide to Historic Dangar Island: Island Gem of the Hawkesbury* (The Dangar Island Historical Society, no date) for the story of the handprint in the cave, and details of the region's flora and fauna. The mining of Aboriginal middens is mentioned in Sue Rosen's *Losing Ground: An Environmental History of the Hawkesbury–Nepean Catchment* (Hale & Iremonger, 1995). Details of Sydney's sandstone have been obtained from Douglass Baglin and Yvonne Austin's *Sandstone Sydney* (Rigby, 1976), Beryl Nashar's *Geology of the Sydney Basin* (Jacaranda Press, 1967) and Charles Francis Laseron's *The Face of Australia: The Shaping of a Continent* (Angus & Robertson, 1972).

The descriptions of painting on leaves (particularly gum leaves) have been greatly assisted by Sophie Ducker's *Story of Gum Leaf Painting* (School of Botany, The University of Melbourne, 2001). For more general art techniques, I have relied upon *The Artist's Manual: Equipment, Materials, Techniques* (ed. Stan Smith & Friso Ten Holt, Macdonald Educational Ltd, 1980) and *An Introduction to Art Techniques* (Ray Smith, Michael Wright & James Horton, DK Publishing, 1995/1999).

The stories of the Cumaean Sibyl in Virgil's *Aeneid* (Penguin, trans., 1990) and Ovid's *Metamorphoses* (Oxford University Press/The World's Classics, trans., 1986) helped me choose Billie's birthplace and artistic medium. These works also related the myths of Cybele, Apollo and Charybdis, and influenced the character of Didóne.

My picture of Italy began with archival research, which was later combined with first-hand observations of Ischia, Naples, Pompeii and Cumae. Important to this process were Loretta Santini's *Naples and Surroundings* (Plurigraf, 1976), *Naples: The City and its Famous Bay, Capri, Sorrento, Ischia and the Amalfi Coast down to Salerno*, issued by the Touring Club of Italy (Touring Editore, 1999), and the sections on Ischia in *Italy's Book of Days: The Happy Isles* (ed. Elena Baggio, E.N.I.T., 1966).

Reading Martin Clark's *Modern Italy: 1871–1982* (Longman, 1984), Christopher Duggan's *A Concise History of Italy* (Cambridge University Press, 1994), James Barr's *Religious Liberty in the Totalitarian States* (Allenson & Co., 1938), Wanda Newby's *Peace and War: Growing up in Fascist Italy* (William Collins & Sons, 1991) and Dennis Mack Smith's *Mussolini's Roman Empire* (Longman, 1976) all helped me understand the political background for Cibelle's early childhood.

Didóne's stories of the angel, the Sibyl and the rotting nuns are tales of Ischia mentioned in *Guide to Ischia: A New Illustrated Guide Containing Useful Information and a Map of the Island* (Edizioni Kina, 1993) and on the following website: <http://net.onion.it/ischia/htmlen/ischia.html>.

For cooking hints (and Piétro's fried rabbit) I have relied upon *Buon Appetito: Regional Italian Recipes*, a cookbook by the National Italian–Australian Women's Association (State Library of New South Wales Press, 1994) and Alan Davidson's *Mediterranean Seafood* (Penguin Books, 1972). The story of the wine made from Christ's tears belongs to the vintners of Naples.

Leo Curran's online photograph gave me the first glimpse of the Sibyl's Cave at Cumae. It is available at: <http://wings.buffalo.edu/AandL/Maecenas//italy_except_rome_and_sicily/cumae/ac880637.html>. Details of the discovery of the cave by Amedeo Maiuri were obtained from Herbert Parke's *Sibyls and Sibylline Prophecy in Classical Antiquity* (Routledge, 1988), Paolo Caputo's *Cumae: Its Archaeological Park and its History* (Electa Napoli, 1999) and from information panels at Cumae itself.

In the Pompeii section, the image of the fossilised bread and the plaster-casts of the victims initially came from Robert Etienne's *Pompeii: The Day a City Died* (Gallimard/Thames & Hudson, 1986/1992), but were later seen first-hand. Other details (including the petrified dog) appeared in Sara C. Bisel's *The Secrets of Vesuvius: Exploring the Mysteries of an Ancient Buried City* (Scholastic/Madison Press, 1990).

Much of the physical detail of England in the novel comes from childhood memories, refreshed by recent visits. Descriptions of wartime Norfolk were informed by Joan Banger's *Norwich at War* (Wensum Books, 1974, held by the Norfolk Records Office), Colin Took and David Scarles' *Great Yarmouth at War* (Poppyland Publishing, 1989, held by Great Yarmouth

Library), microfilms of *The Yarmouth Mercury* (from May to August 1945), as well as the photographic archives of Great Yarmouth Library. More general descriptions of Norfolk were assisted by *The Broads and Rivers of Norfolk* (Ward, Lock & Co, 1963) and Ron Wilson's *Norfolk in the Four Seasons* (The Larks Press, 1995).

Elissa's life was based partially on that of my great-aunt, Isobel. I imagined Elissa's life at the asylum using the archives of Heigham Hall Asylum near Norwich (MC 279, held by the Norfolk Records Office) and Diana Gittins' book *Madness in its Place: Narratives of Severalls Hospital, 1913–1997* (Routledge, 1998). Details of rats eating patients' clothing, thieving, the young woman silenced by rape and Elissa's treatments were drawn from this study. Norman Endler and Emmanuel Persad's work *Electroconvulsive Therapy: The Myths and the Realities* (Hans Huber Publishers, 1988) was also extremely useful.

Reading F.R. Banks' *The Penguin Guide to London* (Penguin, 1977) and Colin Simpson's section on London in *Wake up in Europe: A Book of Travel for Australians & New Zealanders* (Angus & Robertson, 1959) helped me find Queenie's place in the city. Displays in the Bank of England Museum assisted me with details of the city's devastation (particularly the crater in front of the Bank), and of wartime currency.

Aspects of Queenie's life were influenced by Ruth Cullen's documentary about the artist Vali Myers, entitled *The Tightrope Dancer* (Flare Productions, 1989), especially the effect of addiction on Queenie's body and her work. Information on drug addiction and withdrawal was obtained from David Emmett and Graeme Nice's *Understanding Drugs: A Handbook for Parents, Teachers and Other Professionals* (Jessica Kingsley Publishers, 1996) and Kevin Mackey's autobiographical work *The Cure: Recollections of an Addict* (Angus & Robertson, 1972).